Tom Clancy fans open to a strong female lead will clamor for more.

— *DRONE*, PUBLISHERS WEEKLY

Superb! Miranda is utterly compelling!

— *BOOKLIST*, STARRED REVIEW

Miranda Chase continues to astound and charm.

— BARB M.

Escape Rating: A. Five Stars! OMG just start with *Drone* and be prepared for a fantastic binge-read!

— READING REALITY

The best military thriller I've read in a very long time. Love the female characters.

— *DRONE*, SHELDON MCARTHUR, FOUNDER
OF THE MYSTERY BOOKSTORE, LA

PRAISE FOR M. L. BUCHMAN

A fabulous soaring thriller.

— *TAKE OVER AT MIDNIGHT,* MIDWEST BOOK
REVIEW

Meticulously researched, hard-hitting, and suspenseful.

— *PURE HEAT,* PUBLISHERS WEEKLY,
STARRED REVIEW

Expert technical details abound, as do realistic military missions with superb imagery that will have readers feeling as if they are right there in the midst and on the edges of their seats.

— *LIGHT UP THE NIGHT,* RT REVIEWS, 4 1/2
STARS

Buchman has catapulted his way to the top tier of my favorite authors.

— FRESH FICTION

Nonstop action that will keep readers on the edge of their seats.

— *TAKE OVER AT MIDNIGHT,* LIBRARY
JOURNAL

M L. Buchman's ability to keep the reader right in the middle of the action is amazing.

— LONG AND SHORT REVIEWS

The only thing you'll ask yourself is, "When does the next one come out?"

— WAIT UNTIL MIDNIGHT, RT REVIEWS, 4
STARS

The first...of (a) stellar, long-running (military) romantic suspense series.

— THE NIGHT IS MINE, BOOKLIST, "THE 20
BEST ROMANTIC SUSPENSE NOVELS:
MODERN MASTERPIECES"

I knew the books would be good, but I didn't realize how good.

— NIGHT STALKERS SERIES, KIRKUS
REVIEWS

Buchman mixes adrenalin-spiking battles and brusque military jargon with a sensitive approach.

— PUBLISHERS WEEKLY

13 times "Top Pick of the Month"

— NIGHT OWL REVIEWS

GUARD THE EAST FLANK

A NIGHT STALKERS MILITARY ROMANTIC
SUSPENSE

NIGHT STALKERS RELOAD
BOOK 1

M. L. BUCHMAN

SIGN UP FOR M. L. BUCHMAN'S NEWSLETTER TODAY

and receive:
Release News
Free Short Stories
a Free Book

Get your free book today. Do it now.
free-book.mlbuchman.com

The Emily Beale Universe
(military romantic suspense)

The Night Stalkers
MAIN FLIGHT
The Night Is Mine
I Own the Dawn
Wait Until Dark
Take Over at Midnight
Light Up the Night
Bring On the Dusk
By Break of Day
Target of the Heart
Target Lock on Love
Target of Mine
Target of One's Own
NIGHT STALKERS HOLIDAYS
*Daniel's Christmas**
*Frank's Independence Day**
*Peter's Christmas**
Christmas at Steel Beach
*Zachary's Christmas**
*Roy's Independence Day**
*Damien's Christmas**
Christmas at Peleliu Cove

Henderson's Ranch
*Nathan's Big Sky**
*Big Sky, Loyal Heart**
*Big Sky Dog Whisperer**
*Tales of Henderson's Ranch**

Shadow Force: Psi
*At the Slightest Sound**
*At the Quietest Word**
*At the Merest Glance**
*At the Clearest Sensation**

White House Protection Force
*Off the Leash**
*On Your Mark**
*In the Weeds**

Firehawks
Pure Heat
Full Blaze
*Hot Point**
*Flash of Fire**
Wild Fire
SMOKEJUMPERS
*Wildfire at Dawn**
*Wildfire at Larch Creek**
*Wildfire on the Skagit**

Delta Force
*Target Engaged**
*Heart Strike**
*Wild Justice**
*Midnight Trust**

Night Stalkers Reload
*Guard the East Flank**

Emily Beale Universe Short Story Series

The Night Stalkers
The Night Stalkers Stories
The Night Stalkers CSAR
The Night Stalkers Wedding Stories
The Future Night Stalkers

Delta Force
Th Delta Force Shooters
The Delta Force Warriors

Firehawks
The Firehawks Lookouts
The Firehawks Hotshots
The Firebirds

White House Protection Force
Stories

Future Night Stalkers
Stories (Science Fiction)

Other works by M. L. Buchman: *(* - also in audio)*

Action-Adventure Thrillers

Dead Chef
One Chef!
Two Chef!

Miranda Chase
*Drone**
*Thunderbolt**
*Condor**
*Ghostrider**
*Raider**
*Chinook**
*Havoc**
*White Top**
*Start the Chase**
*Lightning**
*Skibird**
*Nightwatch**
*Osprey**
*Gryphon**

Science Fiction / Fantasy

Deities Anonymous
Cookbook from Hell: Reheated
Saviors 101

Contemporary Romance

Eagle Cove
Return to Eagle Cove
Recipe for Eagle Cove
Longing for Eagle Cove
Keepsake for Eagle Cove

Love Abroad
Heart of the Cotswolds: England
Path of Love: Cinque Terre, Italy

Where Dreams
Where Dreams are Born
Where Dreams Reside
*Where Dreams Are of Christmas**
Where Dreams Unfold
Where Dreams Are Written
Where Dreams Continue

Non-Fiction

Strategies for Success
Managing Your Inner Artist/Writer
*Estate Planning for Authors**
Character Voice
Narrate and Record Your Own
*Audiobook**
Beyond Prince Charming: One Guy's
Guide to Writing Men in Romance

Short Story Series by M. L. Buchman:

Action-Adventure Thrillers

Dead Chef

Miranda Chase Stories

Romantic Suspense

Antarctic Ice Fliers

US Coast Guard

Contemporary Romance

Eagle Cove

Other

Deities Anonymous (fantasy)

Single Titles

The Emily Beale Universe
Reading Order Road Map

any series and any novel may be read stand-alone
(all have a complete heartwarming Happy Ever After)

For more information and alternate reading orders, please visit: www.mlbuchman.com/reading-order

ABOUT THIS BOOK

EMILY BEALE RETURNS! AND THE NIGHT STALKERS WILL NEVER BE the same.

Captain Sharelle Vargas may be the best pilot in the 160th SOAR helicopter regiment, but is she ready for Colonel Emily Beale?

Captain Troy Ryland loves three things in his life: his family farm, flying the most lethal helicopter in the US military, and the woman he flies with. Each pull him in a different direction. The clock isn't ticking—it's running out!

A new mission slams them into action as they must infiltrate the notorious "Wind from the East"—Russia. Once in, will their combined skills prove enough to escape with their lives and their hearts intact?

———

A list of characters and aircraft may be found at:
https://mlbuchman.com/fan-club-freebies
Then follow the links.

*And return afterward for a free bonus story
and a recipe from the book.*

1
———

"WHEN WAS THE LAST TIME YOU FLEW?"

"Yesterday. Or was it Tuesday, Emma?" Mark glanced her way, but didn't give her time to respond. "Yep, thinkin' it was Tuesday." He pointed westward at the abrupt upward break of the Montana Front Range. Their twenty-thousand-acre ranch ended there and the million-acre Selway-Bitterroot Wilderness began.

She, Mark, and Colonel Cassius McDermott had stopped their horses in the shade of a white birch copse atop a crest of the rolling landscape. It was one of Emily's favorite views. They were on a lazy afternoon ride a couple hours from the ranch, and this would be their turnback point.

The sun glinted off the sharp peaks of the Lewis Range, emphasizing the alternating light and dark strata that slashed through the mountains like the insides of mile-tall layer cakes. Being born and raised in DC, even six years living here hadn't decreased Emily's wonder at this vista rising in her backyard.

"Took a couple of fat-cat tourists on a spin out there, in our little Bell JetRanger helo. We spotted bear, moose, a couple herds of elk. Gonna be some good hunting for the larder this fall. Good photo safaris, too—we're marketing those heavy this year. You should come on out, Cass. It'll be a good time here at the ranch."

"I don't think that's what Cass is asking, is it, Colonel?" Emily gave Mark the hint, but he missed it. "Six years since the last time we flew a mission."

Then she caught the look in Mark's eye. He'd known exactly what he was doing. Instead of scowling at her for spoiling his game, he offered her one of his broad conspiratorial winks, including her in his play. He'd always enjoyed his games but never been particularly attached to the winning or the losing. Less so with each passing year. The ranch had mellowed him so much that it was occasionally hard to spot the former 5th Battalion D Company commander of the Night Stalkers' regiment.

He pulled out a hip flask. After taking a sip, he offered it to Cass seated on Rollo, reaching over from atop Wind Runner. His big black gelding hadn't slowed with age, but the years had made Mark a better rider—at least he rarely fell off anymore.

"Sorry, didn't get you were talking about *flying,* not flying. Well, why didn't you say it plain, old son?" His horsemanship may have improved; his phony Texas accent hadn't.

Cass was looking at the flask as if there was something wrong with it, or the fact that it was still early afternoon. The early summer finally warm enough for no more than a light jacket.

"None of us on duty out here, Cass, and 'tain't poison. Licensed distiller from just down the valley a piece. All local: water, grain, even the oak for the casks and the cooper who knocked them together—seriously hot, by the way. I'd introduce you, but don't want to tick off your wife." Well, his Texas was a little better, even if she'd never understood why a Navy brat turned Montanan kept toying with it. As far as she knew, neither he nor his SEAL father had ever been so much as stationed there and his mother was pureblood Cheyenne from Wyoming.

"He also has a beard down to his solar plexus, except when he singes it while charring a barrel. You might object to that even more than your wife would." Emily felt it was only fair to warn him.

Cass laughed and took the flask. The whiskey was too harsh for Emily's palate, any whiskey was, but Cass seemed to like it well enough to take a second taste before returning it to Mark, who tucked it away.

It might be Mark doing most of the speaking, but it was Colonel Cass McDermott she watched carefully. He hadn't brought his wife on this trip, which meant he was here on business—the Army's business.

"Did you say six years, Emily?"

"You're thinking eleven." She kept her smile to herself.

"I admit I was."

"The last five were under a different classification, Cass." Meaning operations that her former commander hadn't been cleared for. Always a bitter taste, one that showed clearly on his face.

"Yeah," Mark said in his normal voice. "Classified mission compartmentalization sucks. I always found it as annoying as hell, too."

Cass made it halfway through a nod of acknowledgement when a rabbit bolted from practically under the nose of Cass' horse. When Rollo ran, he had a habit like no other horse she'd ever seen. The gray dropped low and bolted so fast that Cass looked as if he floated in space for a moment before plummeting to the thick Montana grass.

"Goddamn it!" Mark swung his reins over and gave Wind Runner a hard kick. He didn't need it; his horse also loved to run, and he was the fastest on the ranch—because, of course, that's what Mark had insisted on when they moved here, not realizing as a rank beginner what he was asking for.

Rollo offered an easy ride, good for a beginner like Cass—usually. Wind Runner? Not so much. Mark and the two horses raced out of sight over the bluff.

Knowing her own level of incompetence, she'd requested the friendliest of mounts and never regretted her choice. Chesapeake watched the others race away as she chewed her latest mouthful of the lush grass before reaching for another bite. Emily patted her on the neck.

She hoped that she wouldn't have to go rescue Mark next.

Dropping the reins over her mare's neck, she slid to the ground. Nothing much bothered her horse, and she wouldn't run off even if it did.

"Anything hurt other than your pride, Cass?"

"Not much." He remained seated in the foot-tall grass of the July prairie.

The rains had come late—late enough in June to strike fear into every rancher's heart, even a Jane-come-lately like herself. But the so-called million-dollar rains had finally come on strong and set the crops. It had also turned the entire Front Range into a magic carpet of bluebells, buttercups, and windflowers. Their bright colors danced on the air lush with the scent of green. July's typical dusty dry taste had been pushed out into August, making every Montanan walk a bit sprightlier, whether from the prairie or the town.

Cass picked up the cowboy hat they'd given him against the sun, but he didn't put it back on. Instead, he worried the brim around in a slow circle through his hands as he remained seated on the grass. "Six years? Thought you were flying to wildfires."

"That's one way to look at it." They'd also been flying black ops missions under the cover of being helitack firefighters, reporting only to the President and the Secretary of Defense.

She sat down on the grass beside him. Emily felt Chesapeake come up behind her, but she didn't react.

Her mahogany mare picked the hat off Emily's head without catching her long blonde hair in its teeth.

"See? They don't tell me squat simply because I'm the 160th SOAR's commanding officer."

She let her silence tell him that it was going to stay that way, too. Her years flying for the Night Stalkers of the Army's Special Operations Aviation Regiment had been the highlight of her career, but that hadn't been the end of it by a long stretch.

Chesapeake flapped Emily's hat up and down, laughing through clenched teeth. It was an old game between them, since back when they first met and the only thing Emily rode was Black Hawk helicopters. She waited for the horse to hang her head over Emily's shoulder so she could scrub Chesapeake's cheek. The horse sighed happily, dropped Emily's hat in her lap, then turned her attention to ripping up grass.

Cass was thinking hard about her flying career...and something else as well. Didn't matter, Emily was dug in here, but she was curious at what had dragged him all the way to Montana from Fort Campbell, Kentucky.

Picking up her hat, she slid it on. Not for Chesapeake to steal again, but her light blonde hair and matching complexion didn't offer any defense against the Montana summer sunshine even wearing a serious SPF number and sitting in the broken shade of the swaying birches.

"Six years is still too long for us to go airborne again, Cass. A single month off blunts that fighting edge in a top pilot. Six years..." she let that hang.

It would take a minimum of half a year of retraining to regain that edge, if she even could. Flying a Night Stalkers helicopter into a battlespace was *not* a bicycle that your body simply remembered how to fly.

"You knew that before you came here. What's really going on?"

Rather than answering directly, he appeared to be watching the snow-capped ranges behind her. "I saw that you're still listed as active duty."

She was. Mark had finally retired when he'd hit his twenty years—*Same as Dad is plenty good enough for me*—his final four years as a trainer at the nearby Malmstrom Air Force Base. He'd flown and taught leadership courses before finally standing down as a lieutenant colonel. Getting the silver oak leaf had tickled him no end. But when she'd pointed out that a few more years' service might get him a bump to being a bird colonel, he'd scoffed.

Think I'm after Cass McDermott's job? Not even a little interested.

And he hadn't been.

Done my tour.

In the two years since, he'd settled in as if he'd never been anywhere else. His dad still ran the place. Though pushing seventy, Mac was a retired SEAL and wouldn't stop until he was six feet under the sod, if then. But Mark and the ranch had started to fit each other in ways he'd never managed even as commander of the most elite SOAR company.

As the commander of the 5th Battalion's D Company, he'd been a driven hard-ass. The only quality that was good enough for Viper Henderson was perfection—setting the gold standard himself. On the ranch, he was the one behind the scenes making sure everything kept ticking along. It was easy to miss where he slipped in unless she watched for it.

He was also Superdad. Tessa and Belle loved her, but they worshipped their dad—two seriously daddy's girls. Which was okay, she worshipped Mark a little herself.

Cass *knew* Mark had retired; he'd come out to the ranch for the retirement party. Whatever he was after...

I saw that you're still listed as active duty.

"Oh, no. Wait a minute, Cass. I don't want back in the service."

"Saw you earned the same silver oak leaf as Mark, same year too, though you're a couple years younger. Don't seem to recall any invitation to *your* retirement party...unless there never was one. Still on active duty without any missions or any posting showing up in your records at all, at least not any I get to see."

Emily had already answered that one. Five years technically flying to fight forest fires. At least that was the wider perception. By which time, she'd had it running so smoothly that she was able to hand it off.

For the six years since, she'd created and led a clandestine intelligence operation at the behest of the former President. Though now that she thought about it, that operation had finally matured as well. There was little that Lauren, Claudia, and Michael actually needed of her anymore. She been chomping at the bit for a while now, worse than Chesapeake when she scented the barn coming in range after a long ride.

Fully retire like Mark? Leading yet another trail ride didn't exactly fill her cup past a quarter full. Chasing down yet another attack on the Executive Branch sounded equally uninspiring no matter how good she had become at it.

She'd always been a pilot first and last.

Cass smiled. "Eddie Arnson wants to make you an offer."

"Then why are you here?" The Chairman of the Joint Chiefs of Staff, the top-ranking military officer in the nation, knew how to find her. He was Mark's uncle, after all. Only the second Marine Corps general to ever be named to the post. She still wondered what crowbar the President had used to pry him loose from his beloved HMX-1 post commanding the Marine helicopters responsible for Presidential-lift missions.

"Because I asked to make the pitch."

"So pitch."

The ground vibrated slightly beneath her butt. A discontented snort from Rollo announced that Mark had caught the runaway horse unfairly and far too soon into a glorious gallop over the thick summer pastures.

Cass waited for the two of them to come up.

"You hitting on my wife, Cass? Gotta warn you, Emma gets *more* dangerous with age. And she started out plenty dangerous to begin with." He rubbed his jaw where she'd planted his face into an aircraft carrier's ready-room table for stealing a first kiss. A dozen years and a lifetime ago.

Though he never missed an opportunity to mention it, they shared a smile at the memory. She remembered the kiss with searing clarity but had to take Mark's word on what she'd done to him after that.

He also kept the outer bezel of his watch permanently set to the precise minute of that first kiss. She'd tested him a few times; he never had to hesitate longer than a single breath to tell her years, days, hours, and minutes since.

Despite the memory, Emily's smile felt tight on her face.

"Can't say that my missus would take it much better than yours," he winked at Emily, but kept looking up at Mark on his horse. "How do you feel about being outranked?"

"You've always outranked me, Old Man. Simply being older seems questionable grounds for such a thing, but..." Mark shrugged it away.

"You can double that barely concealed envy now. They're bumping me upstairs, commander of USASOAC, giving me a star for my troubles." He tapped his shoulder where it would go.

"Head of the whole Army's Spec Ops Aviation Command? Very fancy, *General* Cassius McDermott, sir." Mark offered a salute sloppier than a recruit fresh through the gate. "Congratulations, Cass, seriously. You're a hundred percent the man for that job. Who's taking over the 160th?" Command of the 160th SOAR called for a colonel, not a brigadier general.

Emily felt the blood drain from her face. Robbed her of the power to speak.

"Funny you should ask that." Cass pulled a small box out of his pocket and tossed it at her.

Emily caught it by reflex. Though it burned against her palm, she opened it. Then turned it to show Mark the winged silver collar insignia of a bird colonel.

He slid down off his horse but didn't say a word. Instead, he stepped up and rested one of those big strong hands on her shoulder. That was good, or the gentle breeze rippling over the grasslands might waft her away easier than an errant bumblebee, never to be seen again.

"There's the pitch. You going to be making the catch, *Colonel Beale?*"

Emily couldn't react as Chesapeake stole her hat again.

The only comfort she found was that, for once, Mark was struck as speechless as she was. Not a single Texas drawl to be heard on the wide Montana prairie.

The sole sound on the wind? Her horse's laughter.

2

"So the new commander's a legend. Someone tell me why I should give a rat's ass." Understated Southern girl had never been one of Sharelle's skills. A decade in the Army hadn't improved matters. Especially not when the heat was turned up to deep fry. The Kentucky sun had cooked the day to a turn. And the falling evening hadn't cranked up the AC one bit.

She followed her crew chiefs as they checked over her helicopter. They didn't *need* her eyeballs on their asses, but they'd long since grown used to that. If she was taking a bird aloft, she was damn well going to double-check everything.

"*Possible* new commander, Captain Vargas," Troy, her copilot, corrected. He was always a stickler for getting it right. She was more of a getting-it-done type, which made them a good team.

"*Possible* new commander, Captain Ryland," she conceded. "But I still don't give a rat's ass." The Good Lord of the Virginia Military Institute—which Lincoln himself had called the West Point of the South—had taught her to only care about performance. Well, VMI had attempted to impart etiquette befitting a soldier, which she barely managed. Anything befitting a *Woman of the South,* whatever that meant, had completely passed her by.

There hadn't been any formal announcements, but everyone knew Cass McDermott had been promoted. The scuttlebutt said that some *legend* was up to replace him.

Problem with the rumor mill was that this time it had churned out only that one bit of useless dreck. The 160th didn't exactly lack for legends. Michael Durant, the pilot captured in The Mog—the disaster of Mogadishu, Somalia, had been scorched into the collective consciousness of the Night Stalkers and immortalized for the public in *Black Hawk Down*—had retired a couple decades ago. The founders of the 160th were either older or dead.

But the insane op tempo of the double dust-bowl wars of the 'aughts and 'tens had provided plenty of chances for pilots to become legendary, at least within the regiment. The less the wider world knew of their missions, the happier everyone was.

The Night Stalkers' tasking meant that they flew Delta Force (typically calling themselves The Unit), DEVGRU (that everyone mistakenly called SEAL Team Six), and 75th Rangers (who were simply known for kicking ass) out to places no one else could go. Then the Night Stalkers flew back in to pull them out when they were done—which had bred a whole new bunch of legends.

But like Daddy always said, *If less than five-gets-you-twenty, don't waste money betting.* But she knew her bet was solid. Like the prehistoric generals who kept refusing to die out of the leadership roles, she just knew they were now going to dredge up some fossil to run the 160th SOAR into the ground the way those OWDs were doing to her military. If they put an Old White Dude in charge of the 160th, she'd...

What? Her inner voice teased her.

Well, she didn't know what, but she'd damn well do it when

she figured it out. Or she'd get her copilot Troy to figure it out; he was better at that kind of thing.

"Not mad at you, girl. Not you." Sharelle patted the black metal skin of her DAP Hawk helicopter to reassure it.

Her nose detected no kerosene bite or honeysuckle sweet, telling Sharelle that her baby had no fuel or hydraulic leaks. Confirmed by no glistening blemishes on her helo's matte-black skin. No marks blotted the tarmac beneath the helo either, not even through the heat haze.

Of course, they were all Night Stalkers—flight crew of the US Army 160th Special Operations Aviation Regiment (Airborne), the 160th SOAR. They all shared the drive for excellence and her crew chiefs always took her oversight in easy stride—after three years as a team, they were as used to her as anyone had ever been.

Not that they needed her watching over them. The only helos with a higher mission availability rate than the Night Stalkers were the Marines of HMX-1. But if you were flying the President and his entourage around, it paid to be seriously anal —easy for a Marine. She resisted the urge to sneer; it's not like anyone shot at them for a living. Sure, Marines occasionally took heat out in the real world, but the Marine One helos weren't exactly front-line weapons of war.

Neither Olsen nor Wright paid her any mind. Both of her crew chiefs were busy, perched high on the bird, popping engine covers for a last look around.

They needed flashlights as the soft evening light of Fort Campbell, Kentucky, turned the high horsetail cirrus clouds blood-red. Storm coming.

No shit, Sherlock. It would help if her inner voice didn't know about her teenage crush on Benedict Cumberbatch. But, as usual, it was right.

"Missing McDermott already?" Troy asked. Troy Ryland kept reading his clipboard. Her copilot was reading through the mechanics' rundown and verifying their bird's status as Mission Ready. He looked like a Troy, ready to enter battle with Achilles and Hector in the ancient city of. Tall, dark-haired Okie simply brimming with all the politeness and tact she'd never even met in a pickup bar, much less become acquainted with.

"McDermott's a pain in the ass, but he recruited me. Been the regiment's boss for most of a decade. I'll miss him like, I dunno, a sore tooth."

"Miss having his boot up your backside too." The accuracy of Troy's jibe, a rare event from him, didn't sit so well. He continued to scan quickly down his clipboard, which boded well for the maintenance log.

"McDermott *did* take a special joy in that. Might be nice to heal for a piece." Of course, he'd taught her plenty about what excellence really meant. Five years in the 101st. Another two years of training to make the Night Stalkers grade, after surviving selection and then Full Mission Qualified status, thinking she knew it all. Over the three years since, McDermott had seriously enjoyed proving how naive she'd been.

"You're just being grouchy about today's mission."

"And you aren't?" Her copilot had been relegated to perching in a spare seat back in the cargo bay.

He shrugged. "Sure, I'd rather be flying, but—" he countersigned and tucked the mechanics' log at the back of his clipboard, then waved the new top sheet at her, "—that's not what they're telling us. I reckon the Army pays for this bird and for us. I 'preciate it any day they pay me to be in the air."

Paper had its place, but still, some things should never be written down—like these stupid-ass orders for tonight's flight.

Sharelle yanked open her pilot's door. "Damned dog-and-pony shit-show." She climbed into the right-hand seat of the MH-60M DAP Hawk, the most lethal helicopter ever sent aloft. The Direct-Action Penetrator Black Hawk was the result of decades of refinement by the very best in the US military rotorcraft business—the Night Stalkers themselves. Sikorsky had done an awesome job of delivering on those designs. Fewer than thirty had ever been built, and this one was all hers.

She heard Wright and Olsen climbing into the rear cargo bay. Meant they'd decided her baby stood ready to kick some ass.

Not today.

Mission brief had been short and simple: *Shake-down demo flight for DoD VIP—Front Seat.* Some Pentagon or, even worse, government desk jockey with enough pull in the Department of Defense to snag a joy ride with the Night Stalkers. Worse than that, some fat-cat senator or bureaucrat drunk on his own power had forced his way into *her* cockpit, which ranked beyond rude and right over into annoying as hell.

Well, Sharelle would stretch him over his pork barrel until he never willingly boarded a helo again. If she worked the flight hard enough, maybe he'd take trains instead of planes for the rest of his life.

She punched on the instrument lights in the dark cockpit, then focused on her final checks before Engine Start.

Sharelle faced Troy, who still stood by her open door, "Let me know when the asshole arrives."

Troy pointed behind her.

"She's here." A woman spoke from the copilot's seat.

Sharelle flinched. She never flinched.

In the left-hand copilot seat sat a fully kitted woman. Her flightsuit looked hard-worn and her helmet far from new. Who the hell had she borrowed that helmet from? It was painted dark purple and had the Night Stalkers' unofficial emblem painted on it—a sword-wielding winged centaur with laser-vision eyes. Sharelle didn't recognize the personal insignia, though it was ringing some deep bell she couldn't place.

"And who are you?" Even with the visor up, there wasn't

much to see except from eyebrows to chin. Nothing past the cheekbones to the sides.

No answer. The woman simply looked over with the bluest eyes ever made. The failing light of sunset did nothing to diminish their message—*Stop wasting my time.*

Sharelle yanked on her own helmet. It was dark tiger-orange with a steel spearhead emblazoned on the side; the spear of Okoye, the female warrior-general of Marvel Comics Wakanda. At this moment, she didn't exactly feel all powerful, and appreciated the deep twilight and her own darker skin because of the heat punching into her cheeks.

Embarrassed or pissed? The woman's look trying to put her in her place...or that she had to deal with some senator's mistress? She didn't know which rankled worse. Except no mistress would be dressed so authentically or slide aboard her bird without Sharelle noticing.

Then she had to tug her helmet off again because, unlike the bald General Okoye, she had thick brown curls that had to be tucked in as she pulled on the helmet—more Halle than afro. Never hurt her ego when a guy did a double take, thinking she might actually be a younger Halle Berry. Better than.

Way better, girlfriend, her voice insisted. *That girl is charging hard toward sixty.*

I'm also five inches taller and a top military pilot, she answered back.

The voice gave her an affirming, *Rock it!*

Once helmeted, harnessed, and plugged into the helo's systems, she dove into the pre-engine-start checklist. Awkward without Troy calling out and confirming each step.

The woman flipped up her helmet's swing-arm microphone, taking her off the crew intercom Sharelle had just finished powering up. Now only Sharelle would hear her.

"You aren't flying solo." Her voice wasn't sharp or nasty, it only felt like that.

Sharelle turned to fully face her.

Those blue-blue eyes didn't change, but there might be the slightest hint of a smile. "I *can* read a checklist."

What Sharelle should do was throw her out. What she did was tap the controller on the woman's display to bring up the checklist. "So, read."

The ride-along flipped her mike down to rejoin the general intercom and read. Step by step. Clear, concise, no civilian hesitation at any of the heavy acronyms.

"Tail Servo Switch to Normal." Without prompting, the woman picked up at the exact next step where she'd interrupted Sharelle.

"Check," Sharelle threw the switch.

"Boost On, Boost Servo Warning Off."

"Check." They continued down the list almost as fast as she did with Troy.

Finally ready, engines running clean and hot, Sharelle contacted the tower for clearance.

"Cleared for immediate departure Runway 23, depart southeast. Range 28, 31, and 42 from zero to ten thousand cleared for operations."

"Uh, Roger, Tower." Sharelle wanted to turn and look at Troy for confirmation at how odd that was, but no way would she be letting this nameless woman spot any weakness to report to whoever she might be a bimbo for. Three of the big training ranges were never open at the same time for a solo flight. Fifty square miles of Kentucky and Tennessee were all theirs tonight.

As always, she shot a salute toward Daddy. He'd be home by now, bedding down with Mama after a quiet evening.

Being a Night Stalker—meaning their training and missions were almost exclusively flown at night—Sharelle lived in a flipped clock world from the rest of her family.

Most mornings, she met Daddy at the DFAC—the base

dining facility—as he came on base to do his dance with the computers. He'd have a second breakfast of a donut and coffee while she ate dinner; it was their special time together, and she always missed it when deployed.

Then she'd go home, hug Mama and tease *Baby Bother* as they headed out to the avionics lab that one headed and the other worked in. Then she and Tigger, the family German Shepherd, headed to bed. Typical Fort Campbell family.

As she saluted, Sharelle felt Daddy smiling back at her from the house she'd grown up in over by the Cumberland River. The Cumberland actually wound through Tennessee, where most of the base lay, but they were a Fort Campbell family and its postal code lay in Kentucky, so they called that home.

One last look around the field and she headed aloft.

———

CAPTAIN TROY RYLAND SAT IN THE SINGLE JUMP SEAT THE CREW chiefs had rigged in the middle of the cargo bay. Because their bird was a DAP Hawk, having the area to himself was less luxurious than it sounded.

The bay on a normal Black Hawk could fit eleven kitted-up troops crammed in tight. But a Direct Action Penetrator wasn't about transport, it was about weaponry. Lots and lots of it.

The two crew chiefs, their twin side-facing M134 Miniguns on sliding mounts, and the multiple four-thousand-round cannisters of 7.62 mm belted ammunition at their feet took up the forward half of the bay.

The view out the large side-door windows was mostly blocked by the stub wings. They weren't for lift like an airplane; they were for war. Tonight, they were mounted with unarmed missiles and a pair of training lasers in place of the half-inch GAU-19 Gatling heavy machine gun, additional Minigun, and rocket pods. With the cargo bay's ceiling at only four-foot-six, he felt like a troll squatting in his cave.

Focus on the mission, Troy.

Three ranges open? That *never* happened. Night Stalkers kept their edge by training constantly—or being deployed. The op tempo should have dropped with the end of the disasters in Iraq and Afghanistan. And it had, briefly. Not anymore.

But three?

Perhaps all cleared for their unnamed passenger?

Unnamed? That made no sense either. Sure, she'd appeared out of nowhere in the middle of the most secure section of the high security military base in Fort Campbell, Kentucky—the Night Stalkers' compound.

She climbed aboard so smooth they hadn't seen her arrive.

Sharelle must have recognized her to not check her ID...but he'd seen no sign of that.

He pulled a red-lensed flashlight out of his flightsuit's thigh pocket and shone it on the clipboard.

No name on the mission orders for tonight's flight.

The orders had included a CAC ID badge code that would have been checked at the gate. And a picture. He'd caught enough of her profile when she'd been talking off intercom to Sharelle to be sure of a match. Like Sharelle's, it wasn't a face that would be easy to mistake anywhere.

So, whoever she was, she belonged here.

And they'd cleared three ranges for tonight's flight.

They'd only do that if...

Troy snorted out a laugh.

"What?" Sharelle's voice, he knew every nuance of it, was seriously stressed. Not softly Kentucky-casual. Or bored for a demo run over the familiar hills and forests of the last rolls of the Appalachian Mountains before they flattened out into the Midwestern plains. No hint of Southern Tennessee charm— not that she typically wielded that either.

He opened his mouth, then the copilot with the purple helmet turned to look at him between the two pilots' seats and the backs of the side-facing crew chiefs at their guns.

Her face remained hidden in the dimly lit cabin, but he felt the steadiness of her gaze.

Keep my mouth shut, got it. He raised a hand palm out to show he understood, and she turned away.

He'd heard the ease with which she'd read the checklist. What Sharelle must have missed was that she rarely looked down at the checklist as she read it out. Knew it cold.

They'd sent a ringer. Hidden her name and rank.

Not a demo flight for some random DoD-head.

An unannounced eval flight by someone from the Spec Ops Training Battalion? That was underhanded, though not unheard of.

Whatever had passed between her and Sharelle in those few moments off intercom had escalated the hyper-focus Sharelle brought to every flight up to behind-enemy-lines extraction-mission levels. Her temper never affected her flying —he'd never flown with a better pilot—only the level of her aggression. At least in the air. On the ground she had the same temper, but no flying outlet to mitigate it. He'd been careful to never cross her.

To get under Sharelle's lovely skin deep enough to escalate her that high on a training mission?

That took a superior officer.

A SOAR pilot who knew a DAP Hawk's checklists by heart and outranked Captain Sharelle Vargas. Perhaps a major, but felt more like a lieutenant colonel or...

What had Sharelle been complaining about earlier? Colonel Cass McDermott being bumped up to brigadier general with his promotion inside Special Operations Command. Going on about some legend. Command of the Night Stalkers was a colonel-level posting. So, some legend who had climbed up to the rarefied heights only a single step below brigadier general.

The Night Stalkers were too specialized to promote from outside the ranks, which meant the woman was from inside. But Troy had thought he knew all the top female officers. They were still enough of a rarity to stand out, dating back to the very first woman to break the gender barrier—the legendary Major Emily Beale. She'd retired a decade ago to fight wildfires and have kids. If she'd stayed in the military, by now she'd be...a colonel. Which meant—

Legendary!

He gaped at the back of the purple-helmeted copilot.

Not merely a ringer.

She was *the* ringer.

He glanced out the window to see if it was too late to bail, but the ground had already fallen away.

The Night Stalkers racked up incredibly high mission success rates. However, though she'd been gone a decade, no one touched Major Emily Beale's record. She made his alma mater's Sooners look like a junior high school basketball team rather than the third-ranked sports program in the nation across all sports.

This time he couldn't stop the laugh—

"What?" Sharelle snapped out again.

By her tone, he no longer felt so assured of his safety in the air. She might have the crew chiefs toss him out at five thousand feet. If she ordered it, Jalissa and Hans might do it. They'd apologize first, but... Well, maybe not, but he wouldn't be risking that.

Colonel Beale—assuming he was right, and he knew he was—didn't turn to look at him this time. Communicating by her very stillness that she knew exactly what he'd figured out.

"Nothing, Sharelle. Sorry. Have a good flight."

"Dweeb!"

Perfect.

Just perfect.

Exactly what he wanted to be called by Captain Sharelle Vargas, the most astonishing woman he'd ever met.

———

SHARELLE PUSHED TROY OUT OF HER THOUGHTS. TO FLY LIKE A Night Stalker required complete focus—perfect mental discipline. After the flight was done and they'd booted their ride-along back to whatever hole she'd crawled out of, Sharelle would find out what he thought was so damn funny.

Time to show their passenger what a proper weapon of war could do.

Aloft to five thousand and past Range 75, which looked busy with the 2nd Battalion running high-speed shooting practice for their Little Birds, she nosed down and dropped low. Moving fast past cruise and up to V-max limits, she carved a high-g pullout, placing them twenty feet over the trees. Moving now at a hundred and sixty knots, a hundred and eighty-five miles per hour, she thumbed the visual control to project the terrain maps inside her visor.

Stick-frame terrain from the helicopter's memory was synced to her position by both GPS and internal navigation systems. The SKR, Silent Knight Radar, overlaid the stick frame with real-time imaging that matched dead-on. And over that, the external camera system painted a combined infrared and night-vision-enhanced image.

It might as well be broad daylight. Except, with the stick frame, she also saw what lay behind the next hill and how deep a river canyon ran.

A glance to the upper right of her visual field inside the visor confirmed that the engines hummed in the sweet spot. A quick flick to a tactical view and back confirmed no other aircraft in the immediate airspace. Normally it was the copilot's task to watch that, but not tonight. She nudged her training to think of Troy as injured and incapacitated. That kicked in a whole series of honed habits that would include frequent scans of aircraft fitness and tactical awareness.

She didn't select the full tactical overlay on the detailed terrain. She could do it, every Night Stalker pilot could, but the strain was severe. The single hardest element of the training for her hadn't been the flying, that had always come to her as naturally as breathing.

It was the full-battle mode of piloting that was hardest.

When needed, she could focus her eyes on separate tasks projected inside her visor. Terrain and navigation to one side and tracking both friendlies and unfriendlies, and targeting the latter, with the other. One person could fly a Black Hawk. But managing the workload in solo flight, especially in battle where weapons' targeting and firing were added in, mapped the fastest route to a migraine ever invented. Learning to do it all, without the headache, proved to be the hardest of all the Night Stalker lessons she'd ever learned.

For tonight, alone in the training ranges, she focused on the flying. A pure joy that felt like floating in a perfect summer lake beneath the sun-dappled trees of Kentucky.

Once the forest below turned to fields, she dropped down as easily as launching off a high dive into that cool water.

Sharelle let the helo plummet to twenty-five feet above the terrain, then slid down until her wheels were a bare ten feet above the terrain. Colonel Cass McDermott had always said that below a hundred feet, halving your elevation tripled the difficulty. A hundred to fifty to twenty-five to ten required over twenty times the skill of flying? It certainly felt that way.

Volleying around the low rolling hills faster than a water skier on a slalom course. Nothing regular and even about flying NOE, nap-of-earth, where a tall bush could tear off a belly-mounted antenna—or worse. She twisted and rolled. Wished she'd thought to hand the passenger a barf bag.

NOE—the ultimate adrenaline rush. Most helos preferred to run high, five or ten thousand feet above the terrain, to stay well clear of any hazards. *A Night Stalker's only happy if they're dragging their belly through the mud.* She'd certainly heard that enough times. And it was true. No challenge matched a flight requiring attention to every nuance of the terrain. Racing full-out with her wheels three meters off the dirt, it took everything she had to keep it safe.

She pushed Troy's odd laugh out of her thoughts—though he'd found something damned funny. Nor did she think of their passenger. Lost in the flow of hill, valley, bush, tree, building, phone line, tree, stack of summer hay bales shimmering in her night vision...she thought of nothing but the flight.

Ten miles by the crow, fourteen by her twisting route, and four minutes-ten by the clock, Sharelle eased up at the far corner of the range. Not a long flight, but enough to shake out the day's kinks and to feel the strain of the most technical type of flying there was. Squids could brag all they wanted about carrier landings and the squid and Air Force *drivers* about running Star Wars Canyon out in the Death Valley—or they could until that Navy F/A-18 Super Hornet driver ate a sidewall and got everyone banned.

Rest of them be damned, *she* was a pilot.

A glance sideways revealed the woman sitting perfectly calmly in her seat, no sign of imminent barfing or even the slightest gag. Instead, her hands were on the controls. Her touch so light that Sharelle hadn't even felt it. How had she...

"You fly?"

"I have."

Not knowing quite how connected the woman was at the Pentagon—she had to be a serious hotshot to successfully beg a ride on a DAP Hawk, most wouldn't be allowed to *see* one—Sharelle figured maybe she should unwind enough to play nice if only because the woman hadn't barfed all over her cockpit. "Want to try?"

Her hesitation was the first crack Sharelle had seen in that chill facade. The woman took her hands off the controls, rubbing them together, then flexing her fingers several times. Even did a quick roll of the wrists to loosen them up. Except it was hard to tell if she was preparing for flight or the controls had somehow burned her gloved hands.

"Don't worry, I'll ride the controls with you. Just a few simple maneuvers."

The woman returned her hands to the controls. Sharelle counted two heartbeats before—

One moment they were hovering over a small stream that marked the far corner of the Range 42 practice area.

The next, the collective shoved her left palm upward and the Hawk rolled hard through a sixty-degree high-bank turn.

Her passenger wove the Hawk back and forth as she climbed to a thousand feet, the same way Sharelle would if testing out the feel of an unfamiliar bird. To most pilots, a Black Hawk would be distinct from a Huey or Chinook, but it would still be a Black Hawk.

To a Night Stalker pilot, every Black Hawk had its own feel. Tiny quirks of tightness of the controls, airframe variations, and configuration. Each flight added another layer of *not just a generic Black Hawk:* weapons load-out, crew placement, fuel load.

Then, a DAP Hawk was a rare beast all its own; nobody except the Night Stalkers had them. A very distinct, and heavy, load. Cutting-edge sensor arrays found on no other bird subtly shifted the aerodynamics balance. Comms enough to oversee a serious battle or a clandestine extraction deep in unfriendly territory added complexity. Layers of gear like no other made it the best battle platform aloft —anywhere.

The woman could definitely fly, though how well was yet to be seen. Her fingertips on the flight controls attested to the surety of the maneuvers that had nothing to do with the nerves she'd seen at the start of the run.

Who the hell was the woman?

Before Sharelle would have completed a full getting-the-feel run, the passenger slammed the cyclic hard right while punching in the right pedal.

The helo tipped all the way onto its right side and continued through a full roll over.

Sharelle ignored the exclamations of surprise from the rest of the crew as she braced to wrench control from the woman— it was damn low for such a maneuver. But the risk of fouling the maneuver had her hesitating just long enough to prove that the woman *did* have control.

Then, as soon as they'd righted safely, she rolled the helo back the other way.

They leveled out again at above seven hundred, a loss of under three hundred feet during two full rolls.

How the hell? The double roll should have cost them most of their thousand-foot elevation. Maybe more than.

Only in memory did Sharelle recall the collective dragging her left hand all the way to the deck and back up—twice. While inverted, the woman had actually reverse-pitched the rotor blades so that they were driving them upward while upside down to decrease the loss of altitude while inverted.

And...her right hand on the cyclic had... No way!

The rotor disk of a Black Hawk was tipped forward to keep the bird closer to level in straight-and-level flight. Inverted, the woman had compensated her angle of attack to point the rotor straight down, offering just that bit more lift for the inverted moment.

Before Sharelle could ask where the woman had learned that, they were diving to earth. She leveled at a hundred feet above the terrain and began following it.

It quickly became apparent that the woman hadn't merely flown helicopters. Or Black Hawks. She'd flown a Direct Action Penetrator.

Then she eased down to seventy-five.

"That's low enough," Sharelle ordered after she dropped to fifty. She could tell that the pilot's skill-level wouldn't do well much below that.

"Agreed." The first word the woman had spoken since completing the Predeparture Checklist. She held *exactly* fifty feet over the terrain, climbing for trees, skirting hilltops, but never flying a foot closer—or farther. For over an hour, she crisscrossed the terrain dozens of times. Sometimes climbing high aloft, others, practicing a hover so low and with such care that Sharelle knew all three wheels kissed a river's surface without wetting the hubs. Then again racing along at that oh-so-precise fifty feet and airspeed pegged two knots below V-max like the number had been painted on the screen.

Even as the woman flew, Sharelle felt her improve. Not day-by-day or even hour-by-hour, but mile-by-mile.

After a while, Sharelle considered clearing her down to twenty-five feet just to see what happened—a flight level below which no one except a Night Stalker flew at speed. But she thought better of it because she'd rather not know quite how good this woman was. She also didn't want to find out the hard way she actually wasn't.

A wandering final double *X* over the joined training ranges, then the woman eased up to five hundred and established a stable hover. "Your bird," she announced in a flat voice as if the last hour had been no more than a short flight across an airfield.

"I have control," Sharelle confirmed, flipping her mind once more from training mode to pilot-in-command. "If you don't mind me asking, who the *hell* are you?"

"I think you have bigger problems."

"I do?"

"Two bogeys close inbound two o'clock low and a distant fast-mover at nine o'clock high."

Sharelle punched for tactical and cursed.

All alone in the midst of an empty training area, trying to figure out the woman in the copilot seat, she'd forgotten to keep an eye out for an unannounced attack. Nothing was *ever* as it seemed in a training range, at least not one run by the 160th SOAR.

If straight ahead was twelve on a horizontal clock, sure enough, off to her right two blips showed low and bright. Down at nap-of-earth. Night Stalkers.

The on-board system decided they were a pair of Little Birds by their radar signature. Not as fast as her DAP Hawk, they'd been designed to slip in where no one else could fit, but they still carried a significant weapons load-out. Right now, they were ducked down in between the trees as they followed an old logging road. Even for a Night Stalker that was a hell of a trick. Worse, they were already inside missile range if they carried simulated Sidewinders.

And at nine o'clock high, thankfully still way high, a jet plummeted in her direction. The system identified it as a T-38 Talon trainer jet. Which offered little comfort—agile and capable of Mach 1.3 versus her own Mach 0.25.

A pincer from two sides, high and low. A vastly superior force. No backup. No—

"Don't think. Act!" Her passenger snapped out.

———

Troy had held onto his clipboard through the neat double roll that Emily Beale had executed. He nearly lost it during Sharelle's roll. Should have stowed the damned thing. Too late now.

Five hundred feet up, she did that exact roll that Beale had performed. Did it in the same way too, not the way Sharelle ever had before. One, well, two demonstrations and she'd already integrated it into her skill set—he never picked up new skills that fast.

He had to grab twice to capture his clipboard as it floated in the negative-g moment of the inverted position aided by the reverse-pitched rotors.

Sharelle let the tumble decay into a deceptively chaotic spin.

He clutched the clipboard to his chest, knowing the next maneuver. Sharelle had done it during that final disastrous evacuation of Kabul, Afghanistan. It meant the crew chiefs and mechanics would have a much larger inspection task before their next flight due to extreme airframe stresses but it made the helo almost impossible to target.

Nothing to do except brace himself. No data to feed to Sharelle. No weapons to arm. Nothing except hang on as she slammed from an apparently out-of-control tumble into straight-and-level flight.

Straight-and-level *sideways* flight. She'd inserted herself between the two Little Birds, just high enough that they couldn't shoot at her without shooting their own rotor blades.

Looking out the cargo bay windows to either side, he saw the tail of one to port and the nose of another to starboard. Sharelle had ended her chaotic maneuver hovering exactly between her two aggressors as they emerged from the trees.

Olsen and Wright, not the least flustered by the chaos, fired their Miniguns, or at least the training lasers that illuminated the two helicopters flying to either side of them. It was a near-level shot at fifty meters—easy as riding a twenty-year-old mare.

"Bang, *du er død,*"Sergeant Hans Halvor Olsen, might be Norwegian right down to the accent and blue-and-red knit sweaters his sister made for him, but he loved the old Westerns despite growing up in some suburb of Seattle. He always picked old gunfighter movies when it was his turn to choose. *Cowboy* Olsen also had a penchant for mixing his parents' mother tongue into his threats.

"He be toast, mon," Jalissa Wright offered a good Jamaican twang that she used whenever especially pleased.

"Now for that fast mover," Sharelle said mostly to herself as she flew clear of the two *dead* helos. A good reminder to the crew that they weren't out of the woods yet.

A single jet. Not a lot of good places to hide out here. Stay low, stay fast, and call for help. Tonight's array of weapons included no air-to-air missiles. Guns against a supersonic jet, one sure to have air-to-air missiles aboard, made a lousy option.

"Not alone," she mumbled so softly that he doubted anyone who didn't know her so well would understand. They'd come through training a class apart, but been on the same bird ever since he'd graduated.

The Night Stalkers often operated far beyond help from friendly ground forces, but it never hurt to ask.

As Sharelle radioed in to do that—and found an *exercise-friendly* drone in the area to distract the inbound jet before it closed to attack—Troy thought about how to hide from it in the Kentucky countryside.

How to hide...

The pair of Little Birds had been too easy, even accounting for Sharelle's spectacular maneuver.

What if they were sacrificial lambs to guide their powerful DAP Hawk to the slaughter?

"Stealth!" he shouted over the intercom. "There's a stealth helo somewhere around here that—"

The bright tone of a target-locked missile ended that question.

They were dead.

———

SHARELLE HATED DYING.

She hated dying even more with a passenger aboard.

The sole blessing lay in the short length of the flight back to base; she'd lost her bird and killed her crew five minutes flight from the Fort Campbell airfield.

No one spoke during those painful three hundred seconds.

———

BY THE TIME SHARELLE HAD SHUT DOWN HER HELO, THE THREE slower Little Birds had settled in beside her. Two were regular AH-6 Killer Egg configurations. The small helicopters had room for two pilots, barely, a Minigun mounted on one side with a single four-thousand round ammo can filling the back seat, and a seven-rocket pod of APKWS—Hydra 70 missiles up-converted to the laser-guided Advanced Precision Kill Weapon System—on the other.

The third aggressor made her blink as it swooped to a hover mere inches above the pavement, then plopped down like someone spiking the ball in the end zone. Obviously, a Little Bird, once upon a time. But it had been chopped up with angular forms, and the weapons hung inside rounded pods with only the business ends visible. It was shut down and rolled into a hangar so fast she barely had time to register its features.

Troy had nailed it even though he'd been stuck back in a cargo bay with no readouts.

Stealth. She knew they existed, but she'd never seen one before. Certainly hadn't known there was one here at Fort Campbell. Then Sharelle remembered, helicopters almost never flew alone. Where there was one bird, there was usually a second. A secret stealth company? She'd never heard a whisper of such a thing.

"Wow! That was a hot maneuver," the pilot of the stealth bird peeled her helmet and was already talking as she exited the hangar. She approached close enough to assess in the dim lighting around the field—about as big around as a sniper rifle and not much taller. Up close, her red hair cascaded down to her shoulders. And her major's oak leaf stood as a testament to her skills. "To do that twisty-tumbly thing, what are you orienting on? When I go to inverted, I—"

"Trisha," a huge man who'd come up behind her spoke the single word with a tone that sound more like a sigh than a warning.

"Right, sorry. I do ramble on a bit. I'll catch up with you in the debrief." She grabbed Sharelle's hand and was done shaking it before Sharelle thought to react.

Killed by a Yankee, Boston by the sound of it. Worse morphing into worser, the name of her day.

"Trisha O'Malley at your service. Pleasure to watch you fly, even if I did kill your ass. Sorry about that, by the way. I'll try not to make a habit of it." She flashed a huge grin that said she looked forward to doing precisely that as often as possible.

"Well, bless your sweet little heart for sayin' so." About the worst insult anywhere south of the Mason-Dixon Line. About the only time she let her Southern out to play.

"My pleasure. You know—" This Trisha completely missed it, just like a Yankee.

Her oversized companion, though, grimaced in sympathetic

pain. Then he clamped an arm across the redhead's shoulders, pulled her far closer than any mere fellow officer would, and turned her bodily away.

Her crew passed by after they finished the shutdown.

"I'm so sorry, y'all." What else could she say after having gotten them killed? It didn't matter that it was a training exercise.

"It is okay, Captain," Cowboy offered.

"It happens," Jalissa's white smile lit her dark face.

But it didn't. Not to her. It had been over a year since she'd been marked with so much as an injured crew during a training exercise. No way to blame it on the woman passenger. Sharelle should *never* have assumed that what she could see constituted the only danger. Though she'd be damned if she knew what she'd have done differently to survive that encounter.

Sharelle saw that her crew chiefs were plenty subdued as they too headed toward debrief. They *knew* she'd let them down.

Troy didn't say a word as he passed by. He didn't look upset, instead nodding back toward the helo. She certainly didn't have the heart now to ask what he'd thought was so damned funny.

She turned to look at her Hawk. The ground crew hovered close around the bird, ready to tuck it into a hangar. But waiting. DAP Hawks weren't left out in the open any more than stealth Little Birds.

But through the big windshield Sharelle saw what had stopped them. The woman still sat at the copilot's controls. She wasn't inspecting the controls, hadn't taken off her helmet, she simply sat there staring straight ahead.

Sharelle glanced over her shoulder to see what the woman was looking at. Nothing much. Twenty-odd Black Hawks, a double-handful of the big twin-rotor Chinook transports, and a scattering of Little Birds—the three primary aircraft of the 160th SOAR.

And yet the woman stared in a way that made Sharelle wonder what she was actually seeing.

She didn't react when Sharelle crossed her line of vision as she circled around to open the copilot's door. On the ground Sharelle didn't mind being nice to the little VIP, especially if it would mitigate the woman's report about Sharelle getting her killed.

The woman had peeled off her fingerless gloves, common among helo pilots, and slowly twisted a wedding ring around and around her finger.

"You okay?"

"I'm...not sure." She didn't turn from her thousand-yard stare. "There should be a single word for describing exceptionally difficult decisions."

"Suckitude!" At least the woman didn't look angry about dying.

She nodded, then she looked down at her fingers. She flexed them exactly as she had the moment prior to taking command of the flight. Except she didn't reach for the now-dead flight controls.

What else might she be grasping for control of?

As if she'd found it, she nodded again, more emphatically this time. Though uncertainty still reflected in those worrying fingers. Sharelle wished she could see the woman's eyes, but it was the middle of the night on a generally darkened airfield.

Then she aimed those hidden eyes at Sharelle. "Thank you for the flight. It has been too long."

"It doesn't show."

The woman's head tip struck like a slap. In a Night Stalker there existed no wiggle room on the truth—especially when it came to operational skills.

"Much," Sharelle amended, managing not to sound too utterly lame in the process. Did it break some God-given rule to be nice to a civilian? Except no civilian ever made a DAP Hawk dance across the sky like that.

As the woman clambered down, Sharelle took a step back. Her height hadn't been apparent while sitting in the copilot's seat; the woman matched Sharelle's five-ten. Where she'd appeared willowy had been replaced by substantial. Not solid, she was too slender for that, but Sharelle hadn't forgotten that quelling look early during the preflight. Nor that she'd had the decency to take herself out of the circuit before reprimanding Sharelle for not soliciting help—a majorly dumb piloting 101 moment. Damned decent in retrospect.

This was *not* some senator's girlfriend or Pentagon hanger-on.

"Is a, uh, salute in order, ma'am?"

She brushed at the area above her left breast, no rank insignia there. She glanced down as if in surprise at finding none. "I was never big on all that protocol; spent too many years forward-deployed."

Sharelle knew that one. Never salute when in a combat zone; it tells the sniper which person is the officer they should shoot first.

The woman pulled off her helmet, releasing a shoulder-length fall of dead-straight hair as pale as sunrise.

Impossible! It couldn't be.

Whoa! was all her inner voice managed.

As the woman turned to go, one of the field lights cast a glow over her chest. The name badge that had been hidden beneath the copilot's seat harness was now visible and confirmed the impossible had turned real.

"Beale," Sharelle managed it as a bare gasp.

"Yes?"

Sharelle couldn't help herself. She jerked to full attention and snapped out a salute.

Emily Beale offered that ghost of a smile, but straightened up and returned the salute formally. "At ease, Captain."

Sharelle dropped into parade rest, knowing that wasn't what Beale had meant, but she had no choice. "You're the reason I get to fly, ma'am. Not a woman in the Night Stalkers doesn't know you busted down that front door."

"That was over a dozen years ago."

"Don't care. You were the woman who was too good to keep out, years before the Defense Secretary decided women might actually have skills. Not a woman in the regiment doesn't know you led the way."

"You're not making my decision any easier, Captain Vargas."

Decision? Sitting alone in a DAP Hawk's cockpit—Emily Beale, Holy Mother Mary, no wonder she'd been so good aloft. But now toying with her wedding ring and acting all...weird?

The ground team moved in and rolled the DAP Hawk toward the hangar. Now they were just two female DAP pilots standing in a field of lesser helos.

Scuttlebutt said Beale had long-since retired with husband and kids. But here she stood in full gear. And that helmet, Night Stalker insignia on a field of sunset purple, it was Beale's own helmet—as if she personally *embodied* the regiment.

Sharelle recognized it now, only ever seen in flashes and not especially noteworthy. She'd been far more absorbed in watching the tactics and techniques of the few videos ever captured of Major Emily Beale's flights. The pilot's helmet had been the same, except in one lame-o CNN piece.

Someone should shoot her. Sharelle had just spent an hour with Emily Beale in flight, a never-possible dream, and hadn't recognized the flight techniques from those videos. But...they hadn't matched. In some ways they weren't as smooth, but in others they'd evolved into whole new directions that would take Sharelle dozens of flights to ingest and integrate into her own.

"Request permission to shake your hand. It's an honor to have flown with you, ma'am."

At Beale's nod, they did so.

They turned in unison to head over to debrief.

"If I may ask, ma'am, what brings you to Fort Campbell tonight?"

Beale responded with what Sharelle was starting to recognize as her normal response, silence.

The image of Beale looking sadly at her wedding ring wouldn't go away. Not like she wanted to take it off, but more like...Sharelle wasn't sure what. Some kind of anchor she herself had never found? Or an irritant?

Beale had a husband and kids. Montana or some such godforsaken place. Here now, flying, and toying with—no —*worrying at* her wedding ring. Here to...

Then Sharelle remembered Troy's laugh.

He knew. Top of the flight he'd known and hadn't warned her. No, he'd started to, but Beale had twisted around to look at him. Hard and fast, like commanding him to silence. Then Troy had wished Sharelle a good flight. Troy was always the smart one in their cockpit. Made him annoying as hell, but also awesome as a copilot.

Emily Beale wasn't retired; she was still in it somehow. And by how she'd been twisting that ring, facing one hell of a hard decision.

Like whether or not to take over command of the regiment from Colonel Cass McDermott? *Colonel* Beale? But that meant—

"Your family. Montana. You..." She didn't finish it. Didn't know why she'd said it aloud in the first place.

Beale stopped outside the heavy steel doors leading into the 160th's operations building tucked between two of the hangars.

"Why do you serve, Vargas?" She asked the question as if it was the most important one ever asked in the world.

"That's easy. Best people I ever met." And they were. After flying with people like this, why would anyone ever leave. It would be a betrayal. Yet, Emily Beale had done precisely that.

Beale nodded solemnly. "And that's the problem, isn't it?"

Sharelle didn't see any problem at all. She loved to fly. To fly the DAP was the ultimate. And to do so with the Night Stalkers? Utterly awesome.

Emily offered that sad smile of hers for a moment. "Perhaps you'll never find out. You can always hope." Beale stood straight and stepped through the doors.

Find out what?

If the woman didn't want to be here, what did that say about her as a future regiment commander?

Sharelle had just peered beneath the legend—and found out something about Colonel Beale that she didn't like one bit.

3

———

"TEN'SHUN!" THE REDHEAD'S CALL SLICED THROUGH THE chatter in the debriefing room. It had been far slower to start than normal after the ugly failures on the training range. He'd been left to contemplate the stench of burned coffee and unwashed pilot sweat that permeated every briefing room he'd ever sat in.

Troy leapt to his feet along with the rest of the crew. Three two-person crews from the Little Birds, including the redhead and her towering copilot—impressive that his shoulders *fit* into a Little Bird at all—and the crew chiefs from his own DAP Hawk. As Troy stood sideways at the front of the room, he saw the others trying to look around without breaking their rigid stance as to why the call had sounded out.

Troy fought his smile as Sharelle and Emily Beale entered the briefing room through the side door. They made an interesting contrast. Other than their height, they shared nothing in appearance.

All the stories of Beale hadn't included her beauty. She stood soldier straight, her bright blonde hair cropped perfectly square at her shoulders. Practically ageless, though she had to be mid-forties measured by her rank alone.

Sharelle's skin showed her self-proclaimed *who-knows* heritage. She said there was African-Scottish blood on her ma's side, and Latin-Japanese on her dad's, though no one knew where the thick mop of dark-amber curls came from. The very definition of melting-pot American made amazing.

Her usual wide, easy smile was missing in action, presently a grim line. In that, her expression matched Beale's. Had Beale reamed her out for tonight's failure? Unfair as hell if she had.

"At ease," Beale's voice had been almost robotic during the flight, hard to read from the few words she'd offered. "Take your seats." Now it had a softness that sounded wrong, especially against the grim set of her jaw. A tiny gesture sent Sharelle to the seats.

His commander came to sit in her usual spot beside him, but the comfortable armchair did nothing to ease the rigidness in her body. What the hell had Beale done to her?

Colonel Beale did not move to stand behind the podium beside the large blank screen that would show tactical views of tonight's flights. Instead, she sat on the corner of a table in an incongruously casual pose.

"First, allow me to introduce myself. I'm Colonel Emily—"

"About damn time," the redhead called out.

"—Beale," the colonel ignored her. "The one with the mouth is Major Trisha O'Malley. I never flew with her in the Night Stalkers—"

"But we kicked ass together back in the 101st."

"And she still doesn't know when to keep her mouth shut." Emily didn't offer the glare that had quelled him during the flight.

"Nope!" the redhead replied cheerfully.

"And her copilot is Lieutenant Colonel William—"

"Billy the SEAL, but only I get to call him that."

"—Bruce. No longer a SEAL—"

"Which is why I'm the only one who gets to call him that."

"—now a permanently embedded liaison to the Night Stalkers from The Unit."

Troy twisted around to look at the pair. They sat in the second row, holding hands. A wedding ring dangled from a chain about her neck, a common enough practice among soldier women who needed to use their hands. Married and yet they served together.

That was...impossible.

No, it wasn't. Colonel Beale had married her company commander, Mark Henderson, though they'd left the military soon after, hadn't they? All ancient history. There were rumors of others, but in the same chain of command? That was crazy, and illegal as hell by Army regulations. So, what, special dispensation by the commander in chief? Not likely. And then Major O'Malley and Billy the Not SEAL? What the hell was going on here?

It was but one of the many reasons he kept his relationship with Sharelle Vargas strictly professional. He could serve with her or risk losing the right to fly with her. And if the feelings weren't mutual, it could screw up everything and she might not want to fly with him anymore. A tough decision that he questioned only ten or twenty times a day.

Bruce returned his gaze steadily, apparently used to the reaction.

But that wasn't the only shocker. Troy had heard of embedded Delta in the Night Stalkers once. Stories of—oh!—then-Major Emily Beale and the equally legendary Colonel Michael Gibson of Delta. Here was their legacy, seated in the row behind him as if it was the most normal thing in the world.

Only after Troy turned back to face Beale did it sink in. Cass McDermott's departure and Emily Beale's arrival might not be the only things about to change in the 160th SOAR.

"First, I want to thank Captain Sharelle Vargas and her crew for allowing me to barge in on their flight. I asked Cass for the best team he had—"

"Hey!" the annoying redhead called out.

Sharelle wanted to gag the woman. Sure, it was fine for her to feel so happy, she was the one who had killed Sharelle's ass in front of the great Emily Beale.

The look that Colonel Beale aimed close over Sharelle's head made her want to duck to keep clear of its power.

"Just trying to keep it lively," but the redhead kept that to a whisper that barely reached Sharelle.

"The best team he had...in a DAP Hawk," Beale amended. And this time her serious gaze aimed at Sharelle and offered the slightest nod of acknowledgement.

Sharelle's spine straightened as if that tiny nod had added inches to her height. That might chill down Trisha, but Sharelle knew that only the very best were entrusted with one of the Night Stalkers precious DAPs.

"I set you up against unwinnable odds, including myself as an unknown quantity for a copilot. You accounted for three of your four opponents. Even with your regular copilot," this time she acknowledged Troy, "it would have been tough. Trisha is almost as exceptional a combatant as she is a pain."

Pain-in-the-ass Trisha O'Malley!

She wanted to give her inner voice a high five for nailing it. But remembering the simulated death of her entire flight at PITA O'Malley's hands, any wind that had gotten lift on Sharelle's wings turned into a hard-shearing downdraft.

Beale again paused, absentmindedly toying with her wedding ring, though she didn't look down at it. Sharelle wondered that the woman did anything absentmindedly. She glanced at Sharelle and must have picked up where her attention had drifted. Her hands went still, then...casually separated.

After another long moment of silence, Beale nodded as if to herself, the motion visible only as the barest ripple along her dead-straight hair. Her left hand was now clenched in a tight fist.

She abruptly rose to her feet. Her stance announced the end of the debrief even though they hadn't reviewed the flight yet.

Everyone in the room rose to attention without the call. Out of the corner of her eye, Sharelle saw even the redhead scrambled up fast.

"There will be a formal announcement tomorrow," she glanced at the wall clock—it literally *was* zero-dark-thirty. "Make that later today. Until then please keep it among yourselves. At the behest of General Cass McDermott, the Chairman of the Joint Chiefs of Staff, the Secretary of Defense, and President Zachary Thomas, I hereby accept command of the US Army 160th Special Operations Aviation Regiment (Airborne). It will be an honor and a privilege."

Suspecting it was coming and hearing it said were two very different things. Sharelle had seen the doubt on Beale's face. Would it be worse to have an Old White Dude in command or Beale when she didn't want to be here? Sharelle simply didn't know.

"Captain Vargas," Beale's attention snapped to her, freezing Sharelle's thoughts in place. "I want that final maneuver of yours against the Little Birds incorporated into training by end of week, with both our own Special Operations Training Battalion and the ACE team down at Fort Novosel. See to that. Don't tell them, fly down with your crew and show them until they get it right."

"Yes ma'am." That was something at least. The Army's Aviation Center of Excellence boasted the toughest trainers anywhere. Coming from someone of Beale's caliber, it was a highfalutin' compliment.

Own it, girl!

She would.

"I will leave you to debrief amongst yourselves. I expect you to focus on what worked, not what failed in each of your tactics. Ask what you each might have done differently to survive the situation. That goes equally for you Little Bird pilots killed by the DAP Hawk. I expect at least three new ideas on ways to run that scenario, from both sides."

Watch out for a goddamn stealth bird! would be at the top of Sharelle's list.

"Further, sacrificing two helos and four personnel to take out a DAP Hawk is an unacceptable solution in any scenario I can imagine, short of an imminent threat to the President or nuclear security—so imagine it for me. I want three more scenarios of when such a sacrifice *would* be called for, then solve how to avoid any losses in each of those scenarios. Don't dwell on it; do it and get it done. Full report from my Number Two before dawn." Emily nodded toward the redhead. "That's a well-deserved rank bump, by the way. Congratulations, Lieutenant Colonel O'Malley."

"What? Emily! No way! I fly for a goddamn living." Trisha O'Malley didn't sound so cheerful anymore.

Sharelle smiled, though she kept that to herself.

Colonel Emily Beale stood silent. She looked around the room, one person at a time—seven pilots, her own two crew chiefs, and a Delta Force operator. Not even the redhead dared break the silence while she did. Sharelle came last and, it seemed to her, the longest. Emily's voice, barely a whisper, reached Sharelle, "So did I."

Had it been doubt, sorrow, or hard acceptance of a new reality in which she no longer *flew for a living?* Sharelle didn't know if she'd seen weakness or been granted a once-in-a-lifetime view of the raw power it took to lead, especially as a woman.

Then Beale snapped to and saluted the room. "Dismissed." And she strode out like... the commander of a Special Operations regiment.

"No way did she just say that. Tell me she didn't say that, Billy." Trisha's pleading voice didn't grate on Sharelle's nerves so much anymore. To be taken out of the sky like that—victorious against a DAP Hawk one moment and relegated to command the next? Freaking brutal. "I knew I should have stayed a Warrant Officer. But no! Goddamn LaRue said I had to go officer! It was for this. She *knew* this would happen. I'm gonna kill her. That woman is fuckin' toast next time I see her."

"Some serious nepotism. Old pal up to Number Two," Sharelle whispered to Troy.

"I don't think Colonel Beale is the sort to make that mistake. And it's not sitting well, is it?"

Sharelle looked at the distress on Major, now Lieutenant Colonel O'Malley's face. Not merely distress. Beneath her rant, tears were streaming down her face as fast as Billy could wipe them away. As usual, Troy had it right. Which meant Beale had done that to the woman because...

"She's got something that doesn't show," Troy continued. "Beale called her an exceptional combatant. Might be that extends to more than in the briefing room."

He always kept it politic and calm, where her preference for confrontation was a smile on her face and a DAP Hawk wrapped around her. On the ground, she simply imagined the DAP Hawk armor and took no prisoners.

Billy looked over at him. With a silent nod, he indicated

Troy, then tipped his head to indicate the podium that Beale had ignored.

"Oh. Uh... Okay, people," Troy spoke up. "As I was the only noncombatant in this scenario, I'll start the breakdown." He moved up to the podium and pulled up the satellite and range tracking of the night's flight. He didn't start at the final battle, but all the way back at the initial departure from Fort Campbell Army Airfield.

Sharelle sat back in her seat. It was going to be a long night. And out there, somewhere beyond her sensor range, the Night Stalkers were changing.

4

A CHILL SEPTEMBER WIND RIPPED DOWN FROM THE ARCTIC. Fairbanks, Alaska, ranked somewhere past crazy as a choice of where to live.

Kentucky had been comfortable in the lush warmth of late summer.

Here, the Fort Wainwright runway lay mostly hidden in a racing swirl of snow. Barely ankle high on Sharelle's army boots, it did create a colorful low mist as it snaked above white runway and blue taxiway lights. Splashes of green and red marked thresholds at either end of the runway. Between, it caught the golden light of the half-moon. A scene she felt in no mood to appreciate.

Only stoic tradition kept Sharelle out in the open, following her crew chiefs through their preflight. Kentucky bred and buttered, she'd lived close enough to Fort Campbell to have helicopter dreams each time they roared through the darkness overhead. Tonight's mission, at least from Mama Nature's side? Prove the bitter snow belonged in mid-September rather than the very heart of winter.

The old military joke of *Behave or we'll ship you out to a radar station in the Alaskan tundra* struck her as much less funny than it ever had. She knew it wasn't punishment; it only felt that way.

Sixty days after Colonel Emily Beale took over and Sharelle wondered if the Night Stalkers would ever be the same.

Combat has changed and we must change with it. Beale had said in her speech at the official Change of Command ceremony that first day. *This is no longer a world defined by the Iraq or Afghanistan War.* She'd said it while standing next to Cass McDermott of all travesties. McDermott had overseen the last years of both conflicts and the final evacuation. Yet there she'd stood, accusing the man of being out of touch.

It had been hard at the time to remember that Emily Beale's entire deployment with both the 101st and the 160th had been to those two wars; a decade mostly flown in the horror show that had been Afghanistan.

Two months, and change them she had.

Jalissa Wright kept pounding her gloved fists together as she worked her way through the preflight inspection. Cowboy, apparently impervious to the cold, had only half-zipped his jacket that flapped in the bitter wind like a trapped crow beating its wings against his chest.

For sixty days, Sharelle and Troy had studied tactics like none she'd ever seen, and flown missions of impossible complexity. The workload so high that several pilots, good men, had burned out of leading forward combat missions and were relegated to the transports. They were still Night Stalkers pilots, meaning they flew deeper into danger than any other unit, but no longer led at the point of the spear.

Not a chance would Sharelle be falling for that. She flew a DAP Hawk. The spear didn't get any pointier, and that's where she, Troy, and her crew thrived.

"We be good, Captain," Jalissa told her. "All ship and shape."

Sharelle hadn't been watching them, instead coming to a

halt in the bitter wind—half watching the swirling snow scoot along the ground in waves, half reviewing the tactical changes Beale had demanded.

"Uh, right. Okay. Then let's get out of this wind and up into it."

Aboard the helo, still freezing until they heated her engines up, she read off the checklists for Troy. He would start as pilot in command. Tonight's flight was a long one and they'd need to switch off several times.

With the engines spinning and the cabin almost up to icebox temperature, Sharelle checked out the windscreen. The three MH-60M transport Black Hawks she'd be flying protection for during tonight's training were all starting their spin-up as well.

As she watched, an unprecedented twenty-four Delta Force operators streamed out of the hangar and loaded up eight to a bird with backpacks the size of small moving vans.

She'd seen the mission plans but could only stare in wonder as they boarded the other birds.

You sent in two or three Delta to take down a terrorist cell. A half dozen to take out an entire training camp, clear an airplane, or scour a cruise ship. Three eight-man squads probably ranked as the greatest single concentration of lethal force anywhere in the world.

Jogging at the front was the ever silent *Billy the SEAL*. The name had stuck, of course, exactly as PITA O'Malley—an unofficial name for Trisha, which the damn pain-in-the-ass woman fully embraced—had known it would. He was half again the size of anyone else on the team, but he ran at the lead. Over the last two months, he'd often had two or three of his Delta Force brethren along, but never three full squads.

Colonel Beale had warned them of new tactics, but what the hell would require a deployment force like this one? Except now she *could* imagine it. The wonders of two months of pressure from PITA O'Malley. A dozen scenarios came to mind far too easily.

Trisha's twisty mind riffed a new scenario faster than anyone she'd ever met—she even pushed Troy in that respect. Being both smart and likeable made her even more of a PITA; seconds-in-command were supposed to be the hard-ass drivers with the commander being the voice of reason. Instead Colonel Beale pushed everyone away personally, not a chance Sharelle would ever consider calling her Emily. But Trisha could make you laugh right in the middle of reaming you out. At least she hadn't managed to kill Sharelle's DAP Hawk again, though there'd been a couple of exercises that came too close for comfort.

Sharelle glanced around, despite the briefing that they wouldn't be there. No Little Birds tonight. They were capable of covering the route but would require four refuelings, which had to be done on the ground for the little MH-6Ms.

Not a problem for the Night Stalkers, they practiced FARPs —Forward Arming and Refueling Points—but each descent, refuel, and climb out took time. That would put the Little Birds another forty-five minutes behind due to their FARP maneuvers. The Hawks' lone refueling could be done in the air.

No FARP would fit in the time restraints PITA O'Malley had mandated for tonight's exercise, especially not with their ten-mile-per-hour lower speed than the Hawks. In the six-hour scenario, they'd be a full hour behind. But she missed them. It was like having several fingers taken away, then being told to play a drum. You could still hold the sticks, but it wouldn't be the same.

"Black Route Alaska, here we go," Troy called out as he took them aloft. The other three helos lifted in smooth unison and turned north. With their superior sensors and firepower, the DAP took the lead.

The Night Stalkers commonly flew Black Route training

missions. Originating in the very first days of the regiment—before night vision functioned worth a damn—the Night Stalkers began practicing long missions under the cover of darkness.

After the death of Lieutenant Colonel Michael C. Grimm while flying a Black Route, the fourth Night Stalker to ever go down, the regiment had focused immense effort on advancing night-vision technology and adapting it to piloting. All the other armed forces of the world might take the technology for granted, but no Night Stalker ever would; its modern-day history was their history, in honor of LTC Grimm.

The early records of the founding of the 160th weren't wholly clear, but most folks believed that Grimm had personally created the Black Route challenge that ultimately killed him. Fly eight hundred miles at nap-of-earth altitudes, stopping at only three locations, but arriving at each one within a one-minute window. Plus or minus thirty seconds because ground troops' lives might depend on it. The moment troops broke cover to reach a landing zone, they were vulnerable. The Night Stalkers were *always* there precisely on time to get them out.

PITA O'Malley drove the teams to hit plus or minus fifteen seconds or she counted it as a failure. Sharelle was completely down with that and personally pushed herself and Troy for a plus-minus-five window.

The normal Black Route course ran from Fort Campbell, Kentucky, down to Fort Novosel, Alabama, and back. Most Army helo pilots still called it Mother Rucker for the brutal demands of the trainers there and its prior name of Fort Rucker —after a Confederate colonel, no longer so honored.

Not Colonel Beale's idea of a Black Route.

Assume a winter war in the Carpathians, the Caucasus, or along the Finnish border, she'd said when she made one of her rare personal briefings twenty minutes ago. Sharelle hadn't even known that Beale had come to Alaska. No need to say against who in any of those places: Russia. *Assume the worst. Then know, for a fact, you've only scratched the surface of reality.*

Tonight's mission felt plenty real.

Black Route—Alaskan style.

A normal airport departure included a steady climb to a thousand feet. Per instructions, Troy never climbed over fifty— to the top of the rotor. That meant their wheels were thirty- three feet, ten meters, above the tundra. At a hundred and sixty knots, that placed them a tenth of a second from impact for a single mistake. And by the mission profile, they'd be riding that knife edge for the next six hours.

An enemy's Primary Surveillance Radar might reach down to only a few hundred feet. But on a flat plane like the upcoming tundra, where ground interference would be minimal, lower was always better—as long as one avoided impacting the ground.

"Okay to stow?" Olsen asked from the back.

In her present role as copilot, Sharelle studied the tactical feed from both onboard sensors and the drone watching from high above. Nobody in their airspace except her three fellow Black Hawks.

"Do it."

Sharelle heard the heavy clanking of metal as the two crew chiefs' Miniguns were pulled inboard, locked down, and the shooting doors closed against the frigid night. They could redeploy in seconds—in battle perhaps a crucial few seconds that might separate life and death—but running alone through the Alaskan wilderness probably not. It made the ride both quieter and warmer.

Olsen and Jalissa would settle in to monitoring the DAP's overall status and taking turns to stretch out on the deck.

"She's pushing us on this one," Troy followed a tiny ravine that the nav software named as Nome Creek, running between the rough hills sixty kilometers northeast of Fairbanks.

No need to identify who *she* might be. Colonel Emily Beale already had made herself a presence, no, a *force* felt in every corner of the regiment. It seemed the woman was always everywhere. Friends in the third and fourth battalions had reported consecutive night visits by her—except they were based in Georgia and Washington state, respectively. And not simple visits, but in-depth inspections, unannounced exercises, and tabletop training scenarios.

One thing to say for Beale, she was utterly tireless when it came to bettering the Night Stalkers' skills. Like Cass McDermott, but without the patience or sense of humor.

McDermott had pushed the best to lead by example and lift the rest of the regiment up with them.

Beale *was* the example! And she drove everyone to be their individual best: man and woman, pilot and crew chief, mechanic and even cook.

"Beale's a crazy woman," Jalissa said on the intercom. The crew chiefs typically didn't say much, leaving her and Troy to provide any entertainment.

"Pushing herself even harder." Troy often talked when flying nap-of-earth, she had found it distracting at first when he'd done the same to her while she was flying NOE, but she'd grown used to it, even preferring it. It forced her to keep a more flexible mindset, rather than becoming too locked in on the task at hand.

"Since Day One," Sharelle acknowledged.

"Before Day One; she flew with us the night *before* taking command." Running out of creek, Troy slid into the icy ravine that ran around the base of a Mount Prindle.

Out her right-hand pilot's window, she gazed up at the three-thousand-foot prominence of the jagged peak, already shrouded in a brilliant blanket of snow and probably just waiting to dump an early-season avalanche on their heads. "And why is this night different from all other nights?"

"Now you're sounding positively Jewish."

"I am? Why?"

Troy twisted them through another narrow ravine, then climbed over a mountain saddle before descending the other side.

Sharelle checked both the radar and the night-vision-enhanced rear view she projected on her visor to confirm that the three helos they were escorting made it through clean. They were Night Stalkers. They did.

They flew with a non-combat spacing of three rotors. For a helo pilot, thinking in *rotors* rather than multiples of the seventeen-meter span of the blades provided simplified communication.

"I was dating a Jewish girl once who took me to a Passover Seder. They ask that question as a part of the ceremony."

"So why is that night different?"

A final turn and the last of the mountains fell away. "Your bird," Troy announced.

At NOE, a handoff made for a much more sensitive technique than up at a thousand. The slightest bobble here could be fatal. First the collective for power, she could feel the steadiness of his left hand as she eased hers onto the lever beside her seat. Then slipping onto the cyclic joystick until they were flying like a single body. Finally, his easing away, breaking that brief, intense connection. They passed control more smoothly than the surface of the dunk tank the moment before helicopter chassis slammed into the pool for escape training.

"I have control."

Troy had threaded them through seventy-five miles of twisting hills and deep valleys. The next two hundred miles would be far simpler but require a different technique, a reasonable moment to switch pilots. From here, as long as she didn't run into one of the radar domes at Fort Yukon Air Force Station—probably the tallest objects in the four-hundred-person town—it was all about scattered trees and occasional river valleys. Once they hit the Yukon River, she'd lead the flight up the Porcupine to the Coleen, letting her fly close above the surfaces already freezing up for the winter.

Troy began flexing and massaging his hands. "Passover is the celebration of the freeing of the Jews from Israel. Ten curses sent by God across ten nights and then the people were freed from slavery."

"Okay, well, why was that night different? It's always bothered me. Beale really, really didn't want to take command of the Night Stalkers."

She felt Troy turn to her simply by the nature of his silence, though she didn't risk looking past the in-visor display during NOE piloting.

"Seriously. The woman practically squirmed in her seat trying to make up her mind. When she did, she looked ready to yank off her wedding ring and chuck it across the room."

Troy was a long time answering.

She picked up the line of the Upper Mouth River well east of Fort Yukon and began chasing its meandering path northeast.

"Jesus, Sharelle. You're the best pilot in all SOAR, but sometimes you can be so goldurn dense."

HOOF-IN-MOUTH DISEASE, TROY NELSON RYLAND, JUNIOR. THAT'S what Momma had always called it, also the only time she used his full name. At least he knew where he'd gotten the gene from, because the other variation often heard around the house was: *Hoof-in-mouth disease, Troy Nelson Ryland, Senior.*

The silence in the cockpit was thundering, even accounting for the masking of engine and rotor noise.

"Da man put his foot in dat one, di'n he?" Jalissa spoke the best English of them all when she chose to, which wasn't when she was busting his chops.

"He did." Sharelle replied.

"Perfect." Maybe he should throw himself out of the bird. Of course, the Porcupine River was freezing up fast. Then Sharelle swung north to follow the Coleen, which looked to already be fully iced. If the ice didn't kill him, punching through into the frozen river beneath certainly would.

"He is right though," Cowboy rode in to put out the fire. *Good man. Brotherhood ruled.*

"How's that?"

Troy retreated to the keeping-his-mouth-shut line and silently urged one of the crew chiefs to step in.

"You know the stats," Jalissa spoke in her natural, slightly Brooklyn, New *Yawk* accent. "No one finished more missions with a higher success rate than when she was aloft with Mark Henderson. Retired out before any of us signed on, yet we know their names and a lot of their missions. I'd wager there are a lot more missions we *don't* know about. Then, *poof*, dey bod be gawn. Oh, so sad."

"Now she is back, like she was never gone." Olsen stepped in. "Husband, two kids, happily retired—but not."

"How do you know she was happy?"

Troy scoffed. Troy, Mr. Always-So-Polite, scoffed.

Sharelle bobbled the flight. Not much. Not enough to kill them. No more than five feet down, then up. But enough for Troy to note it as a major reaction for Sharelle.

He really had to keep his foot out of it.

"Do the math, Sharelle," he kept his tone soft and steady. "Full colonel at forty-two. At least three years ahead of the norm. That means no gaps in her service. She leaves the Night

Stalkers and goes to fight forest fires way back before any of us ever touched an Army bird. Then drops out of that three or four years later. Not a peep. Except, *Pow!* By inexplicable magic, here she is a full colonel. She *wasn't* out of the service. She was doing things none of us will ever know about."

Troy thought about a couple of Cass McDermott's departing comments and began to wonder if *he* knew what she'd been up to all those years. Maybe not? But still he'd chosen her and command had agreed.

"Okay, so she was busy doing who-knows for who-cares," Sharelle hadn't softened her tone much. "I saw her damn face that first night. All sad and lost, wouldn't stop playing with that stupid wedding ring."

Troy wished he could see Sharelle's face. For all of their mutual teasing, there'd been no question between his parents. A-plus marriage? No. But his folks demonstrated at least a rock-solid B. That ring meant something. Funny, now that he thought about it. In three years flying together, Sharelle never discussed her family.

Jalissa sighed but didn't speak.

Cowboy had wisely stolen Troy's plan of keeping his thoughts to himself, which only left himself.

"They fell so in love that when she left the Night Stalkers because she was pregnant, Henderson quit the same day. He was a company commander. Except they didn't really quit. What if they went on to something even edgier than the 160th? I looked them up. They now run one of those seriously major tourist ranches out in Montana. Looks pretty idyllic to this Oklahoma farm boy. Horses, a Michelin-starred chef, military dog trainers, a lot of discounts for active duty and veteran guests."

"Whoop-di-doo."

"And a lot of shots of a seriously happy family. Two cute kids, Lieutenant Colonel Mark Henderson front and center. He retired two years ago after four years running training for the local Army National Guard. What were they doing until six years ago after leaving the 160th eleven years ago? They were *both* into something hush-hush before he went to the ARNG. No sign that she ever stood down. But you see them together and there can't be any question."

———

"You still have an eye on tactical?" she asked to slow Troy down. Sharelle couldn't make the pieces he was telling her fit together in her head. She eased up five feet to buy herself a little more reaction time.

"Roger that. We're showing clear as far as we can see. Overwatch is showing a couple whirlybirds just landing at Fort Wainwright and nothing else for a long way around." Overwatch would be one of the Night Stalkers' MQ-1C Gray Eagle RPAs, remote piloted aircraft, run by someone back in Kentucky.

At least they weren't the only suckers aloft on this miserable night. No snow, clear skies, but that icy wind slashing down from the Arctic definitely kept the flight interesting. More so, there were some hills coming up fast.

"If she was so damned happy, then what's she doing here?"

No one had an answer to that one.

It felt as if she should. There'd been something Colonel Beale had said that night, but Sharelle couldn't drag up the memory. Two months and a great gobsmack of new information ago had erased the moment.

"Turn heading two-five-zero in two kilometers."

Thirty seconds. She toggled to a wider view of her flight path before jumping back to the NOE mapping and letting her mind analyze what she'd seen. They were coming up fast on the Canadian border. Five kilometers from crossover, they ricocheted off it at an angle, switching from a northeasterly approach to a west-south-west departure. Straight into the heart of the Brooks Range.

This far north she'd expected snowy peaks. Instead, the setting moon shone off massive mountain faces that built and climbed layer upon layer as they turned to drive into the heart of the range. No glaciers. And, according to the reports she'd read, even the areas of perennial snow were all but gone courtesy of climate change. The Brooks Range kept heating up far faster than southeastern Alaska, already passing through four degrees C. No snow—yet. At this rate, pretty soon it might be never again.

She turned over the controls to Troy as they plunged into the ridge and valley of the mountains. Now headed south of west.

Per the mission plan, in two hundred and fifty kilometers they'd pick up some godforsaken river, probably with a name wholly unpronounceable by a native Kentuckian, and come slamming down the North Slope to stage a rescue in Prudhoe Bay.

Except the mission plan—not atypical for the Night Stalkers—didn't say who or what they were rescuing. How often had she flown out somewhere deep beyond the lines only to be put on a hold. *Get in close...and wait.* Sometimes they were banking on intel that simply didn't happen. Other times she'd have bet money that command liked jerking her personal chain, though she had no idea why.

Imagine.

That had been one of Colonel Beale's big lessons.

Imagine three scenarios that...

Give me five situations where...

Rethink the Osama bin Laden takedown mission, but with a wholly different set of assets.

Only by pre-thinking variables will you have a sliver of a chance to react instantly and accurately when the situation goes to hell—and you are Night Stalkers; where you fly, it's a given that everything will go to hell at some point.

So she kept one eye on Troy's flying, a second on tactical, and her imagination ranging ahead like a third eye.

What were they after in Prudhoe? It was the northern terminus of the Alaska Pipeline. Eight hundred miles of forty-eight-inch pipe, moving half a million barrels of oil every day. That filled a supertanker every two to three days. A full fortieth of US daily consumption flowed down that one pipe from Prudhoe to Valdez, headed to refineries at points south.

Didn't sound like a huge loss until she'd read the briefing packet. Kill off the Alaska Pipeline and, to make up the difference, they'd have to turn off the country for ten days a year. Everything: electricity, cars, trains, planes, factories, the whole mess.

Prudhoe used to be accessible by sea only a few weeks a year. Now the passage stood open for half the year. Easy access if Russia still had a Pacific Fleet worth talking about. China didn't have deep-water projection, yet, but the pipeline was impossibly vulnerable out there on its own.

———

"THINKING MIGHTY HARD THERE, SHARELLE."

Silence radiated off Sharelle in waves when she was digging deep. But experience had taught Troy that after a certain point, she'd be spinning gears faster than a tail rotor yet not making any fresh headway. How often he played cyclic to her hard yank on the collective. She pumped the power into this outfit, but it never hurt when he added a bit of guidance.

"Uh, yeah." She mumbled, about halfway back from her thoughts.

That was a good place to keep her. "Good thoughts about your dashingly handsome copilot?"

That earned him a snort of laughter, a very indelicate one for a fine Kentuckian.

He knew he wasn't the handsomest guy around, but he also hadn't seen Sharelle going after those much. Or anyone else. She'd hook up here and there for a week, but nothing stuck. He knew the feeling. The one woman he was stuck on worse than barbed wire caught around a combine's cutter remained wholly out of his reach, about half a meter away.

"Okay, so, what *are* you thinking?"

"I'm thinking that Beale's setting us up again."

"Oh, like she hasn't done that a dozen times these last two months."

She shook her head, "This is different. This is a real target, not a practice range."

Troy climbed over some nameless saddle that had probably never been seen before except by a lost caribou or a satellite and let himself fall into the valley on the far side. All the low-altitude climbing and descending chewed up a lot of fuel.

Their two-thousand-kilometer range might barely carry them the thousand to Prudhoe without a midair refuel.

"Beale's up to something."

"You still on that? I tell you, we may not know what's going on in her head but—"

"No! I'm not still on that," as close to a snarl as Sharelle ever aimed his way.

Troy shut his mouth and listened to the heavy throb of the rotors that pushed past his helmet's hearing protection. It was good enough that his ears would feel fine after the flight, though his body would be only too aware of the hours in the heavy bass downbeat of the big rotor blades. His body would be numb and tingling for hours after a flight this long, like it had been set on Agitate for too many rounds in a washing machine.

Sharelle still wasn't speaking.

"So, if not that, what *are* you on about?"

The valley was flat grasslands, nothing taller than his family's dog, a placid-with-age golden retriever named Maxine. He risked a glance over. Her head was up, but he'd wager she wasn't staring at the data displayed inside of her visor. As if to prove his point, she shoved up the visor and, leaning forward, stared out into the night as if trying to see what lay ahead of them.

In fourteen seconds, he'd be climbing up the face of a slip-fault that had blocked the valley. The artificial terrain map showed a lake had built up on the other side, so no simple tipping over the top of this one into a quick descent.

"Imagine..." Sharelle whispered as she leaned forward. "Imagine..."

He imagined a whole lot of things, but they were all about the woman and not the flight. Pushing them aside wasn't as easy as it sounded.

Up the rock slide, boulders the size of a Chinook helo had tumbled down off the mountain and—

"The Chinooks!" he shouted out much the way he had *Stealth!* during that first flight.

"The what?" By the dim cockpit panel lighting, he saw in his peripheral vision how the dark shadow of Sharelle twisted to face him.

In reaction, he almost did follow the terrain over the top of the saddle and down the far side, which would have been bad. The lake was running high. He leveled out five meters off the water and slowly climbed back to ten.

Sharelle noticed, of course. Keeping her silence until he'd stabilized at the proper altitude.

"What about the Chinooks?" she kept her voice steady.

Surprising a pilot busy flying nap-of-earth was never a good thing, and they both knew it.

"Those whirlybirds that Overwatch reported arriving at Fort Wainwright in Fairbanks after us. Who else would be flying a helo on a night like this?"

"Only us," Sharelle whispered. "Chinooks?"

"Chinooks," he confirmed. He'd bet on ones as big as life. The monster twin-rotor helos could carry twice a Black Hawk's load, except they weren't weapons platforms like their DAP Hawk. They were cargo and troop haulers like the three transport birds full of Delta Force they were escorting on this flight.

"Carrying what and heading where?" Sharelle's voice slid into pre-battle mode. Damn but the woman slayed him.

"Prudhoe Bay seems like a popular place tonight."

She almost laughed. "That's Beale all over. That's why she routed us all the way over to the Canadian border and is having us run back along the length of the Brooks Range. The Chinooks would make a direct flight from Wainwright to Prudhoe Bay in under two hours. Flat out, we need three and a half. All of this NOE pushes us out past four hours."

"She's setting us up?" Troy didn't know why he didn't believe it; it made perfect sense.

"Damn straight. Not even PITA O'Malley would have come up with this nastiness. How much you want to bet those Chinooks are inbound to Prudhoe Bay even now to emplace a massive force to surprise us when—"

Sharelle punched to the secure frequency between their DAP Hawk and the three birds they'd been leading. Night Stalkers flew in radio silence on missions to minimize trackable transmissions—except in emergencies.

"Hey, Michella," she called the lead Hawk, "need to talk to Billy the SEAL."

"Bill Bruce here," he answered back seconds later.

"You hear anything about a herd of your former SEAL brothers hanging out at Wainwright before tonight's mission? Waiting for a ride in a couple of Chinooks?"

His typical silence lasted longer than usual, even for him.

"Perhaps a couple of boats with them?"

Again the stretch of silence.

"Got it. Thanks."

"Yes ma'am. Bruce out."

"What?" Troy had missed something.

"No way PITA Trisha O'Malley didn't tell her hubby what was going on. Then she'd have sworn him to secrecy, promising not to say anything. He is absolutely a man of his word."

"What few words he speaks. So, what does that tell us?"

Sharelle didn't hesitate, "We're flying straight into a trap."

"Now we need to *imagine* how to avoid the trap."

"Any bright ideas?"

Troy smiled. "Oh, I've got a few."

5

"WARN MICHELLA. COURSE DEVIATION."

Sharelle did, but Troy didn't reveal what he was up to.

"Call in the refueling birds. Low-level refuel at," he read off the coordinates.

"But that's—"

"Please call it in, Captain Vargas."

She loved it when Troy shifted into his overly serious command mode. She swore that he grew in stature every time he did it. Reminded her of Daddy. He'd always been the strong guardian of his family, the ultimate protective father. Never missed one of her soccer games where she'd put her long legs to good use, winning the high school regionals twice as the center—first time she'd had the rank of captain. Never missed meeting one of her dates either. She'd inherited her height from him. Lean, but at six-two he managed to look down on every boy she ever brought home, even the ones from the basketball team.

Troy was the only man she'd met who might live up to Daddy's gold standard for what his daughter deserved. It was very distracting; kept her from concentrating for long on any number of amenable partners who had crossed her path.

Then she looked again at the coordinates.

Due east of Mount Isto, the tallest peak in the Brooks Range. Near enough nine thousand high and eight thousand feet of prominence above the valley floor, it was more imposing than the fourteen-thousand footers around Aspen's eight-thousand-foot base elevation.

They were supposed to pass south of it and continue another hour through the Brooks. Instead, Troy was guiding them to refuel in a wide valley to the east of Mount Isto. The mountain would block them from any high-flying overwatch pilot who might be guarding the flight of Chinooks.

By the time they made the turn northward beside Mt. Isto, an Air Force C-130 Hercules slid in low overhead. Refueling tankers liked to be at ten or twenty thousand feet. Coaxing them below three thousand, especially in a valley along the base of the tallest mountain in north Alaska, wasn't easy—until she evoked Colonel Beale's name.

Even in the Air Force, the woman had power. Now that was some serious pull.

The lowest known aerial refueling had been done by Iran during the Iran-Iraq War. F-4s and F-14s had refueled from a 747 flying at three hundred feet to avoid Iraqi radar. And they'd done it at three hundred knots.

Her flight did it at half the speed and she could only force the C-130 down to twice the height. Still, at six hundred feet up, there wasn't a lot of breathing room for a breakaway if anything went wrong because of the steep valley sides.

The whole operation took under ten minutes and she was fairly sure she didn't breathe the entire time.

The C-130 held stable at a hundred and thirty knots, splitting the difference between their stall speed when they'd fall out of the sky at a hundred and the helos' V-max of one-sixty. Then, they spun out the hoses attached far out on either wing, with a big three-hundred-pound catch basket at the end—a basket that only looked big on the ground. In the air, being buffeted about by the C-130's passage and tonight's hard winds funneled to curl and accelerate around the base of the mountain, it looked like a thimble on a thread dancing in a hurricane.

Once more in control, Sharelle extended the refueling probe. The big pipe reached outward from where it stowed on the lower right side of the fuselage until it reached a few meters past the spinning rotor blades.

The trick was to fly forward with at least four hundred pounds of contact force, to jam the probe into the dancing basket. If she did, and it hit clean, the valve would latch onto the probe and fuel would flow into her hungry tanks. Once latched, they swallowed a full load of fuel in thirty seconds flat.

But, if the basket swung up on a gust and she didn't back pedal fast enough, she might eat the basket with her rotor blades—which wouldn't be good for either of them.

Being Night Stalkers, three of the four hit clean and the fourth managed it on the second try.

Two minutes later, the C-130 was turning back to wherever it came from, lighter by seven tons of JP-8 jet fuel.

Their flight of Black Hawks would now be arriving in Prudhoe a hundred and fifty miles and forty-eight minutes ahead of schedule with a half load of fuel. Hopefully that would be enough to deliver her Delta Force troops a real advantage.

Except Troy didn't direct her straight to Prudhoe. Instead he kept them heading north. Thirty minutes after refueling, they were out over the dark depths of the unforgiving Arctic Ocean. But the Arctic had two advantages at this time of year. It was dead flat—no icebergs in this part of the ocean, only ice floes, and those would all have melted during the hot summer anyway. They flew very low and at full throttle.

The second advantage—no one would see them coming.

———

Trisha felt as useful as a thumbtack on a teacher's chair sitting copilot to Emily—she knew from nothing about fixed-wing planes. "When did you learn to fly one of these things?"

Emily made it look easy, of course. "Firefighting. Mark always flew them over fires as the Incident Commander – Air. Decided I should at least get my ticket."

The C-12 Huron, a fourteen-seat Beech King Air to civilians, was like five times heavier empty than her Little Bird. She always felt claustrophobic every time she was encased in so much metal. Airliners gave her the heebie-jeebies. She'd take the view out of her tiny helicopter's wraparound windscreen any day. "I hate you, by the way."

"For?"

She waved down at Prudhoe Bay five thousand feet below them. "That should be me down there."

Though the town wasn't all that much to talk about. Three streets wide between the airport and the south shore of a big lake, twenty long as it wrapped around the south and east of the water. The North Slope made paved airport runways in the Lower 48 look lumpy. The only thing that relieved the flatness were all of the lakes that pockmarked the landscape and the manmade structures poking up a story or two.

With the moon down, nothing lit the landscape except the lights at the various pumping stations and the town of Deadhorse where a few thousand temporary workers huddled for the length of a contract before flocking back to warmer climes. Each light bloomed in the thin mist, not enough to obscure, but enough to add a surreal mystical quality to the scene.

"What's that?" she asked to distract herself when Emily didn't answer. A line of well-spaced flickering lights stretched off to the south. Each one a bright flare in her night-vision goggles.

"Dalton Highway. A couple hundred trucks a day come up from Fairbanks along that road with everything from groceries to oil drilling bits."

"Four hundred miles of hell." About how Trisha felt.

"I can put you back in your bird," Emily said as they continued to circle and wait for the action to begin.

"Really?" Trisha twisted to look at her commander. She imagined her Little Bird wrapping around her like a warm blanket on a cold night.

"However, think hard about the last two months."

"I hate it when you do that."

Emily didn't answer, leaving her to actually have to think. It was a trick Billy played on her all the time. He'd fixed the utter disaster she'd made of her relations with her parents that way —as much as anyone could. Billy had also convinced her to fall in love with him that way. Half the reason she still called him Billy the SEAL was to remind herself that the man was like a total sneak.

She felt his silence somewhere out in the Brooks Range as surely as she felt Emily's here in the cockpit circling five thousand feet over a wasteland of tundra, ocean, and massive oil reserves.

In the last two months she'd gotten to know the crews across all five battalions. Until now her view had been only one company wide, two because of her bestie Patty serving in the 5E while Trisha herself had flown in the 5th Battalion D Company —until Emily yanked her ass.

"Most of them are so damn young."

Emily shifted from flying circles to lazy figure eights. Inside the lower loop: the town of Deadhorse and the airport. The upper loop encompassed the messy, wandering delta of the Sag River, Prudhoe Bay, and the bright spots of the various oil production and pumping stations.

Messy and wandering. Her life had always included someone else giving the orders and leading the missions. She'd chafed at that, of course, but all part of the deal. In exchange they'd let her fly way out on the cutting edge. Now her MOS—military occupational specialty—made her the one telling others what to do, which she didn't like a whole lot better.

"I'm stupid." She flipped up her night-vision goggles and rubbed at her eyes.

Emily glanced over at her.

"I'm not getting it."

"Tell me about missions you've flown, not the everyday takedown missions, but the black-in-blacks."

"Shit, Emily, you know I can't do that. You weren't part of the action teams." White ops were released to the newsies as a matter of course—like the takedown of bin Laden. Black ops were quiet. They leaked on occasion, but for the most part they were never more than a whisper outside the community. Black-in-black? No one outside the action team and the President's people *ever* knew about those. They were all hairier than a two a.m. meetup in Boston's Southie, which she'd done plenty enough times too know.

"Somalia, Azerbaijan—" Emily started listing them.

"How the fuck do you know about that one? Michael spill the beans to you? What the hell goes on at that ranch of yours?"

Emily shook her head.

No, of course Colonel Michael Gibson wouldn't break security, not even with Emily. Besides, the man spoke even less than Billy. He'd never once hinted that she and Michael had slept together long before Billy—not even when Billy had flattened his ass in a fight, making him probably the only man to *ever* get the drop on Michael. Only Michael's wife Claudia Casperson ever coaxed words out of him. Claudia, who had led the Azerbaijani operation. But Trisha couldn't see her spilling the goods any more than Michael. Which meant—

"Gods, I *am* stupid! You're where Claudia disappeared to that day." The black-in-black mission to Azerbaijan had kicked up from Pending into full-on Crisis mode, without notice, one day between early morning and late afternoon. And Captain Claudia Casperson had been gone for that entire time. She'd come back all fired up and with a clarity that, in hindsight, only a clandestine meeting with Emily Beale could have instilled.

Emily nodded without looking over.

"Okay, what's your point? And don't tell me to think it through. I'm stumped why you think I'd be any kind of a good commander." She'd stressed out every commander she'd ever had. She knew damned well that only her competence had saved her from any number of demotions and disciplinary actions. Not that she'd ever admitted that to anyone other than Billy.

"Remember my installation speech."

"Shortest Change of Command speech in history for a new commander of an entire regiment in any branch of the service."

Which actually made it all the easier to remember the key points. *War is changing in ways we didn't imagine. To remain effective, we must imagine how it will continue to change. Then we must innovate to prepare for far worse.*

That was one thing Trisha had always excelled at: thinking outside the box. Except she never had to think about it. Hell, she didn't even understand the box that most folks seemed so trapped inside of. There simply *wasn't*, at least not one that she could see. It never made any more sense than why St. Paddy's Day green beer made a girl pee green—though that did make sense now that she'd thought it. Crap! She *hated* thinking. And she'd apologize to her bladder later.

"There are the SEALs now," Emily nodded to the south.

Trisha dropped her NVGs back into place.

Five degrees below freezing out there and the SEALs had rolled out of their Chinook helos ten klicks to the south of Deadhorse. They'd climbed into their RHIBs—rigid-hull inflatable boats—and raced down the river. No one stayed dry riding in one of those at speed. They'd all be ice-coated and hypothermic by the time they arrived. Except Trisha knew from being married to Billy that neither problem would slow down a SEAL for more than a single heartbeat.

The SEAL's mission? Capture Deadhorse Airport—the airport had been warned. The main channel of the Sag River curved within three hundred meters of the airport. Plenty close for the heavy weapons mounted on the RHIBs to offer additional air cover.

"Tell them," Emily ordered.

Trisha dialed in the radio frequency for Captain Sharelle Vargas' flight.

"Vesper One this is Control." Vargas had chosen her bird's name after 007's true love in the Daniel Craig reboot.

"Go ahead, Control," Troy answered, meaning Sharelle was doing the flying at the moment.

"This is an exercise. I repeat, this is an exercise. We have inbound hostiles at Deadhorse Airport. They'll be in full control in ten to fifteen minutes. Be prepared to recapture against heavy opposition."

"Understood, out."

Trisha glared at the radio. "No begging for more details? They're up to something." She considered. Not *thinking*, not really. More...*imagining* what she'd do in their place. With all those Delta operators in their birds, they'd have to know it was more than some simple emplacement exercise.

But what? Trisha had purposely isolated them from any OPFOR information. The opposing force of SEALs and Chinooks being in Alaska at all had been carefully guarded.

Which meant...what?

Emily laughed, once. More of a chuckle than a bark, but still as unusual as hell and grape popsicles coexisting. She was looking down from her side window at an area hidden from Trisha.

"That's what you want, isn't it? You *want* Night Stalkers to break the rules."

"I didn't name you as my second-in-command to lead, though you're better at that than you think you are."

"Then why the hell did you?"

Rather than answering, Emily reversed the plane's high-bank turn so that Trisha's view looked down at the airport from above—the view of something Emily had seen mere moments ago.

Three helos, no, three *Black Hawks*—where there shouldn't be any for another half an hour—scooted into the airport.

A glance to the south, no sign of the SEALs' boats racing down the Sag River yet. That meant they wouldn't see the incoming Black Hawks.

Down below their observer plane, she could see the operation unravel.

The three Black Hawks' side doors slammed open. They hovered so low that two men stepped from each bird onto the roofs of three buildings. At the same moment, two more fast-roped out the other side to ground level.

All three birds then ducked behind other buildings to off-load the four remaining team members in a dust-off style landing. A meter above the pavement, four Delta dropped out each side and the helo lifted and accelerated away.

The first operators who'd roped down from each team raced to the center of the field between the taxiway and the runway, diving into drainage ditches filled with dustings of snow and freezing slush. Within thirty seconds, no sign of movement existed anywhere on the field or around the buildings. Not even any heat signatures, though she couldn't imagine how they'd achieved that—swimming in the slush? She felt a sympathetic shiver.

The three delivery birds were already out over the large lake on the other side of town, headed away to the north.

To the north.

"They ignored my flight plan. Came in over the Arctic. Damn it! I gave them a very specific thirty-second arrival window that's not for another..." she checked the dash clock, "thirty-four minutes. The SEALs were supposed to be dug in by then. Instead—"

Trisha twisted to look the other way. The SEALs slammed up onto the muddy river bank and began tumbling out of the RHIBs. Now they were the ones walking into a trap, wholly convinced they were coming into a quiet civilian airport with plenty of time to set up.

She didn't know where to look.

The SEALs, never ones to take such tasks lightly, fanned out and raced onto the field as if it was a hostile battlespace.

The Delta teams remained invisible even in night vision.

The three departing helos.

"*Three?* Where's—"

She had her answer a moment later when an aiming laser, brilliant green in her NVGs, lanced out to splash over the two RHIBs parked on the mudbank. Cue massive explosion in the real world.

The DAP Hawk swept in from upriver, having circled around behind the SEALs.

The three Black Hawks, which she'd momentarily lost track of, returned. One directly along its departure path over the lake, perpendicular to the center of the runway. But the other two had circled wide to come in either end of the runway.

That's when the Delta operators opened up.

The poor SEALs never knew what hit them.

"Holy shit but those squids are gonna be some kinda pissed."

And still Emily circled.

"Fight's over, Emily. Let's get down there before the SEALs actually try killing any of the D-boys. My man is one of them."

———

"Where are they, Troy?"

He opened his mouth, then closed it. Sharelle could see as well as he did that the SEALs were all accounted for. And their two boats. The pair of Chinooks that had delivered the SEALs had been spotted parked ten miles south of town by the overwatch drone operator.

That left...

"Scatter!" He keyed the mike and called out the command again.

Michella and Sharelle moved fast enough. Drew and Barry didn't.

Coming out of the night, with absolutely no signal on his tactical display, a pair of Little Birds skewered the second pair of Black Hawks.

"I knew it!" Sharelle snarled. "Stealth. Not a peep since that first night. I knew we'd see them again someday."

Troy had kept his eyes on the closer one and managed a positive missile lock on the heat of its engine exhaust—masked enough to be less than one of his dad's diesel tractors, but he achieved the lock and the bird was declared dead.

Michella was hard on the tail of the other.

Barry reported that the sensors had decided he was

downed, but Drew might still be in the game...if he dealt with all of the systems that the training computer was insisting were failing at the moment.

Yes, Sharelle was right. He should have anticipated this. He hadn't imagined hard enough.

But now that he had...

He almost laughed as he quoted Colonel Emily Beale from that first flight. "I think we have bigger problems."

"We do?"

"Two Little Birds a long way from home. A..." he let it hang for a second—

———

—WHICH WAS ALL SHARELLE NEEDED.

"Helos never travel alone," she reminded herself. They weren't the only DAP Hawk in the territory, but the other one had to be stealth like its Little Birds.

If they'd been making an evasive maneuver to avoid the stealth Little Birds, Sharelle now stretched her DAP's abilities into a whole new territory for the probable stealth DAP Hawk. She didn't dare risk her tumbling trick; she'd already revealed that to the flyers in the training battalion and ACE at Fort Novosel. The trainers' reactions hadn't hurt her ego. While she was at it, she'd also passed on the secret of Emily's roll maneuver.

Who knew how far those lessons had been dispersed over the last two months? Against another DAP Hawk she couldn't risk being predictable.

When Wakanda's Warrior General Okoye fought, she floated and attacked from every direction as if they all were united. Okoye always fought in circles but in ones that overlapped unpredictably.

Sharelle jinked and jerked across the sky, making herself a

hard target. Every time she moved, she did it with a spin—sometimes flying backward, sometimes sideways, but never for long.

The constant change of direction would make a missile lock on her hot engine exhaust harder to target. There one moment, gone the next.

As she flew, Troy began calling out, "No indications in Grid One-seven."

She swooped low, then climbed hard facing backward, glad they'd defined a pattern over the entire town as part of their mission planning.

"Nothing in Grid Three-five."

Her wandering pattern also served to clear the sky in multiple directions one after the next. Not in some neat rectangular search, which should be more effective against an opponent hunting her but would also make her an easier target.

"How stealth are these damned birds?" Sharelle growled out as Grid Five and Two insisted on *not* having a stealth DAP Hawk lurking among them.

"Huh," Troy grunted. "I have an idea."

"Don't say, do!" She didn't know how much longer she could sustain this pattern.

———

"LOOK LIKE ONE OF YOUR PATTERNS, TRISHA?" EMILY'S DRY TONE said she full well knew the answer was a big negatory.

Trisha grimaced. She'd never seen anything like what Vargas was doing. She'd be studying the tactical post-action report on this flight for a long time.

"Bill, Vesper One," crackled over the radio. Troy Ryland, Sharelle's copilot.

"Go ahead."

"We need a target to lure a stealth DAP."

"Roger." That's all Billy said.

He and Trisha had both flown plenty of forward ops. They'd met during a hostage rescue mission in Somalia, which had included an immense amount of gunfire aimed in their direction. And now he was being asked to step again into harm's way.

It didn't feel like it was an exercise, not the way Vargas and Michella Perrault were flying it—Michella had finally accounted for the second stealth Little Bird. Now she flew guard above the limping Barry.

Trisha looked at Emily for reassurance. But Emily was continuing her lazy figure eights as she too watched what was unfolding far below.

Two boats' worth of SEALs, twenty of them, lay face down on the cold dirt. There was no other sign of the Delta operators in either infrared or light-intensified night vision. The only way to know of their presence was the unmoving nature of the prone SEALs.

Whatever they were using for cover on the flat ground hid them very effectively, some of them nowhere near the slushy ditches.

"Thermal camouflage clothing?" Trisha guessed. With NVGs so readily available now, Delta had developed some sort of defense against them.

"Stealth Delta operators," Emily sounded impressed. "Haven't seen that before."

Trisha would be impressed too, except—as if out of nowhere—eight Delta appeared as if teleported—clumped to one side and guarding the SEALs they'd overwhelmed.

Less than two seconds later, they were lit up by a training laser so that they glowed brightly in Trisha's night-vision goggles.

———

"Gotcha!" Troy followed the line of the laser. It painted a dead straight line through the mist.

Sharelle pulled four g's as she brought the DAP's nose to bear on where the stealth bird had revealed itself.

Troy anticipated her turn and unleashed all hell on the spot as soon as it was in range.

A pair of simulated Stingers, ten (simulated) 30 mm rounds a second from his M230 cannon, and both of the crew chiefs opened up with their Miniguns' targeting lasers.

Three seconds later the invisible DAP Hawk flicked on its running lights to show that its computer system had declared it was dead.

———

"I *hate* being killed!"

"I know the feeling." But Sharelle had a hard time putting much sympathy in her voice. They were all crowded in a small conference room that Alaska Airlines had loaned them at Deadhorse Airport.

Her copilot and husband Tim just smiled, but Chief Warrant Lola Maloney still looked madder than a snake facing a pack of honey badgers.

"Lola, you shoulda seen *her* face," PITA Trisha O'Malley strode in and hooked a thumb at Sharelle, "when I killed her ass. Some kinda serious pissed. It was so sweet. Total pissa that she shot your behind despite your stealth, though, huh?"

"Go away, O'Malley."

"Love you too, Lola."

She turned on Sharelle with perhaps the first scowl she'd ever seen on the redhead's face. "I can't believe you blew off the scheduled time for your arrival. Night Stalkers have a narrow window that they have to hit every time."

"I made a command decision to deliver my team before the trouble started."

"But that's—"

Sharelle felt the shadow of someone slide up in her peripheral vision. Beale, of course. As if stealth helos weren't bad enough, she had a stealth commander as well. Now she was going to catch it. Though, like the cat that ate the canary, she'd feel good about downing a stealth DAP Hawk for a long time to come.

"How might you have saved the Delta squad serving in your team?" Impossible to read support or censure in Beale's look or tone.

She hadn't forgotten that first night's exercise to create alternate scenarios, and had been trying to ever since she'd landed. Not one idea good enough to offer it a shot of bourbon —not even a cheap one. Sharelle glanced at Troy, but he shook his head.

"It was masterful," Lola was the first to speak. "I knew you had me the instant I fired on your ground team. But, as you know, no time to think up there in midbattle. I reacted instinctively to protect my team and that exposed my position."

"I still don't know. If I'd arrived on time," she glanced at her watch, "four minutes from now—"

"We'd have chewed you up and spit you out."

Sharelle looked up at Beale and asked her question by not asking aloud.

At length, Beale nodded the slightest amount, typically easy to miss if not for the ripple down her straight hair.

It felt worse that not even Colonel Emily saw a way she might have won that battle without sacrificing a portion of her own team.

"O'Malley," Beale called out without looking up.

"Here, boss." Trisha called from across the room. "Just ministering to my dead husband."

Troy whispered in Sharelle's ear, "Probably by lecturing him about how she'd kill him if he ever died."

"Wouldn't put it past her." Sharelle wondered how she'd feel if Troy died. Not a comfortable thought. Far more than losing a copilot. More than friend. Maybe even like a...what?

Beale signaled O'Malley toward the front of the room.

"Okay, everyone," Trisha shouted out. "Shut up and put your butts in the chairs. Let's take this whole thing from the top."

As everyone settled, Beale said softly, "Remember, Captain Vargas, that your enemy's reactions will not always be so dependable."

"Yes ma'am." She filed the thought away for later consideration.

Beale headed to a chair by the door as Trisha started the debrief.

6

THE PAIR OF CHINOOK HELOS HAD GATHERED UP THE SEALs AND their pair of boats at Deadhorse and disappeared south to points unknown. Which was just as well, the SEALs had indeed been as grumpy about their utter and swift defeat at the hands of Delta Force as Sharelle had imagined.

After the much shorter direct flight back to Fairbanks, a C-5A Galaxy transport jet—the largest in the US military—had been waiting for them. Lola's Stealth DAP Hawk, along with her two Little Birds and the three Black Hawks Sharelle had been escorting, filled the entire cargo bay of the massive transport jet. The massed Delta Force team had climbed aboard, including Billy and Trisha, and they all headed south.

That left only Beale's C-12 Huron airplane and their own DAP Hawk on the tarmac at Fort Wainwright.

Sharelle noted that the blowing snow hadn't become any warmer at 0300 in the morning than it had been at 2000 hours last night.

"You have a long flight in the morning. Get some rest." Emily handed her an envelope, saluted, and walked away. She climbed into her C-12 Huron and was gone.

"Morning's like three hours away," she told Emily's departing aircraft.

"Four, but we take your point." Jalissa covered a big yawn.

Exhausted by the flight to Prudhoe, battle, debrief, and far more direct flight back to Fairbanks, Sharelle handed the envelope off to Troy. A hotel minivan pulled up and they all scrambled aboard to get clear of the chill wind. Three blocks later they were standing in a warm lobby and Sharelle felt ready for a solid ten hours sleep.

At 0300, the only sign of life was a clerk who looked as sleepy as she felt while Olsen talked him out of the room keys.

"So?" she asked Troy.

He opened the envelope, which had the standard single-page order. After squinting at it hard, he pulled out his phone and keyed in something. He shifted from squint to confusion.

"What?"

He turned the phone to face her.

It was a map. A red spike marked a location near a cluster of buildings. He zoomed back. Then again. And again. Buildings surrounded by a whole lot of nothing.

"Where is this?"

"Montana," his voice sounded hoarse. "A place called Henderson's Ranch."

He might sound hoarse, but Sharelle couldn't speak at all.

Colonel Emily Beale had *ordered* them to fly to her private home. What in the name of Christendom was the woman up to?

Troy lay wide awake listening to Olsen breathe. At least he didn't snore, but there'd only been two rooms available: a dual queen and a king. He and Olsen had decided to be noble and share the king.

They had four hours to sleep, fifteen minutes to eat, and then an eleven-hour flight including a refueling stop at Ketchikan. More of a nap, really, as they were all used to flying at night and sleeping during the day.

After the long Black Route Alaska exercise, he'd looked forward to that nap before the upcoming all-day transit flight.

But there'd been a brief moment in the lobby, upon hearing only two rooms were left, when he'd imagined sharing a king bed with Sharelle. Even the brief thought had burned away any ability to sleep.

Three years! Three years they'd been flying together and he'd never had this problem. Well, not often and never this bad.

He and Sharelle had long since learned to fly in sync. From the very first day it had felt like something special—a fact confirmed by Cass McDermott telling Colonel Beale that they were the Night Stalkers' best team. It sounded crazy, as he'd met some amazing pilots...but it did feel that way when they were aloft together.

And tonight's exercise had been that in spades. Once he'd even half suggested it, there hadn't been need for another word as they blew off Trisha's mission plan and raced out deep over the Arctic Ocean to avoid detection. They simply did it. In flight, there was no way for things to be better.

Which actually kinda sucked.

Looking at those photos of Beale with her husband and kids had almost knocked him out of the service. He was already a short-timer, coming up fast on the end of his tenth year—not that he'd told a soul he was leaving. Especially not Sharelle.

He'd sat down with Colonel Cassius McDermott nine months before, long before McDermott's promotion to general commanding all USASOAC, and requested early departure. It had been a long, hard discussion.

The outcome had been an executed REFRAD packet— release from active duty—even though he didn't want to leave.

He'd kept it very quiet. Nobody wanted to fly at this level with a pilot who didn't want to be there. Which wasn't the problem, he did.

But he'd been a late child; Momma and Daddy were getting up there. If they'd had corporate jobs, they'd both be retired and living out their Comfort Years as Momma called them. Instead, they were working the old land-grant family farm with too few hired hands and nothing but pure luck keeping them afloat.

The Army ROTC scholarship to become a University of Oklahoma Sooner had seemed like a good tradeoff at the time. He'd crammed a BS and an MS in agriculture into five years—making him the first Ryland to make it past tenth grade. Grandpap's death had ended Troy Senior's education. Momma was the oldest of six and had left school to help raise them.

The Rylands had always been poor farmers on both sides—until him. But they weren't *dirt*-poor; they were dirt-*rich*. The problem being, that wasn't enough in this day and age to keep the farm afloat.

But the Army had identified something more in Troy Junior. He'd graduated along with the rest of the cadets as a second lieutenant, fully expecting to be slotted somewhere stupid for having a degree in farming. Daddy had always been a long-term thinker and passed that onto his son. Four years' service and four years in the reserves, he'd planned to keep his head down, do his duty, and pay back for his education. Then he'd head back to the farm.

It was his reaction time that caught the Army's attention. They'd tried him out in helos, which took a fair degree of finesse and lightning-fast reactions. He'd been hooked and signed up for the two extra years. After five years, and starting the countdown for when he could head home the following year, a Night Stalkers recruiter had dropped by Fort Drum. Because, of course, where had the Army sent an Okie with a degree in farming? To the coldest corner of a Yankee state ever invented. By the time the recruiter showed, he'd have said yes to anything to get out of northern New York.

Almost anything.

The Night Stalkers wanted a minimum five-year signup. That would push him out to ten years total. A nice pay bump and a serious percentage more in his retirement pension—though a long way from the full pay after twenty years. So his highest paid thirty-six months would be ahead of him, not behind him. Every penny would help on the farm; if only that was enough. The numbers still wouldn't work, but they'd be better.

And it was the 160th Night Stalkers asking. They were the best and he'd developed a pilot's ego that he didn't want to turn them down.

We waited this long for ya to come on home, son. We just fine waitin' for a bit more, Momma sounded sad but not upset. Daddy had simply said, *You say no on our account, Troy Junior, and I'll come kick yo' behind.*

Maybe if he wasn't in the service anymore, he and Sharelle...

But he never quite managed to picture the woman asleep in the next hotel room on an Oklahoma farm, married to an Okie farmer.

Coming *home* to a farmer when she was on leave? The service was such a part of Sharelle that she'd never leave until she aged out.

He knew only too well what those visits were like. He went home for every leave. Prepping another part of his plans to save the farm before each visit, he and Daddy would plunge in for every minute he had. And things would be a little better afterward. Better crop rotation. Add a U-pick field along with its higher per-acre income. Work a field through the long process to be certified for organic produce. Piece by piece he'd been delivering on his college education.

Not that it would ever be enough.

The visits always ended so fast—an eyeblink of two weeks' hard labor and too little achieved. Not the way he'd want to run a family.

He stared at the vague shadows on the hotel room's ceiling, the slivers of light leaking in around the drawn curtains. She'd want to be up there, flying like the magician she was.

And he wanted...

Didn't matter much. The farm needed him.

Trying to guess Sharelle's reaction to his leaving the Night Stalkers? Not a single easy or comfortable scenario came to mind.

Then Troy had a thought that jolted him hard enough he almost woke Olsen.

He froze until the crew chief had settled back into sleep.

With all the extra training they'd been doing, Sharelle wasn't the only one who'd be annoyed. When Colonel Beale stumbled on his departure date in the roster, she might cut his head off. Maybe Olsen would wake up in the morning with Troy's chopped-off head under the covers like that prize horse's head in *The Godfather*.

That would be bad.

———

"WHAT'S WITH YOU?"

Troy didn't have a good answer. The sleepless night had included exactly that, no sleep at all. Incongruously, he'd managed a couple catnaps on the flight from Fairbanks down to Montana. Letting his body think that it was *ever* an okay choice to sleep during a flight wasn't good.

Sharelle had let him sleep, which made him feel worse.

At least he'd flown the first long leg down past Juneau. But after that, the steady thrum of the dual turbines and the endless Canadian coastline of rocky shores backed by endless conifer timberland, mostly empty all the way to the Atlantic, only held his attention for so long.

Or the unfamiliarity of lying beside Olsen and the intense familiarity of flying beside Sharelle that had finally put enough nerves at ease to let him sleep? He liked that explanation better; even if it was a load of bull droppings.

"I wore him out," Olsen called over the comm. "He and I, what can I say, a match made in heaven."

"Or at least in the air," Jalissa added in.

"Yeah, that must be it." Troy pushed himself more upright in his seat and blinked hard several times. If he hadn't been wearing his helmet, he'd have slapped his cheeks. "I can take it from here."

"Thanks but no thanks."

He turned to Sharelle to gauge quite how annoyed she was at him. But all she did was tip her head forward as if pointing.

Jagged mountain peaks stretched off to the left and right as far as he could see. Ahead, nothing but rolling hills and flat plains. Directly below them was that crazy break of the Front Range—nothing...then, *bang*, jagged mountains. Or with their present west-to-east direction of flight—mountains...then, *splat*, flat prairie.

He glanced at the nav display, they were only ten kilometers out from the ranch.

Small clumps of trees dotted the soft rolling foothills, more like foot-humps. Streams wandered this way and that, all headed toward a small, quick river that looked like a slim band of gold where it caught the light of the setting sun.

Ahead, like no sky he'd ever seen, "The Big Sky."

"That it is. You've never been here?"

"Big Sky, Montana, no. You?"

Sharelle shook her head.

"You folks need to get out more," Olsen muttered.

"You say that like we've never left Kentucky," he winked at Sharelle. "We've flown to Afghanistan, Alabama, Alaska, and all sorts of other fine places beginning with A."

"We're only a day's drive out of Seattle." Olsen was always on about the little town near there where he'd grown up.

"That," Jalissa scoffed, "is crazy talk. A day's drive from New York will get you to Montreal, Chicago, or Atlanta. Actual civilized places. Your states out here are far too oversized. Empty too, because you've got nothing to put in them."

Troy tuned them out, or tried to as they kept up their banter. He whispered under it to Sharelle, "That is one durn big sky." A few purple clouds were strolling about the upper levels of perfect blue, glowing with the last of the sun's rays slipping over the horizon.

"Like you can see all the way to Kentucky," her whisper back was almost intimate.

They passed over a few remote cabins and a lone campfire near a line of tents and tethered horses along the river before closing in on Emily's coordinates in their orders.

"Holy moly!"

Troy completely agreed. They came low over a final ridge with a big swimming hole tucked in behind it. A tidy ranch sprawled around three sides of the bowl below. A majestic two-story log cabin ranch house commanded the north side with a miniature version of it to the south. Between them, massive barns and equipment garages anchored corrals of horses. Small cabins perched halfway up the gentle-sloped hillsides. Around to the north, beyond the big house...

The operation was huge in comparison to his family's farm.

"Is that a dog-training course?" Sharelle asked.

Troy didn't know what else it could be.

A change on the display snagged his attention as trained habit had him automatically scanning it every few seconds.

"Inbound! Dead ahead, range twenty kilometers." He flipped into the full tactical display, waking up all the DAP Hawk's powerful sensors. "Major EM source from that big barn."

Sharelle heaved up and back on the controls.

Troy heard the crew chiefs' shooting windows slam open, then the slick clank of steel as they slid their Miniguns into ready position without being told.

Sharelle had them back over the ridge before they'd fully crossed it and hovering low over the swimming pond. Beach balls and foam swim toys scattered far and wide out of a storage bin beneath the heavy downdraft of the pounding rotors. Not their problem.

Troy dialed in the Unicom frequency on one of the radios. It was the standard frequency used by general aviation pilots when they were out of a tower-controlled area.

"Hey, hon. Did you just see a big ol' bird a-zoomin' over the ranch?" Deep voice, Texas accent—except it wasn't.

"Heard them approach," an instantly recognizable Emily Beale replied. "Scooted out of sight before I had a chance to spot them. Captain Vargas, come back."

"Captain Ryland here, Colonel." Troy replied, not willing to distract Sharelle once he spotted how close her rotor blades' tips were to a pretty little gazebo at the pond's edge.

"You're clear to land, center of the main lot."

No need to glance at Sharelle, she hadn't moved the helo an inch.

"Unknown inbound and heavy EM source." He didn't make it a question.

Beale replied with a soft, "Damn." Then in a clearer voice on an encrypted Army frequency over another radio. "Forgot your bird would be able to see the latter. That's me. Remember, the Unicom is an open frequency."

He and Sharelle exchanged glances. In addition to the encrypted radio, the EM scans also showed high-volume satellite traffic and a microwave transceiver. Not like a radio sending and receiving, but as if a lot of data was moving in and out at a high rate.

"Yer unknown inbound," Mr. Not-Texas was back on the Unicom, "is the ranch's bird. Just droppin' a few customers off at the Great Falls airport. Meet y'all on the deck."

"Can't you just hear him grinning?"

Troy could, but that didn't help his nerves. The man had called Colonel Beale *hon.* He didn't know if he was ready to meet the his personal idol, Mark Henderson.

———

Sharelle waited a heartbeat. When Troy didn't make any comment, she eased up the shore and slid to the top of the ridge, her wheels brushing the grass.

With a clear view for the SKR—Silent Knight Radar—they saw that the inbound aircraft was a Bell JetRanger, a small five-seat helo. No sign of a weapon's conversion kit. The big electromagnetic source was far more worrying, but the Colonel had claimed that was her.

Troy localized it on the central display and zoomed in. The middle of the largest barn's roof looked normal until she looked more closely. Most of the barn showed a dark roof shingle pattern. One section was equally black, but sporting no shingle pattern. Some radio-transparent material, flat-black like the carbon-fiber covering over her DAP's nose-mounted radar.

"That answers that."

"Answers what?" Sharelle decided that Troy's statement was

sufficient confirmation of their safety and finished cresting the ridge.

The smaller JetRanger arrived first and settled down quickly in front of one of the garages. It did so with the kind of flair no civilian pilot would ever attempt and that no military pilot could ever resist. With a hard final turn and blast of upward power, he landed like a feather.

Once he was solidly down, she gently crossed the large dirt lot at the center of the ranch buildings. The dust kickup wasn't too bad, but she was still glad of the new DVEPS for piloting into degraded visual environments. Landing in dust brownouts or snow whiteouts caused by your own rotor wash had always sucked.

Sharelle swallowed hard to clear her throat once they were down.

Troy somehow spoke easily. "That EM traffic answers how Colonel Beale kept serving and yet had all those family photos. Whatever she was doing is based in that barn."

As they shut down the helo, Sharelle heard the crew chiefs withdrawing and racking their Miniguns.

"I don't care where we are, lock 'em down hard."

"Roger that, boss."

She left Troy to finish the shutdown and update the logs; it was the least he owed her for his getting some sleep on the flight down. Not that she'd managed much herself last night. Sacking out immediately after a major flight had never worked for her, but she knew that.

Instead, she'd settled in to let her body rest while she replayed every twist and turn of the long Black Route Alaska exercise. Especially her second-guessing a prescribed flight plan, one that had specified a precise minute of arrival. It hadn't been a decision she'd made lightly.

And last night, despite Colonel Beale's apparent praise, she still didn't know if she'd been right in making the alteration. How much of it was PITA Trisha O'Malley's doing, how much Colonel Beale's, and how much her own? Trisha's mission plans always pushed limits, until Sharelle had come to embrace them. Every limit had proven to be such only in proven methodologies or in mindset, but never in reality. Beale hadn't been joking, Trisha O'Malley was one hell of a fine combatant—on many levels.

Colonel Beale's constant prodding to *imagine* more had led her to do precisely that.

And her own predilections? To find ways to excel that no one else had before, including O'Malley and Beale, pushed her all the harder.

Besides, she didn't know how Troy slept at all on the flight down. Why had the colonel invited them, and only them, to her home? Something strange must be going on. How strange definitely worried her.

Now? As soon as she stood on the dirt, Sharelle felt herself wavering on her feet from the long flight. Except no way would she let Beale see that. She spread her feet a little wider and masked any unsteadiness in a couple of stretches.

"You're not fooling anyone." Beale spoke as she came around the nose of the DAP. "I know how long a flight that was after a short night, I'm sorry to do that to you."

"Then why did you?" Sharelle gave up on the show but didn't let herself sag.

Beale had traded khakis for jeans, a denim jacket, and a cowboy hat that should have looked ridiculous on her but didn't. Somehow Beale looked exactly the same as always.

Of course, the C-12 Huron would have covered the flight in half the time Sharelle's helo had. Less than, as she'd probably flown the more direct route over Canada, not an option for her fully armed military helo without jumping through a lot of clearance red tape. Beale had probably gone to bed about the same time Sharelle and her crew had lifted out of Fairbanks.

Beale, of course, didn't answer her question. Sharelle wondered what line Beale followed in choosing what to answer or not. Troy had probably been charting that in some back corner of his brain; she'd have to remember to ask.

Sharelle looked at the barn, just as a door opened along the side facing a corral. A tallish woman with a long flow of dark red hair down her back stepped out and started making a clucking sound. Horses whickered and came trotting over.

With the last of the sun out of the sky, twilight was taking hold. The air felt lovely. Of course, after Alaska's bitter winds, anything would.

"So, it's also a horse barn."

"Yes," Beale sighed. "And no, we don't talk about anything else in that barn, not anywhere on the ranch. We're a horse ranch for tourists and that's all we are."

"By your website—"

Beale groaned. "Not my idea, believe me. The place has done some very odd things as if it had a mind of its own."

"Weddings catered by a Michelin-starred chef? Back-country survival courses? And was that a dog course I saw?" She turned to look north past the main house, but the falling twilight now hid it from view.

"Yes, it is. We're a vendor to Delta and DEVGRU, if you must know, with the occasional animal going to the Secret Service."

"Say *what?*" Sharelle tipped her head to see if somehow swimming-hole water had gotten into her ears from hovering over the pond. Those two teams were the Night Stalkers' primary customers and their dogs were legendary.

"You'll meet the trainers over dinner."

A big man came to Emily and slid an arm around her waist. He too wore a cowboy hat, he also wore mirrored shades despite the falling night. With his other hand, he lifted her cowboy hat, lowered it to block Sharelle's view of them, then made a show of kissing her wildly behind it.

"And this," Beale said without looking the least bit flustered afterward, "is my husband, Mark." A woman should at least look flustered after a kiss like that, if not well-mussed on top of it.

"Lieutenant Colonel Henderson." Troy came up and saluted him formally. "Captain Troy Ryland. An honor, sir."

Mark grinned and returned the salute. "Never gets old, Emma. LTC Henderson, who would have ever thought of such a thing. Should I have stuck around until I earned the birds to match yours? Nah! They'd just end up in a drawer with all the rest of that stuff." He flicked his fingers at his left breast where any medals would be as if brushing off a bit of dust.

Sharelle noted that he didn't call it *shit* like so many other officers did, pretending to be cool and dismissive. But Henderson also didn't seem like the type to brag, despite the swagger, so probably tucked away for his kids.

Emily headed toward the DAP Hawk. "I'm sorry that we don't have a hangar big enough for the DAP without folding the rotors. Let's at least get it covered."

With her crew, Beale, and Henderson, it was quick work to pull a camo net out of the cargo bay and shroud the bird.

"Who wants first watch?" Sharelle turned enough to make it clear that she was addressing her crew and neither Beale nor Henderson. She wouldn't be trusting them until she had a much better idea of what was going on here.

"Don't worry, not a soul here would bother it." Beale reassured her.

"Uh-huh. Troy?"

"Yeah, I'm awake enough." He understood the underlying question—was he willing to make payback for sleeping the last leg of the flight. "First round is mine."

"Captain, not a soul on the ranch would—"

"And folks not on the ranch?"

Troy's laugh sounded, again, at some private joke.

"You trying to piss me off, Captain?"

"Remember the map I showed you of these coordinates?" He pointed at the ground.

She did. From here there was a cattle ranch a couple miles across the way and...nothing else she could recall.

"Forty-five minutes or so to the nearest town, Captain," Henderson informed her. Not a hint of Texas. Instead, a command tone that must have cowed whole generations of fliers. "And there's not a truck here on the ranch that doesn't have a rifle in it big enough to face down a bear. Probably safer here than in some dusty hangar at Fort Campbell. Your bird, but you might consider standing down."

Sharelle glanced at Troy. All he offered was a microscopic shrug.

Sharelle turned on Beale. "My bird picks up so much as scratch, it's on you, Colonel Beale."

Beale nodded with the easy confidence of someone without any doubts.

Henderson aimed those mirrored shades at her in the near darkness. "You were right, Emma, I do like her. Welcome to Henderson's Ranch, Captain Vargas." He stepped forward to shake her hand. His grip was firm, as solid as the Earth. He then greeted each of her crew by rank and name.

"Bet he was an amazing commander," Troy whispered in her ear.

"He was," Emily Beale watched her husband quizzing the crew chiefs about the DAP's recent upgrades with genuine interest. She was actually smiling—looking...softer. Sharelle almost didn't recognize her.

———

There were plenty of people sitting around the campfire off the side of the big house. Ranch hands, the Michelin-starred chef who Troy recognized from the website, and enough retired this and retired the other that Troy almost missed being introduced to Colonel Michael Gibson—no one had said retired. The legends of Delta Forces' former commander were told alongside Beale and Henderson's.

"She's the real hero," was all Michael said while Troy was busy trying to untangle his tongue. His nod indicated a blonde woman, a softer version of Beale, playing with a five-year-old who had his father's black hair and both their blue eyes.

"Claudia. Former 160th Little Bird pilot." She didn't say retired either.

"There seems to be a lot of that going on around here," Sharelle stood close enough to Troy's side that people might mistake them for a couple. She was the one who had shifted so close and made no change to remove him from within her personal space. Personally, he liked the feeling of coupleness, even if only in his imagination.

Claudia's smile came far more easily than Beale's. "I still fly a Little Bird for Stan and Jodi's dogs. Part of jump training."

"They really train SOCOM war dogs here?"

Claudia waved over a couple. The light brunette walked like she was tougher than anyone you'd ever meet anywhere—and he actually looked it. He was a big guy with burn scars that twisted up half his face. A pair of beautiful Malinois made sure to arrive first and sniff both Sharelle and him thoroughly.

"Think we'll pass?" he asked as he offered a hand for the dog to inspect.

"Never know," the guy's voice sounded as deep as he stood big. "Whaddya think, Bertram? Good, bad..." then the guy offered a twisted grin "...or dog food?"

The dog didn't look as certain as Troy would have preferred.

"He's Stan. I'm Jodi. That's Brandy," the woman nodded

toward the second dog without preamble. Brandy was decidedly gray about the muzzle but moved with all the stateliness of a queen dowager. Her owner's handshake was up-and-down once and firm. Stan held a beer in his right hand so he shook with his left. It was—cold.

Troy flinched in surprise.

"Oh yeah, I'm so used to the prosthetic that I forget about it sometimes. Full tactile for me in the fingertips—heat and pressure—but not for you." He tapped his beer bottle against his mid-biceps to show the transition point between man and machine. Even looking closely by the firelight, this hand looked normal.

"Sorry." Troy caught himself.

"No problem. I was fine with the two hooks, but Pat and Nate's ma is into biotech. They ganged up on me, recruited the President and Jodie here. Guess I'm stuck with it now."

"He likes to whine," Jodie apparently didn't believe in wasted words.

"Not me. That must have been Brandy." He squatted down until he was nose to nose with the gray-muzzled dog. "You miss being a SEAL like your ma does?" The dog licked his face, which earned her a big rubdown with both of Stan's hands. The dog gave no sign of caring about their temperature difference.

Troy and Sharelle both turned to look at Jodie, who shrugged. "Just the regular teams." As if being a female SEAL dog handler was no big deal.

The timing of her glance at Stan as she said *regular* told the next level of the story. The only *non*-regular SEAL team was DEVGRU, more commonly called SEAL Team 6. What the hell was this place?

"Out of our depth here, Sharelle."

Jodie's smile said she'd heard his whisper despite the arrival of a gaggle of more children with happy shrieks of greeting all around—the eldest two girls unmistakably belonging to Emily and Mark. They were preteen, a couple years apart, and absolute knockouts. The younger matched Mark's black hair and tan-dark complexion, with Emily's blue eyes. The older as blonde and fair as her mother with her father's gray eyes.

"Bionic," Jodie tapped her right ear. "I keep it turned up a bit in crowds so that I can hear conversations better."

"Sharp as a dog's ears; that's my Jodie." Stan's pride in his wife shone out of him.

A call of "Burgers, steak, or chicken" sounded out from a big grill standing off in the shadows.

"What? No vegetarian?"

"You want something? Nathan has this great lentil loaf with Emily's mushroom reduction gravy that—"

Troy held up his hands. "Just asking. I'm fine with a bit of ground beef on a bun."

"Uh," Stan squinted for a moment. "That might be a problem. No beef. I can't remember if it's bear or elk tonight."

Momma had taught him that a guest took what was offered. "Don't have a lot of elk roaming through Freedom, Oklahoma. Guess I'll have to try some."

"Lauren's bear from a couple days back," Jodie answered for him.

"Or bears."

"Not a lot in Fort Campbell either that I've noticed." Sharelle didn't miss a beat.

————

THE DAP CREW HUNKERED DOWN IN A LITTLE GROUP A WAYS clear of the fire.

Sharelle had asked and Emily had promised them tomorrow would be a dark day, so they each had a beer. Pilots were legally eight hours bottle-to-throttle; Night Stalkers were twenty-four hours. Bear kebabs, fire-roasted corn blackened on the cob, and a pile of red-cabbage slaw—with honey and vinegar rather than mayo.

"What's going on, Captain?" Cowboy asked.

Sharelle stopped stuffing her mouth long enough to shrug. After a rinse of beer, she managed, "Your guess is as good as mine, Hans. Beale's not saying a word she doesn't have to."

"Never a wasted word on that woman," Jalissa agreed.

"Hard to beat." Troy wasn't paying attention to the conversation.

She followed the line of his gaze—straight up. With her back to the fire and the main lodge, little light impeded her view. A distant light over a barn door revealed the outline of the shrouded DAP Hawk and not a soul near it. Above that, nothing but the stars of the night sky as thick as Mama's chickpea-and-ham stew.

"Reminds me of home—heck of a sky there, but it seems closer here." Troy continued looking upward.

"We're at most of a mile's elevation," Jalissa was now craning her neck as well.

"Never seen anything like it," Hans agreed.

Neither had Sharelle. Living near a military base meant lights along air field access roads, highways, and a dense suburbia rife with yard security lighting. When deployed, helos and their personal were always back to base when not aloft. Night vision enhanced the stars, but this blaze of light managed to be brilliant all on its own.

"This reminds you of home?" Montana had screwed up her sense of normal enough already. Having DEVGRU SEALs, Colonel Gibson, and gourmet chefs around might be a normal part of Beale's world, but they had nothing to do with her world. Neither of the towns around Fort Campbell were big enough to evoke the word *city*, but they counted near enough two hundred thousand folks in the general vicinity. Choteau, the nearest town to here, lay thirty miles away and under two thousand folks made it their home.

"Not as flat as home, but sure," Troy answered. "Feels like you can breathe here without bumping up against a hundred other folks."

To her it felt as if this place stretched her so thin that she'd simply dissipate in a tiny puff of Sharelle. Sitting side by side with Troy through so many flights—it was a rare day that a Night Stalker wasn't either aloft or in the lab studying someone else's flights—she thought she knew everything about him. This man, staring up at the stars as if he belonged beneath them, she didn't recognize at all.

7

———

"What do you mean, Beale's not here?"

By the time Sharelle woke up, the sun streaming through the cabin's windows had warmed the bed and her face. The party, campfire dinner, hootenanny, whatever it was, had been going strong when the crew had finally faded—about fifteen minutes after finishing the best burger of her life. Bear burger, she remembered, but didn't feel at all queasy about that thought.

Emily had installed them in one of the guest cabins. Small, cozy, bunk beds for four, kitchenette, and a serious bathroom. She'd considered a good soak in the big tub, settled for a quick shower, and the others had been asleep before she was done. She'd been whole seconds behind them.

"Not here," Troy reported when she'd found him by the helo. "That's all I got from the redhead, not Trisha. Taller, darker red. The one with the horses."

"Well, that's some relief." She could do with a break from O'Malley constantly stretching her brain to keep up.

"Then she headed off on a ride with another stunning blonde. They seem to grow them that way out here."

103

Before she figured out of how to react to that, Troy continued.

"Wedding rings on both. I've been awake about five minutes longer than you. Sorry if I woke you." He hadn't.

"No sign of intrusion?" She turned to her DAP Hawk squatting under its camouflage net. At least that was a subject more comfortable than redheads and stunning blondes.

"Intrusion past those guys? Not a chance." To demonstrate, he took one step closer to the shrouded helo.

An angry snarl filled the morning from a German Shepherd suddenly standing at a narrow gap in the camo net. Troy took a step back and the Shepherd quieted, but it didn't settle.

"Forgot about them." Last night she'd mentioned her intent to sleep in the helo.

Stan and Jodie had instead rousted three of their dogs, set dog beds and a water bucket under the helo, and simply said, "*Pass auf!*" Explaining it meant *guard* in German—the dog's command language. The dogs had lain down under the helo and glared at her until Emily had led the whole team away to the cabin.

"So, we can't board our own helo and Beale is gone somewhere."

"About the size of it."

"Morning," Jodie walked up, then called out, "*Gute hund.*" The three dogs raced out to greet her and received dog biscuits and a good rubdown.

When Troy boldly extended a hand, the dogs looked to Jodie, then at him with a bit of a curled lip.

"Oh, sorry. *Freund,*" she pointed at Troy. Then repeated it and pointed at Sharelle.

All three dogs sniffed them carefully, then accepted head pats.

"Sorry, I should have told them you were friends last night. Didn't think of it. They'll remember now."

Sharelle looked at the quiet morning. The horses in the corral tugged at an unraveled haybale in a steel feeder. A line of crows nattered away along the barn's ridge—black blots against the brilliant blue sky. No other people about.

"I suppose we can let them off guard duty."

"Oh, that would be good if it's all right with you. We're at a crucial stage of their final training. Graduation and handler selection coming up next week."

Sharelle was about to ask what that entailed when one of the big doors opened on the equipment garage. Moments later Claudia emerged, using a riding lawn mower to tow an MH-6 Little Bird into the sunlight. Her five-year-old son sat in the cockpit to direct his mother. She waved when she spotted them. Her son jumped down and raced into the pack of dogs who greeted him enthusiastically. Claudia didn't appear to be the least bit worried, instead climbing up the helo's embedded ladder to unfold the rotor blades.

"Six," Troy said.

"Six what?" Jodie asked.

Sharelle looked more closely. Six rotor blades. Only the newest M version of the Little Bird had six-blade main rotors, most only had five. "Rotor blades. You have very current equipment here at the ranch."

"Wouldn't know. All I do is jump from them with dogs. That's what's on the slate for today, final jump training for this year's class of dogs. Claudia flies Stan and me up with a dog each, and we take them through a fourteen-thousand-foot HALO jump including armored vests and oxygen. Twelve dogs to graduate, a lot of jumps today."

"Why fourteen?" Troy's interest, she knew, was completely genuine. He found everything fascinating.

"The climb limit on the helo is eighteen, the ground here is four-plus. Fourteen-thou between one and the other. Little less up to the swimming pond when we train them for water landings." She snapped her fingers and walked away with three dogs and a five-year-old boy following in close formation.

"Any bets on a future Night Stalker pilot?" Troy indicated the boy.

Sharelle noticed that Claudia and Jodie didn't exchange so much as a look at the hand-off of the boy. "Everyone here's just a big happy family."

———

Troy decided that made sense. "Remote, hard winters, hard work the rest of the year. Like my parents' place, but..." He couldn't seem to manage the next word.

"What?"

"Let's go give her a hand." Not that Claudia appeared to need it. Folding a Little Bird's blades so that it would fit inside a jet transport, a ship's hangar bay...or a ranch's equipment barn wasn't a complex task. Each blade was under fifteen feet long and as light as structurally possible. Claudia would be done by the time he'd walked across the dirt lot.

Sharelle grabbed his arm. "She's got this. What were you going to say?"

Troy shook his head.

"Every time you mention the farm, which is half of never, you come over all strange. Spit it out, Troy. That's an order."

He stopped and eyed her.

She took a lesson from Beale's book and let silence be her answer. Now that she'd said something, she understood that there'd been an underlying pattern for some time now. He cared about his folks. Yet something about them had him avoiding the topic.

"This place," he waved a hand helplessly at it. "It works."

"It's functional, in some weird Beale-like way." She spotted J-Right and Cowboy strolling down from the cabin.

They paused, made eating motions, and pointed toward the kitchen end of the main lodge, close by last night's campfire.

Then Sharelle noticed the look on Troy's face and waved the crew chiefs to go without them. Once they were out of sight, she rested a hand on his arm.

He looked at it, *stared* at it, but showed no other reaction. "It's way more than functional. A hundred small things that someone not from a farm probably wouldn't notice."

"Like what?"

He looked around as if waking up, moved a little too casually away from her touch, then nodded toward the horses. When he led off, she fell in to follow beside him.

"They take good care of the horses," he stopped and rested his arms atop the corral fence. The horses at the feeder stretched out their necks to sniff at both of them before pulling out another mouthful of fodder.

"Sorry, no sugar cubes," Sharelle rubbed the nose of one who leaned particularly close. "Only jerks and those who deserve to die don't take care of their horses. I'm from Kentucky, so I know that there's no lower life form—if you don't count drowning kittens and beating dogs."

"No. They aren't taking care, they're taking *good* care." He reached over the corral fence and plucked a handful of hay from the bright red steel feeder. Painted this season. "Fine stems, broad leaf flowers, no seed heads yet." He put his nose in it. "Smells like home. That's top quality. You can see it in their coats."

Sharelle was more used to seeing Kentucky Mountain Saddle Horses and Tennessee Walkers than this mix of Quarter Horses, Paints, and Appaloosas. But there was no denying their splendid condition.

"Did you hear a single squeak when she opened that big garage door to pull out the helo? Trust me, that's the first kind of maintenance task to go when things get hard." He walked into the barn.

Sharelle followed him in. Folks said Kentucky and Tennessee were the only states where, if you didn't own a horse, you sure knew a soul who did. Not in Memphis or Louisville, but most places it held true; certainly around Fort Campbell. She rode some but Troy walked in like it was in his blood.

The main aisle looked recently hosed down. The stalls she peeked into were clean with fresh straw. They found the manager's office, door open with a large salt lick block to keep it that way. Inside, a big-screen monitor on one wall that listed every horse. It tracked health and last time they'd been ridden. Not a one was over a few days, except two that were in yellow at five days. They were also showing as currently signed out to Chelsea and Julie.

"Blonde and redhead?"

Troy's shrug said maybe, but that he didn't know their names.

Sharelle felt a strong sense of relief. Relief that...Troy hadn't shown more interest in them? Not even enough to find out their names? Troy had never given her the slightest indication of interest. He dated, on occasion, but always outside the service. If she could think how to ask him why he'd never asked her out, she would. She didn't know any man better than Captain Troy Ryland—but missed her chance.

Since when did you get stupid about men, girlfriend?

Never! She shouted inside to shut up her inner voice.

Troy strolled out of the horse manager's office and over to the tack room on the other side of the central aisle. He ran a hand over the leather of several of the saddles, all hanging neatly along three sides of the room. The fourth side held halters and bridles in an equally neat array. They showed plenty of wear. But the leather was all oiled, supple with no signs of cracking, and smelled of fresh saddle soap instead of dust and age.

"It's like a showroom." Troy seemed to get sadder with each passing moment. He closed his eyes and leaned his forehead against one of the saddles.

Unable to stand it, she stepped close to rub her hand up and down his back.

He didn't react.

Sharelle leaned her cheek against his shoulder blade.

His heart pounded against her ear; his breathing short and sharp.

It might be ridiculous, as the man wallowed in misery, but she noticed how good he felt. Always there. Someone she could count on at every turn. Times ten these last few months when the proverbial ground shifted daily under their feet.

Every time Beale pissed her off, Troy would break down the *why* like a mission debrief. He'd take the whole situation apart and put it back together in a new light. Letting her see her way through the perceived persecution into a new technique, a new degree of battlespace awareness. And she'd thought Cass had driven her hard.

"Easy, Troy. Just breathe." She slid her arms around him and held on.

Troy froze, then grabbed her hands and dragged them aside. "Don't!" he struggled free of her grasp.

"I was only—"

"Just don't!" He stepped clear until he faced her with his back to the wall of bridles. The metal bits rattled against the wood-plank wall like random gunfire.

—offering comfort.

"You can't do that to me." Troy hung his head like a...beaten horse.

"Do what?" She'd never been stupid about men—until now. It all clicked. He *never* touched her, not so much as an accidental brush while spotting during weight lifting. Never except when answering a high-five, which he never offered. Did he... "You've never said a single word."

"I can't!"

At a loss for words, she held up her hands palm-up in question.

He looked at her in blind distress, then bolted for the door.

The Army hadn't trained her in survival and hand-to-hand fighting for the fun of it. And her Baby Bother fought dirty when she cornered him.

Sharelle managed to snag the back of his belt and pants. A quickstep closer, she slid her other hand to grip beside the first, then braced for the impact as she leaned sideways. They might be the same height, but Troy was farmer strong, always had been, so she'd lose a direct tug of war.

Instead, by leaning sideways, her foot, hip, and shoulder impacted the inside of the tack room doorframe and stopped her cold.

She might not be a farmer girl, but she made her living with her hands and they were strong—her grip on his belt held.

It worked better than she'd expected, other than smacking her entire body and her head into the door frame hard enough to make her glad she didn't bruise easily.

Not anticipating her ploy, Troy's hips stopped as his feet kept moving. Abruptly overbalanced, he fell backward onto his ass.

Sharelle managed to release her hands in time, but not before his fall had overbalanced her as well. She landed hard on him, dropping a shoulder into his gut—nearly as unforgiving as the door frame had been.

Troy grunted, lying still for a moment.

She clambered over him before he recovered. Astride his hips and a fist planted firmly against each of his shoulders, she had him momentarily trapped. At least until he put his hands on her—she'd been unable to pin them with her knees.

But he didn't fight. Instead he closed his eyes. "Give me a break, Sharelle."

Ready for a hard struggle, for being bucked aside by her much stronger opponent, she wasn't prepared for simple capitulation.

"Give or I'll beat it out of you."

He didn't react...or open his eyes.

"Give or I'll *tickle* it out of you."

That earned her a fleeting half smile but it didn't last.

"Give or I'll..." What came past tickle? That's as far as she and her brother ever escalated it. Troy wasn't her brother. He was five-ten of thoroughbred helo pilot.

She didn't question whether the next thought had been lurking in the dark like a stealth helo, if it was a fresh tactic born of watching all those happy couples last night, or their being off any military base together for perhaps the first time ever. Asking questions was Troy's tactic, not hers.

Without planning...

Without thought of consequences or not...

Sharelle leaned down and kissed him.

He convulsed beneath her, clamping his hands around her waist so hard that it knocked half the air out of her and almost broke the kiss. She half expected him to push her up and away. Or toss her aside. Instead he dragged her tight against him.

The kiss gained heat much like a Hellfire rocket motor kicking the missile up to Mach 1.3, seconds after firing from a DAP Hawk.

She lay her body down over his as one hand clamped onto her butt and the other arm wrapped around her shoulders like a friendly boa constrictor made of warm, male—very male. It was—

A loud cough sounded behind her.

It was...

"Well, this is a sight," a deep voice rumbled out. "Can't say I ever much thought of bringing my girl here for a little nookie amongst all this fine leather."

———

TROY OPENED ONE EYE, LOOKING DIRECTLY INTO A MASS OF Sharelle's dark ash-brown curls. The other was pressed against her forehead as she'd shifted from kissing him like he'd never imagined, to hiding against him cheek-to-cheek. He couldn't move; they were both gasping like they'd sprinted the last klick of a 10K run.

He shifted aside enough to look up at the man standing in the doorway.

Guy with gray hair mostly gone white...and built like a small tank. "I thought it a might peculiar to see a set of boots sticking out the tack room door like a man gone down in the line of duty. Now I can see that you young'uns knew what you were doing just fine."

Sharelle curled closer, hiding her face against his shoulder.

Thinking better of his own position, Troy moved his hand from Sharelle's amazing behind to the small of her back. He felt her shaking ever so slightly against his palm.

The man smiled at the gesture, but his gaze didn't take any advantage of the fine angle of view Sharelle must be offering him.

"Uh...hello." Troy managed.

Sharelle's shaking escalated.

"Hullo yourself. That your helo out front?"

Not a sob or a convulsion.

"Yes, sir. Hers, actually."

That earned him raised eyebrows.

"Don't that beat all."

Sharelle's burst of laughter did two things: explained why she was shaking, and almost took out his eardrum at the same time.

"How can you be holding me like this," she gasped out, "and carrying on a conversation like that?"

"Must admit I was wondering much the same thing." The man remained foursquare in the doorway as if it had been built around him. "I think, miss, that you need to question either his priorities or his attention span. Neither would be impressing me much at the moment if I was the one lying in his arms."

Sharelle rolled one shoulder aside enough to look back over it. "You *are* a little distracting."

"Well, it is my barn, so I admit to finding a certain curiosity that is now piqued by your helo. DAP Hawk, same as my boy and Emily used to fly."

"Might be."

His boy. Mark's father. Troy didn't recall meeting him last night.

"Wasn't a question. Didn't play SEAL for twenty years to not recognize those as were saving my ass. Uh," this time he did glance down at Sharelle's behind, assuredly well displayed by how she knelt over him, "if you'll pardon the allusion, ma'am."

Sharelle started struggling out of his arms.

Troy considered not letting her go. After three years, he'd finally held her, for all of about five seconds, and that was a heck of a thing to be giving up.

Then he discovered how sharp Sharelle's elbows were when pushing against his chest and let her loose.

She rolled to her feet in one smooth move and faced the man. Offering Troy a fine view of where his hand had so briefly and happily rested, and leaving him sprawled on his back like a laid-out corpse.

With them both looking down at him, he decided it was high time he stood up as well. Troy landed on his feet so close to Sharelle that—why not—he slipped his hand into her jeans back pocket and let himself enjoy all that wonderful shape.

No sharp elbow to the ribs was all the permission he needed from her. It was strangely more intimate than even their kiss with her lying atop him.

"Mark Henderson Senior, though folks call me Mac."

"Captain Sharelle Vargas," she shook his hand.

Then Troy had to pull his own hand free from Sharelle's pocket, "Captain Troy Ryland. I'm her copilot."

"Yet you were squirming about together on my stable floor. Emily never was much of one for the rules."

Troy and Sharelle looked at each other. Troy wasn't going to miss a chance to find out more about their commanding officer. "How's that, sir?"

"Not a sir, Master Chief Petty Officer by the time the survivors of my class stood down together."

Troy whistled in surprise. If Senior chief chiefs were the backbone of the Navy, a master chief petty officer was the right hand of God. A SEAL master chief said there was far more to the man than met the eye—and plenty met the eye already. It also explained plenty about Mark Henderson Junior.

He turned about and, with a tip of his head, led them once more into the barn manager's office on the other side of the main aisle. There he dug some juice bottles out of a small mini fridge and offered them around. He took a seat, though not the manager's chair.

Troy and Sharelle settled on a half couch. The old leather looked fifty and felt soft as pure luxury. A bit of a slouch in the center had them sliding together in ways Troy didn't mind a bit.

"Let's see," Mac crossed his boots on a low table that had several equestrian and rodeo magazines piled on it—latest issues, well creased. "Marrying my boy, for one. Her commanding officer no less."

"But she left the service after that."

Mac nodded, "A couple years after that."

"A couple years?" Sharelle leaned forward as Troy leaned back, offering him a new appreciation for the shapes he'd held so briefly. Strong shoulders tapering down to a slender waist that had felt just fine encircled by his hands.

Then Mac's words sank in and he sat forward as well. "Wait, what? A couple years? But that's—"

Mac nodded. "As I said, she never much noticed the rules. Michael and Claudia Jean were at least in different regiments, even if they flew together."

"Bill and Trisha," Sharelle whispered to him. Beale's second-in-command and the Delta operator.

"What other ways, Mac?"

"Oh, wouldn't want to be telling any secrets."

———

That jogged Sharelle's memory. What Emily had said right after Sharelle had landed and spotted the heavy EM traffic coming out of the barn.

We don't talk about anything else in that barn, not even here on the ranch. We're a horse ranch for tourists and that's all we are.

So far, everything they'd seen in this horse barn looked like the inside of a horse barn. Yet...

She looked up at the roof. No, wrong side of the building. She glanced out the manager's office door and across at the tack room. It was the right depth to match the barn, no secret room. Then she noticed the stairs leading up to a storage loft. She sat closest to the door so that her angle of view wasn't cut off.

A storage loft up the stairs and to the right. Up and to the left had been enclosed. Windows, which she'd taken to be merely dark. They didn't look normal though. Heavy-duty? One-way glass? If she went up those stairs, what would she find? Would it be...

She glanced at Mac.

He'd been watching her through squinted eyes. Very slowly, infinitesimally, he shook his head. *Steer clear, girl.*

For once she knew something Troy didn't...though she never knew with Troy.

Three long years flying together and she'd never known. "Three years? Really?" She hadn't meant to ask that aloud.

Troy's dark gaze didn't argue or flinch aside.

Mac's big hand slapped down on her knee, jolting her in surprise. He pushed to his feet and tossed an empty juice bottle into a recycling bin. "Now you're asking the right question, girl."

He was half out the door when Troy called out. "Sir? Mac?"

The big man paused and half turned.

"Do you know where we can find your daughter-in-law? We were told she's gone, but not where."

Mac licked his index finger and held it aloft as if testing the wind here inside the quiet barn. Then he tipped it down, pointing—Sharelle checked her inner compass—northwest. "'Bout a half day's ride that-a-way. Family taking her out to see the newest fishing cabin. Julie will be back from her ride soon," he thumbed a finger at the screen showing which horse she was out on. "She can tell you all about the place, as she built it. The cabin came out nice...and *very* private."

And he left.

Somehow, with that last word he made it clear that he wouldn't tolerate them disturbing the family for a single second. Also somehow suggesting she and Troy might do well finding somewhere equally private.

Sharelle pushed off to chase him down and demand some

answers. Halfway to her feet, Troy's hand snagged her belt as neatly as she'd snagged his earlier. She collapsed once more onto the couch and flopped into the curve of his arm.

"Troy!"

"You think you're going to get answers out of a master chief who isn't in the mood to be giving them?"

He had a point. "But what are we doing here? Beale didn't just bring us here to sit on our asses."

"But yours is so very nice."

She twisted enough to look at him. "Do I even know you? What happened to my always-a-freaking-gentleman-until-the-world-ends copilot?"

"You kissed him." Troy looked plenty prepared to rest his own nice ass on this couch till the end of time. "I also find myself encouraged by Mac's stories of—"

Then he froze. Not looking at her; she'd wager not seeing the wall he was staring at so hard either.

"I'm so sorry, Sharelle. I should never have—" And somehow, though she'd been collapsed inside the curl of his arm, Troy slid free and was gone before she reacted.

By the time she did and hurried out into the barn's main aisle, there was no sign of him. She didn't even know which way he'd turned, so how was she supposed to find him again? Sharelle closed her eyes.

Righthanded. Given an arbitrary directional decision, most people's first inclination was to turn toward their dominant hand. Except a Night Stalker was trained against that pattern, against any pattern that might give away their next action.

Had Troy turned left against nature or right, well aware that she'd think left?

Move, girlfriend.

Every second standing still increased his odds of escape. She bolted out the office door, then stumbled to a halt.

"Captain Vargas." Michael Gibson stopped halfway down the stairs from the loft over the tack room. "Looking for you."

Escape? Why did Troy need to escape her? What the hell had she done wrong except receive one of the best and shortest kisses of her life? The memory of his hand clamping her butt no longer felt so exciting—now it felt like a slap.

8

"Whoa there, hoss!"

Troy stumbled to a halt when Stan stepped in front of him. Last night sitting by the campfire's light, he'd looked big. In broad daylight, standing square in Troy's path, he looked huge. Full jump gear, including parachute, spare oxygen bottle, and an HK416 rifle made him even bigger. The massive Malinois seated at his side looked at Troy with his head cocked half sideways, asking what was going on.

Troy tried a sidestep.

Stan's head tip didn't mirror his dog's. Instead it said, *You ain't that stupid, son.*

Take on a DEVGRU SEAL half again his size? Troy no longer knew; he might well be.

Caught up in the moment, he'd kissed Sharelle. More than that, he'd made it damned clear how attracted he was to her. Except that couldn't work. In ninety days he'd be out of the Night Stalkers on the family farm. He was at the end of his career and she, especially with Beale's tutelage, perched at a whole new level of hers.

"Might know that look," Stan rumbled out.

"What look? I don't have a look."

"How stubborn are you?"

"I don't have a look." All he'd done was just destroy the most important thing in his life, flying with Sharelle. The only way it could be worse was when she found out he'd waited until he was leaving the service before kissing her.

Stan studied him too closely for comfort, like Troy stood here naked down to his soul.

He glanced over his shoulder to make sure Sharelle hadn't followed him out of the barn and all the way out past the lodge to the dog training course.

She hadn't.

Did that make him feel better or worse?

How was he supposed to know?

"Bertram," Stan said with such authority that for a moment Troy wondered if he was being given a new name. "Jodie... No. *Nichts. Nein.* Need her for the jump training. Bertram, Ama *such!*"

Bertram sprinted away.

"*Such?*" With a guttural German ch sound like a choking basso hamster.

"It means: seek, track, find. All one to a dog." Stan kept staring at him.

Troy checked over his shoulder again. No Sharelle.

Stan harumphed. "Better get you out of the sun, brother. Before you twitch yourself to death." He clamped a hand around Troy's biceps, which would have been chilling enough even if the hand wasn't cold.

The Terminator's got me.

Stan didn't get him out of the sun. Instead, he led Troy around the back of a dog jump on the training course and shoved him down to sit on the ground and lean against the side of the barrier facing away from the barn. Hidden. Better than any shade—ever!

"Sit. Stay."

"Not one of your dogs, Stan."

"Nope. As my old commander used to say, they at least use the brains God gave them."

The fast beat of a helo sounded overhead. Small. Troy looked up and spotted a Little Bird climb from the barnyard then sliding down toward them.

Stan called out two names. A pair of dogs trotted over from where a whole pack rested in the shade of a larch tree. They wore full Kevlar vests. Jodie and two dogs converged as Claudia landed the Little Bird on the far edge of the dog course. Stan strolled over to join them.

He and Jodie each harnessed a dog to hang in front of them, then sat on the side bench seats that ran along either side of the helo. Within thirty seconds of landing, they were headed aloft for the first jump of the day.

Troy watched them wind aloft in a broad spiral until he once again heard the birdsong and noticed the dusty, brittle scent of grass close to haying time.

Who the heck was Ama that the dog had been sent to find?

———

The saddle creaked as lazily as Chesapeake's walk, and each creak sent ripples of pain against her inner thighs now chafed like a cheese grater. She'd only ridden a few times since Cass McDermott's visit, always a stolen hour here or there.

The long ride to the far corner of the ranch crossed prairie, rolling hills, and steep gullies mostly dry with the long summer behind and the fall rains yet to arrive. It had no effect on her family. Mark rode easily in the saddle, and the girls were born to it.

Now ten and eight, they'd been four and two when she and Mark had finally stood down from any active service fighting forest fires, and other undocumented operations, to live on the ranch. Julie—who had married in from the ranch next door—had spent her whole life riding and made sure that the girls rode as magnificently as she did.

Despite her best intentions, Emily had missed the Calgary Stampede. Julie had won her second first prize in women's barrel racing, proving the prior year hadn't been a fluke. Many from the ranch had attended, including Mark taking both their girls who'd dressed in full cowgirl attire: black for Tessa and Barbie pink for Belle. Tessa had placed second in weaving between poles, Belle placing fifth. The pictures Mark sent had almost killed her as she'd spent those days and nights battling the Army trainers who held so hard to their precious guidelines and training checklists.

They crested a high roll that marked the last of the plains before the sharp break of the Front Range. Above towered the mountains of the Lewis Range. Straight ahead, the sweetest little cabin that she'd helped design but had no part of building perched above a stream perfect for trout fishing.

The girls, obviously familiar with the locale, shifted from walk to canter in a single stride. In moments they were flying down the slope at full gallop, their hair streaming out behind them, their cowgirl hats fluttering against their backs at the end of the rawhide stampede strings. They were far better riders than her or Mark, but it didn't stop her heart from attempting to choke her as she watched them race away toward the cabin.

"I..."

"Emma?" Mark hadn't raced away, instead keeping Wind Runner at a walk. The whole way out he'd ridden close enough that their boots brushed occasionally.

"I..." her throat closed against any more words. "They..." she helplessly waved a hand toward the girls.

He reached out and took her hand across the gap of the

walking horses. She clamped on hard, but it felt as if he too was slipping away.

"This... I can't..." She couldn't. How had she ever thought to leave this? "Didn't I do enough?"

Mark looked at her; then, as if she weighed no more than Belle, he plucked her from her saddle and sat her in his lap. Wind Runner was too big and solid to care. Chesapeake kept nodding along beside them.

She turned and buried her face in Mark's shoulder as one of his arms wrapped around her waist. Breathing him in, he smelled as he always had, warm winter earth, so solid and safe.

He buried his nose in her hair. "You always smell like springtime, Emma."

Emily held on with all her strength.

"We talked about this."

She nodded against the soft flannel of his shirt.

"We're both wired to serve. Not the sort of thing to walk away from."

"You did," she managed out of a throat that sounded very much as if it was choked with tears.

His nod against her hair matched Wind Runner's easy side-to-side rocking. "I've been serving a different purpose."

"What?"

"You serve your people—your teams—to your very core. That's what you do." Mark kissed her atop the head. "Me? I serve the best pilot I've ever met."

Emily pushed back enough to look at him. He didn't appear to be in one of his joking moods, the lack of Texan drawl backed up that assessment. "Me?"

"You were always the best of us, Emma. Ever since I fished you out of the Thai jungle, you've been the best. I read up on your career before and followed it after, all long before we recruited you to the Night Stalkers. I led because that's what Dad and Ma raised me to. But nothing touches the way you flew and, more importantly, the way you build teams. You made me a better commander just trying to be good enough to have you in my company someday. You changed why I formed up the 5th Battalion D Company the way I did, so that we'd be ready when you came aboard."

Emily shook her head. "No, that's not right. You were an incredible commander."

"No, I was merely good, no better than any other hotshot Army helo pilot before I met you. Oh, I took care of my men and the commanders gave me a company, but I wasn't going to be any better at that than the next guy before I met you. You were born to lead the Night Stalkers, Emma."

"But," she waved a hand helplessly at the two girls now halfway to the cabin, their happy giggles at a chance to race carrying down the soft breeze.

"Like we said after Cass' visit. Not a chance it was going to be easy."

"But I didn't know it was going to be so *hard*. I don't know how I can do this." She rested her head on his shoulder, facing outward, watching the world plod past.

"Is that why you brought the DAP crew to the ranch?"

That had her raising her head sharply enough that she caught her head on his chin.

"Ow! Crap, that hurths when you do that."

She kissed his chin in apology.

Her reasons at the time had seemed obvious, but now...

Why *had* she brought them here? Some instinct that she'd learned to trust had issued the order because it was right. But while that might be true, the *why* remained elusive.

———

"I WAS—" SHARELLE WAS NOT GOING TO TELL COLONEL MICHAEL

Gibson that she was looking for her upset copilot. Nor of her desperate need to do so.

"Walk with me." He descended the rest of the way down the barn stairs.

She glanced upward, but he shook his head. He acknowledged that the room up there was something special, but clearly stated she didn't have the clearance for it. Well, at least she knew from *where* if not *how* Colonel Beale had stayed involved between firefighting and her return to the Night Stalkers.

Gibson turned to her right. Troy's dominant-hand turn exiting the office, if he did that. Though the way they'd entered lay to the left.

A moment's debate. Go find Troy or...

But this was Colonel Michael Gibson. The best Delta Force operator in their history. Even Bill no-longer-the-SEAL Bruce spoke of him in hushed tones the few times he'd mentioned the colonel over the last two months. Trisha's stories were so glowing that—Sharelle almost laughed at Gibson's back—that there just had to be some history there. Wasn't that too precious. Good history, but history. And by the memory of Bill's smiles when Trisha went particularly rhapsodic, he knew, though she'd wager Trisha still thought it all her own big secret.

Her hesitation almost lost her guide. Gibson reached the far end of the barn before she gave in and trotted after him to catch up. Along the way, she kept an eye out, half afraid she'd find Troy collapsed in a horse stall. But she didn't. She caught up with Gibson as he stepped through the door at the end of the barn, opposite the one they'd entered, opened to the south.

Outside, a glance left between the corral and equipment garage showed the DAP Hawk still shrouded in its camo tent. Once past the garage, she spotted a grass volleyball court. Her crew chiefs Wright and Olsen, joined by a half dozen others who looked like tourists, not ranch hands, were starting a game.

Gibson led her on by.

They passed a smaller barn, another equipment garage, and the small version of the massive log cabin lodge across the compound. A carved wooden sign stated: Ranch Manager. He didn't slow when they hit the edge of the dirt and started climbing the bluff that defined the south edge of the bowl that encompassed three sides of the ranch. The path was wide enough and well-maintained for tourists, even with log stairs cut into the steeper sections. A dirt service road wound around the west side of the bluff, but they didn't follow it.

Sharelle wished they'd stop for a moment so that she could survey the ranch below and perhaps spot where Troy had gone, but Michael didn't slack his pace for a moment. Her one quick glance behind had her stumbling hard on the next step and she gave it up.

The path didn't even offer a decent switchback where she could glance sideways.

Straight up and over.

In a small swale past the ridge, Michael stopped so abruptly that she walked square into him—and bounced off almost landing in the grass.

He neither spoke nor moved a single step—without turning around to see her coming, he'd anticipated the force of her impact too perfectly to stumble. Guy was spooky.

Michael looked around once, so Sharelle did the same. Other than Claudia's small helo climbing aloft, the ranch was invisible. To the west, the mountains towered above them. To the east, cattle dotted the prairie onto forever. At the lower edge of the bluff, before it turned to grazing land, a slender dirt road led off into the distance.

"Julie's family herds cattle," the beginning and end of Michael's explanation.

"Never been so far from civilization before."

He looked around as if surprised by the thought.

"Where?" she asked him.

"There are places."

"Do I need hot branding irons to extract a complete sentence out of you?"

"That was a complete sentence." Gibson's smile slid sideways. He might be twenty or more years her senior, but he shifted from grim to seriously handsome, in a very rugged sort of way, with that slight smile. "Been taking lessons from Claudia?"

"No. I figure I can deal with a ground pounder like you all on my own."

"My wife is a good teacher."

"At how to beat words out of retired Delta operators?"

Gibson's very non-reaction at the word retired said that he too was still in active service somehow. This place was going to make her crazy.

"Claudia has many gifts."

"Says the biased husband."

"Yes," he didn't hesitate a moment.

She knew how people talked about her: driven past sanity, pushy, always on the attack... Except, how might Troy talk about her? That one she didn't know. "So, what are her skills?"

"She's a fine archer. Runs classes here. USA Archery certified instructor."

"Haven't shot a bow since high school gym class." That's when she noticed the line of hay bales arranged to make a perfect backstop for target practice. "What else?"

A glance aloft, she saw a pair of black dots against the brilliant blue sky. They resolved rapidly into a pair of human-dog teams, but they kept plummeting downward. A third black dot, a tiny helicopter, descended not that far behind them, racing earthward.

All three kept coming.

And coming.

She was about to cry out when the chutes deployed at a bare thousand feet. Seconds later, the helo carved a hard pullout, sweeping into a tight turn around the jumpers and their dogs. It was a combat pilot's maneuver—a Night Stalkers combat pilot's. In seconds, all three disappeared below the line of the bluff.

"She's also an exceptional Little Bird pilot."

"Shit!" Sharelle's heart was still pounding with how low they'd come before popping their chutes; high-altitude low-opening indeed. With a helo simulating an attack. Those dogs had to be amazingly well trained to do that. "I guess *so*."

"And..." Gibson didn't finish. Instead, he tapped his ear and indicated a circle around them.

Sharelle opened her mouth to ask, *What the hell?* But Gibson's look commanded silence. So she listened. And the longer she listened, the more she heard.

The helo's rotor sound washed briefly over them, then faded away. It must be settling behind the bluff to fetch the next pair of jumping dogs.

Bird calls sounded back and forth. She knew the sharp call of the crow and the laughing chirps of the chickadee. The others were a mystery. Though now that she was paying attention, she also spotted several birds gliding silently along the high thermals—hawks, vultures, or maybe eagles—all too high to make out.

The cattle had little to say, but she did hear the occasional lowing moo. A breeze rattled the tall dry grass. The rising note of the Little Bird helo once more climbing aloft with the next jump pairs seated on either outside bench soon faded away.

A steady rhythm she couldn't identify. High energy. Low. Pounding. Not like a helicopter but aggressive. Low enough to be directionless, she kept turning slow circles to locate it. Not the ranch. Not the road. And growing louder. Until—

A pair of racing horses crested the bluff at a full gallop. The riders hunched forward over their mounts. Blonde and red. Chelsea and Julie. Or Julie and Chelsea.

By some mutual consent, they veered sharply and came straight at her and Michael.

They passed close enough to either side that she could have touched one and Michael the other.

Once past, they both shouted with a loud whoop and slowed their mounts as they arced around to return to them.

"Who won?" the redhead called out on a breathless gasp. "Come on. Was it me? Did I finally beat her?"

Michael kept his silence.

"What's the blonde one's name?"

"I'm Julie. She's Chelsea," the blonde answered in a soft voice.

"Doesn't matter? Which of us *won*?" The redhead walked her horse closer.

"By a nose..." still nothing from Michael, "...Julie."

Sharelle half expected Cheslea to plunge a fake dagger into her heart and tumble to the ground as Trisha O'Malley would have. Instead, she only had one remark, "Well, Pooh."

"Poo like in horse poo?"

"No, like in Pooh Bear." Chelsea shrugged. "I hate it that the best rider on the ranch always wins." She leaned over to hug Julie across the gap between them.

The horses were still puffing and blowing from the run. Lifting one hoof and then another as if shaking out their muscles.

"You should walk them a bit," Sharelle knew that much about horses.

With his usual not-a-word, Michael stepped forward and took both sets of reins. The two women slid off their horses.

Michael looked at her, tapped his ear as he had earlier, telling her to listen. Then, after inspecting her briefly, he made a show of clamping his mouth shut to tell her to keep quiet, then turned and walked the horses toward the longer side road.

Well, screw him. She stepped up, held out a hand, and spoke loudly, "Hi, I'm Sharelle."

As they greeted her, she could feel Michael roll his eyes.

She stuck her tongue out at him, but he'd never turned from leading the horses down the road to the barn.

———

THE SUN'S HEAT HAD ALMOST LULLED HIM TO SLEEP WHEN A shadow blocked the heat and light against his closed eyelids.

Troy squinted one eye open.

Bertram's massive face inspected him from inches away. He whined in worry.

Troy patted his head and whispered, "Good dog."

Behind him, two riders sat atop horses, all four of them silhouetted by the blazing midmorning sun and looking down at him. Five. A third, riderless horse also gave him the once over. Six, Bertram still sat front and center.

"Good boy," he reassured the dog. It took a moment but he finally recalled the right command, "Bertram, Stan *such*."

Bertram inspected him as if unsure of the command.

Troy repeated it more emphatically.

The dog's face turned to joy. With a happy bark that had Troy banging his head hard enough against the boards behind him to see stars, Bertram leapt to his feet and raced away toward the area the helicopter had been working over by the kennel building.

That still left two people and three horses. He doubted the same trick would work on them.

"Up, son. Between the barn and here, I think you've done enough lying about for the day."

"Hi, Mac," he struggled to his feet.

A cautious glance over the dog obstacle course wall that he'd been leaning against—oh face it, hiding behind—revealed no sign of Sharelle. In the distance, the Little Bird helo swooped around a second, or was it third set of jumpers with dogs. They were close enough that he saw the dogs watching the helo with interest but no sign of panic.

"Another pair passed."

"Yep," Mac also watched them. "Stan and Jodie make one hell of a team."

Troy opened his mouth, then closed it. He hadn't really focused on the second rider. She was a towering Native American, almost as tall on her horse as Mac on his. Her hair flowed to her waist, black sheened with silver. Mac sat like a skilled rider. The woman sat so naturally it was hard to decide where woman ended and horse began.

"You must be Ama."

She inclined her head in response.

"Hi, I'm Troy." He tried to imagine what story Mac had told his wife, then wished he hadn't. "Let me guess. You talk as much as Emily or Jodie."

Ama tipped her head in possible agreement.

"Yet Stan thinks I need to talk with you."

"Ah," Mac nodded. "That's why he sent Bertram out looking for her. Can't say I was surprised, except for Stan thinking that deep. That's more Jodie's style, she must be rubbing off on him. Figured it was something like that. My wife and I been off the ranch for a week and were headed out for a ride to sorta say hello to the place. We brought along an extra mount if you want to join in. You ride?"

"Placed top ten statewide in calf roping as a teen." What was wrong with a simple yes? Maybe he needed to feel grounded in his past because his present rocked worse than seasicker on a Navy ship.

"Then stop standing down there on the ground, son. We got a prairie out there with our names on it."

He greeted the horse, a big gray, and tightened the girth before climbing into the saddle. He'd be sore unless it was a very short ride—he hadn't been in the saddle for most of ten years since his parents had to sell off the last of the horses. A farm didn't need an animal that cost more per year than a new quad bike they so desperately needed. But letting go of Shane had been tough. He'd been a fine horse for a growing boy. At least they'd found a place with a new boy for him to teach.

Ama rode off in the lead, heading north along the edge of the bluff.

Over the first rise he reined in sharply. A massive cow, with horns as wide as a pickup truck and sharper than the tips of Hydra 70 missiles, glared at him. A calf, its horns no more than a couple hands long, shifted behind the cow's bulk.

"Don't mind Lucy none. She belongs over the road a piece, but no one's ever figured out how to keep her there." Mac pulled off his hat and waved it at the beast. "Get on home, Lucy. At the rate you move, you'll be missing your supper, though it isn't half-morning yet."

The cow pulled up another mouthful of grass and ambled on ahead of them, eventually drifting off the trail to sample a lush patch of blue and gold flowers. The calf made sure to stay on Lucy's far side.

"Fool beast," Mac said with some affection and trotted ahead to catch up with Ama. She'd ridden past the cows as if they were too natural in this place to disturb.

"So, what are you supposed to be talking to Ama about?" Mac asked when Troy caught up to him. "I'm guessing it's more than that pretty young lady up to the barn."

Troy didn't want to think about Sharelle. He didn't want to

think about losing her when he'd never had her to begin with. And he *definitely* didn't want to talk about that moment in the barn.

They passed over a low rise and the vista completely changed before them.

The whole length of the Front Range lay before them. It stretched into the distance until it seemed that the Canadian border eighty miles away lay within easy reach.

Across the dirt road and perhaps a mile ahead stood a farm far bigger than Henderson's Ranch. The house wasn't a quarter the size of the ranch's magnificent lodge, but well-used barns spread about the muddied yard in a vast array. Cattle were everywhere. Men moved about purposefully on horses and quad bikes, though they were too far off to hear over the lazy thump of horse hooves and the creak of leather.

Straight ahead, Beale's C-12 Huron was parked at a pullout. He glanced over his shoulder and saw that a long stretch of the dirt road was in good shape and straight as a ruler. Plenty wide to be a runway for a C-12. Actually, big enough that a C-130 Hercules transport might roll in if the pilot was good.

Yet one more part of everything that worked right at this ranch.

"How do you do it?"

Ama slowed until they were three abreast—himself, Mac, then Ama plodding through the grass whispering against the horse's hocks.

She looked at him with eyes so dark they were almost black, nodding for him to continue.

"I mean," he waved a hand helplessly behind him, "this place, your ranch, it...works."

"Nothing as simple as it looks, Troy," Mac answered. "Lot of hard work and sweat these last twenty years."

Some part of him wanted to put the man down. Former

Navy SEAL, he wouldn't stand a chance, but that didn't stop the wanting.

"My parents, their parents, and on back have worked the land since the 1893 Land Run. They put everything they had into that land. Every generation has worked it since. Extended family, we won adjoining parcels for fifteen hundred acres. Fifteen hundred acres grew to six thousand as one neighbor died or another went to the cities. But now we're whittled down and again some more. Not much past a thousand acres left. Too small for hunting *and* farming. Hosting hunting groups doesn't pay enough, and no chance of beating the massive agribusinesses at farming. All the folks that left, my line is the one that stuck. But it's bleeding my parents to death." By the end of it he'd reined in not far from Beale's airplane and was shouting. Loudly.

He swallowed hard as if he was the seasicker being tossed about by towering waves.

"Sorry."

He wished he flew fixed-wing. He'd steal Beale's plane and fly away. Fly from Sharelle, the Army, this place, then—

"You cannot fly from yourself." Ama spoke for the first time, her voice low and warm.

"Do you read minds?"

"Not often," her smile said she might. She rode ahead again.

Mac's grin said a definite *yes* on the mindreading, before he clucked his horse ahead to follow his wife.

"Are you one of Emily's?"

"One of Emily's what?" Sharelle had spotted three horses crossing over a hill to the far side of the ranch compound, leaving on a ride. Too far to see details, yet she knew Troy was one of them. She simply knew. Two with cowboy hats, one without. Absolutely Troy. Though he'd look good in a cowboy hat.

After spotting him, she'd dropped to sit at the bluff's edge. Chelsea and Julie sat to either side of her. Out ahead lay the flat prairie dotted with cattle. It looked like a fake quilt someone had tossed down over the land. It simply ran on forever until it disappeared into the distant heat haze.

The fore slope of the bluff appeared to be butterfly heaven, in the right proportions that they could be distant flying cattle instead. Black wings with white trim, brilliant blue, orange with black dots like a Monarch. The whole place like some fairytale kingdom with a butterfly ranch instead of a castle.

Not one of her little girl dreams.

Chelsea nudged her with a shoulder. "Come on. You just gotta be one of Emily's. Your type drops in every now and then like they're voyaging to a holy Mecca. Though I've never seen a helicopter quite like that one," she nodded behind them toward the ranch.

"A holy Mecca? I'd like to..." Sharelle noticed her own hands clenching the air in front of her as if it was someone's throat—Beale's throat. Everything had made sense until she'd landed here and Beale had bugged out, leaving her to deal with it all on her own.

She flexed her fingers and dropped them into her lap.

"Wow! She musta seriously pissed you off. Does that sound like Emily?" Chelsea leaned forward to look across at Julie.

Julie had been making a braid of the dry grasses, plucking them one by one. "Sometimes."

"Oh, c'mon. She's awesome." Chelsea turned back to Sharelle. "You see, she had her kids way before either of us. So she like knows everything before we do. We've adopted her as our big sister...well, she adopted us as her little sisters. What's better than awesome?" Chelsea didn't wait for an answer. "I used to be governess to her first kid back when they were both flying to fire. She was unreal. I mean I don't know anything about fighting wildfires from helicopters. Well, I didn't. Now I guess I kinda do, and she was amazing. She and Mark—but mostly she—built Mount Hood Aviation into the best wildland helitack firefighters there are."

They'd been with MHA out in Oregon? Hell of a reputation. It had slipped her mind that's who Emily flew with. There were rumors, very quiet ones, that fighting wildfires wasn't all they did. No word on what else, but she'd spent the last few months poking the grapevine about Beale. One old helo mechanic, who'd never flown with MHA, told her all sorts of things about MHA one night. Sounded like a conspiracy theorist, so she'd dismissed what he'd said—until now. Now that she'd met Beale, she wished she'd paid more attention.

He'd said MHA had started out when they bought all of the CIA's old aircraft from Air America—an illegal part of the US operations during the Vietnam War, especially drug- and weapons-running in Laos. Since then, MHA had flown to a lot of odd places for a firefighting team—when really interesting events were taking places in the countries they'd flown to, according to the old mechanic. But she couldn't recall much more than that.

Black Ops in foreign countries as a firefighter? It somehow fit the hazy picture that she was building of their commanding officer. She should have told Troy about that, he might know more. But now there was this...thing between them.

"Why does there always have to be this...thing?" She still didn't have a better word. "You know, with men."

Julie stopped with her grass-braiding.

"Not my department," Chelsea spoke first, of course. "Doug and I were gobsmacked at first sight. We kissed within ten seconds of meeting, kinda by accident. It was Tessa's, Emily's kid's fault. We didn't know each other's names yet. And he was so gorgeous and so clueless." She sighed happily.

"Hussy," Julie teased.

"For Doug? Always." Chelsea proved wholly unflappable. "But you had a real man...*thing* with Nathan. He's our hot, hot chef," Chelsea explained in an aside.

Julie nodded.

"Tell Sharelle how you got around it."

Julie studied the horizon, then barely whispered. "Almost didn't." One of the black butterflies circled her hat once or twice before settling on the crown and slowly waving its wings.

"Do better than that," Chelsea chided.

Sharelle had worked with Trisha enough to know better than trying to shush a redhead, she simply didn't look away from Julie.

Julie pointed her latest piece of plucked grass toward the cow-spotted horizon. "I was out past Choteau, heading only the Good Lord knows where, chasing a construction job I didn't want because it was the farthest I could imagine running from this place. Emily tracked me down; sent Mark in a helo to stop me in the middle of a dusty road to nowhere. I'd feel stupid, but she'd sent Mark all the way to New York to, as Nathan puts it, *smack him upside the head*." She studied the grass blade before pointing it at Sharelle. "Are you needing a smack upside the head?"

Sharelle still felt the heat of that kiss on the barn floor. She wanted more of that. A lot more now that she thought about it.

She looked at the two women. Happily married. Kids. Knew who they were and what they wanted.

Julie's butterfly soared aloft, fluttering off on some new mission.

All Sharelle had ever wanted was to fly.

Until...

She scowled over her shoulder in the direction Colonel Michael Gibson had walked away.

Listen.

Well, she'd listened. And heard more than she'd wanted to.

"A smack upside the head?" Sharelle wanted to bury her face in her hands, but she was a Captain for the 160th SOAR, dammit, which was the only reason she managed to resist the temptation. "I think Michael already took care of that."

———

TROY HAD NEVER RUN FROM ANYTHING IN HIS LIFE, BUT THE URGE still had him digging his knees into the saddle like a first-time rider. His big gray turned to look back at him. Forcing himself to relax should have been as easy as it sounded. It wasn't.

When he finally managed, his mount trotted to catch up to the others.

They left the plane behind where the trail they'd been following met the road. At the end of the dirt and gravel one-lane, it turned in at the cattle ranch. They rode past the gate with a wave that several of the ranch hands returned. Beyond, it turned from lane to a track that would require a heavy-duty truck or a quad bike to navigate. By the look of the growth, neither had passed this way in some time.

Mac fell back to ride beside him. "When we took over the place, the only thing worth a damn were the two houses and the main barn. And they'd been empty for onto a decade. Too far from town to attract trouble, and Nils," he nodded toward the cattle ranch, "kept an eye on the place."

Troy kept an eye on Ama riding ahead of them along the track as it wandered close above a horse-wide crick splashing alongside. Was she listening or not?

"I'd learned something important in the SEAL teams. Sea,

air, and land aren't what you'd call the important part of the equation; it's *team* that makes or breaks the day. Once we landed here, I put out a careful word. A few military men showed up here through my former commander, a couple old cowhands through Nils. Had some happy accidents too: Patrick, Chelsea, and Nathan. But we're mostly vets here. Vets know hard work. Got the men and women moved here, built a team by setting a tone, only *then* tried figuring out what we were doing."

A tip of Ama's head, as if turning an ear in his direction, had Troy answering, "Just Momma, Daddy, couple'a hired hands."

Mac nodded. "That's a tough row to hoe, all right. We have hired hands for the summer season, have to or we'd never keep up. But they're begging to come work here now, not like early days. One's a university professor who's been leading rides here for nigh on a decade and his wife handles our social media part-time because she loves doing it, and this is where they met. But the core? They've shown up often as not before we knew what to do with them. Stan spent a whole winter alone up against the Bitterroot before we thought up the dog training idea."

As if on cue, the helicopter whooshed by. As it passed, Claudia waved by rocking back and forth before shooting off toward the ranch and the latest pair of parachuting dogs.

"Nils has his three boys. Those four men work hard. Cattle need tending year-round, and their hands live on the ranch. Like as not, their women move in rather than the men leaving when they get hitched. But cattle's a hard life, even harder than horses."

Troy felt worse, if possible. "That's why I'm heading home."

Ama stopped so abruptly that he and Mac had to rein in hard not to run into her, even at a slow walk. With so little command that Troy had to admire the horsemanship, Ama turned her horse about in place until the three horses were nose to nose. Once they saw nothing else was happening, all three tore a mouthful of tall grass from beside the track.

"Home," she said as if placing the word on the ground between them.

"I'm a farmer by trade."

"Got an odd mount you're riding," Mac chimed in.

"The flying was an accident. My degrees are all in agriculture and farm management. My reaction time had the Army sending me aloft."

"*Captain* Troy Ryland." Ama left this statement to float in the air above the horse's heads. Her slight emphasis spoke of someone who'd stuck when walking away would have made more sense.

"Extra rank and a higher MOS means a higher pension for the farm."

"This morning, Mark said you were ten years in. Another year or two of good service makes major. Yet you're talking like you're leaving soon."

"Ninety days today."

"Who knows?" Ama asked.

Troy attempted to answer. Honestly he did, but he couldn't get the words out.

"Not your pilot," Mac didn't make it a question. "That's why you hightailed it outta the barn. Stepped across a line and can't figure how to step back."

"Something like that." If it was Mac alone, he'd turn and ride away. But Ama's dark eyes held him there, demanding truth. "Fine. Yes. Sharelle's the best pilot I ever met. She's an incredible woman. But I can't ask her to be a farmer. And I can't stay because the farm *needs* me. I'm a late kid. My parents are probably close to your age and they can't do it alone. The farm isn't big enough to support as many farmhands as it needs anymore. I have to go."

"Choices. We *all* have choices." Ama nodded as if that

ended the conversation. To drive home the point, she pivoted her horse again, with no indication of how. Troy was a good enough rider, he should have seen it. Was her horse a mind reader too?

She and Mac rode ahead, but Troy remained stuck where his horse stood.

Choices.

The one thing he didn't have.

They were long out of sight before he turned his big gray and headed back to the barn.

————

"Which one are you wanting to face down?"

Sharelle looked at Julie. The two women had started talking about kids and horses. It didn't take long to understand that redheaded Chelsea was the one primarily responsible for the incredible care of the horses and the immaculate barn. Smart, driven, and cared with all her heart.

Did PITA Trisha O'Malley do that? Really care about her people?

Would she show it if Sharelle gave her half a chance?

Julie was practical in a different way. The ranch's top rider, and their resident building contractor.

Yes, I'm listening now, Michael.

"Which one what?"

"Emily is a half day's ride that way," Julie pointed northwest. "Short helo flight. If you really want to take the battle to Emily."

"If you insist on strangling her," Chelsea imitated Sharelle's earlier chokehold, "don't do it in front of the kids, okay?"

"Sure. But you asked which one. Which one what?"

Julie nodded toward a lone rider returning from the north.

No cowboy hat.

Moving slow.

She was up on her feet and hustling toward the path down to the barn before she realized that one of her legs had fallen asleep—forcing her to face-plant in the tall grass.

"Not much of a trick question, was it?" Chelsea's laugh floated overhead like a whole flock of butterflies.

9

———

By the time he reached the barn, Sharelle stood in the foreyard. Her chest heaving for breath. Grass stains on her jeans, her black t-shirt untucked, and bits of hay in her hair. It would help if she didn't look so wonderful.

She also had her fists planted on her hips as if ready to beat the crap out of somebody. Well, him.

Knowing he was a likely target, "Let me take care of the horse before you kill me."

Her nod didn't include a smile.

He rode all the way to the tack room and tossed the reins around a handy railing. Saddle, switching out a halter for the bridle, he gave the gray a quick brush and checked his hooves for gravel. Unsure which stall was the gray's, Troy shooed him out into the corral.

Closing the gate, he turned to face the music, which was standing about a foot behind him.

"What the hell, Ryland?"

He took a calming breath, which worked in battle but not this time. "Which question are you asking?"

"How in blazes should I know?" Sharelle shouted in his

face. "You kiss me like there's no tomorrow, then you run like a rabbit who accidentally hopped into a greyhound kennel. What's going on?"

He nodded. She deserved to know, but how was he supposed to tell her without ripping his heart out of his chest and stomping on it? He wasn't. That's what it was going to take.

Voices sounded near the far end of the barn.

"Walk with me?"

At her nod, they headed out the other end. The volleyball game had ended and everyone was headed to the barn. Probably going out on a ride. Or doing chores. Or... It didn't matter.

The yard was busy as well, though there appeared to be a *Don't Get Close* bubble around the covered helo, causing people to swing wide around it. The last thing he needed was to be reminded of how much he'd miss flying.

Behind the barn, they picked up a path that led to a line of cabins tucked all along the western slope. They all had tree names and most were surrounded by plantings that matched: Aspen, Larch, Fir, and so on. Beyond those, a cluster of cabins in a tiny compound of their own, and a group of yurts beyond those. Half up the slope, a trail branched off to the right with a sign, *Swimming footpath*.

He turned onto it because it fit his mood, like he was swimming through a sewage pit.

"I don't want to swim."

"Neither do I," but he kept going.

"Are you going to speak or am I going to have to drown you in that swimming hole?"

They crested the low ridge. From here the mountains soared aloft to the west beyond a vast expanse of rolling prairie. In the foreground was the swimming hole they'd hovered over last night upon discovering the unexplained EM source in the big barn. Someone had gathered all the float toys that their hovering had scattered. A stout cabinet of rough pine was labeled *Beach Towels*.

"They've thought of everything."

Not a soul around. Good. No one to ask him impossible questions about choices he didn't have. Except Sharelle Vargas, of course—the hardest of them all to answer. At least from here the ranch lay hidden or, more importantly, the helo that he loved to fly. Only ninety more days. He turned aside to head for the gazebo.

It was a pretty thing. It touched the shore to only one octagonal side, standing on stout pilings a couple feet over the water. Like the decking, the benches were stout planks of Doug fir, the canopy shingled in the same. Rather than any railing, it remained open to the water, with the benches placed back to back so that a convivial group could face inward or contemplative couples might face out toward the water and mountains.

He walked around the perimeter until he faced due west with the still water reflecting the distant mountains and the achingly blue sky like a mirror. He sat.

Sharelle followed but stood rather than sitting. Her arms crossed so tightly that it must hurt.

He knew the feeling. "I don't know where to begin."

"The beginning?" her voice was rough with tension.

Stepping into his first post-training briefing. Two years from surviving the brutal month of tests to join the Night Stalkers, he'd finally been deemed skilled enough to board one of their helicopters for a live mission. And there she'd been.

Her stance provided her answer: the beginning.

He looked up at her dark eyes but had to look back to the reflected water before he could speak. "First moment I saw you." He raised his hands to show his perplexity. "Never saw anyone like you. Never expect to again."

"So, what? A secret crush that you didn't act on for three years and suddenly you do this morning?"

Troy shrugged a *yes*. "I know every nuance of your face. The way your smile stays even but it reaches your right eye before the left. How your hair flops over one eye when you're really concentrating."

"Why?"

He tried to laugh and almost choked himself. The morning's breeze had gone. The air pressed close, unmoving, as if he'd used up all of the oxygen where he sat, leaving behind no energy to stand and move.

"Why do I know your face so well? Why you? Why didn't I act on it before?"

"Yes, to all of the above. And why you're so miserable after such an incredible kiss."

"Give me a break."

"Not a chance." At least she finally sat beside him.

He still didn't look at her. "The best pilot I've ever flown with. The way you do what you do across the sky," he drew an arc through the air and pictured her crossing through the reflected sky. "It's magic, Sharelle. Like you're making love to the very air as you move through it. How could I not fall for that?"

Her silence kept him from stealing a glance.

"Why didn't I say anything?" He closed his eyes but still saw her face. "To fly beside you... There's nothing like it. I didn't want to screw that up."

"Well, that at least makes some sense."

He noticed that she hadn't said a word about her own feelings. Captain Sharelle Vargas, always in perfect control.

She rested one of those fine hands on his shoulder, so incongruous on such a powerful woman. The heat of the connection almost burned.

"And why did you run away this morning?"

And there it was. The one question he least wanted to answer. "I ran out of choices." No matter what Ama said, in his case she was flat wrong.

"Choices to do what?"

"I ever tell you about our family farm?"

"You know you haven't. You never do anything by accident."

"Except kissing you." He hunched, trying to keep the words inside.

"Thought it was a happy accident at the time. Now stop avoiding the question."

"I'm not." And he told her about the farm. The wide fields of wheat and rye that had been his playground as a young boy; now gone to massive agribusiness along with soy, corn, sorghum, and even oats. "We've been forced into the less profitable crops of beet, potato, and onion. On leave, I've been going home to help build direct-to-consumer channels for my folks, but that takes more time, more hands-on care. They're old and getting squeezed out of existence."

"It sounds awful," her hand still rested on his arm. "But what does that have to do with running from a perfectly good kiss?"

The contact felt so good. Connection or something. Warm. Solid. "I can't see you living on our farm."

"Maybe in my dotage. Though I wouldn't place big bets on it." Her laughed splashed into the pond. As if evoked by her amusement, a light breeze rippled the surface and shattered the perfect image.

But sometimes you had to rip off the bandage.

"That's where I'll be living in ninety days. I'm leaving the Night Stalkers. The Army. I'm going back to Oklahoma—three months from today."

———

Sharelle was sure they were words.

Troy had spoken them so they must be truth.

But they'd turned into a buzzing in her head messier than her hair after a full day trapped under a helmet.

"You…"

She shook her head; it didn't clear.

"Leave…"

Nope. No way.

"*What?*" Sharelle knew she was shouting. Could feel her fingernails digging into the flesh of Troy's shoulder. She never shouted. Cool and steady was her command mantra. *Show confidence as a leader and your people will follow,* one of her brain-dead instructors had insisted.

Troy wasn't following! He was veering off on an unimaginable course.

"Oklahoma? That's a place people escape from, not go back to."

Troy shrugged as if her tight clench on his broad shoulder wasn't even there.

She tried to imagine the cockpit without Troy beside her—

Nope. No way.

"No. Request denied."

"Not your call, Sharelle."

"Yes it is. You can't leave, Captain Ryland. You're an officer, a *Spec Ops* officer. You serve at the pleasure of the President just like I do."

"I submitted my REFRAD packet nine months ago with McDermott's signoff. A full year off-ramp. I've got initial approval for a ninety-day out."

Her thoughts spun worse than a helo with a shot-off tail rotor. "He did what? And you didn't tell me?"

Troy shook his head.

"You fucking idiot!"

Again that noncommittal shrug that didn't deny the charge.

"You're kidding me?"

Again the head shake. He'd always been the positive voice of reason in their crew. Now, he looked beaten worse than the last horse across the line in the Derby.

"But..." No, he *had* told her why. His farm. His parents' hardship farm. And he was leaving the Night Stalkers because he cared that much about his family. Small wonder he never spoke of it, a point of pain for him since... Probably since he'd left home to begin with.

Troy rolled his shoulder, knocking her grip loose.

Then he stood and looked down at her. "I'm so sorry, Sharelle. For..." he looked up at the sky and down at the water, everywhere except at her. "For everything."

He turned on his heel, circled the outer rim of the gazebo, and walked away.

A slapping sound had her ducking low.

Slap like a distant gunshot.

She had half turned to make sure Troy was okay—when she spotted the source. The duck-and-turn let her see up past the edge of the gazebo's canopy toward the sky.

Two jumpers, with their dogs strapped to their harnesses, fell under parachutes—still showing the hard swing of a fresh opening. Not a gunshot, it was an incredibly low chute deployment.

They plunged into the pond. A fountain of water erupted from their landing points. Seconds later, they all surfaced. Freed from the harnesses, the dogs played for a moment until Stan and Jodi grabbed onto their war-dog jump harnesses.

The dogs swam for shore, towing their trainers along with them. Once ashore, Jodie waved, then began gathering her chute. Sharelle managed a wave back. She'd never been in a position to witness the end of a HALO jump, only the beginning as she and her DAP Hawk guarded the helos they were jumping from. So up close and personal that she'd caught a bit of spray. SEALs were even crazier than she'd thought all along.

By the time Sharelle remembered to look, Troy had once again disappeared in some unknown direction.

———

AFTER LUNCH, THE STREAM THAT RAN CLOSE BY THE NORTHWEST Cabin proved to be a sufficient distraction for the girls. It needed a better name now that Julie had finished building it but Emily couldn't seem to focus.

Following in her father's hip waders, Tessa at ten had already taken to fishing like an old hand. She had a fine pair of rainbow trout circling in a bucket of water, waiting to become dinner over tonight's campfire. Switching to a barbless fly she'd wound herself, she shifted to trying her luck at snagging a catch-and-release cutthroat trout. Like a true fisherwoman, she didn't care that the ranch lay at the very edge of their territory. Or that one had never been caught on the ranch in the twenty-five years the Hendersons had run the place.

At eight, Belle could still be endlessly entertained by her fantasy worlds. She had created some sort of fairy kingdom upon a small bank of sand that had gathered at a lazy curve in the stream. She'd built a sand castle, woven grass roads, and one-leaf trees with their stems stuck in the sand like trunks. Then she'd peopled it with leaf men, stick men, rock horses, and other beings that Emily resisted asking about. Her questions always seemed to break Belle's world as she tried to explain the social hierarchies and the different voices of a Y-shaped stickman versus an L-shaped one and why that should be obvious to anyone.

Mark eyed the two girls, then slid his hand into Emily's and led her a little way upstream. She knew he'd rather be fishing beside his daughter, but he hadn't forgotten Emily's near breakdown this morning.

Night Stalker pilots do not *have breakdowns. Ever!* The fact that her *new flight* was commanding an entire regiment rather than a helo meant she couldn't afford a momentary lapse on the ground either.

"Look, Emma, I can only guess how hard it is. I know how much the girls and I miss you. Out there alone it must be ten times worse."

"It's awful. They either don't want me there because I'm not Cass, or they can't unwind enough to speak in my presence because I'm," she made air quotes with her free hand, "The Great Emily Beale. If it wasn't for Trisha, I'd lose my mind worse than I already have."

"Look, Fort Campbell's a nice enough place. The girls and I—"

"No! Don't even offer it or I might say yes. They'd be miserable leaving the ranch. So would you. And Mac needs you here. This *place* needs you like it never needed me."

Mark was silent as they strolled along the stream bank, always staying in sight of the girls.

"I believe in what I'm doing, Mark, I really do. But is belief enough?"

"If not you, Emma, then no one on the planet."

"Come on. You know as well as I do that everyone's replaceable. The 5D barely stumbled when we left it. Lola, Trisha, Claudia, Justin...they stepped in clean."

He stopped them at a formidable glacial-drop boulder planted alongside the stream, coated with blue-green lichen. They climbed up—Julie had strategically placed a couple smaller boulders to make a natural-looking stairway—and sat on the top. From here, the cabin and the girls were in clear view. The Front Range break and the rolling prairie. The big Montana sky...

And the distant horizon that told her to stop wasting time sitting still.

"What did you tell Zack?"

"A year. I promised the President a year. It's been two months and I'm already losing it. There are," Emily held out her hands as if trying to grab fistfuls of reins, "so many threads. It's all—" She buried her face against Mark's shoulder. She needed a good blasting storm to plummet down from the face of the Rockies so that her outsides matched her insides.

Be careful of what you wish for, Emily.

Mark let her find some sense of control before speaking again. He'd always understood the power of silence yet knew when there'd been enough of it as well.

"See that cabin?"

Emily raised her head. It was a lovely piece of work. Julie had scavenged lumber and fixtures from several old buildings dating back to the ranch's heyday running cattle, fifty years or more before. It looked old on the outside and authentic Western on the inside. A cabin, not a house, but one for well-heeled tourist groups. A ground floor with three rooms barely big enough for the four bunk beds stuffed in each one. The rooms were small to encourage folks into the large central area with the cast iron stove, comfortable chairs, a decent field kitchen. Julie had wrapped it in a wide porch under a reaching eave. A comfortable horse barn stood nearby.

Solar electric, propane tank cooking, and a woodshed full of split logs delivered in a dump by their helo. No road. No cell service. Only horse and hiking trails, and an emergency radio that reached back to the ranch.

Patrick, with his fine filmmaker's eye, had photographed it well. Reservations for next year had sold out the first week it had been on the website.

"It didn't spring out of the ground fully formed. I scouted from the air. You rode out with Julie and Chelsea to decide on the placement. Mac and Julie near enough arm-wrestled over the design. How many hours went into building it? A team effort. That's the trouble, Emma."

"The trouble with the cabin? I think it's wonderful the way it—" She bit her tongue. "You're talking about the Night Stalkers now, aren't you? Never mind, you are."

"I am." He kissed her on the temple and she let herself sink into it.

She'd always been the straight-ahead one. Subject changes, at least ones not about the regiment, tripped her up all the time, still. "So, what about them?"

"Look, Emma," Mark held out his big hands as if he had the power to reshape the world. He'd certainly reshaped hers. "You can see the finished vision. You can already see the 160th in the form it needs to take to stay relevant in the future. It's one of your many gifts." He made a point of looking down at her body and smiling. "Many gifts, my love."

She let herself get lost in the kiss that followed. If the girls weren't in sight, she'd drag him down into the tall grass here and now. He gave her the moment to recover as the man still made her weak in the knees.

"You were the one who saw the mission complete before it was started, yet maintained the flexibility to adapt when the situation went dynamic. Never told you, but Michael had been with the outfit for five years before you came along. Getting antsy, knew I was about to lose him and not a damn thing in my power to do about it. He was too good to stick around for what I had to give him. Then you showed up and dragged him off that cliff face in the middle of a gun battle. Colonel Michael Gibson stayed five more years—because of you."

Emily shook her head. That couldn't be right. Michael was the top soldier in Delta Force, or any military for that matter. Stayed for her?

"You aren't so easily replaceable. You have skills that only you can pass on. Trisha's a better commander than she thinks she is. Goes times ten for you."

"But I can't keep doing it." She felt as if she was fraying around the edges. Except it wasn't a gradual wearing away like a bearing that needed replacing. It was the imminent failure of a swash plate about to make her rotors fall off, plummeting her down to the Earth from some great height. She'd been there and done that, still not able to believe the miracle she'd somehow pulled off so that she hadn't killed her crew in the process.

"Then let's solve that, because you can't walk away from it and live with yourself. We both know that."

Well, Mark might know that, she didn't. However, she'd never once found a reason to mistrust him.

"You've plowed nonstop through the first two months and you wonder why you're strung out. Made a hundred changes by the sound of it. Good. Well done, you. But now you need to leave time for those lessons to bake in a bit before the next round. From this month forward, you're going to run the regiment from here at the ranch for one week a month."

"That would never—"

"Emma," Mark cut her off. "It's already done. Why do you think you're here?"

"It's because..." But it hadn't been. She'd thought it was a stolen moment between the Alaska training mission and returning to Kentucky. But...

"Already talked to Uncle Eddie and Zack about this last week. If the Chairman of the Joint Chiefs and the President say it's fine, then it's fine."

"How?" It was a gift past anything she'd ever imagined. She looked up to see Tessa tossing another fish back into the river. Belle had drifted away from the river. About to jump down from the height, Emily finally spotted her at the cabin's small corral talking to her pony. A glance showed that, of course, Mark had tracked her move. Superdad.

"Think I don't know your voice after all these years, Emma? Can hear how it's choking you. Girls and I will fly out and visit you in Kentucky more often now that tourist season is mostly done. I already picked up a lovely used Super King Air 350, hangared in Great Falls. Fetch them straight from school and we can be to you in time for a late dinner and a long weekend."

Emily had only cried a few times in her life. Now wasn't one of them, but she couldn't loosen her throat enough to speak either. She'd never expected such a gift. She leaned her head on Mark's shoulder, the most solid place she'd ever come to rest.

"Now, about the Night Stalkers."

Emily shook her head.

"Be here now?"

She nodded.

He slid an arm around her waist. Some timeless time later, Belle chased a butterfly past the big boulder, then climbed up to join them. Not long after, Tessa finally decided that she'd stood knee-deep in a glacial-fed stream for long enough and joined them as well.

For the rest of the afternoon they talked about nothing more important than the shapes of passing clouds.

Emily was pleased to note that none of them were storm clouds—yet.

10

When Troy had arrived at the ranch's main compound, he'd been wondering quite how chicken he'd been, dropping the bomb of his departure, then walking away from Sharelle. Giving her time to cool down? Giving himself time not to be embarrassed more than he already was? Or too busy feeling like an untended manure pit by betraying everything she'd believed in, including her belief that he felt the same, to care?

"It's supposed to feel better."

"What is?"

Troy twisted around. "Dang it, Colonel, how do you keep sneaking up on me?"

Gibson's wintry smile said he'd find no satisfaction here about how the man moved so silently.

"Fine. Isn't telling the truth supposed to make me feel better? Getting something off my chest. Speaking my truth. All that noise."

Gibson's smile faded fast enough. He actually grimaced at some foul memory. "Never that easy."

"Well it should be. Shouldn't it?"

At least the man had the decency to nod in agreement.

"Though it never is." He stared up at the sky for ten seconds, then twenty... By thirty Troy wondered if the man had fallen asleep standing and staring at the clouds scattered across the sky.

As abruptly, Gibson looked at him once more. "Wait here."

"Like I have anywhere else to go." But again he stood alone and was talking to himself. Man, the guy was slippery.

He returned before Troy thought of anywhere else to be. He carried two knapsacks and a pair of .350 Ruger rifles with shoulder slings, handing one of each to Troy. "Five shot."

"We going hunting?"

"Walking. Bear aren't common this side of the ranch but we do get them. We're at the edge of the wolves' range but we do get them, too. They're more likely to be spooked by us than attack, but I'd rather be the live one afterward. You?"

"Uh," Troy finally caught that this was the peak of humor to a man who was deadlier barehanded than any wolf ever born. "Sure."

Not even that hint of a smile before Gibson headed off northwest. Their shadow lay to the northeast, well past noon by the human sundial.

"Did you pack lunch? I think I missed breakfast too." Unsure of that as everything else didn't bode well for his future.

Gibson veered toward the lodge. At the western end, close by the last night's campfire, they entered a massive kitchen.

"Holy cats! Let's stop here. Right here." To the left lay a massive kitchen all down one wall with an island that could fit a dozen chefs or two whole sides of beef. A crazy mix of normal pots, pans, and so on, next to industrial size mixers, a massive multi-burner range, and a bank of ovens worthy of a cooking show. To the right, a big family dining table, and beyond that a large sitting area cluttered with comfortable sofas and kids' toys grouped around an unlit fireplace.

Gibson had stepped over to a man sorting through a pile of tomatoes in every size and shape imaginable.

"Got some sandwiches or other hand food, Nathan?"

Nathan glanced over. "For two?"

Gibson nodded.

Troy's stomach grumbled in answer. He offered the cook a smile. "How about for three? One for my stomach and one for me."

"Preferences?"

"On bread? I'm not particular. Like most anything."

"My favorite kind of eater."

In minutes, Nathan had whipped together four massive sandwiches. Gibson had also taken two.

"Oh, man," he managed a mumble. A BLT made with farm-smoked bacon, fresh-picked spinach and tomato, and a thick layer of fresh avocado and another of homemade mozzarella on fresh-baked rye sourdough kaiser rolls and toasted in a panini press redefined his idea of heaven.

Not believing in sitting still, Gibson led them out the door mid-first sandwich. Troy managed to mumble a *thanks* around a mouthful as he sucked in air to cool the scorching hot cheese. Nathan stuffed a baggie in Troy's jacket pocket. "Fresh-made pretzels. I'm trying a new recipe so let me know."

They headed behind the lodge, upslope of the dog training area, and struck out over the hill to the northwest. Like most Night Stalkers, Troy typically ran a 10K most days, which should have made keeping up with Gibson a nonissue. The man wasn't running, but he walked up the steep slope with the same steady gait he used on level ground. Troy reluctantly tucked his second sandwich, wrapped in foil, into his pocket because it would be impossible to eat and breathe hard enough to keep up.

At ten minutes, Gibson stopped to tighten his boots. At ten minutes and fifteen seconds, before Troy could think to ask where they were headed, he set off again. Down into a ravine, over a log crossing a fast-rushing stream as if it was a paved bridge rather than the springy branch slick with spray, and up the far side.

After an hour, Michael stopped and pulled out his water bottle.

He started to move off before Troy had even fished his out. Too out of breath to speak, he grabbed Michael's shirt. A hand clamped around his wrist like a vise and twisted just enough outward that another millimeter would either send him plummeting to the ground or dislocate his elbow.

Gibson let him go. "Sorry. Was thinking about something else. You surprised me."

Troy massaged his elbow. "Like what? Best methods for ripping out a person's arm?"

Gibson shook his head.

"Well, if you're not going to answer that question, mind telling me where we're going?"

He glanced to the northwest.

"That's not an answer."

"Someone you need to talk to."

Troy probably needed to talk to Sharelle. He'd left the conversation in a far more awful place than he'd intended. *I'm leaving the military,* would have been bad enough on its own. He had set the ninety-day mark as his own internal deadline for telling her, so at least he'd been spared the temptation to blow that off. But to do it immediately after his revelation that he felt...whatever it was he felt about her, rated as cruel.

But the path to Sharelle now lay a couple miles behind them.

"Some kind of hermit guru of the prairie?"

Michael shook his head and almost smiled. "Though he might like that image. Give him a good laugh at least."

"How far away is he?"

"A ways."

"Couldn't we have taken horses?"

Michael squinted for a moment, then shrugged.

"Didn't think of it? But you live on a horse ranch."

He shrugged again. "Prefer to walk." To prove his point, he turned and headed off before Troy could stop him.

At least it was a *he* they were headed toward. Troy wasn't ready to tell Colonel Beale about his upcoming departure, a revelation he'd wager would go worse than telling Sharelle—if possible.

———

DINNER WAS A JOVIAL AFFAIR IN THE BIG KITCHEN. SHARELLE FELT about as jovial as... Each metaphor she came up with turned out grimmer than the one before.

"Where the hell is he?" she asked her crew chiefs.

She sat with Wright and Olsen at the end of the big table crowded with folks. Though there was plenty of elbow room. Even if Beale and her family hadn't gone camping, her team didn't add much to the crowd.

Mac, the old owner who'd surprised her and Troy on the tack room floor, sat to her left and her crew to her right. At the moment, he was having an intense discussion with Stan and Jodie about the dogs' training today. Farther down the table, Julie talked earnestly with a couple of very genuine-looking cowboys. Sharelle had never really expected to see such a thing outside the movies. Others ranged down the table to the matriarch who ruled the far end of the table, a gorgeous native American woman with a long fall of dark hair going purest silver.

Chelsea sat as queen of the nearby kid's table. A couple of empty chairs must be for Emily's kids, but high laughter filled the table as Cheslea turned dinner into some sort of game.

"Michael took him for a walk," the chef announced as he set down a bowl of pasta thick with fresh veggies and smelling of a garlicky basil sauce.

"Where?"

"They headed out that way," he waved northwest with another pair of bowls before setting them down in front of Wright and Olsen, "four or five hours ago. Packs and rifles." He turned back to the open kitchen for more bowls.

"Where?" she asked her crew, but it was Mac who answered.

"With Michael, that's often hard to predict."

"When do you think they'll be back?"

Mac twirled up some pasta, pinned it in place with a finger of sautéed zucchini, and ate it leaving her to answer her own question.

"With Colonel Gibson, that's often hard to predict."

"Smart girl. Emily said you were."

"She say anything else?"

Mac smiled and tapped the side of his nose like a corny spy signaling a secret.

———

TROY HADN'T CAMPED OUT UNDER THE STARS SINCE BEING WITH Mary Ann between high school and college. Now that had been a fine summer, so many nights spent together out under the Oklahoma sky. From two ranches down, she'd been as happy sleeping wild as he had. In the deep grass of the high knoll overlooking his family's ranch had become a favorite.

They'd gone ROTC together though they'd already shifted from lovers to friends—their past wasn't their future. She'd hadn't survived the training.

Out on an exercise, their team had been captured by the opposing side and stuffed onto a swamp boat for transport back to a compound as POWs. Under cover of darkness—and lax guards—she'd managed a slip off the side. Before she let go of the gunnel, she'd shot him a final grin and dropped out of sight. One of the guards had spotted the move too late. They'd circled back but found no sign of her. Good at hiding or…

They'd found her with a foot jammed in an old bit of boat wreckage; long drowned by the time they dragged her body from the muddy water.

Several of the cadets on that boat had dropped out, but he'd refused to do that to her memory. That memory had driven him to stay long enough to discover flying.

Out here, under the stars brought back the many good memories without dredging up too much of the horrific one.

Helicopter pilots didn't camp much. Multimillion-dollar machines, especially forty-million-dollar DAP Hawks, rarely slept anywhere except in a hangar. He could count his nights camping wild since on one hand with enough fingers left over to handle a horse's reins. Even by year twenty of Afghanistan, when the best officers' quarters' mattresses had been beaten to death with five thousand nights of use by a long succession of pilots, it had still been on fortified bases. Michael probably thought it was normal to have a single blanket along and not much else.

He'd shot a pair of rabbits and cooked them over a near smokeless campfire. Didn't even bother with the rifle, pulled out a pistol Troy hadn't known Michael was carrying and, *bang,* straight through the head at fifty yards. Salt, pepper, and a side of stream water lightly seasoned with purification tablets and a package of electrolytes. Now they lay atop a hill, one rise closer to the stars.

"You like living rough. Delta teach you this?"

"Camped rough as a kid. Claudia Jean too. Kid comes along. Now when we camp, it's an event. Tents, packed food, bags, pads, and all the rest of it. Miss this."

"You'd miss the wife more." And why had he said that? It

took him from the star-spangled sky straight back to Sharelle. Did she ever camp rough? Like this? He didn't know, but he could easily imagine her lying here beside him, which sucked. It sure wasn't going to happen now.

Michael's silence was the only answer he heard before the long hike and the short night caught up with him.

Next he knew, the sun stood well clear of the horizon.

Michael sat twenty paces to the northwest, so still he might have been a part of the landscape.

"If you were so hot to get to this guy, you should have rousted me."

"As good a spot as any."

Troy discovered a half pot of coffee kept warm close by the fire, and a trout baked on a hot rock, though the nearest stream lay a half mile off. Two sets of fishbones and one skin in the fire told him this fish was all his.

Sitting next to Michael after eating the succulent fish, he lingered long over the coffee, enjoying the quiet of the day broken only by birdsong, a high raptor call, and a deer family strolling slowly across the facing hillside. Michael merely...sat.

"I'm always impatient when waiting."

Michael nodded. "Pilot thinking."

"Right," though Troy had never thought of it that way. "Not happy unless we're on the move."

Michael stayed focused on the distant mountain horizon. Or on nothing at all.

"You Delta operators train to wait for the right moment."

"It usually shows up if you wait long enough."

The right moment to talk to Sharelle. He sure hadn't found that. Returning to the farm, already years later than he should have. Leaving the Night Stalkers? With the way his track record had been running, he might find his worst timing yet, though he couldn't imagine how.

"And we're waiting for some non-guru guy."

In answer, Michael simply stood. As he made no move to depart, Troy didn't bother standing.

Minutes later, he moved his arms twice like telling time on a clock. Then he sat.

Like a clock. Semaphore.

Left arm straight out to the side, right arm angled down to the side. Then right arm straight out and the left crossed over to angle down toward the ground.

Troy was more used to reading an air marshaller's baton gestures, but he'd been drilled in Navy flag talk in case of communications failure.

"M-H?"

Michael nodded but made no other motion.

Not watching the distant horizon. No, he was Delta Force and probably watched everything at once. Probably behind them, too, without needing to turn. The warriors of The Unit were downright spooky.

Troy scanned the hills and finally spotted a group of four horses cresting through a low saddle in the far distance. No bigger than fingernails, yet somehow, Michael had known when they were looking his way and sent a signal.

M-H. That would be...

Oh no! This was going to be *far* worse than facing Colonel Emily Beale.

———

"Who's that with Michael?"

"Durned if I know, Emma. You're the one in the family with the eagle eyes." Mark knew there was no doubt Michael awaited him atop three hills over. No one else would have chosen his perch on the hilltop's curve that carefully; he and his companion sat fully silhouetted against the blue sky for maximum exposure. It also had the earliest possible view of the trail from Cutthroat Cabin, as the girls had named it last night, back toward the ranch.

"That was an M-H, wasn't it?"

Mark sighed. "Can't imagine why he wants me instead of you, but ours is not to question why." He turned to the girls and laid a little Texas on them. "Got a mission for you two young'uns. Y'all make sure your mama gets home safe for me. Can you do that fer me?"

It earned him two enthusiastic nods and an eye roll. He leaned over to kiss the woman giving him the eye roll, then turned off the track. If not for that eye roll, he'd have given up the silly accent years ago. Maybe. He'd become fairly attached to it over time and it never failed to get a rise from Emma.

He let Wind Runner have his head and he soon saw that Michael's companion was that DAP Hawk copilot. Easing Wind Runner to a walk for the climb up the hill might frustrate his horse but it gave him a moment to puzzle at the possible reasons they were all the way out here. Mark wasn't in the habit of stepping into situations where he didn't know at least something of what was going on.

No sign of horses, these two had walked long and hard yesterday to reach this far across the prairie. Nothing except two knapsacks and a well-doused fire about the size of a saucepan. Classic Michael, but still no clue.

"Morning, Michael. Captain Ryland." He reined Wind Runner to a halt.

Michael nodded and Troy looked about to barf on his own boots. Well, this might be fun after all. He pulled his canteen from the saddlebags and slid to the ground. Only as his feet hit the ground did he realize his mistake.

Wind Runner had always been smart. Mark on the ground, with the tied horse's reins still lying across his neck? Mark had only half turned by the time his horse bolted out of reach. Three strides to a full gallop and he was racing back the way he'd come. He'd catch up with Emma and the girls, trotting happily back to the barn without him. Nothing he could do about it now.

Looking southwest, he shook his head. "You just had to walk this far out, didn't you, Michael?" It was going to be a long, long hike back to the ranch. He kept an eye out.

Wind Runner caught up with the others fast enough. Emily snagged his reins, looped them through a ring on her own saddle without so much as breaking stride, then waved as she continued down the trail and out of sight around the next hill. No help from that quarter—though he could practically hear her laugh over the long gap.

He turned back to Michael. "What's up?"

Michael simply nodded to Troy, then he began walking southwest along no track that Mark saw. He and Troy fell in behind.

"What's up, son?" Christ, was he actually old enough to say that with a straight face?

Troy merely shrugged, trudging along in silence.

Silence that stretched long enough for Michael to speak without glancing over his shoulder. "Ama said you two needed to talk. I brought him to meet you where you weren't likely to be disturbed."

"We walked six hours yesterday. Was meeting Colonel Henderson by the swimming hole completely out of the question?"

Michael ignored Troy's protest.

"So, *son,*" he could get used to this, it worked fine for John Wayne after all. "What in tarnation made Ama think we needed to be doin' some talkin'?"

———

T\ROY CONSIDERED PUNCHING HIM WITH A RIGHT CROSS TO THE Texas. Was it technically possible to punch the annoying, condescending accent without punching the man? If so, did it count as punching a superior officer or was hitting his accent a non-actionable offense? What if he was retired?

Troy was a total mess for even thinking about it.

"I don't know. I yelled at her a bit and—"

"You *yelled* at Ama?" Even Michael had stopped to turn and stare at him.

"I don't know. I didn't mean to. One moment she was looking at me with those all-knowing eyes of hers and the next I was screaming at her and Mac. Never done anything like that in my life. Didn't even have a chance to apologize. She just nodded like everything now made sense and rode off."

"And Mac? You yelled at a master chief SEAL's wife. Why aren't you walking about half maimed?"

"Lucky, I guess."

"Fool's luck. You yelled at my mom and you aren't dead. Dad must have a real weak spot for you." Mark laughed. "Don't that beat all, Michael?"

Michael nodded in agreement, then continued leading them down the slope.

"What were you yelling about?"

Troy never talked about the farm—or its problems—away from the farm because he'd never figured out how to talk about one without the other. Yet they'd come all this way, so he had to say something. And once he started, it all came dumping out.

But Mark understood more about ranch operations than any military man he'd ever met. He asked hard but good questions, forcing him to dig deep for the answers. They chased around ideas for a couple miles at least.

Henderson's was about tourists and horses, his own family's was mostly about produce for market. Tomatoes, beans, peppers, and eating corn rather than cow corn. Beets, squash, and cabbage in the fall. Opening up to U-Pick had helped some, but there would be no turning a flatland Oklahoma farm into a tourist destination.

"Not even a good tubing river?" Mark asked.

"Deep wells. We're just one of the million-odd folks drawing down the aquifer hard."

"Tough row to hoe."

"That's what your dad said."

"Was that before or after you lit into him and Mom?"

Troy stared down at the thick grasses hard. "Not sure. After, I guess. Before we talked about Sharelle."

Mark's hand crashing down on his shoulder almost drove him into the sod to ride out the seasons planted right here. "That pretty pilot of yours? Now we're talking my language."

"No," Troy shook his head. "No, we aren't. She's no farmer's wife and I'm going home in ninety…eighty-nine days."

"Any bets if Dad laughed his ass off at that?" Mark called to Michael loudly enough to spook a couple of ring-necked pheasants who shot aloft in a great flapping of wings.

Troy was either imagining things or he actually felt one of Michael's smiles without the man turning around.

"He didn't laugh and I *am* going."

"More you protest, son, the harder it's going to be when it's time to change your tune."

"Good. Harder the better. Because I can't be changing my mind. Harder to take back my word just makes the going easier."

"If Dad didn't laugh, what in tarnation did he say?" Mark squinted at him in confusion.

"Nothing," at least not that Troy remembered.

And Ama had been so wrong that it wasn't worth mentioning. He didn't have *any* choices.

11

———

Emily looked at the welcoming committee awaiting them by the horse barn.

Chelsea sat on a bale of hay, leaning on the barn's cladding, with her trademark bright red cowgirl boots crossed lazily in front of her.

The moment she met Claudia's gaze, the woman indicated up and behind her with a glance. Some information had come into their secure operations center that needed immediate attention.

Captain Sharelle Vargas stood with her arms crossed in the same aggressive attitude she'd given Emily during that very first flight. It hadn't been on such obvious display since.

Mark had been absolutely right. *That girl is gonna be some kinda teed off at ya parkin' her behind there and riding away for two days without any explanation.*

Not one of Emily's smoother moves. However, a commander had to make her mistakes appear as brilliant as her best maneuvers.

Chelsea shoved to her feet, reset her pink cowgirl hat—woe betide the person who called it a *cowboy* hat—and took

Chesapeake's reins. "I think these two will stress themselves to death and destruction if you don't do something about it, Emily. I'll take care of your horse, uh, horses." She patted Wind Runner's nose as she turned to the girls, "Was it an awesome ride?"

Belle set into a breathless description covering every detail of the two-day trip. Emily slid to the ground and listened to Chelsea's fascinated *Uh-huhs* when Belle left her enough room to slip one in as she led them off. Tessa offered her a knowing smile, then followed her younger sister.

Emily turned to face Claudia and Vargas, wrapping Mark's words around her, *If not you, Emily, then no one.*

Command mode, she ordered herself.

Prioritize.

"Captain Vargas," she offered a nod, then turned to Claudia. In her peripheral vision she saw Vargas going up on her toes ready to do battle.

"SecDef Stevenson," Claudia spoke softly.

Vargas' stumbled a half step forward before regaining her balance.

Yes, Vargas, I am the commander of the regiment. The Secretary of Defense does call me directly. The fact that Archie Stevenson had been her copilot throughout her time in the 101st and later in the Night Stalkers, until he was injured out, did make her look forward to it. No matter what bad news such a call presaged.

She nodded for Claudia to lead the way, then turned to Vargas. "You, stay here. We'll talk."

"Damn straight we will, Colonel." Emily could practically see the flames coming out her ears. *This was* not *going to be fun.* Though no matter how angry, she remembered to give respect, which was a point in her favor.

———

Sharelle had gotten no satisfaction from anyone last night. No Troy in the cabin. No one knew Emily's schedule. Everyone admitted that only Emily or perhaps Mark would know why her crew, her forty-million-dollar Hawk, and her own personal ass were parked on a Montana ranch.

Glaring at their backs through the open barn doors didn't gain her anything. Not so much as a glance in her direction as they turned and climbed the stairs up to that secure comms room that Michael Gibson had descended from yesterday.

Why wouldn't her fists unclench though her hands throbbed? Years in the military had included plenty of hurry-up and wait. But now, with each passing second, she felt Troy slipping farther away, leaving her utterly powerless to do anything about it. Powerless did *not* belong in her repertoire.

From the first time she'd seriously thought about the future, during her first-ever major make-out session in the woods along Fort Campbell's perimeter fence, she'd made sure she was the one in control. Grabbing the valedictorian ring gave her choices, including a full scholarship at the Virginia Military Institute. Captain for the volleyball team and a forward on the soccer team gave her enough status to run over anyone who tried to hold her back or tell her what she couldn't do.

Cass McDermott had fed into her need by being the first person to push her as hard as she pushed herself. And he'd made her pilot of the best helo anywhere as a reward.

Colonel Beale played from some other card deck. Every time Sharelle thought she had the woman figured, some new card got turned up that had nothing to do with anything before.

She should have had her ass reamed for breaking that mission plan up in Alaska. PITA O'Malley had been ready enough to do that. Yet somehow Beale made it a lesson about those operationally involved owning the battlespace they were in.

Now she was—

Beale reappeared halfway down the flight of stairs up to the loft and waved her to come over. By the time Sharelle arrived, Beale sat on the fourth step, placing them close to eye level.

She'd be damned if she was going to speak first, because sure as hell she'd get it wrong. Which... What the hell. Who cared?

"Why did you haul my ass to your personal ranch, Colonel? You dragged me here, then rode away as if I'm supposed to figure it out somehow. A lesson in what? And please don't say patience. That drowned out in your swimming lake about this time yesterday."

That earned her an eyebrow quirk of a question but she refused to be knocked off topic. Beale waited a long moment, then nodded to herself. "Your question is valid."

"Thank you so very much. I'd never have guessed."

"Me either. I'm not exactly sure why I asked you and your team here." And once again Sharelle was facing the woman rather than the commander.

"You know, it would really help if you gave out signal cards about which mode you're in."

Again with the eyebrow.

Sharelle decided she was frustrated enough to bite down on the bullet. "Most of the time you're the scary-as-shit commander—playing her cards so close that no one knows what she's thinking, except her ten-year-old daughter."

"Mark too," the woman admitted.

"Goody for him. It doesn't help those of us you're scaring to death. Then," Sharelle waved her hand a little helplessly, "suddenly you're you. Still cryptic-as-shit, but at least approachable."

Beale stared hard enough over Sharelle's shoulder that she almost turned to look. But she'd been fooled into that before, after that first flight—Beale's thousand-yard stare, except this was Colonel Emily Beale so her stare probably covered a thousand klicks.

"She's right you know." At the voice close behind her, Sharelle would have leapt out of her boots if they weren't so well tied. Chelsea had stepped out of her office across the main aisle of the barn. "Do me a favor, if you're gonna fight ugly, can you give me enough of a heads-up so I have time to make popcorn and sell tickets?" Chelsea patted her on the shoulder in a friendly fashion. "And if you want a clue, ask Emily about her dad." Then she sauntered off on some errand.

Beale hadn't spoken by the time the echoes of Chelsea's red cowboy boots had completely faded away.

"Your father?" Beale. Father Beale. The— "FBI Director Beale."

The colonel nodded.

"Well, shit. No wonder you're inscrutable."

"You're not the only one to think that about me." Emily tapped her own chest, then pushed to her feet and descended the last few steps. She began walking along the aisle of open stalls.

Sharelle fell in beside her. At the midpoint of the barn, a big set of side doors stood open to the sunlit day. A gate kept the horses out in the corral, but a few watched them walk by. She'd never had a horse of her own, but still it smelled of home and made her miss her family all the more. And her parents were doing well. What must Troy be feeling?

They'd walked the length of the big barn twice before Beale spoke again.

"What do you think of me versus Cass McDermott as a commander?"

Sharelle laughed. "Answering that is a seriously no-win scenario."

Beale nodded. No, in a weird way it was Emily who asked, not Colonel Beale. She could answer the former, or at least try.

She just hoped that the repercussions didn't land on her head from the latter.

"Okay, at the risk of putting my ass in a sling...Emily," she tested the name but elicited no negative response, "you're right. I look back at how McDermott treated me as a pilot. It's like he was, I don't know, sculpting me in his own image of a perfect pilot. Not that I got close, but I sure as hell tried. You..."

"Yes?" Emily prompted her while she debated the safety of continuing.

"You've burned out a number of good pilots, Emily."

"I'm well aware of the statistics."

"Don't go all Colonel on me now."

Rather than smiling or snarling, Emily took a deep breath, let it out slowly, and nodded for her to continue. Her... humanity continued to surprise Sharelle each moment.

"But what we were able to do in Alaska, we were your test case, weren't we? Tactics and coordination at levels I never managed before your training. Sure, Trisha O'Malley is your wild card, but I can feel you watching over my shoulder as I fly and pushing me to be better. To be more...I dunno, myself? Myself instead of whatever perfected form McDermott drove me toward."

Another length of the barn and halfway back passed in silence before Emily stopped them at the base of the stairs up to the loft room above the tack storage.

"So, ready to kick my ass?"

Emily offered a ghost of a smile. "I haven't been doing that enough already?"

"Might have." Sharelle made a show of rubbing her back side—and wished she hadn't. Rather than her own hand, she remembered the feel of Troy's touch for that brief moment he'd slipped his hand in her back pocket after a stellar far-too-short kiss. She pulled her hand away. "Why do I get the feeling that the ass-kicking isn't over?"

Emily nodded, "As much as I think this conversation has merely begun, other matters press."

And suddenly, with no visible change, Sharelle faced the colonel. She stood straighter and waited.

"Captain Vargas, how familiar are you with the Kamov Ka-52 Alligator?"

She snorted out a half laugh. "I know its battlefield abilities." It was perhaps the world's most impressive gunship after the DAP Hawk. She'd even put it up against Bell's AH-1 Cobra-Viper-Zulu family of helos.

"How's your Russian?"

"Plenty good enough to fly an Alligator if you ever get your hands on one." Which was about as likely as her forgiving Troy for leaving her—for leaving the *Night Stalkers.* She was fine the way she was. To fly an Alligator? That would be exceedingly cool.

"And Captain Ryland?"

"Troy's Russian is better than my English. He *is* the brains of this team." *Had been?* "You know he's quitting?"

She'd finally surprised the unflappable Colonel Beale, perhaps Emily as well. Her natural stillness turned frozen, not so much as a hair follicle moved.

"Ninety days. McDermott accepted his resignation."

"Why?"

Sharelle felt a twist in her gut like she was spilling secrets, someone else's secrets. She didn't have a lot of experience with it. Security clearance boundaries she understood fine. But her family were a verbal lot and personal secrets rarely lasted past the dinner table. If he hadn't run away. Or evaporated into outer space without another word. Or wherever...whatever...

"Shit! Sorry, Colonel. Not mine to tell."

Beale waited until Sharelle finally answered with a sharp shake of her head.

"His to tell."

Beale nodded. "Remember what I said to you?"

"You're kidding, right? How much have you dumped on my head these last two months, not counting everything you said through PITA O'Malley?"

Beale raised a single eyebrow.

"Sorry. I meant Lieutenant Colonel O'Malley."

"What impresses me is that you managed to make that nickname stick. Trisha was always a pain in the ass and she used to get fighting mad about being called on it. You've helped her embrace who she is. It will make her a better commander someday."

PITA O'Malley in charge of the Night Stalkers? Sharelle didn't know what to say. She took a line from Emily's playbook and kept her mouth shut for a change.

"It's something I said to you before we entered that first debriefing session."

Sharelle cast her mind back to that first flight where she'd made a total idiot of herself, getting Colonel Beale and the rest of her flight *killed* that night at Fort Campbell.

"You hoped I never found out something or other."

Beale nodded, declining to explain what.

She puzzled at it for a minute. "Nope, you'll have to explain it to me."

The colonel offered a sad smile. "It means you aren't there yet. I'm still hoping for your sake that you don't get there. Come along." She turned and climbed the stairs.

———

SHARELLE ASCENDED THE STAIRS WITH SOME TREPIDATION.

A sign above the door stated it was the Tac Room, not the Tack Room where she'd first kissed Troy immediately below. She considered asking but understood that she already knew the answer—Tac for Tactical. Of all the unlikely things to discover today, Colonel Emily Beale having a sense of humor might well be the strangest. If she had any doubts about the room's purpose, Emily clearing the lock with both keypad *and* retinal ID answered them.

Inside?

One-way glass, which had looked so dark from outside, offered a wide view of the horse stalls in either direction. Part of the action without being part of the action.

Claudia Gibson sat at one of two stations that looked capable of navigating a starship. Tiers of screens curved in front of both stations: a comfortable chair, keyboards and controllers, and enough computing horsepower and comm gear in a side rack to easily explain the EM noise the DAP Hawk's sensors had picked up emanating from the hidden antennas atop the barn.

Most of the screens were blanked with a screen saver. Hidden because she'd entered the room. Even on the few screens left active Sharelle recognized only parts of the information; no way to absorb it all at once. She knew from flying her DAP that it took practice and deep familiarity to comprehend this level of data as anything more than bits and pieces.

Still, US airspace stood out clearly on one screen. Another revealed disposition of the world's navies across the oceans.

"Claudia?" Beale said after closing the door and taking the other seat. That left Sharelle nowhere to be except standing behind their two chairs.

In answer, Claudia pulled up a pair of images on the two active screens. One was unmistakably the long, cross-shaped Ka-52 Alligator. The other, a Kamov Ka-27 Helix, a boxy transport that made the butt-ugly Mil Mi-8 Hip look graceful. Both sported the unusual coaxial double-stacked main rotors that only one or two US birds had ever boasted. Both were parked in a hangar. But what she found fascinating about them was the background aircraft.

"Those are American hangars. Where? Out at Groom Lake?"

Beale nodded. "Yes, you'll fly there tonight under cover of darkness. Two days familiarization. Again, flying only at night to avoid Russian satellite identification of the aircraft."

"And then where? Into Russia, obviously. Or occupied Ukraine?"

Her expression remained flat, her tone in command mode. "If the mission is given clearance, you will be notified at that time. Also, the information so far provided is not authorized outside this room except Colonel Michael Gibson and Captain Ryland. There is one more controller you haven't met."

"What about my crew chiefs?"

Emily shook her head.

"Then it's a no-go, Colonel. Sorry."

"The Ka-52 Alligator is a two-seater. They won't be accompanying you on any mission."

"I don't care. They're the ones who've kept me aloft and in one piece for the last three years. I don't fly a bird they haven't vetted."

The silence that followed wasn't like any stare-down contest Sharelle had ever won—and she never lost. Instead, she could see the wheels spinning in Colonel Beale's brain. Finally, without so much as a sacrificial blink, she turned to the screens and simply said, "Claudia."

Within seconds, all of Wright's and Olsen's details were up on side-by-side screens. Not merely service records and security clearance interview transcripts, but also social media accounts, school records, parents' backgrounds...

For five minutes of stone-dead silence, the two women rolled through information Sharelle didn't know about her own people after three years together. Some of it she deeply wished she still didn't. Neither one had an easy childhood.

Finally, they exchanged glances and Beale nodded. "They're provisionally cleared through the prep phases of the mission. They are not," Beale faced her directly to drive home her point, "I repeat, *not* authorized for any information regarding the operational phase."

"That's easy. You haven't told me shit either, Colonel."

"And for now it's going to stay that way." Would it kill the woman to blink a little more often? "I will leave you to discuss this with Captain Ryland."

Sharelle's stomach clenched. "I'm not sure that's the best idea. We've—"

"You'll find him..." Beale nodded toward Claudia.

Claudia brought up a map of the ranch. A beacon flashed a moment later about a mile from the ranch—it bore a label *Mark sat.* with the period. He carried a satellite phone. A moment later, his track appeared, complete with hourly time markers counting back through the morning. It traced a path with one sharp turn, all the way back to a distant cabin. This system had just accessed, processed, and projected a historical track of satellite data. She looked up at the ceiling, where the antennas she'd detected on arrival must be mounted. How connected were they here?

An overlaid trail map showed that they'd recently joined a trail and would be coming back past the swimming hole where she'd last seen him.

"You're dismissed, Captain." Colonel Beale turned back to the screens and Claudia. "Let's look at those last reports on the equipment for the emplacement team." Sharelle didn't waste a glance at the heavy-duty schematics Claudia projected.

She didn't duck and run away. But she didn't exactly stroll away either.

You running from Beale or headed into battle with Troy?

She didn't waste time answering her own voice.

12

———

"Oh no! Please tell me this isn't happening."

Mark and Michael looked at him, but Troy ignored them. They both turned to look in the same direction he was.

Please let it be an illusion.

Mark blew that hope up with one of his pile-driving shoulder thumps. "You *are* the music man. Time to go face the music, Captain Troy Ryland. Just remember what I taught you."

"Always hang onto the your horse's reins?"

"Ouch! Low blow, son, though that kinda works, too. I actually meant about which part of all this is important."

"All this?"

"Life, pardner. That filly there. That's what's important. C'mon, Michael, gotta see if the young'uns made it back okay."

The two of them turned aside, leaving Troy to stare down at the swimming lake. And there, on the lake side of the gazebo precisely where he'd left her yesterday, sat Captain Sharelle Vargas.

Choices? Ha! Not a one.

He tramped down the last of the trail and stepped into the

gazebo. Tracking around the perimeter, he sat where all of this had started twenty-four hours ago. "Please tell me you haven't been sitting here all this time."

Sharelle shook her head but kept staring down at the water.

"Sorry. I'm sure there were better ways to handle all this, if I only knew how, but I don't."

"We've got a mission."

"What is it? No. Wait. Never mind. We need to talk first."

"About what?" She looked up at him. Absolutely deadpan.

Troy didn't even know where to begin.

That he was leaving?

That he hadn't included her, his pilot and closest friend, in the decision?

That they'd kissed, thoroughly negating three years of careful control and respect?

"Fine, what's the mission?" The biggest cop-out of his entire life.

"Top secret. We aren't cleared to know yet. But we're out of here at sunset to Groom Lake where we'll be training on a Ka-52."

An Alligator, the *Hokum* to NATO but he liked the Russian name better—either way a seriously nasty piece of Russian war machine. The only reason to train on it was if they were doing some mission around Russian airspace. Some sort of a deception flight? "Ukraine?"

She shrugged and turned her attention once more to the water. "Beale said I should tell you. I've told you."

"Thanks. Now can we talk?"

She shook her head, but she didn't appear to be saying *No.* What if her confusion ran as deep as his?

What had Mark said? Focus on what was important.

"I really enjoyed kissing you."

———

OF COURSE THAT WAS THE ONE HE STARTED WITH. ALL THE questions that had scrambled in her brain, that was the one she kept coming back to as well.

But it didn't mean she could look at him.

Yet she'd raced out of the barn. Too fast to be merely escaping from Beale and the strangeness of the Tac Room. She wasn't much of one for fooling herself, but she wished this once she was. Escape might have been the impetus that kicked her into motion, but she'd been driven here to await Troy's return by something far deeper.

As she'd waited for his arrival, the world had narrowed, as if collapsing in on itself.

He wanted, no, he *needed* to return to his family. If there was one thing Sharelle would never question, that was it. She might question her company, the regiment, even the service before she questioned family.

"You're that close to your folks?"

His hesitation was long enough that she almost looked up at him, but not. "Yes."

Just that. A flat yes.

"And the farm. Been a Ryland on that farm for a hundred and thirty years. It's nothing special, but it's ours."

The Vargas home sat on a half acre and had been in the family for most of her life, but not all of it. She and her parents had been in a Clarksville duplex until her younger brother came along six years later. She assumed the place was free and clear by now, but she didn't even know that for sure. "A hundred and thirty?"

"Six generations. Eight if you count that my many-great-grandpa was still alive when his kids and grandkids won adjoining land grants. Farm generations happened fast back then. I was the first long generation, my folks are pushing close to seventy. Only kid. I have to get back before the farm kills them."

She'd been right, there was no arguing with that.

"I wish…"

Sharelle looked at Troy, now he was the one with the thousand-yard stare. "What?"

"It's stupid."

"Tell me anyway."

He turned to look at her. Troy brushed a line of fire along her cheek with his fingertip. "There's never been anything like flying with you, Sharelle Vargas. I'll miss it every day."

This time, when he pushed to his feet, she felt neither anger nor abandonment. All she felt was numb.

———

SUNSET HIT HENDERSON'S RANCH AT 1950 HOURS. IT ACTUALLY hit fifteen minutes earlier because the bowl of the hills that surrounded the main compound cut off the western horizon. Ten minutes later, it shifted off the hilltops and the distant plains as it dropped below the jagged horizon of the Rockies, lighting a few high contrails. Finally even those thin strips of gold faded against the purpling sky.

Troy tried to shrug it off. The place had included plenty of the horrible, but it had also included a lot of good memories he wouldn't forget anytime soon. Yet it felt strangely empty with only Stan and Jodie to help them pull the camouflage net off the DAP Hawk and see them off.

Mac and Ama were standing in for Mark and Emily by putting the girls to bed. Mark and Chelsea's husband, the ranch manager who he'd never met, had flown off somewhere in the ranch's helo shortly after Mark's return, now hours ago. Emily and Michael had boarded the C-12 Huron and left shortly after dinner because the road section they used as a runway didn't have night lights.

"Good luck with the dog trials," Troy made a point of shaking Stan's bionic hand, which earned him a grin.

"Four days and counting," he grinned. "Makes me shrivel up every time. They only send me fully trained DEVGRU and Delta handlers. Hard guys to impress."

"He worries too much," Jodie patted his arm, but her tight shoulder roll gave away her own nerves.

"What I saw from the ground," and it thumped into him so hard that he had to look away and survey the ranch, "you're in good." He gave Jodie a nod and clambered aboard because he'd run out of words.

They were in good. With the ranch and with each other. This was a place for military vets to find purpose and raise families. He'd never fit in. He hadn't finished his service, instead he was bailing out.

Sharelle was doing her standard preflight habit of following Wright and Olsen around the helo as they did their preflight. Whatever she'd said to Stan and Jodie earned her a hug from each. He kept his eyes on the checklist in case it earned him any scathing looks.

Twenty minutes after true sunset they fired the twin GE T700 engines and were aloft as soon as they were up to temperature.

"I'll miss this place."

Sharelle didn't reply.

"Going off line for a minute."

"Roger that."

So, now she wasn't talking to him except for running checklists. Perfect. Just perfect. The faster he returned to the farm, the better off he'd be.

He made sure he was fully switched out of the intercom. Then he patched in his cell phone and called home.

Paw was the one who answered. "Hey, son. Everything okay?" The first question every time.

"Sure. Just wanted to hear your voice before I went into blackout." Past experience had taught him that outbound calls were not looked on favorably from inside the NTTR. And while the Nevada Test and Training Range that occupied five thousand square miles of the state was all a highly secure site, Groom Lake in Area 51 was far, far more paranoid. It was there that the most cutting edge and secret technologies were tested and developed. Getting permission to phone home from there practically took an act of Congress.

And if there really was a mission? They'd most likely be on full comms blackout for the duration. Not a Special Operations family didn't know about that.

"Well, that's a change. They actually gave you a heads-up before locking you down?"

"Wonders never cease. Everything okay there?"

"Sure. Sure. Same as always." Which meant the farm was far from okay but no disasters.

"Wish I could say how long—"

"But they aren't telling you anything and, if they did, you aren't cleared to pass it on."

"You always were a sharp one, Paw. But you'll know I'm okay—"

"As long as the chaplain doesn't show up at the door. We know the drill, son. Don't worry about us. Go off and do what you do."

Troy couldn't resist glancing over at Sharelle. Barely visible as a silhouette against the last fading light of the night sky, she remained focused ahead. "I promise, Paw. Won't be much longer."

"What are you talking about, Troy?"

"Nothing." He hadn't told his family about his plans either. He planned to show up in eighty-nine days as a surprise, then they'd take on the farm's future all together. "Momma around?"

"She's run off to the store. We've got some guest coming in, says he's an expert on farms and ranches. Wants to talk to us some. Name of Doug Daniels."

The name didn't mean anything to him. He almost asked Sharelle, but she wasn't talking to him at the moment and he didn't blame her. "Don't get caught out by some shyster."

"Not born yesterday, son. Your momma's the soft touch, getting them orange juice and who knows what all to serve breakfast tomorrow."

Troy didn't need to hear a thing to know they shared a smile. Momma was as tough as they came, but she was also a woman of the South who took her role as hostess very seriously.

"Asides, says all he wants to do is talk some."

"Dangerous stuff," they said in unison and laughed together at the old family maxim. Freedom, Oklahoma, might be their home and the biggest town in the fifty miles between Alva and Buffalo, but with a population under two hundred it suffered from a severe dose of small-town disease: once the workday was done, not much else to do *but* talk. Two hundred folks meant three hundred different hard-held opinions.

"Love you, Paw. I'll call as soon as I come out the far side."

"Don't worry none, Troy. We're takin' care just fine. You do the same."

"I promise."

And Paw hung up.

Troy was slow to disconnect his cell phone and tuck it away. That was how they ended most of their calls. Paw had never been one to say he loved his son, not that Troy doubted it. No, the strange part was that Troy wasn't much of one for saying the words either.

The pressure was mounting, but even with the last two months of training, it didn't feel like anything new. Night

Stalkers missions were inherently dangerous and the whole family had adapted to that being a part of their lives. But what had prompted him to tell Paw that he loved him?

Something else was changing, though he'd be trussed up like a rodeo calf if he knew what.

13

"I don't know if I hate it or love it." Troy's voice echoed strangely in the vast hangar.

"I've faced them enough times that I'll go with hate." Colonel Beale had crossed over from another hangar when they'd arrived.

Sharelle leaned toward the love side.

Reaching Groom Lake at midnight, they'd been shuffled straight into one of the hangars and there it was: sixteen meters of Russian-green gunship. Two meters shorter than the DAP Hawk didn't take anything away from it. She figured that fifty percent of Russian military design was about making their weapons war-ugly.

No graceful curves of the Hawk; it looked sharper, more angular, more like the Ka-50 Kamov Black Shark, its predecessor. The Ka-52 Alligator sitting on the clean concrete floor before them looked like what it was—lethal. Instead of four hard points on stub wings for mounting guns and missiles, it boasted six, plus a heavy dual-barrel machine gun mounted along one side of the nose.

Unlike the DAP, there were no crew chiefs. No one with a

side-mounted Minigun to be directed at attackers or ground targets. An Alligator was all about killing whatever lay ahead of it, with lots and lots of missiles and massive 23 mm rounds.

The only thing that broke its long lines was the compound rotor that made it look a little like a potted palm. Two frail-looking three-blade rotors were stacked like two dinner plates where her DAP's single rotor of four massive blades stuck out meters longer to either side. But the stacked compound rotor offered high maneuverability, especially in tight spaces. Also, there was no tail rotor to shoot off, which not only would be catastrophic on her DAP, but it was also the source of much of the aircraft's noise, far more than the main rotor.

Troy stood staring up at the central hubs of the rotors with his arms crossed.

"What?" She looked up but didn't see what had riveted his attention.

"Notice the extra wire?"

She did now that he pointed it out. It ran from the central hub about a half-meter along the blade where it terminated in a thickened area.

"Explosives. To blow off the blades."

That's when she remembered. This was one of the few helos with ejection seats. The first trigger blew off the six rotor blades, the second shattered the canopy above the side-by-side pilots' seats, and the third fired a rocket to extract the pilots.

"Better than mincemeat."

Which, she admitted, was what would happen in almost any other helicopter—no way to eject past a spinning rotor. Jumping out of a flailing rotorcraft was not a solution either. Almost always, riding down the helicopter would be the safest tactic anyway; proper auto-rotation landings had high survivability potential. The key word being *almost*. She'd lost friends whose helicopters were so damaged that they offered no such forgiveness. A part of the career of being a military helo pilot, not an easy part but a part.

Over the next two hours, Groom Lake specialists led them step-by-step through the systems and observed performance characteristics. They did *not* say how they'd acquired the bird: stolen from the Russians, purchased from Egypt, or captured in Ukraine...and she didn't ask.

Slowly, the impenetrable silence that had grown between her and Troy—making for the painfully silent four-hour flight down from Henderson's—wore away under the friction of mission prep. A long way from easy, but they managed to shift most of the way back to teammates over the last few hours.

Beale hovered close beside them through the whole thing.

Sharelle had been on the edge of asking if she didn't have something to go command when she recognized the look on Beale's face: longing. It was the pilot, not the commander, who stood beside them—a woman Sharelle hadn't seen since that first flight together. She too felt that need to know; the eagerness for every nuance of controlling a drastically different aircraft.

"You sure you don't want to be the one flying this mission?" She recalled the way Beale had flexed her fingers after flying, as if they hurt. As if she missed flying so much that it was both physically and emotionally painful. "Sorry, I shouldn't have asked."

"It's okay. I'm finding being a colonel far more challenging than being a major and, before you ask, no, I'm not sure I appreciate that change. Besides, I'd still be suffering from too big a skills gap."

"Some days I find being a captain challenging enough." And Sharelle glanced at Troy, currently sitting in the cockpit with one of the trainers going over the EO system, the Russian electro-optical sensors operated quite differently from the American ones.

"Give it a little time, Captain." Beale actually smiled at her. "I personally found some...difficulties in accepting Mark's interest in more than flying together."

"How did you make it work?" Sharelle didn't know where the question came from. It left her both embarrassed and desperately wanting to know.

Wright and Olsen practically shoved them aside as a technician opened another section of hull to expose the aircraft's inner workings. They too were on a steep learning curve.

Beale retreated by several steps, somehow indicating that Sharelle should follow. Even aware of her subtlety, Sharelle missed how the Colonel did it.

They both turned and faced the aircraft. There was a hustle of activity that had gained a focus. At first, it had simply been wonder and an awkwardness with the unfamiliar airframe. But she saw each of her team settling into the familiarity until it looked more like the smooth flow they all exhibited with the DAP Hawk. She'd never noticed the difference until the smooth flow wasn't there.

"It's not easy," Beale said after they'd watched the team for several minutes. Apparently this too was a lesson.

Sharelle had to think for a moment to recall that she and Beale had been discussing something very different than a Ka-52 Alligator.

"I've seen many couples grow from flying together. It is almost inevitable given the level of life-dependent cooperation required to fly. At least inevitable with the right person. I flew with my copilot for most of a decade, but he married one of my gunners."

"But that's officer to enlisted. How fast was she thrown out? The woman took the heat, of course?"

"Neither. It built—and broke and built again—over many months, but it was over the course of a single mission that they truly came together. He was injured-out while completing a mission no one will ever know about."

What if...Troy injured? It conjured up a horrific image that she definitely didn't want to face.

Wright and Olsen shifted from internals to weapon mounts, walking through every step of attaching and arming the missiles. And verifying that all of it matched what the instructors were saying.

"But...how?"

Beale's smile was back to one of those enigmatic expressions she so preferred. "My advice? Focus on *if* not *how*. How may seem awful, but it's the easier of the two. For now? Focus on this mission and let everything else take its course."

Then *Colonel* Beale, abruptly in her shroud of command once more, turned on her heel and strode out of the hangar.

———

THEY MANAGED A TWO-HOUR PREDAWN FAMILIARIZATION FLIGHT on the first night. On the second night, they managed two three-hour sorties, finishing strong on the NTTR gunnery range by killing targets, battering old tanks, and facing attacks by other helos.

At the dawn post-op briefing, the trainers had broken down all three sorties, offering detailed notes. Troy felt wrung out, but few of the trainers' comments were above the level of nuance. He and Sharelle had acquitted themselves well.

They'd hardly seen Wright and Olsen as they'd shifted to daytime operations, working over every inch of the helo when he and Sharelle didn't have it aloft. But it was never out of the hangar in daylight where a passing satellite might spot it.

The most useful part of the training, other than the flying, were their two shared meals at the beginning and end of each other's day. The chiefs offered massive info dumps of key systematic differences of the Alligator versus the DAP Hawk that played out well during the nights' flights.

Trisha was there with Billy the not-SEAL-now-Delta and Michael Gibson. There was also a flight crew she hadn't met before, who instantly set out to prove that they were a two-man comedy team: a broad-shouldered black man and a much taller slender white dude.

"Rafe and Julian at your service." the taller one spoke up without identifying which he was.

"Which is which?" Troy took the bait.

"Doesn't matter, we answer to either one," the shorter one confirmed.

His buddy didn't miss a beat. "Please do *not* be calling us C-3PO and R2-D2 like our last commander." Practically begging to be called that.

"Or you can just call us Awesome because we—"

"Trisha," was all Beale said.

Trisha's hard smack on the back of the nearer one's head earned her a laugh instead of a scowl.

"Better him than me," the farther one said but shut up after that.

"Where are Wright and Olsen?" Sharelle asked.

"As I agreed, preparation only. They were never cleared for the operational side of this mission."

Troy studied Sharelle's scowl, but she didn't argue. Neither did she look happy. For two nights and the day between, they'd discussed nothing but the Russian helicopter. Meals were held over ops manuals. Any time not aloft or asleep was spent in tactical and performance briefings. Of the last thirty hours, twenty-two of them had been deep immersion in the helicopter and he hadn't thought of anything else.

Now, he felt like a prairie dog popping its head up and looking around for the first time.

Two helo crews, a pair of Delta operators, and the top two

commanders of the entire regiment all parked in a secure conference room at Groom Lake. Something heavy was definitely going down.

Michael's and Bill's grim looks confirmed that assessment.

"Flashbacks," Emily said to Trisha, who nodded.

"I know. Seriously weird. Do it up, girl."

Troy might have thought they, too, were joking around if Bill hadn't looked slightly ill, his shoulders ever so slightly hunched. *Uh-oh, incoming round.*

The comedy team froze and showed no sign they'd ever laugh again. Or had ever laughed before.

Emily turned to them. "I can't believe I'm giving this lecture again, but here it is from the top. Any of you four know what a black-in-black operation is?"

The comedy boys nodded very carefully.

Sharelle shook her head.

Troy's face must have given him away as he didn't recall moving.

Emily sighed before turning to face him and Sharelle. "White ops are published to the press. Black ops stay inside the chain of command, at least they're supposed to. Black-in-black *always* do. And I mean that in the strictest sense. You will never discuss this mission with anyone not directly involved." She turned fully to Sharelle. "That includes not talking about it with your crew chiefs—ever. They're now outside the envelope."

No one spoke.

"This mission is by direct order of the President, the Secretary of Defense, and the Chairman of the Joint Chiefs of Staff. The *next* President asks you about this, you lie to his face. If you're called before Congress, you lie to theirs. This is not an intelligence mission, this is a military-action mission so the Gang of Eight have not been informed."

The Gang of Eight were the top party leaders and ranking

intelligence committee chairs of the two houses of the US Congress.

Colonel Beale looked at them in turn. "Not drunk. Not on your death bed. Not in a tell-all book."

"Don't worry about C-3PO," the shorter pilot hooked a thumb at his companion. "He can't read or write anyway. I mean. *See Dick. See Dick watch Jane's butt. See Jane slap him silly.* How lame-o is that?"

Beale's glare shut him down without Trisha's intervention this time.

"Your helicopters—"

"Helicopters plural?" Sharelle whispered to him. Troy had no idea.

"—are currently being loaded into a C-17 Globemaster III. In seven hours you will be landing on Attu Island near the far end of the Aleutian Island Chain. The island is uninhabited and is our farthest west airfield in the North Pacific. At Attu you will offload and fly a thousand-kilometer night transit to meet your ship for refueling and a thirty-hour transit aboard to the west coast of Sapporo, Japan. There your ship will have a mechanical failure and anchor offshore."

"Eastern Russia or..." Troy's breath caught in his throat. Or fly a Russian helicopter into North Korea? Or South Korea...in Russian aircraft?

"Are we starting a war?" Sharelle had the same thought he did.

He didn't like the sound of that at all.

"No," Colonel Beale shook her head. "We're fighting one that's already ongoing. Except it can't be known—ever—that the US has intervened."

14

———

As Sharelle walked up the big rear ramp of the C-17 Globemaster III, she saw that they weren't the only ones to board the military's second-largest cargo jet. Beyond their Alligator, nearest to the rear ramp, a pair of Russian Ka-27 Helix cargo helicopters were chained in.

Sharelle had forgotten that she'd see them on the screen in the Tac Room at Henderson's Ranch.

Trisha, apparently along for the trip, patted one on its blunt nose. The Droid Boys, as Troy had dubbed them, made a beeline to check over the tie-downs on the other. All three helos had their rotor blades and the mast that held the hubs removed so that they fit aboard. The C-17s always felt cavernous —their cargo bays were most of ninety feet long, eighteen wide, a dozen tall—until they were packed solid with large helicopters.

The few people aboard in addition to the Globemaster's four crew were almost an afterthought.

Close by the forward helicopter, Bill joined a six-person team from The Unit. None of the operators she'd seen in Alaska; this was a crazy mix of three men and three women.

Sharelle hadn't know that *any* women had made it into Delta Force. As usual with Unit operators, they didn't say a word as they worked. They were checking through three large carrying cases, in addition to the massive packs that rested by each one.

Clearly three different teams had been training here: she and Troy on the Alligator, Trisha and the Droid Boys on the Kamov Helix helos, and the Delta team working with Michael.

There were two service techs she recognized from the Ka-52 training. Beale was damned lucky she'd stayed behind with Michael and wasn't here for Sharelle to browbeat for not letting her own crew chiefs serve in their place. She'd put them up against any tech in the service.

Out of options, she dropped into the last of the notoriously uncomfortable fold-down seats next to Troy. With the others forward and their big helo in the way, they might as well have been alone on the plane.

Troy sat with his head back against the hull and his eyes closed.

Her brain and body felt pummeled.

"Sleep, we need sleep."

"Uh-huh," was Troy's helpful reply.

"Sex, we need sex."

"Uh-huh."

She waited a beat.

"Wait. What?" He bolted upright and twisted to look at her.

Now that she had his undivided attention, she wasn't sure what to do with it. "Not the worst idea I've ever had."

"So, what? We have sex and that cures three years of need that I've built up for you?"

Nobody ever *needed* her. Nor she them. Especially not three years' worth. Now it was her turn to close her eyes and thump the back of her own head against the inside of the hull. "How did this get so complicated?"

"Other than my leaving the Army to save the family farm?"

"Other than that."

Troy was silent long enough that she opened her eyes. Besides, the banging wasn't doing anything but making her head hurt. Knocking in some sense seemed too unlikely to be possible.

"Troy?"

"Well, it would help me a lot if you weren't you." The smile that tugged at the corner of his mouth had her returning it against her better judgment.

"You don't really know me." Which was wrong. No one knew her better, not even Daddy. "Okay, scratch that. Maybe our body chemistry is all wrong."

His smile grew.

Precluding all conversation, the big loading ramp began grinding its way shut, folding in upon itself, then meeting the massive section that had swung down from the ceiling to meet it. A final loud whirr of actuators pinned the two big sections together, making an airtight seal on the inside and forming the underside of the plane's tail to the outside.

If she'd only had that lesson a few beats sooner, she might have kept her mouth sealed shut.

"Okay, that was an amazing kiss," Sharelle admitted once she again had a chance of being heard.

"And amazingly brief."

"That you made no attempt to follow up on. That's not a reaction I usually cause in men." It had happened to her a grand total of once and he sat next to her. *She* was the one who ended relationships, not the men.

The engines kicked to life with a high whine that rapidly descended into a deep-throated roar. The four engines, each not much smaller than her DAP Hawk, hung mere feet beyond the uninsulated metal wall they were leaning against. The sudden pain had them both digging for earplugs and jamming them in.

Which turned this...romantic...conversation into a yelling match.

"Sleep." She as much read Troy's lips as heard him.

Between night flights, day training, and not much sleeping since Alaska, she knew he was right. The most common way troops traveled on a C-17 was rolling out air mattresses. Neither of them had one in their packs, but there were spares jammed into gaps between the seats and the hull.

By the time they were up at altitude, they'd inflated a pair of pads, zipped up their jackets against the chill in the plane, and lain down.

It caught up with Sharelle like a hammer blow. One minute wide awake and the next dead to the world.

———

THE CHANGE IN THE TONE OF THE CARGO JET'S ENGINES WOULD wake any pilot.

Sharelle listened but heard no other changes, simply the easing of the throttles to initiate a descent from altitude. No combat descent necessary, which meant they were thirty minutes to landing. So she'd slept most of six hours, a luxury after the last few days.

On the verge of stretching her muscles gone soft with sleep, she froze in place. Not because she was cold, which was typical of the big transports, but because she wasn't.

A warm heavy arm draped around her waist.

She lay spooned with her back against...

Not merely spooned. Someone's—Troy's obviously—face was tucked intimately against the back of her neck. They'd served together long enough for her to know that he woke far more slowly than she did.

Roused by the same cue that she'd been, his first sleepy reaction was to tug her more tightly against him.

Her first reaction—wide awake—was to let him. Not her anticipated response. A sharp elbow to the ribs seemed more appropriate to the situation, but it wasn't happening.

Man's leaving the regiment, girlfriend.

Uh-huh, the part of her that didn't care acknowledged as she pressed back against him.

He's your copilot. Under your command.

Yup.

He's leaving you.

Shh. The inner admonishment couldn't be bothered with such trivialities.

"I've always dreamt of waking up this way with you." Troy's voice was soft beside her ear as she noted that somewhere in their sleep his arm had become her pillow. So close to her earplugs that she could hear it anyway.

She slid her arm over his other arm and interlaced their fingers over her belly. The heavy drone of the four jet engines formed a sonic shield as if it was only the two of them in this world.

"This sucks, Troy."

"Can't we forget about that for the moment?"

Sharelle considered. Her body didn't; it rolled over inside the curve of his arms and hooked a leg over his hips. The Sharelle part of her did glance around; no one in their end of the cargo bay. Her body then closed her eyes and let herself sink into Troy's kiss.

They'd left the brief, frantic heat on the floor of the Tack Room. Now, he slowly wrapped around her like a climbing vine with no kudzu nastiness. The arm her head lay on curled around her shoulders, his hand reaching all the way around to slide between her arm and ribcage. His other hand slid over her hip and into her back pocket before dragging her against him—as if lying tight against him she'd been so far away.

When he shifted his attentions from her lips to her neck, she tipped her head back and let him.

Now! Her inner voice had a definite opinion on what happened next and she had no intention of arguing.

Her eyes flickered open for a half second, then closed again.

In that instant, they captured an image of PITA Trisha O'Malley standing over her—grinning.

Another blink revealed a thumbs up.

"Go away!" she mouthed.

"What?" Trisha mouthed back despite her wide smile showing that she understood exactly what Sharelle had told her.

She managed to free the hand she'd dug into Troy's hair enough to give Trisha the finger.

Trisha slapped a hand to her chest as if mortally shocked.

Troy, sensing some disconnect, stopped the several wonderful things he'd been doing simultaneously. He too glanced up, then groaned in pain rather than pleasure as he buried his face against her shoulder. "Not one break."

She managed a nod in agreement.

They slowly disentangled themselves.

"That looked like fun." Trisha dropped to sit cross-legged at the foot of Sharelle's air mattress as soon as they'd managed to sit up.

"It was. Now go away and we'll get back to it."

"No can do for two reasons." And she uncharacteristically shut up.

"And you're going to make us ask." Sharelle considered the advantages and disadvantages of choking a superior officer and decided against it. Close, though.

"I have to. I don't want to risk my Pain-in-the-ass status. Very difficult to get that back once it's gone."

"So, if we don't ask, are you just going to sit there like a leprechaun perched atop her pot of gold all day?"

"I would, but we don't have that long."

"What's the other reason?" Troy spoiled the game by asking.

Trisha only needed a pointy green Irish cap to go with her mischievous grin. "We should probably do a little flight planning before we land as there won't be a spare minute once we're down. There's an early storm kicking up noise in the North Pacific. Worse than predicted when we launched out of Nevada."

Before Sharelle thought of a good comeback, Troy spoke up. "Is that the same North Pacific that we have to fly across to reach our boat?"

"It sure is. You're right. He is the smart one. Cute too. You should keep him."

I'm trying! her inner voice moaned.

You'd last ten days as a farmer's wife, even coming up the outside —and you know it. That silenced her inner self.

Sharelle looked around. The flight had been smooth so far.

Actually, no it wasn't. In Troy's arms, she simply hadn't noticed anything else. The jiggering about of the massive plane explained why Trisha had sat down as quickly as they'd cleared a spot.

An extra hard jar had all three of them scrambling to fold-down seats and belting in. No big drops, but what had started as a slap rapidly grew into a series of rattles and metallic groans as the hundred and seventy-foot wingspan flexed and fought the shifting load strains.

"Good thing the storm isn't here," Trisha sounded no less merry at the implied news.

"How bad?" Sharelle had flown far more Atlantic-side missions and didn't know how the storms played out in the vast Pacific.

"We'll be punching through a goodly passel of headwinds and tailwinds. They should roughly balance out."

Headwinds cost them fuel to cover a distance. Tailwinds

saved them fuel by pushing them along. With their ship a thousand miles out over open ocean, they were close enough to the range limits of the Russian helos to be very cautious.

"Of course," Trisha continued blithely, "they're happening in the opposite order."

Tailwinds first, then headwinds.

"Well, that sucks," a foul curse for Troy.

Sharelle pictured it as her teeth clacked together in another jarring air pocket.

Headwinds then tailwinds meant that if the headwinds proved too stiff, they could literally turn tail and be easily swept back to their airport of origin without risking fuel limits.

However, hitting tailwinds first meant they'd be swept more quickly away from their launch airport. And if the headwinds on the far side of the storm increased, they could fly into trouble fast with no bailout—the North Pacific was woefully low on safe landing places. Especially in *acquired* Russian military helicopters that no one could ever know about.

Trisha booted a tablet that she'd had tucked under an arm and brought up the weather map.

Troy leaned hard into Sharelle to look across at the map, reminding her of all the pleasant warmth of a moment ago. And then she focused on the map herself.

"Uh, Troy?" Warmth shifted straight to chill.

"Yes, Sharelle?"

"You might want to work on upgrading your curse vocabulary." They weren't even to the heart of the mission yet and a world of ugly lay ahead of them.

"Um, yeah. I'll work on that."

———

Attu Island lay twenty-four hundred kilometers west of Anchorage. The most remote US Coast Guard Station in the

Aleutians had closed in 2010 and looked it. The only reason the windows were still intact was probably because the utter treelessness of the terrain didn't give the horrific storms here any debris to toss.

It was a land abandoned except for the occasional service crew and the annual pilgrimage of crazy birds watchers. Mid-September was too late for them, winter had already arrived, driving most of the birds south.

No hangars here. Just a crossed pair of runways upon one of the few flat stretches on the mountainous island.

Troy tried to beat some life into his hands, the thick gloves weren't enough. With a predicted mean temperature for September in the forties, they were punching for a record low in the mid-twenties Fahrenheit. And the sea damp air, turned bitter wind and ripping south from the Arctic, felt far worse that the fifteen degrees of additional wind chill it dropped on their heads.

Shifting the helos from the C-17's cargo hold onto the open runway had been easily achieved with the small wheel tractors that the Air Force had thoughtfully brought along. But reattaching the heavy masts and then the two tiers of rotor blades had become an all-persons' challenge. Ladders were blown over, the metal chilled fingers toward frostbite faster than they could work, and the wind clearly thought rotor blades were toys to flap about like wheat chaff.

He, Billy, and a massive Delta Force guy named Chad became the anchor men, bracing ladders and handing off tools to those better suited to scrambling about. So the three of them didn't get to move about much.

Icy needles that might have been snowflakes at a lesser speed began spiking through the air.

"Shit, send me back to South America anytime you're ready, man. At least there it's the people trying to kill me, not the weather." Chad looked more Iowa farm boy than Latino.

"How did you ever pass undercover there?"

Chad grinned as he fought the latest gust. "I got skills, man. What's impressive is so does Tanya." And the look he aimed up the ladder at the tall blonde woman holding the outer end of a rotor blade answered a lot of questions and raised even more.

"Married?"

"Oh yeah, brother." Chad looked back down at him with a definite cat-ate-a-whole-pet-store-display-of-canaries smile.

"But *serving* together?"

"Only way we'd get to see each other." Then he frowned. "Got its troubles though."

"Like what?" Troy didn't want to admit why he was asking, but seeing Sharelle constantly at the heart of the reassembly process, managing every step like a hawk, made it hard to think of anything else.

"Well," Chad helped raise the outer end of the next rotor blade aloft to Tanya while still keeping a foot on the base of her stepladder.

The team atop the helo spun the rotor through a third of a turn and began attaching the other end of the new blade she held up. He, Chad, and the ever-silent Billy settled once more into serving their roles as frozen ladder sandbags.

"My best buddy fell in love with this intel officer. Turned out to be a serious wine heiress, too, though we didn't find that out till later. We all had a couple good years together until things went seriously sideways."

"Sideways?"

"Kids! They went and had kids," Chad sounded completely disgusted. "Chose raising grapes and kids over The Unit. Over sticking tight. Don't that beat all?"

Sharelle strode across his vision from one helo to the next. She walked like it was a summer's day, quick and purposeful, not wasting time keeping her face protected from the stinging wind.

He hadn't quite gone there in his thinking. No chance of Sharelle fitting in on the farm. But Sharelle with a kid was definitely a vision of a different kind.

Chad followed his gaze and started laughing. "Oh, bro. You got to stop thinking like that."

"Thinking like what?" Troy did his best to evade.

"You see our three women?"

"Yeah?" Unsure what he was supposed to be seeing. The three female Delta Force operators were pure business.

"Sofia was always a sweetheart of a gal despite being secretly wealthy as snot. Damned brilliant, but never quite had the attitude of a seasoned operator. But your gal, she'd fit The Unit just fine if she wasn't a Night Stalker."

Troy nodded in agreement as he watched her headed back the other way. She was one of the top helo pilots alive. *This* flowed in her blood. It was his problem that it flowed in his as well.

———

THE HEAT THAT BATHED THE CABIN ONCE THE ENGINES WERE UP to temperature was such a relief that it hurt. It sent prickles almost as painful as the blowing snow rippling across her frozen face.

"You sure about this?" Sharelle had seen the math, but she'd also seen what it meant on a map.

"Yep." Troy never was one for wasting words.

She checked the intercom to make sure they were private, then remembered for the hundredth time that the crew chiefs weren't aboard. The Ka-52 Alligator was strictly a two-person helo. The cargo area was small enough that it barely fit their personal go-bags. All other space belonged to the weapons and ammunition.

"Honestly. The math definitely works better this way."

For all Sharelle's wishing she hadn't, Trisha had made her the flight lead. *You're the lead pilot in the lead gunship. I'm an over-ranked commander in a transport bird carting around a flock of Delta operators and their gear. You have command.*

Troy had somehow cooked up the idea, while they'd all been freezing their asses off to reassemble the birds. Massive chunks of navigational math done in his head, only checked later on the NavComps.

Rather than heading southwest, following the shortest route to the ship and risking unpredictable headwinds, Troy wanted to head southeast, ninety degrees away from their waiting ship—and directly away from any hint of land.

"We'll ride the tailwinds clean around the heart of the storm. In the same six-hour flight time, the present winds should add three hundred miles to our range. It's a lower-risk flight with a similar fuel profile than facing the headwinds in the second half of the flight. Especially as they're predicted to continue ramping up."

"And if the tailwinds die off?"

"We arc closer to the heart of the storm, cutting off a corner of the distance."

"And if it fully dissipates?"

Troy offered her a shrug and no accompanying wry smile.

"Oh God!" Sharelle looked skyward, nothing to see but more scudding gray. The pair of Ka-27 Helixes squatted in the building storm. The C-17 Air Force cargo plane parked fifty meters farther away blurred in and out of the building blizzard. "So our last option is floating around in the middle of a Pacific storm in a Russian inflatable life raft?"

"Yep."

"Stop being so damned agreeable, Troy." There, it hadn't hurt to say his name.

Much, her inner voice's dry tone didn't help in the slightest.

Instead, she keyed the mike to connect to the other helos.

"We're following Flight Plan Ryland. If we all die, feel free to blame him, but please keep my name out of it."

"Do it up," Trisha answered.

One of the Droid Boys answered, Rafe the shorter one with skin darker than hers but the higher voice of the two. They'd been name switching just to mess with her but she'd finally caught on that R for Rafe equaled R for R2-D2, the shorter droid. "Let's take the easy path and kill him off right now. Just, you know, push him out the door here on Attu and let him freeze to death. Then you could fall in love with one of us; we're both seriously hot guys. Though I'm, you know, better in every way."

"Not a chance. But thanks for the image I'll never be able to scrub from my brain. Plan Ryland, execute. Air Force, thanks for the ride." She eased the collective up and the two Helixes followed her aloft.

Fall in love? Her inner voice asked.

Not on the agenda. Shut up and go back to sleep. Oddly, the voice did.

"Fly safe, Army. Air Force out," the C-17 crew called. A glance back showed they were already accelerating along the runway. Once aloft and turned for home, her team would be on their own.

At double their maximum range, Hawaii, Chuuk, and Guam lay in a distant arc to the south. If not for the storm, Hokkaido, Japan, might be only a few hundred miles past their maximum range. In reality, they reached their ship or they hit the water and, if they survived that, they then prayed a cargo ship lay close by. With the Pacific water temperatures, very close indeed.

On the direct route, the one they weren't taking, they'd at least have a chance of aborting to the Kamchatka Peninsula. If only they weren't trying to hide from the Russians.

She turned southeast and the others followed her.

Below, the midday ocean looked angry and blue-black. Above, the clouds tried to convince her the day had already ended, and an evil twilight of the storm's core hung somewhere off to their right.

"Talk to me, Troy."

"About what?"

"About anything other than the weather or this flight." On reaching five thousand feet, she leveled out, checked the other two birds were off to either side and a little behind, and set the autopilot. However, her attempts to relax didn't grab hold.

A glance showed Troy looking around. Not as if checking their course and flight status, though she was sure he did that as well, more as if trying desperately to find a safe topic.

"Tell me about your farm."

He latched onto that topic and told her about its history. How his ancestors had grown it together, only to have the exodus of successive younger generations to the urban centers rob them of their future hopes. He led her all the way to the pressures of rising worker and seed costs, falling produce prices due to agribusiness, the costs of trying to revive soils played out by a hundred and thirty years of farming, and aging parents.

"Why are you going back?"

Before he opened his mouth—

"No. I've heard all of your reasons. But why—I don't even know what I mean by this—*you?*"

"I've answered that enough times that I'll just repeat myself."

"No, not *you* Troy Ryland, heir to an Oklahoma farm." This wasn't her kind of discussion. Give her hard facts, tactics, performance envelopes, and rules of engagement any day. "But *you.* You know, the guy who's flown next to me for three years without mentioning once that you were lusting after my body."

"It's more than that," his voice, already deep to begin with, dropped about an octave.

With the instinctive part of her brain, she focused on eking every additional kilometer out of their flight profile that she could find. They'd had enough practice in Nevada to make her safe flying the helo, but now she strove for the next level of integration with the machine. "You know, the Alligator fits me better than the DAP in some ways."

Troy squinted over at her.

"She—"

"He. It's Russian, they call it a *he*."

"*He* lacks any hint of nuance. We both walk the blunt side of the track: me by choice, the Alligator by design."

"And why did you choose that? Not complaining, it's but one of the many things I like about you."

"What are some of the others?"

"I'll make you a list. Why have you chosen to live an unnuanced life?"

"Asking me to be a deep thinker really goes against the grain." Sharelle fought through an air pocket that dropped them fifty meters—the Russians had finally abandoned the world standard of setting flight levels in feet and gone completely metric. Most aspects of the US military had switched over as well, so the thinking wasn't hard, but neither was it instinctual.

She waited for the lift out the other side of the air pocket, but there wasn't one. Finally, she expended the fuel to return them to five thousand feet. She'd rather be at ten, but that would be fifteen degrees colder. Down here the storm raged with more water than ice. At ten thousand the opposite would be true and the helo wouldn't like that. At the worst, it would drop them into the sea. At the least, more layers of ice meant less efficient flight surfaces, meant running out of fuel and dropping into the sea anyway.

"Try." Troy's tone of pleading left her little choice in attempting to explain herself.

"Before my baby bother joined the family, we lived much closer to the fort proper. I used to lie in bed as a kid and listen to the helos rising out of Fort Campbell. Probably listening to bloody Beale and Henderson doing their training qualification flights now that I think about it."

Sharelle considered. No, the timing was wrong, but not by much. Beale, at least, would have still been in the 101st Airborne Screaming Eagles...who also flew out of Fort Campbell. She'd been listening to Beale fly since she'd been a little girl. Which was too weird for words.

"I insisted that my curtains be left open so that I could watch them. Always so full of purpose and intent. When I watch a big jet claw aloft, all I see is the improbability of throwing so much metal into the sky. With a helo, I just know that its going somewhere definite—it always knew what it was about. I liked that. Wanted to be like that."

"Turn south to one-eight-zero. We've made enough easting, I think. Now it's a matter of riding as close to the center of the storm as we can without icing up."

"Wonderful. Flying into high-icing conditions in a Russian helicopter."

"At least they designed for it."

Sharelle supposed so, but her instincts didn't like it. "Hey, wait a minute. You dodged my question."

"Rats! I hoped you wouldn't notice. The one about me and the farm, or the many ways you mesmerize me?"

Sharelle laughed. "Your attempts to tantalize my interest with the second isn't going to get you out of the first."

"I can try. I'd start with—"

"My body."

"—the way you fly. It's damned magic, Captain Vargas."

He actually swore, but Sharelle's breath stuck too hard in her throat to point that out. She knew her body wowed some, her looks others, and, creepily, her dark skin a few more.

Weren't they past that one *yet*? But one of the most highly qualified people to judge, a Night Stalkers pilot, claimed it was her flying that captivated him.

"I see all the other aspects of you as a very pleasant bonus, because you are a knockout. But what you can make a helo do is, well, making me repeat myself—very attractive."

She hoped her helmet hid the heat rushing to her cheeks. "You're still avoiding the core question." And she knew that no matter what the helmet hid, the roughness in her voice gave her away.

"Bearing one-seven-zero. We're a little close to the storm."

"One-seven-zero." She confirmed. The other helos, being Night Stalkers, simply held formation with her, not breaking radio silence. Even in a simple ferry run like this, no Night Stalker wanted to be tracked by their transmissions.

Then, like her radios, she kept her silence.

TROY WISHED THAT THE STORM WAS BEING MORE DEMANDING BUT his original plan remained right on track, perhaps even a little better than.

So, why *did* he want to get back to the farm so badly?

Sharelle had reached back to when she was a kid. Did the answer lie there? What had he been like?

"How am I supposed to remember what I was thinking that far back?"

"I do," Sharelle teased him.

"All I remember is chores. We're a produce farm, but we have a small herd of milk cows, some chickens and pigs, and my horse. I fed them all before I fed myself. Too slow and I'd end up with a PB&J on the bus and get teased for being so slow in the head that I had to eat my breakfast on the way to school. No sports after school—and sports were *big* in our school. Back to help with animals. When I was little, working the kitchen garden. Older? Working the fields. My only escape was my horse."

"And you find it weird that you ended up in helicopters?"

Troy had always known he was headed for the farm. Helos were merely some strange aberration of his agriculture degree.

"Troy! Can you be so dense?"

"Apparently." Not exactly the kind of review he wanted from either his pilot or this woman beside him.

Sharelle actually twisted to face him, trusting to the Russian autopilot for the moment—which they'd both learned was a dicey proposition for more than a minute or two in such harsh conditions. It behaved only with constant attention. "Seriously?"

What else was he supposed to say? "Seriously."

Instead of some harsh rebuke or laugh, Sharelle reached across and brushed her fingers along his exposed cheek. "My dear sweet man. You really *are* trying to break my heart."

"No, I'm not."

"The only part of your past you ever talk about is your horse, Shane. I bet I'd know him out of an entire herd from your descriptions. He was your *escape* from farm life. And this?" Sharelle tapped the center of the Ka-52's console. "This is a little boy's rodeo horse grown man-sized."

Troy had no way to answer that.

None at all.

15

THE PASSAGE AROUND THE CORE OF THE STORM PASSED WITHOUT incident, or much else to say between them. They traded off pilot-in-command a few times, and they both wished for the more comfortable American seats. Long haul in a Russian helicopter seat was a cruel abuse of the body.

Troy hadn't returned to anything personal, not *anything,* and Sharelle didn't want to break that either.

Six hours after leaving Attu Island, they raised their ship, the USS *Peleliu,* near sunset. The LHA, Landing Helicopter Assault ship, had a deck over two football fields long and two-thirds of one wide—essentially a small aircraft carrier without any catapults for jets. The LHAs specialized in helicopters and Harrier jump jets on top, and landing craft carrying troops and heavy armor in a large sea-level well deck coming in from the stern.

There weren't any other birds on deck except for a lone search-and-rescue Seahawk, the Navy's version of the Black Hawk. They probably waited to see if anyone on their flight fell into the sea and might need rescuing—if they survived.

Normally, any class of assault landing ship at sea was as notoriously crowded as an aircraft carrier. Not this one.

"No sign of a reinforced battalion of Marines." LHAs typically hosted seventeen hundred jarheads in addition to the thousand crew and officers. Except for a couple of deck crew and the personnel behind the glass high in the command tower, Sharelle didn't see anyone aboard.

"That's because she was decommissioned in 2015," Troy looked up from his tablet and peered out at the ship to confirm his information.

"No way. It's right there in front of us. Big as life."

Even though it was big, the landing presented the greatest challenge of the whole flight. Arriving with only fifteen percent reserves still in her fuel tanks had been nerve wracking; doubly so for their two accompanying Ka-27 Helix birds down to ten percent. These birds weren't Night Stalker Hawks or Chinooks with refueling probes; when they ran out of fuel, they fell from the sky.

The *Peleliu* possessed plenty of deck space for all three aircraft to come down, but there weren't enough deck personnel. That wouldn't be an issue, except for the storm.

The rough seas made the deck rise and fall a good ten feet *while* it swung side-to-side with the occasional unexpected twist thrown in. *Not* the conditions for landing clean without deck guidance. Added to that, storm-riddled twilight made for the poorest seeing conditions.

The crews brought each successive helo to a stable hover ten meters above the deck.

Then the dance began, with Trisha going first.

Counting the waves and watching the deck action, they signaled her to hold the hover until—

The deck rose on a high wave, coming up square to meet the helo. As it crested, the marshaller signaled Trisha down.

Wheels touched at the moment the deck rose highest. Then, by shoving the collective to the floor and reversing the rotor lift, Trisha pinned the helo to the deck for the descent. Once solidly down, she taxied over to one of the elevators where another crew hurried the Helix below and out of sight. Not that any satellites would be peeking through the evening's heavy cloud cover.

By the time Sharelle reached the deck, the other two birds were already below.

The ship's crew didn't hesitate long enough for them to disembark before their bird too was riding down the big elevator. The hangar deck, two-thirds the size of the deck above, should be packed solid with helicopters, each with their rotors folded to save space. In addition to their three birds, there was only one additional Seahawk in a space designed to fit ten of the monstrous CH-53 Sea Stallions, the largest helicopter in the US military. Their little helos left it echoingly empty.

"What the hell are we in, Troy?"

"Deep end of the manure pit."

Sharelle laughed. "You can say *deep shit,* Troy Ryland. It's okay."

He shrugged an acknowledgement.

As they went through the barely familiar shutdown lists, they both kept looking at the strangeness of the empty hangar.

————

WHAT TROY NEEDED WAS FOOD AND SLEEP.

What he and the rest of the team got was time for finding their quarters and grabbing a quick shower before a formal meal with Commander Boyd Ramis.

"Brace yourselves," Billy the not-SEAL had warned them

with a rare comment as they approached the commander's cabin.

"Not your first mission aboard this ship?" one of the Droid Boys asked.

"Two years," Trisha's grimace, then happy artificial smile was all the warning they had. She walked with the same stiffness Troy felt after the long, weather-beaten flight.

The captain's cabin wasn't some steel box below decks. He'd taken over the flight deck-level pilots' ready room. And Troy saw where he'd cut out the intervening wall with another space of equal size. He'd turned it into a spacious, daylit, combined office, conference space, and dining room.

"Lieutenant Colonel Patricia O'Malley, a pleasure as always." The tall, spare man in the Naval officer's uniform sporting silver oak leaves on his epaulets had gray at his temples. He shook Trisha's hand after they'd traded salutes. "And Lieutenant Colonel William Bruce," received a friendly nod. After introductions, they were waved to seats: the five pilots, plus Bill in his role as Trisha's copilot or the lead Delta operator.

The other operators had either dodged the invitation or been considered too lowly to be invited at all. They were probably off carousing with the ship's crew—except he couldn't imagine one of the Silent Warriors, yet another nickname for Delta Force operators, carousing much. They were more a quiet-beer-in-a-dark-corner types. Or, since this was pre-mission, experience had taught him they were surely ensconced in some deep hold of the ship, reviewing their gear...again.

Presiding over the meal at the head of a long table, Ramis would have fit right in with the British admiralty of the nineteenth century clear down to the stilted tone and British idiom. But for all that, he remained kindly enough.

The space reflected the ship's age and hard use. Age-faded paintings of Marines charging beaches did little to add cheer. The high-gloss polish of the table that the seven of them sat around didn't hide the scuffs and stains in the dark wood.

First, Ramis offered them a welcoming drink—Navy ships were all *supposedly* dry. "Just a spot of sherry to be social that the Navy brass doesn't need to concern themselves with."

The Night Stalkers were often effectively dry as well. Not by Army rules, but because the Night Stalkers demanded twenty-four hours from-bottle-to-throttle. As they could be deployed on short notice, they needed to be fully stood down to have a drink. However, they'd be aboard this ship for over a day, so a glass of sherry wouldn't upset anyone.

Over a starter of creamy potato-and-leek soup, Ramis discussed the ship's proud history, starting all the way back to the Battle of Peleliu she'd been named for when two thousand Marines died and another eight thousand were wounded while clearing that South Pacific island of twelve thousand Japanese, few of whom had survived.

The entrée of individual steak-and-ale pies—

"Chef insists on using Guinness but steak-and-stout pie doesn't have quite the proper ring, does it?"

—covered her twenty-year peacetime service history. And the dessert topic, the ship's fourteen years ducking in and out of the Dustbowl wars of Southwest Asia and other duties.

Of the nine years since her decommissioning, all he said was, "I took command the year of her retirement. My assignment, to see her properly put to rest, was preempted by you Special Operations lot taking her on as a mobile operations platform. Seen a fair bit of the world since then, I must say."

And finally Commander Boyd Ramis made sense to Troy. An underperforming officer, competent but not excellent, definitely on the late side of promotion age, had found perhaps the only niche to keep him from forced retirement. Who better to shepherd around an aging and lightly-laden platform on the behalf of Special Operations.

After tea, with milk recommended, during which he offered a brief talk on the proper technique for dunking shortbread biscuits, he concluded with, "You may think me an awfully dry bird."

Troy managed to bite back his automatic agreement. Others caught themselves with less grace, but Ramis merely nodded to himself as if confirming his own truth.

"I'm well aware of the importance of the tasks you lot perform. But do please consider the challenges of command I face. Going on nine years, I've been granted command of this craft, mind you with a skeleton crew more befitting a Coast Guard's patrol boat than a Tarawa-class assault ship. On only a few occasions over these years have I been granted the privilege of knowing what missions were launched from the *Peleliu's* decks."

He left a longish pause, which no one answered. Then Ramis sighed and rose to his feet, making a show of taking a final sip from his china cup.

"And I see that this occasion will be no exception to that rule. Therefore, I have done what I can to heartily welcome you aboard."

He checked his watch, a move imitated by everyone around the table.

"You have been aboard for two hours. As commanded, we're at full steam to the west coast of Hokkaido, Japan, and will be arriving there in approximately nineteen hours. Until then, I'll take my leave. Do please let me know how I or the US Navy may be of service."

He offered a salute. Everyone at the table rose to return it and the man departed.

After he shut the door, most of them collapsed once more

into their chairs. Troy saw the weariness of a heavy meal after a long flight hammering them all down.

"Not quite the crashing bore we'd thought," Rafe spoke up.

"Way better than you," Julian had an answer, of course.

"Okay, everyone," Trisha cut them off before they really started rolling. "It's 2100 hours in our mission time zone."

Everyone set their watches to that because from this point on, that's all that mattered.

Though Trisha just had to rub in the challenges of Spec Ops. "That makes it 0400 on Attu Island, 0500 where we were training in Nevada, and 0800 back in Fort Campbell."

And 0600, just coming up dawn, in the Big Sky Country where he and Sharelle had spent a day and two nights in Montana.

"Take your pick. We depart at 2000 hours tomorrow mission time zone, which is eastern Russia at GMT plus-ten, by the way. Final go/no-go and pre-mission briefing at 1800 hours, in our birds by 1930 and ready to launch. I recommend staying awake, whatever time zone your body is in, for at least another six hours."

Going from night missions in Alaska to daytime at the ranch to yet more night exercises in Nevada and now shuffling nine hours backward—but a day forward for crossing the International Date Line in the mid-Pacific—Troy figured staying awake for six more hours was good advice.

"Who's up for a ship's tour?" Trisha called out. "Billy and I flew off this ship for several years and she boasts several very fun quirks." She managed a saucy wink at Troy but somehow included everyone else around the table. Which told him precisely what kind of *quirks* she and Billy had explored during their time aboard.

He did his best to be casual about glancing in Sharelle's direction.

Her eye roll told him he'd botched the casual part of that.

"That boat's long since sailed," Julian managed the first word this time.

"They definitely have something to explore but it's not the good ship *Peleliu*," Rafe agreed.

"Besides," Julian added.

And Rafe continued, "we don't need a tour either. We had a posting aboard—"

"That we can't mention, of course."

"—though Captain Ramis must have been on shore leave—"

"—as we missed his fine lecture."

"This was all—"

"—sometime after you departed the ship, Lieutenant Colonel Trisha."

"That's PITA O'Malley to you two. And don't think it won't be literal if you don't cut that out for this mission. You Droid Boys make my head hurt."

"Yes—"

"—ma'am. Whatever you say—"

"—ma'am."

They both jumped to their feet and offered sharp salutes before departing.

Billy rose slowly, neatly folded his napkin, and glanced toward the door.

"Sure, go," Trisha waved him off. "Easy guess as to where the other Delta went to ground. Make sure they've got the timing."

Billy circled to stand behind her chair, wrapped his big arms around her slender frame, and kissed her atop the head before going.

Watching Trisha's expression go goofy had Troy carefully *not* glancing at Sharelle once more.

After the steward had cleared the cabin and the three of them were alone, Trisha spoke up. "You two have a problem."

"Several of them." And Troy wished he hadn't said that.

Trisha nodded, for once completely serious. "Emily didn't see fit to warn me," her look said they'd definitely be having a few words about that, "though she always plays her cards close, all the way back to the day I met her. Anyway, a couple of your issues are pretty damn obvious."

"Any easy answers?" Troy kept his attention on her.

Trisha's laugh sounded bitter. "No such thing! Lola kicked me out of the regiment. Actually put the proverbial boot on my ass and shoved—hard. Mandatory leave until...if...I got my head screwed back on. Or maybe screwed on half right the first time. Anyways, close enough to gone I figured to be done with the 160th. Billy was the one who saved me from utterly blowing the second best thing in my life. God but I love to fly. This being in command shit cuts into it something fierce, though I'm kinda getting used to it. The occasional mission, like this one, will make a nice break."

Like this one? He managed not to asked that question. Instead, "What was the best thing?"

Trisha dug into the neck of her blouse and pulled out her dog tags, which included her wedding ring, and rattled them at him.

"Oh, right."

"One more answer for you. I received a confirmation of REFRAD date form to make sure you wouldn't be on a mission." She dug a crumpled envelope out of her back pocket and tossed it at him. "Don't be stupid, Captain Ryland."

Then she stood and walked out the door.

Sharelle remained silent until he'd extracted and scanned the two double-sided pages. "Is that what I think it is?"

Troy folded it carefully and tucked it back in the envelope.

He didn't rip it in half.

Didn't crumple it up and chuck it at the garbage can in the corner.

Instead, he smoothed out the envelope enough to tuck it into his own pocket and button the flap where it burned like a magnesium signal flare before answering.

"If you think it's my final DD214 Certificate of Release from Active Duty awaiting my signature on the day, you got it in one."

16

Sharelle led the way back to their assigned cabins. With the ship running a skeleton crew, even visiting Army captains were upgraded from visitor cabins into the heart of officer country. Their cabins were side by side.

She saw Troy hesitate at every step. How he didn't look at her much over dinner. How he handled that envelope. And the clear pain as he now stood facing her outside their steel gray doors.

Checking in with herself would be a waste of time, she already knew her own answers.

She pushed open the door to her cabin and stepped in without shutting it behind her.

Her personal go-bag sat where she'd dropped it on the only chair. The wardrobe was designed to hang up a dress uniform and not much else. The twin bed. The mirror barely big enough to see her face over an equally minute sink; a toothbrush would overwhelm that thing. But they had that rarest of privileges, their own bathrooms with a one-person shower. It sported signs about ten-minute shower limits, the luxury of such a large ship.

She couldn't see Troy's face in the mirror without ducking down, but his chest hadn't moved from close outside her door... hatch...whatever the Navy called such things. Wishing she had something sexier to do it with, she shrugged off her polar fleece vest. Peeling off her black t-shirt and tossing it aside revealed a battered sports bra. She was Army; it's how she dressed.

A careful side glance, still no movement.

Maybe he isn't interested.

Rarely was her inner voice so dumb. Then she remembered the last thing perhaps-not-such-a-pain-in-the-ass Trisha O'Malley had said.

"Don't be stupid, Captain Ryland."

Unable to stand looking in the mirror, she closed her eyes.

She lost count of her heartbeats before her door-hatch-thing clicked shut. No amount of straining her ears told which side of the door he'd chosen. Another twenty heartbeats before his hands came to rest on her bare waist. They slid so slowly around her that his touch became tortuous.

But he didn't stop. They kept sliding around her and pulling her back against his chest until they were so tight it became hard to breathe. Or perhaps her pulse sliding off the engine governor to approach a new high-throttle record had robbed her of air.

When he rested his head on her shoulder and turned his face into her neck, she slid a hand up into his hair and grabbed on to keep him there. She felt herself falling backward into his chest and simultaneously leaning against an unmovable stone wall of his warm flesh.

With his kiss on her jugular and her fist in his hair, his hands began to roam. The soldier-flat plane of her belly. The smooth muscle over her rib cage. And the long slide up her breastbone until he cradled her neck, a rough thumb tracing her jawline.

Laying a hand upon his other arm, she guided him up to cradle her breast.

She enjoyed a lively round between the sheets as much as the next girl. But at the moment, all she craved was Troy's touch. Her body against his. His hands on her skin.

When she tried to turn in his arms, he kept her pinned as she was.

Sharelle had been with enough soldiers to understand Army-strong, but Troy existed on another level. Born to hard physical labor, the Army had honed him into something else entirely without any over-muscled weightlifter physique. He didn't clamp her into place, there was simply no resisting his solid grasp. She knew he'd stop if she said a single word, so she made sure not to.

His kiss traced up to her ear. Then with the gentle guidance of his thumb, she turned to face into his kiss. Never had she felt so...desired.

Or so exposed.

Troy delivered the hot sweaty ravage she'd been anticipating as a slow exploration, his exploration of her from behind—with no action on her part. The submissive moment grated against her nature.

She shifted her hand from dug into his hair to clamped onto his ear.

"Ow. Ow. Ow!" Actually, "Mmph. Mmph. Mmph!" as he followed her leading pull until they shifted chest-to-chest, never fully breaking the kiss.

She leaned back enough to speak—and rip off his t-shirt between them. "Who says boys are the only ones who get to have fun. Because," she looked down, "you are so very pretty, Troy Ryland."

His slow smile indicated the same without once glancing down. In fact, he didn't look away from her eyes.

How had she missed her bra disappearing at the same time as his t-shirt?

Walk careful, girl. Might be real trouble here. Her voice didn't sound like it was talking about sex and that's all she cared about at the moment. So, since turnabout was fair play, she ignored the voice.

Troy began working his way down, stripping her bare of far more than her few remaining clothes. Everywhere he touched her, she felt...not exposed...revealed. As if he created her anew with every caress. After he'd unlaced her Army boots and removed the last of the clothing they'd trapped about her ankles, he took his time inspecting her from where he knelt.

It was the intent look he used when studying a helo upgrade: cataloging and memorizing every nuance of the installation. His gaze and attentions drove the heat upward until it had all climbed into her face. Men saw her, complimented her with a lusty grin, and dragged her into bed.

Troy studied her like some Greek statue. Dark marble, but still—

"I'm right here, you know. Alive. Breathing. Made of flesh."

He shook his head like a surprised horse; she half expected his ears to flap as he did so. "Sorry. My imagination seriously underplayed this moment."

"Been undressing me with your thoughts?" Finding a smile proved easy.

"Might have a time or two." He returned the smile. "Might have a few times more than that."

"Prove it."

He tipped his head to the side ever so slightly as if saying, *You asked for it.* Easy to imagine the horse he'd learned that from. It was also the last coherent thought she managed for some time.

Where his mouth didn't travel, his hands did.

Like the great copilot he was, Troy was always exactly

where she needed him most. One instant his two strong hands clamped over her buttocks to hold her tight against him and the next teasing her until, unable to do more, she begged for him to finish her off.

Only stage by stage did she understand that he was controlling the flights of her body *exactly* as if he was flying a masterful route in their DAP.

To any other woman, it would probably be a turnoff.

To a Night Stalkers pilot?

She'd never imagined anything even half so arousing.

———

Unsure when he'd finally crashed, Troy blessed that he'd set his watch alarm half an hour early.

Low thrum of the ship's engine. USS *Peleliu*. Right. Mission tonight.

When he'd set the alarm, he'd been thinking about a pre-mission run around the deck, two laps per kilometer.

Shorts, sneakers, and, if they hadn't cleared the storm yet, rain slicker.

He managed to open one eye—to see Sharelle looking down at him.

Big smile.

Close.

Very. He looked up at the finest breasts it had ever been his pleasure to manhandle. Full and rounded without being large. Athletic rather.

Last night they'd—

"Whoa!"

"And he's finally awake."

"Uh-huh." He... And Sharelle... And last night...

"How early did you set that alarm?"

"Uh. A run. Thirty minutes."

"Oh. You'd rather run? Okay." And she rolled out from under the covers.

She made it halfway before he woke up enough to realize his arm remained around her waist where it had probably been the whole time they'd slept. The logistics of two people in a twin Navy bunk didn't offer many other options.

Using that arm, he dragged her back under the covers.

"I thought you wanted to run. It's like a ritual with you before every mission."

"It is. Want to know why?" His body was fast waking up to the idea of a naked Sharelle Vargas sprawled half over him.

"Not really." Her fake puzzled expression didn't fool him for a second. "But if you *insist* on telling me, go ahead."

"Well, since you don't really care..." Troy cupped her cheek with a hand, still amazed that her skin felt so soft, and left a gentle kiss on her nose.

With the same brilliant lack of subtlety she'd shown last night, she slid her hand down his torso and grabbed onto him. "So tell me!"

He grunted hard at the strength of her grasp but she didn't ease off. Not hard enough to hurt but not comfortable either. "I run," he managed a steadying breath, "to burn off my need for this seriously hot Night Stalkers pilot. You know, before sitting side by side in a cockpit with her for hours."

"You run because of...me? All those years and miles." Her voice became a whisper. And her grip eased—slightly.

"Keeps me in shape as a bonus."

"A very nice bonus," she leaned down to return the kiss on his nose, still not releasing her grasp. "No morning-after regrets?"

"It's impossible to regret a single moment I spend with you —ever. Moments like the ones we spent last night? Well, that's like comparing folding paper airplanes to flying a DAP Hawk. You're a top flight craft, lady. Top flight."

"If you start singing *Ruddigore,* I'll..." Sharelle tightened her grip enough to make his breath catch.

"What's a Ruddigore? Is that a ship?"

She studied him for a moment before easing off, much to his relief. "An old operetta that Mama likes. Very British. Captain Ramis probably played all the Gilbert and Sullivan hero roles in his college theater group. There's this whole song about the heroine being a *neat little, sweet little, bright little, tight little, trim little, prim little craft.*" She sang the last to a catchy tune.

Troy knew it was a bad move, but he laughed in her face. "Prim is not a word I'd ever use to describe you. Kick butt, sure as shootin'."

"You mean kick ass."

He slid a hand to cradle the object in question. Sharelle Vargas had the most amazing behind. "Sure, whatever you want."

"What I want..." she shifted to kneel over him, holding the covers like a tent.

He reached out a hand for another packet of protection.

Exactly what he wanted too.

17

"WE'RE ALOFT IN TWO HOURS," TRISHA ANNOUNCED AS THEY SAT.

They were back in the large conference room for breakfast by the lowering sun. One advantage of Ramis' expanded office was that it spanned the base of the ship's island—the sea to one side and the flight deck to the other.

This time without Captain Boyd Ramis but with the entire action team, including the other six Unit operators who'd managed to duck out of Ramis' welcome party.

The big screen at the head of the table lit up, split in two. To one side, Colonel Emily Beale looking as cool and collected as ever. To the other, Secretary of Defense Archie Stevenson.

Sharelle had never met him before and inspected him with interest. He'd been Beale's copilot for most of his service.

Battle stations, girl!

Right. Now, he was the second-in-command of the entire Department of Defense after the President himself.

Even though it was still just a monitor screen, she felt awed. He and Beale had come up out of West Point together, yet he was already the SecDef. A testament to his service record and how sharp he was.

Sharelle knew they were headed into the deep end of the dunking pool—one of the hardest training events for any Night Stalkers pilot. A fully rigged cockpit, blindfolds to simulate night and full systems failure, and a twisting plunge to slam upside down into the water. Now rescue yourself and your people before the training divers decided they had to save you from imminent drowning. They tended to wait a very long time to truly drive home the lesson. She learned to excel in that skill very quickly to avoid ever having to repeat the exercise.

Facing the SecDef for the first time on such a personal level felt precisely like that: short of breath, edge of panic, fear of dying in the next few seconds.

Stevenson smiled pleasantly. "Colonel Beale informs me that you people represent the best action team possible for this mission. Congratulations and thank you."

"Ready when you are, Mr. Secretary." Again, Trisha O'Malley proved her abilities; Sharelle doubted she could have formed more than a squeak if required.

"Colonel Beale has, I believe, briefed you all on the black-in-black security level of this mission. This is your last chance to step out the door. No judgment. No marks on your service record."

No one moved.

After fifteen long seconds, the tiniest nod from Beale was all the compliment that Sharelle needed.

"Again, thank you. Moving along. Since 2006, the UN has imposed heavy sanctions on North Korea to deter their nuclear program. Supreme Commander Kim Jong Un has decided that weapons development is more important than feeding his people."

Sharelle glanced at Troy. On the flight down, they'd been certain that they'd be flying into easternmost Russia. That was one challenge, but into North Korea? They were believed to possess more antiaircraft weaponry than any other nation.

His uncertain head tip didn't encourage her at all.

"Running out of munitions themselves," SecDef Stevenson continued, "the Russians have traded food for at least seven thousand containers of North Korean shells and other weapons for shipment east to the Ukraine War. Last month, Russia used its veto power on the UN Security Council to disband the committee that had been investigating Russia's violations of these sanctions. We are going to disrupt these shipments."

Someone let out a low whistle of surprise. Sharelle couldn't manage to look aside to see who.

"Uh, Mr. Secretary?" Troy raised his hand like a boy still at school.

"Captain Ryland?" Stevenson didn't glance down at any list. It meant he'd studied each of their dossiers enough to be familiar with them.

"There have been multiple prior attacks on the Trans-Siberian Rail, over sixty since the start of the conflict in 2022. Only a few have resulted in notable damage. How will anything we do be different?"

Sharelle smiled to herself. Leave it to her Troy to ask the intelligent question. *Her* Troy? She needed her head examined. All they'd had was a single night of life-changing sex.

Life-changing, huh?

Go away. I'm busy!

The voice went silent but she knew that constituted only a temporary reprieve.

"Because, unlike those sabotaging the rail with explosives to stop the flow of arms, we won't be targeting the railroad itself."

"But—" Then Troy stopped himself. She wondered what he'd been about to say before thinking better of questioning the Secretary of Defense. She knew he'd be three steps ahead of her, but that still left her with no real hint.

Beale glanced down long enough to tap in a few commands. She and the SecDef were relegated to a pair of boxes at the right edge of the screen. The rest filled with a map of Russia. Only three lines traced across the vast distance from Moscow to the Pacific: the two rail lines of the Trans-Siberian Railroad, and a single fragile road only fully paved in the last decade.

The northern rail track ran in a straightish line all the way from the coast back to Moscow. The southern leg curved around a great northward bulge of China before plunging another seven hundred kilometers south. There, at the very southeastern tip, the rail reached the junction point of Russia, North Korea, China, and the Pacific Ocean.

A lone city, the second largest in the eastern half of Russia, commanded that critical junction point—Vladivostok.

"You were about to say," Beale spoke up, "that all trade from North Korea to Russia must pass over the slender Friendship Bridge into Vladivostok. And that if we destroy that bridge, it will be very obvious that the US has intervened."

Troy confirmed that.

Beale tapped a key and a red X appeared on the screen along the rail line—but five hundred kilometers north of the city. It was the closest point to the northern tip of Japan; finally the *Peleliu's* planned anchorage made sense.

"Two hundred kilometers over the Sea of Japan. Three hundred more over a largely uninhabited stretch of Russia."

Troy estimated the distances. It intercepted the rail connection between North Korea and the main trunk of the Trans-Siberian Rail.

"Flying into Russia in Russian helicopters."

"Yes," Beale answered. "Even now, full Russian kits have been delivered to your cabins, right down to your socks and shoelaces."

Troy nodded, "That should be doable then."

That was her Troy. No hint of nerves, or how wild such a mission sounded. Calculating the odds and challenges.

She noted that no one else spoke up. She also noted that she didn't flinch internally at *her Troy* this time.

Beale, as voluble as ever, made no comment as she zoomed out the image, revealing a second rail line out of Vladivostok. Rather than striking north, then west around China, this line sliced through that great bulge of China. It rejoined the Trans-Siberian another fifteen hundred kilometers later, cutting the distance by forty percent.

"The Chinese Eastern Railway. Secondary objective," she placed a second red *X* where the rail line reentered Russia.

A gasp echoed around the table that echoed her own.

The two *X*s intercepted the only two rail lines on their long journey through the barren wastes of central Siberia toward Moscow.

Sharelle swallowed hard and wondered if slipping into North Korea might be easier. That second *X* lay thousands of kilometers inside Russia.

Troy offered no quick assessment. He simply stared at the screen perhaps as aghast as she felt.

It was a long time before anyone spoke.

"Please tell me this isn't a one-way mission?" Even Trisha sounded breathless.

"No," Beale answered. "The action team has full mission-abort authority at any time."

Another lesson from the Black Route Alaska mission. Take ownership when defining the limits of your own battlespace.

"Team safety is our highest priority on this mission," SecDef Stevenson confirmed. Yet he was sending them over two thousand kilometers *into* Russia. How desperate was the situation?

"But...how?" Sharelle waved at the screen. They'd managed a thousand miles across the North Pacific, mostly by Troy's exquisite Flight Plan Ryland slinging them around the storm.

This was fourteen hundred miles each way—triple the distance.

———

"Well shit, man!" Julian was the first to speak after Beale explained.

Troy turned to look at him; Julian's face had regained no more color than anyone else's. Even Sharelle's still looked bloodless.

The Unit operators would be riding with Trisha—all of them, rather than spreading across the two Helixes.

"I guess we *do* give a flying FARP," Julian noted.

"That'll be a real super stinker." Rafe proved he was recovering.

Julian made a predictable fart noise, then glanced at the SecDef and blushed bright red.

A forward arming and refueling point—F-A-R-P. The Droid Boys' Ka-27 Helix would be along as a flying gas can, refueling the other two helos at stops along the way.

"Your mission," Beale spoke before Rafe responded to embarrass Julian further, "is to deliver the Delta team to three locations. They estimate thirty minutes minimum required at each location. The first two along the Trans-Siberian Rail: one twenty kilometers west of the Amur River Bridge at Khabarovsk…"

The easy *X*.

"…and the second a similar distance north of Zabaykalsk on the Russian-Chinese border."

The one threatening to give Troy and the rest of the team a heart attack.

"The third location, the lowest priority placement, will be along the Trans-Siberian Highway in this vicinity." A third *X* appeared along what had to be their return route.

"Can't we fly the direct route?" Even from the first *X* well to the north, that large bulge of China pushed far up into Siberia, following the line of the Amur River. "That would save us four hundred kilometers each way. There is little more Chinese population south of that border than there are Russians north of it."

"Under no circumstances are you to risk an incursion into Chinese airspace." The SecDef made it a flat statement.

Troy supposed that having a few American military invading Siberia would cause one issue, but being caught traversing their supposedly friendly Chinese trade partner's territory would be many times worse politically.

Troy glared at the screen and hope to *hell* it was worth it.

Then he smiled. No one asked, but it did earn him several questioning looks.

Wouldn't Sharelle be pleased that he'd finally managed a decent curse, even if it was only in his head.

———

TWENTY-TWO HUNDRED KILOMETERS EACH WAY.

Eight hours' flight time—each way.

That didn't count the stops for whatever the Delta operators were going to be doing.

Once the SecDef had dropped out of the picture, route planning had become the top priority. Precise landing points would be determined on-site, but some unnamed image analyst somewhere had created a handy list of primaries and alternates.

As an unregistered military flight, it would be nice to have codes for airspace authority at a minimum.

"As far as we can tell," Beale informed them, "they don't have them."

He'd known that Russian air defense was utter crap. The

Ukrainians had proved that with strikes against oil refineries, heavily protected technology factories, and even the heart of the country—Moscow itself—hundreds of kilometers past shared borders.

"Are you saying we can simply wander freely around the Russian countryside because we possess Russian military helicopters? That's crazy." Yet Troy almost believed it.

Beale went on to describe that, until the long-delayed fiber optic cable through the Arctic passing for twelve thousand kilometers along the country's entire north and east coast was completed, the answer was essentially...yes.

"Their primary communication across the continent remains satellite based. We have a team that will make every effort to jam, intercept, and respond to those signals before they can cause you trouble." That had him looking at the steel ceiling of the briefing room and wondering quite what kind of tech they were flying up there in space. Jamming a satellite would be plenty obvious to the Russians.

When he looked down, Sharelle was watching his face. His expression must have given away his thoughts as she looked no happier than he felt.

"Of course," Beale said before sending them to their helos, "it would be better if you weren't spotted at all."

Perfect. Just freaking perfect.

18

HALF AN HOUR PAST SUNSET, WHEN VISIBILITY TO OUTSIDE observers—like Russian satellites—would be at its worst, the three helos rode the elevator up to the *Peleliu's* flight deck.

Three minutes later, when their engines stabilized at optimum operating temperature, they started their take-off rolls in unison.

Sharelle was glad that the deck was clear except for the search-and-rescue Seahawk, lurking like a sad bird of prey.

She didn't try rising to a hover at all. The techs had stashed every possible ounce of fuel aboard, pushing calculated max takeoff load limits in ways she'd rather not know about. She used every inch of deck the *Peleliu* offered to gain forward speed before easing aloft.

"It wallows." Which told her how hard they were up against the airframe's limits. No sudden maneuvers until they'd burned down some of the fuel.

Rafe and Julian carried a massive fuel bladder in their Helix —an extra eleven thousand pounds of fuel—sixteen hundred gallons. The techs had stripped out every non-essential item, loading only a massive rubber bladder and two high-speed pumps into the cargo bay—Chinese rather than Russian so that they'd actually work.

Like a giant waterbed, Julian had observed when they'd all looked at the tank. It filled the entire eight-foot width of the cargo bay, fifteen feet of its length, and stood two feet high.

On steroids. Rafe agreed.

Don't be thinking you're going to get lucky with me, flyboy. Julian tried to make a sexy hip check, then pretended he'd thrown out his back.

Not getting off that easy... And so it had probably continued through preflight and the ride up the elevator.

They flew to starboard of her Ka-52 Alligator.

To port, Trisha and Billy were aloft with the six other Unit operators and their gear. She half wondered if Trisha had shed her skivvies to load a few extra ounces of fuel. Wouldn't put it past her. Recalling that the techs had weighed each of them in their full gear before finishing the fuel load, and thinking about the long flight and hazards to come, Sharelle wished she'd thought to do it.

Then she recalled quite how Troy had taken them off her last night and needed something else to think about. "What the hell are The Unit folks carrying anyway?"

Troy sat left-seat and glanced out his side window at them. "Uh, we never got around to that, did we?"

"No shit!" How had she let that slip by? She couldn't risk calling them up on the radio to ask at the moment. They'd entered mission communications blackout when they flew out of the continental US. Leaving the ship, they now flew in mission communications blackout. If all went well, the next time they'd touch the radio would be landing back aboard the *Peleliu.*

And the chances of everything going well while flying forty-four hundred kilometers over Russia on a top-secret US operation?

Sharelle took a deep breath, closed her eyes long enough to count to three, then turned west. The last rosy color above was fading into darkening blue. By the time they had crossed the two hundred kilometers of the Sea of Japan forty-five minutes from now, the Russian coast should be pitch dark. They'd pass through the sixty-kilometer gap between the thousand residents of the Svetlaya fishing village and the hundred residents of Yedinka with, hopefully, no one the wiser.

"Any guesses?" Sharelle had taken off from the *Peleliu's* deck, which lay ten meters above the waves, and decided that they'd hold that until they were nearer the coast.

Troy considered for long enough to worry her. "Well, Secretary of Defense Stevenson said we weren't going to blow up the train."

"Right."

"And Russia voted to disband the UN sanctions monitoring team for North Korea contraband."

"Yes." Sharelle decided that ten meters to the *top* of her rotor rather than the bottom of the wheels would make her happier. But that would put her wheels at five meters while flying at night over a black ocean without any running lights. No, she'd save that draining, white-knuckle skill for later when they knew they needed it.

It's just nerves. Airport radar rarely reaches below sixty meters. Just chill, girlfriend.

One of these days she was going to *chill* her inner voice square between the eyes.

She compromised on eight meters: wheels-to-water.

"I can't see us flying all this way to install a monitoring system."

"Why not?" Sharelle had thought that was a decent bet.

"We could never admit to how we obtained any data from that system."

Which was why Troy was the brains of their outfit. "Meaning?"

"Meaning, I don't have a clue. We'll have to ask at the first refueling stop."

That lay over six hours ahead, well past the first installation.

The Russian coast slid closer and closer by the second, as if it had transformed into a tsunami wave looming up to crush them. "Okay, new topic."

"Fire away." She saw Troy flipping between tactical, navigation, and onboard systems screens. Once every four to five seconds, watching for shifts in patterns.

"If you keep doing that for the next sixteen hours of flight time, you'll go blind."

He nodded, paused long enough to rub his hands together as if washing them clean of the same nerves she felt, then returned to flipping screen views every *ten* seconds. Unlike their DAP Hawk, far less information was projected inside the visor at any one setting. They each had a heads-up display, but its primary function was weapons targeting.

Send aloft another prayer that we won't be using any of them.

She did. Because when the voice was right, it was majorly right. A missile battle deep in Russia would not be turning out well for anyone.

One thing that had shocked her during the training, though she hadn't truly acknowledged it until this moment, was what a lame machine this was.

In comparison to a Black Hawk, she found little to complain about. The Alligator's glass cockpit provided full navigation and weapons management. Her...*His* firepower ranked top-end like few other birds brought to battle. And his agility—unbelievable that the Department of Defense had canceled the Raider and Defiant compound rotor programs— blew Sharelle away at every turn.

But up against a DAP Hawk? No contest, baby. Her Direct-Action Penetrator could track the direction an incoming bullet had been fired from, directing the crew where to answer back—hard. Beyond that, when it came to terrain-following, tracking or blocking EM transmissions like phones or radios, or even reporting air-frame health, the Alligator felt generations back.

"Ever been to Russia before?"

The relief that coursed through her at Troy's question surprised Sharelle. Why wasn't she bringing up last night's amazing sex? Their relationship? The envelope containing the release from duty form that she'd felt in his pocket during the lovely full-body hug before they'd changed into their Russian gear? Yet it was definitely relief that she felt.

Not brave enough? She asked her inner voice.

Doesn't sound very Night Stalkerish, girlfriend. Being smart for a change?

That answer didn't sit any better.

"No. You?"

"I was a broke scholarship boy; I never went anywhere the Army didn't pay the ticket on. ROTC said I needed a language, so I landed on Russian because the farm next to ours was owned by Russian immigrants. I'd heard it enough as a kid to pick it up quickly. Plenty of deployments into the southwest Asia mess where a bit of Pashto, Farsi, or Arabic would have been nice, but never into any of the Russian-speaking countries. Except for the bits Russian soldiers left behind after *their* Afghan War. Why did you learn it?"

"There was this cute guy..." At least that's how she usually told the story.

This time she felt Troy's stony silence.

He can not be thinking you are a virgin, girlfriend.

Not after last night. Her sarcasm shut up the voice—for the moment. To avoid more rebuttals from within, Sharelle decided to shoot for the truth. "Had a professor at the Virginia Military

Institute who figured there were two possible wars to face in the future, at least big ones. And I didn't want to learn Mandarin. Little did I know it would place me in the seat of a Ka-52 Alligator on an invasion of Russian sovereign territory."

"It is an odd bonus, isn't it?"

Whatever level she and Troy had of any implied commitment would have to wait; the Russian coastline was approaching fast.

She slid down to five meters above the waves. A glance aside showed that the other two aircraft had followed her cue. She'd expect no less of Night Stalker pilots.

That reminded Sharelle of her response to Beale that first night; she served because these were the *best people I've ever met.* She still couldn't recall quite what Emily had said in reply and was out of time to think about it.

The idealized Earth horizon at their current altitude was six miles and two minutes out. Jagged surf cut off a third of that and the Ka-52's crappy radar resolution cut that in half again. Inside of two minutes, they'd crossed over the mouth of a tiny river midway between the two towns.

"Straight line?" she asked.

"Sure," Troy agreed. "First, we have insufficient fuel to follow any meandering course."

Sharelle climbed to treetop height and raced inland up the broad valley.

"Second, we're now a Russian military flight. Unless a missile takes us out in the next thirty seconds, it's time to act as if we belong."

Sharelle didn't know why he chose thirty, but if Troy said it... She counted them out slowly, only releasing her held breath when they were clear. "I guess we're in good."

"Thirty seconds *was* arbitrary."

"I did *not* need to know that."

"Sorry." Troy studied one of his screens. "Do you still prefer passing close by their airport radar or flying within two miles of the Chinese border over swinging north of Khabarovsk city?"

"Sounds like a trick question when you put it that way. What's at the border there?"

"It's where the Chinese and Russians hand over prisoners and such. So, I'm thinking test the airport passage."

Sharelle considered. "Show me."

Troy put the map on the middle screen for them to look at together. "It's another sixteen kilometers to loop north of the city, but—"

"We stick with the southern route, close, but not too close to China. We belong, right? You just said so."

She flicked on her running lights to prove the point. Trisha and the Droid Boys did the same. They were now an official *looking* military flight.

"But mostly? Who knows when we'll want that extra sixteen kilometers. Use that as the baseline measure for all future navigation."

"Roger that." And he gave her a new heading, a few degrees to the south of their present course. The two Helix helos followed.

"But don't be stupid about it."

"Yes, ma'am." He didn't sound happy.

"Sorry about that, Troy. You're the smartest man I know. It's just..." she didn't know what.

"I'm just being stupid by PITA O'Malley's and your standards."

"No. Last night you weren't stupid for a single second."

His grunt said he wouldn't be arguing with that.

"Once you finally got smart enough to cross over my cabin threshold, that is."

"Well...crap."

From Troy, she'd take that as a heartfelt curse.

TROY, PRESENTLY THE PILOT-IN-COMMAND, SLOWED AS THEY neared the first stop. They'd cut their running lights and once again flew dark. They'd made it fifty kilometers past Khabarovsk—and four hundred klicks and eighty-nine minutes past the Russian coast—with no one reacting.

No challenges.

No border patrol jet slipping up to check them out. Or to shoot them down.

With each klick of non-event, Troy felt his body getting tighter and tighter rather than relaxing.

He surveyed the generally flat terrain. It was a mixed bag. They wouldn't be gaining much altitude anywhere in the mission profile, which saved fuel. It would be nice to climb into slightly thinner air—both the Alligator and the Helis were more efficient at two thousand meters than at twenty—but then they'd be visible to every radar out there.

However, the usual advantage of flying so low—saving fuel due to ground effect as the rotors drove the air down against the ground, causing added bonus lift due to air compression under the blades—wouldn't help. All except the very end of their run would be at or below twenty meters, but that would be measured from the treetops, not the ground. Trees did nothing to help create ground effect; in fact, they dispersed it brilliantly. At least they also muffled noise, which would be a small blessing.

They'd flown by a village ten kilometers to the east and were out past the orchards so common in that area. The road and railroad ran east-west here, with little variation for the next six thousand kilometers.

The road, little more than a two-lane strip of pavement, would change only near the biggest of towns between here and the Ural mountains. The rail was in better shape. It had dual tracks that looked solidly placed.

For five kilometers to the north of the road, the Urmi River had twisted so far over the flat terrain that it created thousands of hectares of cut-off oxbow lakes and muddy swamps.

To the south of the rail, swampy lands stretched all the way to the Amur River at the Chinese border.

The highest points anywhere were the built-up dikes under the road and railroad tracks that lay a kilometer apart here. The road had diverted north to firmer land. The engineers of the early 1900s had decided that a straight shot across the wetlands was a better route for the railroad.

"Nobody in their right mind would come here."

"We're here," Sharelle answered.

"I rest my case." Though the *we* bothered him. "I'm a short-timer, Sharelle. You don't want to be with me."

He eased to a hover over the precisely chosen nav point using GLONASS, the Russian version of GPS.

"This is it." He cut off anything she might say.

They both concentrated on making a careful sweep, with the instruments such as they had. No traffic along the road or the tracks; though they couldn't see traffic a half hour out, Beale could. No signal from her on the satellite radio frequency they were tuned to meant they were in the clear—for now.

"Clear?"

"Clear," he responded.

Troy clamped his eyes shut to protect his night vision as Sharelle flashed the interior cabin lights twice. The other two helos, watching for the signal, responded by settling down in a nearby field. The moment they were wheels-down, the Delta operators streamed off their bird.

"Aloft or down?" he asked.

"You tell me."

Troy did the math. They needed to be able to respond to

any trouble quickly, they were the hammer of the outfit responsible for protecting the other two. Yet at an estimated thirty minutes for Delta to do whatever they were doing, they'd burn hundreds of pounds of fuel if they stayed aloft.

"You said save the kilometers. We go down, trust Beale and her team at the ranch to be our eyes, but keep the engines hot for immediate lift."

It took Sharelle turning one more slow three-sixty circle of the site before she responded. "Do it."

Troy brought them to rest on the other side of the Trans-Sib's tracks, as the Russians called it, from their own birds.

"You keep an eye on tactical, I'll do the gawking."

Not much to keep an eye on but Sharelle was right. He rode the throttle down to a fast idle and pitched the rotors dead flat so that they didn't expend fuel on excess drag. Another eye on the comm radios.

From her Tac Room at Henderson's Ranch, which Sharelle had described in fascinating detail, she'd be keeping an eye on them. She'd know that they'd chosen to settle and would be doubly vigilant about watching from on high. No body with a heat signature larger than a bicycle would get within ten klicks of them. Or fifty klicks if they were a jet or missile.

They'd also timed their landings to the known train schedule, but that was dicey at best. Russian trains ran closer to on time than American ones, which was saying almost nothing.

Sharelle filled him in on the team's actions so he didn't have to watch. "They're using a plasma cutter to make four slices in the rails, each about a dozen meters apart."

"That's not very subtle," Troy carefully inspected the feed from the infrared camera. The camera hung below the nose, almost in the grass, but he kept it focused down the track. There was a slim gap in the trees where he could see a short section a kilometer away; it would give him some warning of a train from the west. "Oh. Twelve and half meters is a standard Russian railroad rail. Why would they need to cut it?"

"Got me, Mr. Genius. How in the world do you know that?"

"The farm isn't far from an old abandoned stretch of track. I looked into buying a few sections of the track and a couple rail cars to set up as glamping guest houses on the farm. Learned a lot about rail beds, track, and cars. Turned out to not be worth doing, but I tried."

Sharelle rested a hand on his shoulder for a moment.

He wasn't going to let the sympathy affect him. His plan was clear, no matter how much he wanted to yank that final REFRAD form from his jacket pocket and shred it. It was a good thing the jacket he'd tucked it into was back on the *Peleliu*. They'd changed together into the Russian gear shortly before departure. The only way to do that reliably was to strip naked, step away from everything, and dress in the new gear. His underwear didn't fit right at all. He'd enjoyed watching as Sharelle had adjusted her bra again and again, sadly without success.

Everything Russian—except for whatever the hell The Unit operators were working on.

Sharelle's hand had drifted away after he refused to react. Her voice was tighter than before as she continued her narration. "They aren't removing the rail. In fact, it looks like they're filling the gap in again. That's done. They're now working both ends of the center section. Running a wire across one end, buried in the roadbed gravel. Making a much bigger excavation at the other end."

"Big enough to bury one of those boxes they loaded aboard?"

"I guess. Mean anything to you?"

"It might. It just might." Troy considered. Two steel rails, cut at either end, only made sense if you were removing the rail. But derailing a train this close to Khabarovsk? They'd have a team here in hours and have the whole thing fixed and the train back on the tracks in a day.

Blowing up the track, they wouldn't need to get so elaborate. But the result wouldn't last that much longer.

That left—

"*Tort! Desyat!*" Squawked in on the satellite radio. A transmission so short he barely recognized Beale's voice. It could be a wide area broadcast blanketing half the hemisphere and they were the only ones tuned to the right frequency who would understand its meaning. Or Beale was using a narrow beam pulse that no one outside their bit of a landing zone could pick up at all. Either way, it worked.

Tort desyat. T for *train,* not the Russian *tort* meaning *cake.* And *desyat,* the Russian number *ten* for how many minutes until they were going to be so screwed. For a helo, she'd have said *Khameleon* for the hard-aspirated H sound to match. *Arbuz,* watermelon, for airplane. *Ryba,* for the road that lay a kilometer to the north here, or for the fish who swam in the nearby river. No English language broadcast in case the transmission was intercepted.

What it really meant was: time to hustle!

All three helos flashed their cabin lights once in acknowledgement, then doused their running lights so that they'd be invisible in the darkness. At least everyone was on the ball and, if Beale had a satellite properly positioned—and she would—she'd see the three brief flashes of light to show that her message was received.

One of The Unit operators, Trisha's husband Billy by his sheer size, turned on a narrow-beam flashlight and clamped it under his arm so that it shone on his hands. He held up seven fingers, turning for each helo to see clearly.

"Oh. My. God!" Sharelle groaned. "A whole three minutes' leeway."

Then Billy waggled one hand sideways, as if saying, *Kinda, sorta, maybe, if we're lucky!* before he doused the light and turned back to the task at hand.

"Of course the trains had to be off schedule. But with that little warning, where the hell were they?"

"Parked on some siding?" Troy stared out into the darkness. "Ten minutes. They can probably make sixty kilometers an hour on this roadbed. Ten minutes would place them ten kilometers away. We can cover that in under two minutes."

"Which way?" Just because she didn't like the idea, didn't matter. Sharelle knew the team needed more time. She'd already spun the engines up to full throttle the moment the transmission came through, the Ka-52 danced light on its wheels. Easing up on the collective, she began the climb.

Troy didn't answer as she climbed up to fifteen meters, then twenty. She was *not* going to pass thirty, even if they couldn't spot the train.

"There! East."

She dropped back down to five meters and raced east. "You're going to shoot the train. That's going to be pretty damn obvious."

"No. Not the train. At least I hope not." He brought up the targeting system. "Crap!"

She risked glancing over as he stared at the weapons' selection. The code for a Vikhr anti-tank missile showed on his screen. "Troy!" That would set off every alert from Vladivostok to Moscow.

"Give me a moment."

To her relief, he switched over to the side-mounted Shipunov 30 mm cannon. It would still punch a plenty big hole in a train, certainly one big enough to stop it functioning. It would be glaringly obvious, but at least it wouldn't light up the skies.

Riding the edge of the never-exceed speed—and burning

fuel at a prodigious rate she wouldn't think about right now—
they raced toward the train.

"Get me a half kilometer to the side of the track, Sharelle,
two kilometers ahead of the train. Get me a clear view of the
track but not the train itself. Just past a curve would be best. I
don't want them seeing us or what I'm doing."

"Anything else while I'm at it?" It was a crazy set of criteria
to locate in unknown terrain at night while flying over three
hundred kilometers per hour.

"Sure. I'll take a rib eye steak, Oklahoma beef, medium rare,
and a Dr. Pepper with extra peanuts."

And she laughed. Racing to kill a Russian train before it ran
down her Delta Force team in eastern Siberia, he made her
laugh. This was the man she wanted in her life.

The rest of your life?

She'd covered three more kilometers before she had her
answer. *Yes!*

How you going to make that happen, girlfriend?

Sharelle ignored her voice's snide tone and focused on
finding the locale of Troy's odd request.

———

TROY WAS AFRAID SHE WAS GOING TO OVERRUN THE TRAIN BEFORE
she found an acceptable shooting point.

Less than two kilometers before they would pass the train
racing the other way—now visible on radar even at their low
altitude and by distant flashes of light through the slender trees
—Sharelle slammed into a turn so hard that he almost
depressed the trigger on the unfamiliar gun while bracing
himself. She circled away from the railroad, making a wide arc
to the south before nosing up just as violently. Not to climb, but
to use all of the rotor's power to slow them down.

Sharelle had integrated the Ka-52 into her reflexes far faster than humanly possible, yet she'd done it. In a single integrated motion, she brought them to a dead halt facing the track at a height of five meters.

He looked. The train ran deep in the trees off to his right—fifteen hundred meters and closing fast. The track lay visible dead ahead at eye level on the built-up roadbed, a peekaboo view through the trees. And he'd wager she was within meters of one half kilometer from the track.

The Shipunov 2A42 could throw 30 mm rounds up to four kilometers, two with accuracy. And do it at twelve rounds a second. But he wasn't trying to hit an armored vehicle or even a person. He selected high-explosive HE rounds rather than armor-piercing AP ones, and low-speed firing, a mere three rounds per second. It was a fearsome weapon.

A round would only take half a second to make the traverse from their helicopter to the railroad. It would drop one and a quarter meters during that flight time. The cannon was zeroed at a thousand meters for a two-and-a-half-meter drop, and he didn't have time to reset it.

He took his best guess, nudged it down ever so slightly—then a little more until it felt right—and lightly tapped the trigger, managing to fire a single round.

"You chewed rock. A meter low."

"How the hell did I—" Then he glanced at the side of the hull. The barrel of the gun mounted on the outside of the helicopter rested even with his ankles, not his eyes. During testing in Nevada, he'd been far more worried about learning the targeting system and getting to the point where he could think in Russian again to cut down reaction time. During range practice with the helo's Shipunov cannon, he'd aimed at an old tank and hit it, not noticing it was a meter low. His Black Hawk-trained instincts were used to the side-mounted guns sitting at head level.

He eased his aim up to where it felt a little wrong and fired again.

The flash of the explosive round shone as a brilliant white spot in his night vision. The auto-shuttering on the Russian equipment wasn't as good as the American ones and he ended up seeing spots instead of the actual results. That's why he'd wanted the curve in the rail. He didn't want the train engineer seeing the explosive's flash and stopping prematurely to take a good look and listen around.

"Busted rail," Sharelle practically crowed. She must have remembered to close her eyes. "You're so good, Troy!"

"That's what you said last night. Up five meters."

She climbed. "You were."

He fired again and the far rail of the second track busted out. "Just trying to keep up with you, Sharelle. Absolutely magnificent."

Without needing to be told, Sharelle dropped them almost to the dirt.

"Twenty seconds," Troy called out.

The train's headlight, which had been flickering through the trees, straightened out as it came off the curve and onto the straightaway leading up to the breaks he'd just created.

"Ten."

No reaction from the train.

"Five. Four..." Then he shut up and just watched through his night-vision goggles, ready to shoot the engine if he had to.

At zero, the train raced straight over the gap.

Had he shot the wrong track? No, he'd shot one rail out of both sets. He was sure of it.

Then the engine dropped. Not much, only a few hand widths. Its forward momentum had carried it on straight after crossing the gap he'd blown in the rails. But the wheels hadn't managed to span the gap. They'd dropped off the rails to roll on the ties. Then, almost in slow motion, the outer wheels crossed off the edge of the dike and the engine tilted. Farther and farther until it rolled out of sight on the north side of the dike.

Ten, fifteen freight cars followed it off the rail and into the marsh that lay north of the railroad bed's dike. Finally, they piled up in a zigzag accordion as the forward cars had nowhere to go and the aft cars were still moving. They jounced off the rails to the right and left before stopping.

Long before the screams of rending metal would have stopped, Sharelle headed toward the rest of their team. They'd be long out of earshot before the train's engineers' hearing recovered enough to detect any beating rotors.

"There've been a number of sabotages along the Trans-Sib since the start of the Ukraine War," Troy told Sharelle as much as telling himself. "Hopefully they'll think it's yet another attack by sympathizers or anti-war protestors who don't want to be shipped to the front lines. I'm banking on the wreck itself destroying any evidence of how the rails were broken. They'll take a day to fix it. Maybe two. Can't imagine anyone guessing it was a Russian helicopter."

"I repeat. You're the best."

He wasn't sure what to say about the best sex of his life. Except it hadn't been the sex. Not *only* the sex. Curling up with her scattered every fantasy he'd ever built onto the wind like so much chaff.

"I'm jealous, by the way."

"Of what?" She had no competition in his head, not even from his very best memories.

"You didn't swear once last night."

"And?" He turned to look at her and saw her smile in his night vision.

"You swore when you missed that rail. I guess you cared more about that rail than me." She eased to a low hover by the team; they were still working hard.

This time it was his turn to laugh. He'd never cared for anything in his life as much as he cared for Sharelle Vargas.

THEIR FIRST REFUELING STOP, HUNDREDS OF KILOMETERS TO THE west, lay far out into an empty field where no one would look for them.

The Delta team had needed nine minutes to complete the task that should have taken another twenty. They'd have beaten the train, but not by enough. Taking out the section of rail had been a good call.

Sharelle chose a clearing in the taiga forest barely bigger than their three helos together. Before she thought to react, the Delta operators had swarmed the Droid Boys' FARP helicopter. Inside of thirty seconds, they had hoses run out to both her and Trisha's birds.

Troy, herself, and she was pleased to see even Trisha, were moving like geriatrics as they climbed out of their helos and met in the middle of the clearing.

"I'm going to shoot the next Russian seat designer I meet." Trisha began doing backbends to loosen up.

"No. I have a better idea," Rafe groaned as he attempted to emulate Trisha's lithe movement.

"Make him sit in his own chair for long flights—" Julian

simply lay on the thick grass.

"—every day for the rest of his life." Troy finished for them, doing his own stretches.

"Now don't you be starting in with the likes of those two," Trisha waved a hand at the Droid Boys. "Or—"

"—we'll have to hurt you so bad!" Sharelle agreed.

"I dunno," Rafe said. "Think we can take 'em?"

Julian shook his head after an unusually long moment's contemplation. "No, I've heard that even Beale can't beat O'Malley in hand-to-hand combat training."

Everyone turned to look at Trisha, who merely smiled.

Troy, being a smart man, didn't say a word.

Delta had them refueled long before Sharelle's body was ready. One of the women came over to them. Thick brunette hair ran long to her shoulders, her complexion somewhere past well-tanned with mostly native American features. She stood only a few inches taller than Trisha. It was hard to imagine that she'd made it into Delta. Of course, it was hard to believe that Trisha was a tougher fighter than Colonel Emily Beale.

"Fuel consumption is three percent better than projected. We're ready." And she turned for Trisha's Helix.

The rest of them returned to their torture seats.

Troy stopped halfway, then trotted after the Delta operator.

Sharelle paused to listen.

"Excuse me." Polite even in the middle of a mission.

The woman turned to look at him.

"Induction loop?"

She nodded.

"Heat or electro-magnetic?"

"Door Number Two."

"With a limiter?"

She smiled.

"Got it, thanks." And Troy came trotting toward her.

"What was that?" Sharelle asked him.

"I'll explain once we're aloft."

"Someone is being very smart," Troy said once they were aloft again and flying deeper into Russia. "I definitely want to meet whoever thought up the devices Delta Force is planting."

Sharelle barely resisted asking how such a smart man could consider leaving the Night Stalkers for a *farm*. She had less than no interest in being a farmer's wife.

Wife? Her voice practically shouted.

What did you think for the rest of my life meant? Sharelle was less certain about her own reply than she felt.

"What are they doing?" Because she definitely needed a distraction.

"Induction coils."

"I heard that, but I don't get what they're doing with them."

"Okay," Troy held out his hands far enough apart that one of them showed up at the edge of her night vision and she glanced down to see what he was doing. "A section of track, with four equal cuts." He made a chopping motion at either end, and then again at one-third and two-thirds as if cutting up three equal sections.

She turned her attention back to her flying. "Four cuts, three sections. Got it."

"You can ignore the outer two sections. They're cutting those and filling in the gaps with nonconducting materials, in other words not more steel or iron, because they need them to be electrically isolated from the rest of the rail."

"Uh-huh." Though she still didn't understand why.

"It's the center section that's important. They wire together one end turning the two tracks of the middle section into a big electrical loop. Got it?"

"A giant U-shaped conductor. Two isolated lengths of track and a wire at one end."

"Right," Troy's voice was climbing with excitement, more and more with each step of the process. "At the other end of the big loop, they buried those devices they brought with them, then connected them to both of the other ends. The ones at the top of the loop."

"Now you have a big circuit. But what does it do?"

"You shove a piece of steel through a wire loop and you get an electro-magnetic field, right? High school physics demonstration."

"Sure. And some day we get Mag-Lev trains and efficient rocket ship launches from that same idea." Sharelle remembered that much.

"Right. Now, they've created a big loop and—"

"They shove a train past it." Sharelle could almost see what it was doing, but the details didn't fit together yet.

"And a train engine is a massive chunk of steel. It's going to create a big electro-magnetic field as it rushes over that induction loop of railroad track. They store that energy, then release it in pulses at every freight car behind it."

"But why? And why did you ask *heat or electro-magnetic?*"

Troy clapped his hands together in his excitement.

Sharelle used that as a reminder that she was flying a mere ten meters clear of the forest trees and kept her attention ahead instead of focused on the mental images Troy was painting.

"The train engine creates this big charge that's stored, now there are two things you can do with it as the rest of the train passes by—say a train filled with North Korean ammunition and rockets. You can use it in turn to induce high temperatures in anything that comes after it—heat."

"But if you induce heat, you'll make the ammunition explode. It's not much more effective than the piece of track you shot out."

"Or, they induce an electro-magnetic pulse which—"

"Oh my God. Which fries any electronics in the rest of the train cars."

Troy laughed again. "Which means that when the weapons arrive at the front line, anything with electronics will be worthless. And the Russians will become furious with the North Koreans for supplying defective arms."

Sharelle saw it. "They'd never think to look at a lonely stretch of track in Eastern Siberia as the cause of those failures."

"Neat as can be. And the whole system will recharge itself with the next train to come along."

"No, wait. What about a passenger train? It's going to charge up the device, but then it will release and kill all of the passengers' phones and computers. They'll know exactly where to look for the problem."

"That's why I asked the last question. There's a threshold limiter. A passenger train car weighs only *five* more tons if you load it with people and luggage. A freight train that's empty weighs even less. But a loaded one can carry an extra *hundred* tons. The device senses the bigger induction footprint of a loaded freight car and *Zap!*"

Sharelle had no problem picturing the look on everyone's faces when load after load of North Korean weapons failed at the Russian-Ukrainian front line. It would be...probably about how her face looked when she'd found Colonel Beale sitting in her cockpit for that first flight. A contortion of fury and injustice desperately seeking somewhere to lash out. Except the Russians would know exactly where to do it. The Russians would take North Korea to task in the worst ways.

"That's why we have to sabotage *both* legs of the railroad. The Russian line, and the Russian end of the line through China. We don't know which route they're using when, but the

SecDef didn't want to place a sabotage device on Chinese sovereign soil."

"Because they'd be a much more dangerous opponent than Russia is already proving they aren't." Sharelle saw it. Both convoluted and elegant.

Now if only you could find that kind of solution for you and the luscious Captain Ryland.

The problem is, Troy is the thinker. Not me.

Her inner voice didn't have a good answer to that.

20

———

THE SECOND DEVICE PLACEMENT, BETWEEN ZABAYKALSK AT THE northern Chinese border and Chita where the Chinese Eastern Railway met the Trans-Siberian, proved to be much less trouble but many times more harrowing than the first.

No surprise trains.

But also no tree cover. The southern taiga forest had bled out to harsh steppe in the area, which had felt terribly exposed.

For forty minutes, during which the Alligator's dash clock had moved so slowly that Troy was certain from minute to minute that it had broken, they operated undisturbed.

At least undisturbed by outside influences.

Troy had been trying to ignore a logistics itch.

Everyone was so relieved to be done with the two emplacements and finally turning east that he didn't want to bring up the problem.

But that itch was growing. He hadn't approached Sharelle or Trisha with it yet as he wanted to be sure.

Be good if it was localized.

Their next refueling was also their overnight stop. Or rather over-day.

They were close to the equinox; day and night were both twelve hours long. There had been endless planning debates about the risks of simply flying straight through the day and getting out of Russia, versus laying over through the day and departing at night.

A twelve-hour night mostly spent aloft was one thing, crossing it all in broad daylight when they'd be visible to both people and satellites was another. Compounded with that, pilot fatigue had been the final deciding factor.

The route planners back at Henderson's had located a clearing in the trackless reaches of the southern taiga forest, a spot two thousand kilometers and nine hours' flight time from safety. The first order of business on landing was covering the three birds with camouflage nets. The next, loading the fuel from the FARP into the other two helos. By the time they were done, it was full sunrise and they were all careful to remain under the edges of the joined nets.

This time it was one of the male Delta operators who came over to meet them, accompanied by a tall and slender blonde.

"Do they both look worried?" Sharelle leaned close to ask as they approached. "I don't like the idea of a Delta operator looking worried."

Neither did Troy—and they did.

"Hi, I'm Richie. This is Melissa. Have you guys done any calcs lately?" He plunged in before he or Sharelle managed to introduce themselves.

"Why? What's up?" Sharelle asked.

"He has," Melissa pointed at Troy.

He nodded, wishing his look hadn't been quite so transparent. "I wanted to get the refueling numbers before I alarmed anyone."

"You're alarming me plenty," Trisha spoke up, who had wandered close enough with the other pilots to overhear.

"Being alarmed two thousand klicks into Russia isn't my idea of a good time."

Richie and Melissa didn't look any more interested in speaking than Troy felt.

He wanted to sit or even lie down. Except the grass was dusted with an overnight frost that hadn't yet melted away. The sun would clear the trees soon and melt the frost, at least outside the shading of the camo nets. Today's predicted high was a roaring four degrees above freezing. And they couldn't risk running even one helo's engines for heat.

Especially not now.

"There's a wind coming out of the east. It's common here this time of year, but it shouldn't be picking up to more than a breeze for another few weeks."

They all looked aloft. It was an instinctive part of all their training. From a hiding place, like this clearing deep in the taiga forest trees, look to nature for what was happening out in the wider world. While camo nets were hard to see into, they weren't hard to see out of.

The first sunlight skimmed along the high branches of spruce and larch. A few birch trees with startlingly white bark pushed their leaves as high. The branches swayed in the breeze. Not only the smaller branches, the whole trees were swaying.

"Beaufort Five," Richie observed. "Climate change is bringing it earlier than anyone anticipated."

"That's twenty miles an hour." Troy tried to convince himself it was only a Four with no luck. "That's a thirty-klick headwind. In eleven hours' flight time from our turn around point, that's a deficit of over three hundred kilometers. At least an additional hour of flight time to cover that additional distance, two if it keeps building. We were already marginal fuel for this mission—planned ten percent reserve for that last leg. It just got a whole lot worse."

"Gonna ease off later?" Rafe sounded serious for once and Julian offered no quick comeback.

Troy let his silence answer that and no one argued with him.

Sharelle stared up at the trees again. "Well...shit."

———

"C'mon, Trisha. You're the one who's supposed to be the brilliant out-of-the-box thinker." Sharelle really hoped she could think them out of this one.

"Me? I'm just the pain in everyone's ass." She rubbed her butt. "Including my own."

They were on patrol. Everyone had moved into the cargo bay of Trisha's Helix helicopter to conserve heat. At first Delta had offered to handle the patrols so that the pilots could sleep, but no one was sleeping on the cold steel, even with the sleeping bags and camping pads they'd brought with them.

An icebox packed to the limits with nerves.

Besides, the longer she sat there beside Troy, the worse the realization of his departure became. It felt as if he'd be gone the minute this mission ended, not three months from now.

She'd insisted on taking one of the patrols and didn't know whether to be pleased or upset when Trisha called dibs on going with her before Troy did. They walked slow circles under the outer edge of the camo nets, not much warmed by the sun but better than squatting inside the steel can of the Helix.

They made a full lap before Trisha spoke again, not as if there was anything to see. This part of the forest grew thick. Sharelle could see three-trees-deep into the woods, but no more. After the region's brief summer, the undergrowth grew too thick for anything except animals to penetrate.

Keep an eye out for wolves, the prior patrol of two of the Deltas had warned them. Sharelle didn't know if they were being practical or spooky. Either way, she carried her PB suppressed sidearm, an SR-2 Udav as a backup piece, and a PP-2000 submachine gun hung across her chest. Each of them carried some variation of the same. Their weapons alone, the newest and best, would prove their superior status if they met with any Russian military.

They were also backed up by a team of Delta Force operators, which Sharelle knew could take on any force short of, well, an utter disaster. Part of the gamble of serving in Special Operations Forces.

"Well, there was this mission," Trisha finally spoke up. "Place unmentionable, of course. But it was a mostly deserted airfield. We snuck in and tapped a fuel truck in the middle of the night. Meter wasn't working, so I doubt if they ever noticed."

"You're saying we should fly into a Russian airport in Russian military helicopters and steal fuel."

"You got a better idea, Ms. Smarty Pants?"

Sharelle didn't. At the moment, all she felt was brain-dead.

Does that make your pants smarter than you?

At the moment? Yep.

They were made in Russia.

Sadder but still true, she answered.

"Gotten any smarter on any other fronts?"

"Are you always this subtle?"

Trisha grinned, "That's as subtle as I get. Me and the 82nd Airborne. We're both real subtle-like."

All the wishing in the world wouldn't give Sharelle a different answer. "No. I don't know what to do about Troy. Three years we've served together, nothing going on. Only it's been going on for *him* the whole time, though he never got around to telling me. Now it feels as if it has all caught up with me too. It's been at least a year, maybe two since the last time I did more than look at a man."

"Had it bad and didn't know it, huh?"

"That's about the size of it."

"I'm gonna steal your earlier line: Well, shit!"

"Thanks. That's super helpful, Trisha."

Trisha did a shoulder bump as they circled behind the Alligator and turned for the refueling Kamov. Except due to their height difference, it was more of a shoulder-biceps bump.

"Hey!" The word was forced out of Sharelle.

"What? Can't take the heat, girl? Get a grip, you're a Night Stalker."

"No, a different *Hey!* I need Troy."

"Well, duh!"

"No. Now!" Sharelle ducked under the Alligator's tail section and raced over to Trisha's helo.

"Don't worry about me," Trisha called after her. "I'm fine patrolling against the wild wolves of Siberia all on my lonesome."

Sharelle stopped, turned to Trisha, turned back to the helo; her mind raced, too busy to make any decision about what her body ought to do.

"Oh, brother." Trisha strode over, hooked her arm through Sharelle's, and dragged her over to the helo everyone else was pretending to sleep in.

When Sharelle hesitated, Trisha shoved her aside and yanked open the cargo-bay door herself.

"Captain Troy Ryland. Front and center, soldier. And I need someone to join me on patrol while they do whatever they do."

"No. Wait! Not that."

Troy stumbled out, bleary eyed, as if he'd actually managed to fall asleep.

"You don't want to ravage his body?" Trisha squinted up at her.

"That's right up there with when did you stop being a serial killer," Sharelle protested. "I need to talk to both of you."

"We've got the patrol," the biggest Delta operator other than Billy said as he stepped out, not bothering to zip his jacket against the chill air. He looked like the stereotype of a clean-cut, blond, farm boy. But he was Delta, which meant he was also a hundred percent lethal. "Who knows what you eggheads are up to. C'mon, babe."

A statuesque blonde, though not the one Troy had spoken to before, stepped out. She looked as robust and excessively healthy as the farm boy did. Chad and...Tanya she finally remembered. They both had Vintorez sniper rifles slung over their shoulders. They'd all be far safer with the two of them on patrol than her and Trisha bumbling about.

She turned to Troy as soon as they were out of earshot. "Just warning you, do *not* ever try using *babe* on me."

"Okay." And there was Troy. Not teasing her about it. Not saying, *Whatever you say... babe.* Instead he simply cataloged her instruction and stored it away in that amazing brain of his.

"You called us all out here for that?" Rafe and Julian, as well as all the other Delta had come out to see what was going on.

"No. And you be quiet," she aimed a finger point blank at Julian's nose.

He held up both hands in surrender. "Sure. Not a word... Babe."

Trisha shoved him back into the helicopter hard enough to crash onto the cargo deck, slammed the door in his face, and leaned on the outer handle so that he couldn't reopen it.

She offered Trisha a nod of thanks.

"Anytime, girlfriend."

Which, much to her surprise, Sharelle rather liked the sound of. Not her inner voice at all—which was the only girlfriend she hadn't pissed off in the past. It was far easier to imagine being friends with Trisha than with the austere Colonel Emily Beale. Except, Sharelle could almost imagine that as well.

"So speak already," Trisha prompted her as Julian opened the copilot's door up forward and dropped down to the ground to rejoin them.

"At what point can all of the fuel on the Droid Boys' helo be loaded into our two birds?"

"Planning on leaving us behind?"

This time Rafe was the one to elbow jab Julian into silence.

Richie and Troy stared at each other in silence for most of a minute.

"Is it enough?" Richie finally asked.

"I think...yes?"

Sharelle wished Troy sounded a little more certain.

"What am I missing?" Rafe whispered to Julian, who shrugged.

Trisha was smiling. "We need a lake. A nice, deep lake."

21

———

"Why is that so sexy?"

"Isn't it amazing to watch?" Melissa leaned on the inside of the Helix's hull beside Sharelle.

"I meant to ask that with my inside voice."

"Doesn't change the reality, does it?"

It didn't. Sharelle kept watching Troy and Richie. They were hunched over a Chinese Huawei tablet computer, a common import into Russia, trying to convince it to be useful.

Trisha had finally authorized a directed squirt transmission. They packed all of their questions into a twenty-millisecond encrypted burst transmission, very carefully directed at an NRO satellite that shouldn't be near any Russian satellite at the moment of transmission.

Twenty minutes later, Beale had flashed back the answers.

The third-priority target of the Trans-Siberian Highway, the third red *X* the SecDef had discussed during the pre-mission briefing, was deemed nonessential. If it became necessary, a separate team could infiltrate a few kilometers north of Vladivostok and bury an induction trap in the road. At this time, it was believed that all North Korean arms shipments moved by train.

Someone had scoured their fuel, flight, and wind data—and confirmed their conclusions.

The new wind predictions were noted, less than encouraging, but looked workable.

Now the two of them were debating the best lakes for sinking unwanted helicopters. Beale had sent them bathymetry as well as inflow analyses for reasons Sharelle didn't try to follow.

"They are a little bit intense, aren't they?" Melissa asked in a tone of such massive understatement that Sharelle's own mouth went dry.

"For all they know, the world might have stopped spinning in the hour since Beale dumped that data down to them. Maybe that's the sexy part," Sharelle tipped her head, trying to see past that. "Is Richie just as focused when you're alone? No. Sorry. I didn't ask that."

"Is Troy?"

He was. Sharelle only had that one night to judge by, but the intensity of his focus had made her miss her own internal world tilting on its axis.

Sharelle glanced around the cargo bay. Their body heat and the little bit of the sun's that filtered through the netting had raised the temperature high enough that her breath no longer made vapor clouds. And as the air warmed, it began carrying the odor of spec ops warriors who'd hustled until they sweat and had been too long between showers.

Over ten square meters, a hundred square feet, didn't mean that there was enough room for all of them to lie down at once. There were only ten of them, plus the two out on patrol, but there was also the third induction unit, Delta's tools, the survival packs they'd all need if they were unexpectedly stranded in Russia and had to find a way to survive until they were exfiltrated.

And the low ceiling, which she could touch easily while sitting, added to the troll's cave dwelling feel. It was actually a relief to go out on patrol. Though right now it was the Delta leaders, Kyle and Carla's turn to tramp about the circle under the netting's edge.

"We need to shift some gear," Troy announced as if he'd been talking all along and not spent the last hour in a whispered huddle with Richie.

Welders, pry bars, shovels already battered by digging the railbed rocks, and the third induction unit were all moved into Rafe and Julian's Helix. They set up a human chain and had soon shifted across everything they could. A lighter payload in Trisha's Helix meant that they could carry more fuel and stretch the flight farther.

That done, everyone sort of ground to a halt.

She'd gravitated to their own helo, the Ka-52 Alligator.

Troy stood next to her.

"Now what?"

He pointed up at the sun, hanging due south in the sky. "Now we wait for sunset."

Only midday? "Busy morning."

"Quiet afternoon." Troy prompted. "Hopefully."

So far all they'd heard here in the forest was birdsong. The nearest sign of human activity in any direction lay over seventy kilometers away, and that had been a logging road still twenty kilometers from the nearest settlement. A lone red fox had been spotted trotting through the clearing out beyond the camouflage nets. It had paused directly downwind to inspect their scents on the air before moving on. Billy had spotted it and said it looked healthy and decently fed—ready for the hard winter to come.

She hoped that meant that any grey wolves would feel much the same, well sated.

In fact...

Trisha and Billy passed close by; they were now the ones on the circling patrol. Billy's attention remained out to the perimeter though, being Delta, he probably knew exactly where they stood. And she'd bet that they'd trigger some weird secret extra-sensory perception if they moved unexpectedly.

Trisha, however, watched them.

Sharelle kept her hand by her side as she pointed toward the forest.

Trisha grinned and made an *only a little way* gesture with her thumb and forefinger.

"I saw that," Troy whispered as he took her hand. As soon as Billy and Trisha moved out of sight, he led her to where the camo net had been extended to reach the verge of the trees in case they needed to make good an escape on foot.

The forest here was mostly larch trees. They didn't grow past twenty-five meters high or a meter across. They also didn't grow in dense forest, even here in the southernmost reaches of the taiga.

Worse, their branches started well above their heads without drooping down, making visibility from the helicopters all too easy. The undergrowth was mostly waist high but leaned heavily toward impenetrable. Not that it was so thick, but everything moved much more slowly in the taiga than in the forests of Kentucky. A downed tree might take fifty years to rot rather than five. The tangle of deadwood scattered over the rough ground underfoot, hidden by the thick undergrowth...

Troy picked up some small animal trail hardly worth the name and followed it.

Sharelle was beginning to feel this was an embarrassing waste of time that everyone on the team would be laughing at. Well, perhaps not Trisha. The regiment's chaos demon had a surprisingly romantic heart. Sharelle wondered if that bothered her...or if she was even aware of it. Was it the sort of thing she could ask? If—

If she hadn't still held Troy's hand, she'd have fallen on her face as the trail, such as it was, dipped downward. Once she had her balance again, she looked around.

They were in a wide bowl, several meters deep—enough to hide their location from the helos. But that wasn't the wonder of the place.

It looked as if some giant had scooped out the hollow with a single swipe of his hand. The larches and their thin branches perched all around the depression were enough to provide cover against observation from above. One of the few deciduous conifers, they hadn't started dropping their needles yet, but they had turned a lovely golden hue. That warm amber color stood out against the stark blue sky all the more vividly for having spent the morning beneath the gray-green camo nets.

"A golden canopy." The scent of drying pine but backed against the lush richness of sun-warmed late summer soil.

"A canopy above where I plan to bed you."

Sharelle looked down at the ground. There hadn't been time or opportunity to grab a sleeping bag, but the protected depression was carpeted with lush grass. It also blocked the cool wind and seemed to concentrate the sunlight, the first time she'd felt any sense of warmth since they landed here.

Then she looked at Troy's face and felt the warmth turning to heat. Though they still held hands and had come to the woods expressly to have sex, he waited. He gave her time to think when he should be jumping her bones. And though they now stood face-to-face, a bare half step apart, still he didn't act.

"What?"

"How am I supposed to..." he shrugged and brushed the

fingers of his free hand along her cheek. "I can't walk away from this, from you, but…"

She silenced him with a finger on his lips.

"But—"

"No. Don't think about that. There must be a solution, we just haven't seen it yet."

"I've thought of almost nothing else for a long, long time. If there was a solution, I'd have seen it by now."

That *long, long time* almost took her knees out from under her. In a funny way, the few days since that first kiss in the tack room on Henderson's Ranch made this the longest relationship she'd ever been in. It had somehow made the last three years of flying together connect into a single cohesive piece. In a strange way, everything behind them made sense.

"We'll let the future figure that out. Let's focus on the now."

By his slow smile, he liked that idea.

Unlike their night aboard the *Peleliu,* she didn't feel the need to take control when he guided her to him by the lightest pressure of his fingertips brushing her cheeks. He pulled her past a kiss and into an embrace that continued to grow tighter and tighter until she almost laughed.

"You trying to make our bodies merge into one?" Not that she was complaining. The firmer his hold, the more they came together, the more complete she felt.

She wanted to tug off their heavy jackets and Russian flightsuits until they were skin to skin…

Yet…

Troy's embrace made her feel as if she must be the most desirable woman in the world. Not the overachiever dusting everyone who couldn't keep up. Held, cherished, wanted. A heady mixture that…went straight to her head.

When he shifted away until a breath might slip between them, she still felt loathe to act. The ticking of the large-toothed zipper of her jacket sounded louder in her ears than any bird call. It equaled the roar of a cataract though he did it so slowly she felt each individual tooth releasing, echoing into her breastbone and rippling down her body.

When he did the same with the zipper on her flightsuit, exposing her inch by lazy inch, it felt as if she were being freed from her past, the worries of the mission, and the fears of the uncertain future.

He exposed far more than her skin when he eased her clothes off her shoulders.

"You should always be in the sunshine," Troy's voice brushed against her like a whisper.

An odd thing to tell a Night Stalker.

It was good her inner voice spoke the thought because she was already beyond speech.

Where his glance led, his fingers and soon his mouth followed. He didn't tease or entice. Again it felt as if he studied her, memorizing every shape, every reaction. As if she was worthy of such attention.

He circled inch by inch until he stood behind her as he had that first time in her cabin aboard ship. Except this time she stood naked from the waist up, with the hot sun heating her front and Troy's warm chest heating her back. He slid his hands around her, cupping, cradling, cherishing.

All she managed was to close her eyes against the bright sun and tip her head to lay against his shoulder. With one hand caressing her breasts and the other sliding down between her legs, Troy carried her upward. Pulse roaring, breath a gasping afterthought, it wasn't his hands that tipped her over the edge. It was the lightest nip of his teeth on her earlobe and the words he whispered that sent her plunging off the deep end.

"Fly for me, my love."

———

Troy held Sharelle close as they lay curled up together on their spread jackets. This was how he wanted her, every time: sighing, laughing, groaning, shuddering with need and again with release. He wanted her now more than he wanted to fly.

But the westering sun said their time here had ended.

She'd given as much as she'd taken. Riding him deep when he was able, touching him with smooth palms while their bodies recovered. Sometimes talking of nothing important, a remembered flight or a funny story, sometimes just listening to the sounds of the forest.

This moment, curled up together in utter peace and contentment was a wholly new experience for him. That both of their bodies were momentarily spent wasn't the difference. He'd had a few very active sexual partners in the past. And when finally worn down, he knew enough to understand that women liked to be held afterward. Something he'd never found reason to be averse to.

But with Sharelle resting in his arms...

"Penny for your thoughts," she whispered.

"That won't even buy a licorice whip. Besides, that's far too high a price for any thought I'll achieve—ever. But..." he caressed the side of her breast, "...this..."

She hummed happily. It was almost a purr. He felt it thrumming through her spine against his breastbone. The woman's body was going to kill him. Heck of a— No, *hell* of a way to go.

"You're thinking awfully deep thoughts back there."

He'd been thinking many thoughts—past and future. But Sharelle had commanded him to be in the now. "I was trying to think if I've ever been happier than in the simple act of holding you close."

"After all the great sex."

"That's just the mission bonus." He pulled her more tightly

against him. "*This* is the core mission element." Which sounded stupid now that he'd said it out loud.

Sharelle went very still before turning slowly in his arms until they lay face-to-face and she hooked a leg over his hips.

"Sorry. I could probably find a less romantic way to say that, but I—"

She kissed him...very slowly...and very thoroughly, before whispering, "You can talk to me that way any time you want to melt my heart. Most men, past men, see the body. Oh, they may like me and we'd have fun—"

"I hate them already."

Her lips brushed against his nose in thanks. "But none of them see me as what I am first and foremost, except you."

"A pilot."

"Exactly."

"But you're wrong."

She pulled back a little and her expression shifted from goofy to glare. "I think I know who I am."

"Sharelle Vargas, you're the best damn pilot I've ever met. But you're still wrong." She didn't react to his curse, so he figured he'd better finish the thought. "You're an even more amazing woman."

That stopped her. She checked in with her inner voice, but it had no comment.

She knew she had the body, enough men had been gobsmacked by it to make that clear. But she'd always figured she was about as unfeminine as could be. She worked hard and she played hard. It had made her a serious contender on the soccer field in school and as a Night Stalker. She'd rather be learning about upgrading her DAP's Hydra 70 missiles into precision-guided AGR-20s than anything women were supposed to care about.

Like no good Southern girl, scrambling an egg marked the pinnacle of her culinary skills. She ate base food or flew well clear of the kitchen at home, typically with Daddy, while Mama and Baby Bother managed to put something together. None of them were brilliant in the kitchen, but she was a certified disaster. The last time she'd worn a dress outside of a wedding, she'd probably been about four. And most of the weddings she attended were military, so she'd worn her Army Green Service Uniform that permitted women to choose slacks over a skirt.

"No. I'm a disaster as a woman."

"Not by my or the Army's standards." And there it was. That simply, Troy forced her to reassess. She was an *Army* woman.

Never thought of it that way, did we, girlfriend?

She managed no more than a *Huh!* She hadn't.

Lying naked with her lover, deep in Russian territory, she felt more herself, more of a woman, more *female,* than she'd ever felt before. As if she finally made sense as a *person*—as well as a woman in a Spec Ops man's world.

"Well, shit."

"What?" Troy asked.

"If I'm such an amazing woman—"

"—and pilot—" he teased.

"—and pilot, this should be a snap."

"This?"

She'd meant the future: this mission, their relationship.

But *this* also included the warm man in her embrace beneath the shining afternoon sun.

That she absolutely knew what to do with.

22

———

THEY CLEARED THE NETS OFF THE HELOS AT DUSK AND WERE aloft at full dark. Four and a half hours and eight hundred kilometers later, they set down on the shore of the Bureyskoye Reservoir at straight-up midnight.

On the far side of the sprawling fifty-kilometer-long lake stood the Bureya Dam and hydroelectric plant credited with electrifying much of Eastern Siberia. A tiny service town of Talakan, under five thousand people, huddled by the fifty-story-tall structure.

With Richie's help, Troy had chosen an arm of the reservoir that veered north from the general east-west line of the lake because it was well shielded by hills. They landed on a small rocky beach, one of their few choices. In most places the forest ran straight into the water where it had been drowned as the reservoir filled fifteen years ago.

They ran the FARP fuel bladder dry, rolling it tightly to squeeze out every liter. Then they pumped most of what remained into the tanks of Rafe and Julian's Helix.

"You've now got under ten minutes of fuel," Troy calculated.

"Perfect!" Rafe got in the first word this time.

"You're right. Besides, I'd enjoy a bath in ass-freezing water after these big flights." Julian turned for the cockpit.

"No! You aren't going." Rafe grabbed his arm and sounded dead serious for once.

"You're just gonna screw it up. Everybody knows that, right? Short guys like you always do. Gotta be me." Julian had missed that, for once, Rafe wasn't joking.

Close behind him, he heard Sharelle whisper, "This is why you get the big bucks and the silver oak leaf."

Then Lieutenant Colonel Trisha O'Malley stumbled forward as if she'd been shoved from behind. No question who had earned the scowl she sent back over her shoulder.

Rafe and Julian were talking at the same time. No sense of humor. No more witty comebacks. They were both earnestly insisting that they were ready to fly the disposal of their Helix into a frigid lake—solo.

No matter how it was done, it would be incredibly dangerous.

Fly out into the middle of the reservoir where the waters were deep but where the feeding rivers would still provide enough silt to cover it quickly once it sank to the bottom.

Land on the water, which most helicopters, including the Helix, were *not* designed to do. Actually, some Helix helos had emergency inflatable buoys mounted to either side of the fuselage for exactly that purpose—but this wasn't one of them.

Once on the water but before they sank, the pilot would have to kill the engines, then dive clear, even if the rotor hadn't fully stopped. That meant getting at least twenty meters away before the helo tipped and the blades touched the water. Then the other Helix would come in low and winch the pilot aboard.

"You want me to risk two pilots on a one-man job?" Trisha started. "I—"

"No!" Troy cut her off. "It has to be one man only."

Trisha turned to face him with her fists on her hips. "And

why is that, *Captain?*" She'd already made a decision and was pissed at being cut off. Except that didn't match her expression, which he couldn't read at all. She looked as if she was...hiding a smile? How much trouble did it imply when PITA O'Malley smiled? Easy answer—

"Now you've done it," Sharelle whispered from behind him, reaching the same assessment. Then she gave him enough of a shove that he had to take a step forward.

"Well?"

Troy focused on the technical issue at hand. "With a solo pilot, they can control the final direction the Helix tips, away from the direction they'd need to swim to get clear. With two pilots, it's fifty-fifty who has to race clear of the rotor blades before it goes over."

Trisha grinned outright, which was even weirder. "So how do *I* decide?"

Troy glanced over at Julian and Rafe, both exceptional pilots, both up on their toes and ready to go. He dug in his pocket and fished out a five ruble coin, "Call it."

They both called *heads.*

Troy flipped it in the air, "Heads is tall, tails is short."

———

JULIAN LOST THE TOSS. HE TRIED ARGUING OVER WHICH WAS THE head of a Russian coin: one side had the value and the other the two-headed eagle emblem of the Russian Federation. "The eagle had *two* heads. That must be the head."

Sharelle pulled a coin out of her own pocket and decided that he had a point, but Troy overruled such quibbles.

Then Julian started mother-henning Rafe. "Go over the timing again. Empty your pockets. Nothing heavy. You can't use a lifejacket in case you need to dive, but you don't want to sink either."

To Sharelle's surprise, Rafe didn't offer a word of complaint. Repeating, nodding, reviewing, whatever Julian demanded. Except it wasn't so surprising. Rafe and Julian had flown together for years before she and Troy met. But she easily imagined Troy doing the same thing, double-checking everything to make sure she came out safely.

It would be...nice.

Lame-o! You're not fooling me, girlfriend. You'd love it! Someone showing they cared that much about you.

You ever get tired of being right?

Her voice didn't answer.

Per the plan, Rafe didn't even start his engines until she and Troy had taken the Alligator aloft and done one more sweep of the area. No one on the lake tonight by visual or thermal imaging.

Trisha powered up her Helix next, and then finally Rafe. Sharelle saw their exhaust heat plumes in her infrared night vision.

Rafe didn't waste a second. As soon as he was up to temperature, he pulled aloft and headed for the center of the lake with his pilot's side door rolled open on its track and locked there.

Julian was hanging out the rear cargo door of Trisha's helo, already lowering the winch wire so they'd be ready to pluck Rafe out of the lake.

The easterly winds had built half-meter waves on the big lake. Rafe flew with his wheels a single meter above them. She and Trisha flew five rotors and slightly trailing to either side to not kick any air turbulence toward him.

To avoid creating any oil slick attracting future attention, Rafe paused far out over the lake. For three interminable minutes, he hovered with his wheels in the water.

Then she saw the temperature drop as one of the engines

sputtered before flaming out due to lack of fuel. The other engine would barely have fumes.

Rafe settled onto the water.

The Ka-27 Helix balanced there, momentarily afloat and kept level by the spinning rotors.

Then Rafe must have lifted the covers and thrown both Engine Fire Extinguishers. Both engine exhaust ports dimmed rapidly in her vision as the burning fuel was cut off and halon flooded into them. The rotors barely slowed. No longer driven, they still spun easily.

Rafe held it steadily upright, allowing them to slow as much as possible, then the Helix tipped to port.

Several things happened simultaneously.

As the helo tipped to the left, the right door rolled upward. Rather than being able to dive out the door and getting a good start away, Rafe waited a second too long and had to struggle over the lower sill. He flopped into the water with all the gracefulness of an albatross.

He'd barely started to swim when the blades struck the water on the far side. It was the crucial moment and Sharelle couldn't manage a breath.

The outer tips of the rotor blades would still be spinning at nearly the speed of sound—fast enough to span three end-to-end soccer fields every second. The helicopter might weigh seven tons but the rotor blades were one and a half tons of that.

In a crash, there was no predicting how it would fail.

The briefers at Groom Lake hadn't had a good answer to Troy and Richie's question on that point. Too little was known of Russian rotor blade construction—and destruction.

If everything simply broke off, it would fling parts far and wide, the reason they'd opted to have Rafe tip the helo away from his exit. And the reason they were holding well back and to the sides from his landing point.

But if the blades held, everything would depend on how

they caught the water. And the fact that they were two disks of three blades spinning in opposite directions made the scenario all the more complex.

Because of the water temperature, it had been decided that exiting the helo fast, rather than riding it partway down in the relative safety of the cabin and then swimming for the surface, was the safer option.

Sharelle prayed and watched.

Rafe had swum perhaps five meters out from under the fifteen-meter radius of the rotor disk when the blades hit the water. Swimming in a flightsuit and boots, he didn't swim fast.

In the worst possible combination, the Ka-27 Helix did both failure scenarios. Meter-long chunks of helo blade were fired outward and upward in a spinning disk. The force of some blades snapping against the water and others not, caused the helo to clock around on the surface, swinging the heavy tail toward Rafe.

It looked as if he saw it coming and dove, but it was hard to tell in the momentary chaos and churned-up spray. Viewing it through night-vision goggles didn't help.

The one mercy was that helicopters died very fast in water, especially with the engines already shut down.

The instant that bits of rotor stopped raining from the sky, Trisha was racing her Helix forward.

Sharelle had to fight every instinct to do the same. With her DAP Hawk, she could cram a few people aboard in an emergency. The Ka-52 Alligator had two seats and no cargo bays—it was a dedicated gunship.

Julian dove out of the cargo bay before Trisha had even stopped, the momentum casting him forward in Rafe's direction.

"There!" Troy shouted. A body floated to the surface—face down.

Julian must have spotted it too and raced over. In seconds,

he reached his fellow pilot and dragged him face up. A fountain of water spewed from Rafe's mouth as he coughed and struggled.

In seconds, Trisha hovered close overhead with the winch cable dangling. Julian snapped it onto the lifting ring integral to Rafe's flight harness and she hauled him aloft.

"Does his leg look wrong?" Was it the night vision or should it really not bend that way.

"Let's hope that is the only thing that's broken," Troy confirmed.

She was glad that, at the moment, he was responsible for the flying. Her hands didn't shake, but they wanted to.

In under a minute, they had Julian inside the helo as well— and still Trisha didn't move. Thirty long seconds they both hovered over the center of the Bureyskoye Reservoir, then Trisha turned her helo nose-on to them before flicking on her cabin light.

Trisha made the hand sign of *Go! Fast!*—a forward slice of a flat hand and then a vertical double pump of her fist. They were still three hours inside Russia, hovering on marginal fuel, and another hour over the frigid North Pacific rife with Russian shipping to the *Peleliu*.

Sharelle didn't have time to acknowledge.

Troy simply slewed them around to the southeast and laid down the hammer.

She barely had time to look at the mass of bubbles that rose to the surface. The Delta team had rigged charges with pressure detonators to destroy the third induction unit and also blow holes in the empty tanks so that they'd flood rather than float. After next spring's melt out, any wreckage would be buried by layers of mud washed down the rivers into the still waters.

Of the Helix that had served them fuel for over three

thousand kilometers, no other sign remained on the surface of the Bureyskoye Reservoir.

————

THOUGH IT WAS AGAINST HER MORAL CODE, EMILY FIDGETED. And there wasn't room to pace in the Tac Room. Claudia and Lauren sat in the two control chairs. She'd never anticipated running these kinds of operations from here on the ranch. What had been a secretive intelligence gathering and security *recommendation* operations center was never designed for this—a full-on Night Stalkers' mission. Black-in-black, they couldn't outsource it to the main command center back in Fort Campbell.

She'd need to talk to Julia about expanding it to take up the rest of the loft over the tack room below.

Lauren's black Malinois, Rip, was invisible in the shadows beneath the desk. Rip, short for Rip Van Winkle, was never happier than asleep on the lumps of Lauren's feet.

That left her and Michael to stand in the narrow space between the chairs and the back wall. The four of them were the only ones authorized in the entry system. Anyone else, like Captain Sharelle Vargas, needed to be escorted—only after the room was scrubbed of any possible information. Even Mark had only crossed the threshold once, made a few suggestions, and never come up again. Somehow, he'd left behind the life that was threatening to consume her.

Since the action team had departed Attu Island, the others had rotated in and out of the room. Slept, gone for a walk...

Aside from rushing downstairs for a quick nature break, she hadn't left the room once since the team had lifted off the decks of the USS *Peleliu* thirty hours ago.

"Play it again." Emily was so exhausted she left the control desks to Claudia and Lauren.

Michael offered one of his trademark looks.

"Never mind. There won't be anything new."

But Lauren already had the satellite feed rolling.

From orbit, at night, there wasn't much to see. Infrared from the engine exhausts of the three helos constituted most of what there was to see. No running lights. No infrared marker beacons. No tracking signal.

Three helos, racing over the water. Two slowing to a halt, the third continuing a short way before coming to a halt. A sudden dimming of the third helo's exhaust that simply had to be the flaming out of the engines. Cooling rapidly toward darkness, their heat signatures disappeared abruptly —immersion.

Then one of the helos racing forward.

And it didn't move for ninety seconds.

Pilot recovery? Body recovery?

Either way, it was too long. They should have had him aboard in under thirty seconds.

And yet, they'd remained there for another sixty seconds past that. Lauren and Claudia had offered guesses—Michael had kept his silence—but no one could make sense of it.

After the achingly long minute and a half—she could feel every ounce of fuel being inhaled by the greedy engines—the two remaining helos turned abruptly for the distant coast, moving fast.

"I—"

Michael opened the door and gestured for Emily to step out.

She shook her head.

Michael reached out and gently took her arm. She didn't need to think to recognize the grip; Trisha O'Malley had taught it to her when they first met going through Airborne Assault School together. With the least pressure of his thumb, Michael could drop her to her knees and make her beg for release. Not that he would; she'd bet only unconscious habit had him grabbing her in the potentially most advantageous way.

She let him guide her out. He followed and closed the door behind them.

Emily blinked against the brightness. Fighting the general dimness of the old wood horse barn, the big eastern doors had been flung wide and the sunrise streamed in. Chelsea and her crew were going down the row, feeding the horses, preparing others for morning trail rides. Fresh hay on the air, soiled straw scooped up with multi-tined pitchforks and thunking into steel wheelbarrows.

"It's all so...normal."

Michael nodded, leading them out into the sun. Not far, as if he saw the bonds between her and the ongoing events in the Tac Room were strained to their limit. But far enough that they were clear of the ranch's morning routines.

She shivered against the cold air, a presage of the coming winter.

Michael handed her a jacket. Her own from the back of the Tac Room door. She pulled it on gratefully. For a while, they stood side by side, watching their cloudy breaths dissipate in the rising sun.

"You're trying to do what I couldn't," he broke the silence first.

"That's hard to imagine." Colonel Michael Gibson had been the most highly decorated soldier in Delta's history. Ten more years in the field than the majority of The Unit's operators. Eventually he'd taken command of the Special Forces Operational Detachment-Delta, SFOD-D, their official name.

A role that *hadn't* lasted.

"Oh."

He nodded without turning to her. "I never found a way to do this." He tipped his head toward the barn.

"To..." Emily knew what he meant, but couldn't shift it into words.

"To watch my people risk their lives, people I ordered into the field while I sat safely in some office. I talked to others about it."

"You *talked?*" Michael was the epitome of the silent warrior. The only people he really talked to were the almost-as-reticent Claudia and their son.

His slight smile acknowledged the tease, but no more than that. "It is a skill you must learn if you're going to survive as commander of the Night Stalkers."

"To be honest, I don't think I can do that."

"You have to." His voice brooked no argument. A simple flat statement more serious than any command.

"Why?"

"Because the Night Stalkers need you far more than Delta Force needed me. Combat is changing. The Unit will still carry out counter-terrorism missions with few changes in their tactics. But the shape of warfare is shifting rapidly. The Night Stalkers can either fall behind or find a new way to remain at the tip of the spear."

"Mark said something similar. So it's all up to me." That was an utterly ridiculous—

"Yes."

"Please tell me you're joking."

He turned to her. His long black hair going salt-and-pepper, his eyes still the sky-blue they'd always been. Too perceptive. Too clear a view of the world. She saw the pain of experience there.

"Colonel Emily Beale. You are the right woman, in the right place, and at the right time. You must find a way to accept that and move forward."

"And if I can't?" If commanding the regiment had seemed

monumental before, now it felt impossible. If she made the least misstep, the results could be catastrophic.

Had she just killed a pilot?

It didn't take much of a leap to picture the Night Stalkers Memorial Wall at Fort Campbell. All the way back to Chief Warrant 2 Bobby M. Crumley in July 1980. Would she be overseeing the addition of another name in the next few days? She already had enough friends' names on that wall, but she'd flown with them, been one of them. Now?

But if not her, then who would stand in her place? Mark was retired. Had he done so because he'd seen this next step coming and didn't want any part of it? She'd never thought to ask and now didn't want to know. But he'd been the natural leader, not her. She'd led her teams by setting the best possible example and others had simply followed.

If not her...

Trisha wasn't ready. Lola? Justin? Pete or Danielle?

And the mission wasn't even over yet. Exfiltration was typically the most dangerous phase of any operation. She hoped it didn't become more dangerous than it already had proven to be.

"I have to get back."

Michael nodded and turned to keep her company. A companion, but the regiment was hers to lead.

23

____

"Does this seem too easy?"

Sharelle groaned. "You had to ask that out loud, didn't you?"

"Hmm... You have a point." They'd kept a watch behind, but there was no sign of any alarm at the Bureyskoye Reservoir. They slid past Khabarovsk, well to the north of where they'd implanted the first device under the railroad. They were low enough that they didn't once pick up even a scattered signal from the airport there.

They went feet wet ninety minutes later after sliding down the same river valley that they'd followed inbound. The *Peleliu* lay two hundred and fifty kilometers away. In just over an hour he could climb out of this torture chamber of a seat. They'd slept two days ago and flown through two consecutive nights. That meant they'd only missed the one day of sleep, but it felt like a week since—

"Shit!"

"Report!" Sharelle snapped out, not even wasting time to comment on his expletive.

"That small boat ahead isn't a fishing trawler. They just scanned us with a high-power AESA radar." An active electronically scanned array at this distance meant they had a very clear image of their two helos.

"The second you detect anything more than a local transmission, jam them hard."

"Military helo flight," crackled over the VHF radio. "Turn about or be fired upon."

Troy flipped on the jammers so that they couldn't call in a report or call for help. "They think we've stolen a pair of military helos and are defecting to Japan with them."

"Suggestions?"

Troy only had one, and he didn't like it at all.

They were so low that they'd cracked the horizon line of sight a bare nine kilometers and a hundred and fifty seconds from the patrol boat. They'd been scanned hard at eight kilometers and were fast approaching four. At this range, it wasn't a question of whether the boat shot their helos, it was what weapon would they choose to do it with.

But he didn't have to answer Sharelle's question because the patrol boat answered it for them.

The attack radar lit up with an incoming track—something moving fast.

"Hold your fire! Hold your fire!" Troy shouted over the radio in Russian.

Too late remembering that he was already jamming their radio frequencies.

"It's a Grinch." A Russian SA-24 Igla-S surface-to-air missile with a reach of six kilometers at Mach 1.5. "Time to impact, eight seconds."

"Countermeasures."

He was already dumping flares and chaff. The moment he did, Sharelle turned hard behind the shield of them.

Trisha, who'd been trailing close behind, turned as if they were one bird, not two. Then, per prior plan, she dropped to wave-skimming altitude and peeled off to the south.

Sharelle stayed high enough to remain the target and purposely flew slower than the Helix, despite the Alligator being capable of flying a third faster. But the math was simple. Trisha's Helix had no offensive weapons aboard and ten personnel. The Alligator had the two of them and they were armed to the teeth.

"Give me a three-sixty spin," Troy called out.

Sharelle didn't ask or hesitate, spinning completely around the vertical axis while still hurrying away.

As the patrol boat came up on the forward radar, Troy set a target marker, then he launched a flight of ten S-8OFP missiles. They were the new high-explosive, fragmenting version, able to penetrate light armor—hopefully like a patrol boat.

The first Igla, fired by the boat, died against the first chaff screen as Sharelle completed her spin.

"Four more inbound. Seven seconds."

"Countermeasures," her voice remained dead calm.

Surviving a barrage of four Igla-S missiles was *not* a good bet. But under battle conditions, you didn't waste time on any *final* words.

He released the chaff and flares in a triple-layered wall as Sharelle opened the throttle wide and eased down within a half-meter of the ocean waves. There was no outracing an Igla, so she swung northwest, curving around the patrol boat. Hopefully it would keep any attention off Trisha's helo as it raced clear.

"In two, one..." He closed his eyes and looked down knowing Sharelle did the same to protect her vision.

He counted to four and looked up in time to see the results of his barrage striking the patrol boat. Good hits, the boat still showed painfully bright from the explosions. Then a secondary explosion proved that he'd hit a weapons store. It would be like a movie scene if he dared look—metal shredding in every direction and the boat already heading to the ocean's floor.

Instead he watched the Alligator's threat radar. Two missiles fired by the now-dead patrol boat died in turn against the chaff-and-flare shield he'd set up.

Two made it through.

Mere seconds out.

He fired another set of chaff and flares.

"Shock wave," he called out.

"Surface clutter," she answered.

By staying low they risked any shock wave from a nearby missile's explosion knocking them into the ocean. But staying low also might confuse the missile's radar with all of the confusing noise off the ocean waves, hiding them in the clutter of multiple reflections of the missile's targeting systems.

Another missile died.

But one made it through.

A final blast of flares—

"Going to be clos—"

He never had a chance to finish the sentence.

———

THE FINAL MISSILE BLEW WITHIN FIFTY METERS. SHRAPNEL rattled against every surface.

Warning lights began flashing in yellows and reds.

A *lot* of reds.

"Turning east." Rock steady in a crisis, Sharelle eased them around again to head for the *Peleliu*. He felt the mushy slip in the turn that indicated the tail was gone. He hated to admit it, but if this was a DAP, they'd already be in the ocean. The rear rotor on a Black Hawk was essential for controlled flight. The Alligator, with its stacked rotors, used airflow over the tail to assist in turning the helo's body, but it wasn't as essential.

Too bad that wasn't the only damage.

"Talk to me, Troy."

"Most of the targeting systems are down, so don't overrun any more patrol boats. Flares are spent, but we still have a couple loads of chaff. Hydraulics Number Two," he flicked a few switches off, on again, then he left them in the off, "gone. Don't bother with the wheels, they're gone."

He shut down alarms as he reviewed each system.

The last trace of the sinking patrol boat disappeared as they flew over it. No heat signature of survivors. It would either be written off as *lost at sea* or, if some other craft saw the flash of light, perhaps as *unexplained explosion.* He'd bet all the rubles in Siberia that the Russian Navy would never admit to the latter even if they spotted the explosion.

As to a satellite image, their departure was *hopefully* timed during a gap in Russian satellite coverage. Russia's first priority would still be watching Eastern Europe for drone attacks.

He returned his attention to the failing systems.

"Nav is up, weather radar is down. And—" he finally cleared enough alerts to see something that wasn't buzzing, bleating, or flashing. "Oh, that's not good."

"What?"

"Fuel." He thumped the indicator, though why he was hoping for any kind of a change from tapping an electronic readout was beyond him.

"*Peleliu?*" she asked.

"Not even close." He and Richie had pushed more fuel into Trisha's Helix because she was carrying the most people. Per that plan, their Alligator would be landing on fumes if they were lucky.

Not anymore.

"Told you it was bad form to say this was too easy."

"Guilty as charged." Troy didn't believe in such things, knew Sharelle didn't either. But it definitely ranked as highly ironic.

"Time and distance?"

"One-sixty kilometers. Thirty-one minutes at V-max. Fuel at

V-max and current leakage rate," he ran some quick math in his head. "Halfway—if the gods are with us."

"How's your relationship with the gods these days?"

"I'm in pretty good with a goddess of a pilot. Does that count for anything?"

"Let's hope so, call it in."

They were still closer to Russia than Japan, so there was a risk in breaking radio silence. But that risk was decreasing with each kilometer.

He felt a shudder. There, then gone.

In unison, they both looked upward though there was little to see of the rotors spinning close overheads.

"Damaged blade," they both said.

Troy didn't hesitate any longer. Rather than taking to time to cue up his message and send it up to a satellite on an encrypted micro-burst transmission, he called up the *Peleliu* directly. He just hoped that they had a bird or drone up at a couple thousand meters to relay the signal past the horizon.

"*Peleliu*, this is patrol flight," they didn't have a call sign set up for a non-Russian transmission. What would identify them easily? "Sharelle-one." Not brilliant, but he liked the idea of flying with her too much to come up with something else.

"Proceed, Sharelle-one," the radio operator was right on it.

He read off their position and estimated time of dumping into the ocean.

"Roger, SAR aloft. Tango-one reports inbound."

"Roger. Thanks." Troy clicked off the mike. "Forgot about Trisha."

"We've been busy," Sharelle agreed. "So..."

"What?"

"How do we do this? I didn't like watching what happened to Rafe. I like my legs."

"I like your legs too. But you're forgetting one thing about this helo."

"What?"

He didn't have to wait long before Sharelle remembered one of its unique features.

Her curse was emphatic. And *not* happy.

———

"ARE WE IN OR OUT OF WINDOW?" TROY HAD INSISTED ON calling Colonel Beale directly; at least the woman had answered immediately. Overhearing the background interactions, Sharelle could hear that Beale had a whole team up in that Tac Room of hers. That was the only thing comforting about this whole situation.

Sharelle knew there was a Russian satellite somewhere above the horizon at the moment.

"Three minutes *within* window," one of the voices responded. It wasn't Beale, Claudia, or Michael Gibson. Her sense of hope plummeted down to the ocean and sank faster than made any sense. They were all there, but that tiny bit of unfamiliarity proved hard to bear.

Three minutes. That was the first problem. A Russian satellite now flew over the southern reaches of the Sea of Japan, which meant that here in the north, it would be low to the horizon with a poor viewing angle and only in range for minutes. Somehow, Beale knew it was oriented in their direction. Not precisely, perhaps searching for the patrol boat that had gone so abruptly silent, but it wasn't something she wanted attention from.

Three more minutes. That was thirty seconds more fuel than Troy estimated they had remaining in their tanks.

The second problem had been thoroughly demonstrated by Rafe. If one man barely escaped landing a helicopter on a calm lake, the chances of both her and Troy surviving a bailout on the rough ocean were not good. The prevailing easterlies had combined with the remains of some storm, perhaps the one that had lashed them departing the Arctic, to build story-high waves that would kill them for sure.

The third? The autopilot had been one of the fatalities. For the last fourteen minutes she'd felt as if she rode a bucking bronc. Every flight control she tried was overcompensated, under-corrected, or just plain ignored by one failing system after another. Establishing a stable hover twenty feet over the waves, giving them time to safely bail out, simply wasn't going to happen.

That left only one option.

But they were still too close to the Russian sea lanes to risk climbing higher to make it any less crazy than it already was.

And a brilliant launch rocket of a seat ejection system would definitely snag the satellite's attention.

"Two minutes," the voice announced.

"Troy?"

"Maybe." He was splitting his attention between the fuel gauges and fighting to keep enough of the helicopter operational that she didn't kill them in the meantime.

"Talk to me about something."

"Well, if we don't die together—"

"*That* is not the kind of thing I meant." The bottom dropped out of the left rudder pedal.

Troy did something that brought it back online, partly. She could control the flight direction, but they slowly spun to the right. First, they were nose-on to direction of travel, then sideways, but still headed toward the ship as she compensated with the cyclic. She pulled up the collective to grab an extra five meters above the waves as they turned tail toward the distant *Peleliu.* Then sideways to the north and finally full circle.

"Sorry, best I can do."

She wasn't sure if he was talking about the topic or fixing

the rotation problem. It was the latter, as they once more headed through the loop around.

"Anyway, if we live through this, do you want to live together first or get married?"

"One minute," the radio voice announced.

"You're proposing to me during an *imminent crash?*" The helo wasn't the only one making her head spin.

"No," Troy reset something that again killed the left rudder pedal but then restored it to normal—mostly.

They now spun at fifteen seconds per revolution instead of five.

"I wasn't proposing if you want to just try living together first."

"Thirty seconds."

Troy's tone changed. "Gonna be tight."

But neither engine was sputtering yet.

"There's one," he called out before she felt it.

A...hiccup shuddered through the airframe. An engine making a last desperate gulp for fuel that was no longer there.

"Ten seconds," over the radio.

"Screw this!" Sharelle heaved upward on the collective and backed the cyclic trading speed toward the ship for rate of climb. "C'mon, baby Alligator. Give Mama some lift."

"Ten meters," Troy called out. "Twenty. Thirty..."

"Five. Four. Three..." the voice counted down.

"That's fifty."

"Still three," the voice compensated for her rate of climb, "now two—"

"Seventy-five," Troy grunted out against the g-force.

"—one. Clear window. I repeat, clear window. The Russian satellite is below the horizon."

Sharelle leveled the flight, took a deep breath, then made the call.

"Eject! Eject! Eject!"

———

In unison, they both reached down between their legs and yanked up on the red loop handle between their legs.

It wasn't something any helicopter pilot outside of Russia had ever done. Even though the trainer out at Groom Lake had drilled in the instructions, they were far from automatic.

One! Troy repeated to himself. Pulling the ring had leveraged the handle upward and into his lap. That positioned his shoulders against the back of his seat.

Two! Position your head. Upright, centered, no twisting last glance aside at Sharelle, lean against the back of the seat.

Thre—

The thought was interrupted by the first detonation. Explosive charges in all six rotor blades severed them close by the mast. The rotation flung two blades forward, one to either side, and two backward, hopefully—or else they'd spin around in a moment to kill them. Troy only had a moment to wonder if they were going to fly into one of the tumbling blades no longer attached to the helo.

—e! Position his arms solidly on the seat's armrests.

The second detonation went off mere centimeters above his head. Zigzags of det cord sliced through the cockpit canopy, which tumbled away in the wind.

Unlike a Martin-Baker seat used in jet fighters, the seat didn't shoot upward on rails, then fire a big rocket under the seat to clear the aircraft.

The Russian system ejected the rocket up and out from the top of the seat. On reaching the end of twin straps attached to the back of his seat, it fired and bathed him in the stench of hot sulfur.

The rockets yanked them aloft, eating exhaust the whole way up.

Side by side, angled outward for elbow room, racing upward for over a hundred feet.

Then they were free, and with a final loud bang that felt like someone had punched him in the kidneys, the straps released the rocket and a great round parachute bloomed out above him.

He'd missed a detail, or perhaps the trainers had: his night-vision had been powered by the helicopter. Now disconnected from the helo, he was rocket-dazzled and floating in the dark above an ocean some indeterminate distance below.

His vision recovered enough for the starlight to reveal the helicopter plunging into the waves and disappearing without hesitation. Above, a great white circle, made nearly black by the darkness, obliterated a wide expanse of the stars.

Other than the soft whistle of passing wind, the world had gone quiet.

Troy had no references to judge speed or distance. Parachute drops weren't something helicopter pilots were typically trained in. So all he could do was...count the swings back and forth.

When he remembered to look for Sharelle's chute, he didn't see it anywhere.

Troy called out her name...and plunged into the frigid ocean waters with his lungs empty and his mouth wide open.

—

THE WAVES, WHICH HAD LOOKED SO FEARSOME FROM THE HELO, each one threatening to snag her staggering airframe and plunge her beneath the ocean, were no more than giant rollers once Sharelle had splashed in and surfaced.

Her parachute had failed to open. All that had saved her was Troy reviewing the steps of the process from the Russian

Pilot Operations Handbook in between fighting to keep the systems running.

She'd found the manual release, falling in terror to a hard plunge after slowing her fall just enough to not kill her. Frigid water flooded in the front of her flightsuit. Russian suits were not designed for cold water landings.

Sharelle surfaced in time to see Troy's chute drifting away until he landed several waves to the—she checked for the North Star—west. Why was the man going back to Russia? Oh, the easterly winds. Someone had better rescue them before they were washed back to those shores.

She hit the harness release, unsure of what to do with the parachute. It had come out of a bag smaller than a briefcase.

Find Troy first. Worry about parachutes later.

Right! Good voice. Wise voice. She wanted to pat it on the head.

She checked the stars again and struck out swimming.

Troy ultimately revealed his position by his choking cough that carried clearly over the big rollers.

Too tired for more, they clung to each other's jackets and awaited rescue.

24

Emily stood outside the Groom Lake hangar where the team had departed from forever and five days ago. This time she'd come alone. She didn't need Michael beside her.

She hoped.

The Delta operators had done their usual fade routine. They'd all taken transport from Sapporo, Japan, down to Okinawa and over to Joint Base Lewis-McChord in Washington State. But the C-130 Hercules to Groom Lake didn't include them on the manifest. And indeed, after the cargo plane had rolled up, finally spinning down the four massive turboprop engines and leaving the thick smell of kerosene on the hot afternoon air, they weren't aboard.

As far as she could recall, Emily had never been so happy to see a crew return.

Trisha sent her a cocky salute before she was half down the rear ramp. Billy's was more formal. Julian wheeled Rafe's chair down, leg in a cast from thigh to foot. Three broken bones, two of them compound, one half-cutting an artery. The medic from the Delta team had saved his life aboard the hovering Helix, and the *Peleliu's* Navy doctor had made sure he'd fly again.

"Personally, I think he's milking this," Julian complained.

"For all I'm worth. Nurse! Nurse!" He snapped his fingers close by Julian's nose. "A Coke with ice cubes. And none of the diet stuff. Stat!"

They both saluted and Emily felt a tsunami wave of relief at their big smiles as they rolled off toward the DFAC.

Last down the ramp came Sharelle and Troy.

They were so changed that she barely recognized them.

They walked together with a synchronicity that meant they were now truly a couple. It was the first thing she saw about them. Even as Troy turned aside to help Julian with his and Rafe's gear.

But it was as if all her life's training had been brought into focus in this moment.

From her FBI Director father to her Washington socialite mother. Mark's easy way with people—even as he scared the shit out of them if they wandered out of line—to his mother's awe-inspiring peace (so thick and sure that it radiated from her). Even Michael's silence found a place inside her.

And the woman now standing before her was somehow her creation. Captain Sharelle Vargas was no longer merely an exceptional pilot.

The salutes they exchanged were all about respect and not at all about rank.

"Good mission?" Emily asked. It should be inane...but it wasn't.

"Good mission." Sharelle replied. Then she smiled, but it held a sadness as well as she nodded toward the team. "Best people I know."

Emily nodded. She'd never forgotten their conversation two months ago, after that first flight. Standing in the dark with Captain Sharelle Vargas, her palms sweaty with anxiety even as her fingers had itched for the controls.

"You were right. It does make it harder. I wasn't the mission commander, Trisha was, but somehow, these were my people."

Emily nodded again. Precisely the lesson she had learned so long ago helping each woman climb into being her best self: Kee, Connie, Lola, and all the others..

"It was an..." Sharelle looked out toward the dusty hills encircling Groom Lake, turning red beyond the setting sun. "The word is wrong, but it was an honor."

"No. It's the right word. The problem is that it isn't enough to explain the feeling."

"Yes," Sharelle nodded. "Yes, that's it. Thank you."

———

THEY BEGAN STROLLING AFTER THE OTHERS, BUT MOVING SLOWLY. A part of Sharelle wished this moment wouldn't end and she wanted to stretch it out.

Emily was the first to break the slow silence. "You and Troy? Feel free not to answer."

"Is that a question from the colonel or the friend?"

"I'd like it to be both."

Sharelle considered, "Me too. Okay, bottom line for the friend. If I've ever met a better man, I'm not aware of it. We..." she meshed her fingers, "...fit. I'll never be as good a pilot as he sees me and he'll never believe he's as brilliant as I know he is, but it won't stop either of us from trying to live up to those standards the other sees so easily."

"And to the colonel?"

She stopped. "To the colonel? How in holy *hell* do I make this work?"

"Does it help to know this was Trisha's swan song?"

"What does that have to with Troy and— Wait, what? She's quitting? She's an exceptional pilot. And a far better commander than she thinks."

"No, she's still my Number Two. But did it feel as if she wasn't quite in command?"

Sharelle managed a nod.

"That was intentional. She was there as a stopgap for you and Troy. Her report said that, other than a few gentle nudges, neither of you needed it. She and Billy are lifers, they'd never leave the service by choice. I'm building her into a commander who still has a long military career ahead of her. But she was doing the same. Do you feel ready to command a company, Major Sharelle Vargas?"

"*Major?*" she barely choked it out.

Emily didn't even have the decency to break stride. "I'd suggest Major Troy Ryland as your Number Two."

"Major?" No more than a whisper this time. "Who's in the company?"

"Rafe and Julian sound like a good start? I have some others for you to look over."

"Have you lost your mind?" Nothing could make less sense.

"Not recently."

"But...how?" Even as she protested, she saw it. Emily Beale and Mark Henderson had become known simply as The Majors. Even a decade gone from the service, the phrase evoked no others. A chance to challenge that. She and Troy would...

And she stumbled to a halt.

"No." She pulled herself upright and turned to face Emily. "I'm sorry, Colonel. As much as I appreciate the offer, it's not going to happen."

Emily merely raised an eyebrow in question.

"I'm not going anywhere. But Troy is headed back to take over his family farm from his parents. We have no idea how we're going to make that work, but we'll have to find a way."

"Hmm."

"That's all you have to say, a thoughtful hmm?" And

Sharelle remembered quite why she'd wanted to throttle Colonel Beale so often in the past.

"May I suggest that in returning the DAP Hawk from here to Fort Campbell, you make a small detour. It's less than twenty kilometers off the route."

"A detour to where? What's going on?"

"Well, if he's the love of your life, you're going to want to meet his parents, aren't you?"

25

SHARELLE STILL DIDN'T UNDERSTAND HOW IT HAD HAPPENED.

One afternoon they were landing in Groom Lake after a harrowing mission invading a foreign and unfriendly power. The next, she was standing on a high roll of prairie grass holding hands with the love of her life.

Love of her life? Beale had certainly slipped that one by her, hadn't she? Not that she was wrong. Sharelle knew *that* without even thinking about it—until Beale had made her think about it.

Troy's farm was beautiful in a different way than Henderson's...and more awful.

They stood upon the farm's highest elevation, barely higher than the tired two-story house at the lowest point other than an algae-thick pond. The DAP Hawk, under its net, was nearly as big as the disused and collapsing barn. An equipment garage and processing sheds completed the farm.

"Home?"

"Yes." It would be easier to understand if not for the unconscious sigh that followed his statement.

No matter how much heart and soul was plowed into this

soil, it would never be Henderson's. In fact, she saw Troy folding up and dying here. Maybe there was potential here, but not for someone like Troy. There couldn't be.

"I've seen how much you love to fly. How can you even think of..." She closed her eyes and wished her inner voice had been the one to say that. "I'm sorry, Troy. It's not my place."

"What part of spend our lives together don't you understand? You get an equal say."

"Not in this."

"Say it anyway." Was he begging her to state the obvious? She held his hand tighter, but she couldn't deny his plea.

"This isn't you, Troy. The challenges would be a heartbreaker for anyone who doesn't love the land for the land's sake. Not for its heritage, but for the actual land. I know you. I know what you love; remember, I've seen you fly. You can't deny that truth."

He didn't answer, but neither did he shove her away. They stood a long time in silence, watching the irrigation arches rolling slowly over the land in a great line of steel trusswork.

"There they are," he pointed at a white pickup truck turning into the long driveway. The farm had been empty when they'd arrived. A quick phone call had elicited cries of pleasure and promises to return to the farm as soon as their errands in town were done.

Together, hand-in-hand, they walked down the hill.

Sharelle didn't know which would be harder: meeting Troy's parents, or her plan to beg their help in cutting their son loose from his perceived duty to his heritage. Not that she had any right to do the latter. What did she know about heritage?

But nothing about this place spoke to her of Troy. Even the old corral that he used to practice his rodeo tricks in was gone, wiped away by necessity.

She hadn't thought about the color of her skin as a factor until the four of them stood together. But other than a brief widening of his eyes, his dad showed no reaction. And even that, she finally realized, had much more to do with their clasped hands.

They were very excited about something, even beyond Troy being home. And bringing home a girlfriend—apparently something he hadn't done since high school.

It wasn't until they were sitting on the shaded porch with tall glasses of iced tea that she understood it wasn't only excitement. They were worried about something.

Perhaps how soon their son would be coming home from the Army?

Or was the farm in even more trouble than it looked?

Think like Emily.

Emily?

But her voice had had its say.

Think like Emily. A brutally tough taskmaster...in making people their best selves. Always finding a way around her own reservations to help others past theirs. Emily Beale could be subtle, like the way she'd sent Trisha along on the mission as a *non*-commander.

Stay focused.

Right. Think like Emily.

Well...at times she also could be about as subtle as an axe.

"What's worrying you about the farm? There's something you don't want to tell Troy. Don't worry, we'll figure it out together."

She saw Troy had inherited his natural reticence from both parents. Each opened their mouths, then, in turn, closed them again.

"We had a visitor," his father finally spoke first.

"Two of them, actually," his mother corrected.

"They came down from a ranch up north."

Sharelle felt a tingle ripple up her spine.

"One a Mr. Doug Daniels, he manages some big horse ranch."

"T'other a Mr. Henderson."

"*What?*" Troy's shout scared his parents like rabbits in headlights.

Sharelle smiled for what felt like the first time since Troy had mentioned he was leaving. She remembered that Mark and the ranch manager had left Henderson's even before she and Troy had. To come here. Doug *Daniels?* She hadn't met Chelsea Daniels' husband, but she knew he managed Henderson's Ranch.

"Let me guess," she winked at Troy.

He simply gawked back at her.

"They did a review of your farm operations."

"They did that right enough," Troy's dad agreed. "Laid out all sorts of truths that were hard to hear."

"And did they give you any ideas of what to do about it?"

"They did. And once they said it, it made perfect sense. But then..." his mother eyed Troy very carefully and seemed to lose the power of speech.

And Sharelle saw the clear path ahead, turning to the man she wanted to fly with every time she went aloft. "Troy, I need an honest answer."

He squinted at her, but finally nodded his assent.

"One word only."

He nodded even more carefully. Such a smart man, with a few blind spots.

"If this wasn't your family's inherited land, would you rather farm or fly?"

"Fly. But I can't—"

His parents' laughter of purest relief overwhelmed anything else he tried to say.

———

SHARELLE SAT ATOP THE LOW BLUFF AND LOOKED OUT OVER THE sleeping farm lit by the half-moon. She then looked down at the happily sated man fast asleep on the blanket beside her. The warm September night caressed her bare skin as gently as her lover had.

Sell the farm.

Troy's parents were well past sick of it.

Troy would rather fly.

The time to let go of the land lay years in the past and had arrived in present.

Because they'd managed to scrape by, with Troy's help to keep them from incurring debt, they owned it free and clear.

Rodion had been the answer. His family had held the big ranch next door for almost as long as the Rylands had held theirs. Rodion also had the large family, the passion for the land, and the water rights to make the farm flourish. He made a generous offer for the place; more than enough for Troy's parents to retire on.

All it had taken was thinking in a new way.

Think like Trisha. It would take practice, but her new friend, PITA O'Malley, would also be a great teacher.

And she'd think like Emily.

Subtle. Even when sometimes that subtle was like an axe —*Major Vargas.* She liked the way that sounded. First Emily, then Trisha, then perhaps someday, with Troy at her side, Colonel Vargas?

Michael too had taught her what was important.

Sharelle listened to the night for a long time before she lay alongside Troy and woke her lover beneath the starlit sky.

AFTERWORD

As this title was finished and entering its final edits, Russia used its veto power on the UN Security Council to remove sanctions monitoring of North Korea—not the sanctions themselves, merely any tracking if they were being enforced or abused. These sanctions were originally imposed eighteen years ago in 2006, and renewed annually since, as a deterrent to North Korea's nuclear weapons development program—for what little good that has done.

Amid an ongoing investigation into Russia violating the sanctions by purchasing weapons for the Ukraine War from North Korea, Russia's vote disbanded the watchdog committee responsible for the monitoring and investigation into those precise violations.

I've incorporated this into the story with great reluctance. I'm so often disappointed at how fast reality catches up with my fiction.

Writing for a better world,

M. L. Buchman – March 2024

AFTERWORD – PART II

And just as this title was entering final production, *BBC News* reported a failed North Korean ballistic missile fired from Russia that crashed in Kharkiv. To make matters worse, its control systems were rife with smuggled US computer chips typical of phones, washing machines, and the like. These are typically purchased by Hong Kong front companies using stolen or printed cash (North Korea is the world's foremost counterfeiter of US $100 bills as was mentioned in my Dead Chef series #1 *One Chef*). The contraband is then transshipped across the Chinese-North Korean border to be turned into weapons, presently being sold onward to Russia.

A part of me wishes that the failure was due to some scenario like the one in this book rather than mere incompetence or a bad chip.

M. L. Buchman – April 2024

AFTERWORD – PART III

Curiously, the day before final layout of this book, I happened upon a single article following up on the missile failure. It cited an unconfirmed rumor that over half of the missiles sold by North Korea are failing at the Russian-Ukrainian front. Maybe I wasn't so far wrong when I thought up this mission for my Night Stalkers and Delta Force.

M. L. Buchman – May 2024

AND DON'T FORGET...

If you enjoyed Guard the East Flank
please consider leaving a review.
They really help.

Keep reading for an exciting excerpt from:
Miranda Chase #15, Wedgetail
(Coming summer 2024)

Be sure to visit:
https://mlbuchman.com/fan-club-freebies

- *Bonus Scene/Story*
- *Recipe from the book*
- *Character list, place maps, plane pictures, and more*

WEDGETAIL (EXCERPT)

IF YOU ENJOYED THAT, YOU'LL LOVE THIS TALE!

WEDGETAIL (EXCERPT)

CHANGI AIRPORT, SINGAPORE

"Look, I agreed to Australia. I never, *ever* agreed to Tennant Creek." Holly hadn't won the argument in Seattle. Or on the flight across the Pacific to Singapore. In an hour, they'd be in the air to Darwin, and she'd probably lose the argument there again as well. Why was she doomed to revisit her childhood home deep in the Outback, a place she'd never intended to see again? And for some reason, the other three members of Miranda's NTSB air-crash investigation team were along for the ride.

"Not my doing, Hol."

"Mike, seriously. I keep making the same points and it keeps getting me the same result. The definition of dumb-ass stupid. Get me out of this!"

"Out of this? But it's lovely." He waved an expansive hand.

"You goofball." She poked her finger into his ribs, not sharply, but enough to let him know she was serious.

He was right, though, it *was* lovely. They stood in a giant butterfly garden built inside Singapore's Changi Airport. Fifty meters long, half that high and wide, and roofed with a great curved glass ceiling like a crystalline Quonset hut. Inside grew a flowering tropical forest, complete with an actual two-story waterfall, viewing platforms high and low, and a thousand or so butterflies in every color imaginable.

Mike had taken her to a much smaller butterfly garden in the Seattle Arboretum once. An actual date, which had been oddly sweet. Dating was a new aspect in their four years of sleeping together.

Strangest of all, she'd been charmed. Mike deserved another sharp poke for that, but she forced herself to behave.

The large tent, with a double-screened entrance, had been raised on the Arboretum's grass. Inside stood pots of flowers to entice the hundreds of butterflies released inside. In retrospect, she could see that most of the creatures had clung mournfully to the screening, dreaming of flapping about in the wider world beyond.

Not here. Amidst Singapore's jungle, they hid in trees, rested on flowers, fed on pineapple slices left out for them. Safe from predators and weather. Living out their lives in perfect security. More comfortable, but still a gilded cage?

She sure as hell didn't want to crawl back into the dog-kennel-sized cage of her past.

"Seriously, Holly?" Mike slid an arm around her waist. "I think you're fighting a lost cause. How many people do you know who can change Miranda's mind once she gets an idea?"

"You?"

"I honestly tried, Holly. I mean, I'm curious to see where you grew up, too, but I tried. It didn't work."

"Damn you for being decent. It makes it that much harder to complain." She stared at a white, yellow, orange, and black-trimmed butterfly that a nearby sign identified as a Painted Jezebel. Perfect. Just perfect.

A painted, immoral lady who always got what she wanted. *Stupid butterfly.*

Holly was doing her best to be a good and moral member of

the team. What had it earned her? A trip to Tennant Creek. And once Mike or Miranda saw where she came from, they'd never think decently of her again.

It had all begun over dinner a few months ago.

The four of them hadn't talked once about Andi's betrayal, her subsequent departure, or her return—not even tangentially. But the topic of a vacation came up. Their first attempt at a team vacation, hiking the Herriot Way around the Yorkshire Dales, had been the prelude to the unmitigated disaster of Captain Andi Wu leaving the team.

Go somewhere different? Andi had suggested.

The antipodes from the UK, Miranda had declared. That turned out to be in the Pacific Ocean south of New Zealand. Which had brought up the topic of Holly's homeland in Australia. Miranda had declared that as sufficiently *antipodal* and noted that she had an interest in the Australian Outback, based on Holly's stories of her survival adventures there. *You grew up there. You can be our guide.*

Somehow that had decided everything—leaving Holly to fight the line with all the effectiveness of a dying fish dragged onto the parched sands of her past. Her adventures? More like her *escape* from Tennant Creek into the tablelands to get *away* from her past.

"Andi? Should I ask Andi to try?"

Mike kissed her on the nose and almost earned a fist on his own. "Andi is still on tenterhooks around Miranda. She's not going to risk rocking the boat for a single second."

Holly sighed. It was too true. Andi had only been back a couple months after eight months gone. Everyone was much happier—even Holly herself, which she hadn't expected—but Andi was playing it very cool.

Even now, neither Miranda nor Andi wandered here with them inside the garden. Meg wasn't permitted in the garden despite her status as an autism therapy dog. *If my dog can't go, then I won't go.* To which Andi had added, *If you don't go, then I don't.*

Instead, they sat out by the blue tile pool in the middle of the concourse, with Meg perched on the wide ledge to watch koi as big as she was swimming lazily by.

"If I pray for a miracle and actually receive a dispensation from this abuse, does it mean that I need to believe in your Catholic God?"

"Hey! Not my God!" Mike held up his hands defensively. "He and I had a permanent falling out a couple decades ago. If I had to pick one, I'd probably go with worshipping Diana the Huntress. A scantily clad Holly Harper look-a-like, with a bow and arrow, running through the woods with her long hair streaming in the wind. Speaks Greek instead of Strine, but I can learn that. There's a definite image to improve my mood." He scooped his fingers through her gold-blonde hair and brushed it out behind her. He played with it more than ever since she'd started growing it out for him. Down to the middle of her shoulder blades and he was a goner. Guys were the strangest critters anywhere.

"Isn't she also the virgin goddess and the protector of childbirth?" Holly wondered where she'd picked up that tidbit as a bright orange something fluttered inches past her nose with wings as big as her palm. "So, are you saying you never want to have sex again or that you want to have a child with me? How do those two go together in one goddess, anyway?"

When Mike didn't answer, she looked over at him. He was studying a blue-and-black butterfly no bigger than the end of his thumb—too intently.

"No way, Mike Munroe. Tell me you did *not* just go there."

He grimaced. "Only for a second, and I assure you that it wasn't intentional."

"I should've stopped at the scantily clad image of me running through the woods."

"Don't forget the streaming hair." He wiped his forehead and didn't quite meet her gaze. "Uh, yeah. Let's stick with that."

Their relationship, since the mess in Sweden, had been better than ever. But there was this growing thing about taking The Next Step—or not. So far, they'd both remained careful not to go there, *until* she'd put her Army boot in it. *Real smooth, Harper.*

———

39,000' above Singapore

"I hate this place."

"Wouldn't be the Strait without you saying that," she replied as usual. Though Royal Australian Air Force Group Captain Rowena McCain couldn't argue. She'd flown more than two hundred patrols above the Strait. So often that she'd come to know it as well as her own hand. And now she could see the entire mess on her display.

It was a tactical nightmare, which had become like that itch that no amount of scratching eased. Constantly on the verge of collapse on every level: sea, air, and space. Even minor problems could have global ramifications.

"I *really* hate this place." Wing Commander Nick Neally completed the ritual that had existed since they'd both been lowly Flight Lieutenants on their first patrol here.

Nick, a great hulk of a man, sat at the console to her left; atypically dour for an Aussie, and brilliant at his job. She'd chosen him to sit at her left hand as the senior Surveillance Officer the moment they'd bumped her to the command seat— all of yesterday.

The Wedgetail—technically the Boeing 737 AEW&C, Airborne Early Warning and Control plane—was the hottest flying command in the RAAF. It was the only plane staffed by a

Group Captain, the equivalent of an American colonel. She had the responsibility *and* the power to order immediate action if needed.

"It's just a bit of clutter, mates," Squadron Leader Grant Felton laughed. "Place is bound to clear out someday." The diametric opposite of Nick, Grant would be chortling at some joke during his own funeral. Too bad he wasn't as funny as he thought he was—though he was definitely as handsome, but she'd long since refused to fall for that.

With her promotion last month to Group Captain—raising her to the highest ranked Black Australian in the RAAF—made her twice the target she'd ever been before. Especially in the eyes of a swagman like Grant. How could someone be so convinced of their own magnificence as a gift to the female gender? At least he tried to be funny about it, ever since she'd offered to recommend him for a lifetime of latrine duty in her next review. Which he referred to weekly, as if it was a bonding joke between them rather than an unvarnished threat.

They occupied the first three consoles in the main cabin of the E-7A Wedgetail patrol jet. Grant's title was Systems Officer, placing him at the forward end of the cabin closest to the main entry door and the cockpit. His job was to communicate with the two pilots forward and make sure that the plane stayed aloft and secure.

She sat next in the command seat, with Nick to her left managing the surveillance team.

Down the main cabin ranged seven more consoles, a total of ten. Six were along the left side of the plane and the remaining four to starboard. The count was split because of the large radio cabinets occupying the first two positions behind her and Grant's seats along the right side of the cabin.

Each station was mounted sideways against the hull and had a headset-wearing operator in a comfortable swivel seat facing outward. Every console was equipped with twin displays and radio controls that could talk to a nearby jet or anywhere on the globe via satellite with equal ease. Some flights only called for a few operators, but all ten stations were manned continuously when patrolling the Strait.

Nick oversaw six of the seven down-cabin stations. He had responsibility for surveillance of everything that happened outside the plane. He always managed to make sure that she was looking at the right thing at the right time. Nick had been doing that since their first day aboard; now she had the absolute faith of experience in him.

Grant managed his own console and the comm tech's at the first seat of the starboard row, close by the radio cabinets if there were any problems. Grant and the comm tech oversaw communications and the aircraft's operational integrity, including every type of radar and radio that could be packed into a single airframe.

Everything either Nick or Grant saw landed on her desk. At the moment, she was in command of security operations for the entire length of the Strait of Malacca.

Which left her in the middle...again. Story of her life.

She'd been a middle sister with two gung-ho brothers. One now a Footie star and the other a world-class sailor. But *she* was the commander set between the surveillance officer and the plane's systems officer. Not to mention being a single woman caught between a pair of RAAF bachelors. One with puppy-dog-sad eyes that saw the world all too clearly; the other convinced he knew far more about her than he did.

Nick tapped his screen, which highlighted a ship icon on hers.

Too fast for a fishing vessel, too small for a container ship.

"Satellite?" she asked.

"UK bird coming up over Sri Lanka. We'll have a visual five-minute window in three minutes."

"Roger that." Rowena went back to studying other shipping

activity while waiting to see if some pirate was desperate enough to commit his crime in the middle of the Strait itself.

In her two and a half decades of service, Rowena had seen plenty of ugly around these parts. Malacca wasn't going to be clearing out anytime soon, no matter Grant's prediction. The only thing that would stop this glut through the Strait was war. She'd gamed that all too often at headquarters; one of the ultimate no-win scenarios no matter how they looked at it.

The only way to bypass the Strait was a long haul south around Indonesia for the Strait of Lombok or on toward Australia and New Zealand. Their two countries were well out of the way, and they both liked that just fine.

At the three-klick-wide choke point where the Malacca opened out at Singapore, it wasn't unusual to have ships three hundred meters long that needed half an hour and six kilometers to stop, lined up a kilometer apart and sometimes two abreast. With the same passing in the opposite direction. And that was merely the big trade boys. Add in more little boats than bugs in a Outback termite mound, world sailors and local fisherman, and the occasional US Navy carrier groups complete with submarines. Then it started to get interesting.

The real trouble came because where there was congestion, there were pirates. The pressure of eight billion people on the planet made for a lot of poor—near enough half a billion of them within shooting distance of the Strait of Malacca—and a lot of those bearing no qualms about taking from the rich.

One poor ship had been robbed four times in a single passage. The first time for the crew's cash and valuables. Then someone pulled alongside and cross-pumped a hundred thousand gallons of diesel at gunpoint. Another pirate took twenty thousand more leaving her almost dry. The final pirates, finding the ship stripped, had ridden along for two days eating as much food as they could before disembarking. Thankfully, that hadn't been on Australia's watch.

As there were no flotillas of military ships passing through at the moment, the pirates were the focus of today's mission.

Of course, from up here in the Wedgetail, they could also keep an eye on the pissing match China led in much of the South China Sea. And not to forget Myanmar at the other end engaging anyone who'd listen to the latest military junta, which was no one with a pinch of common sense.

"Never two days the same," Grant teased.

"Each worse than the one before," Nick embraced his moroseness like an art form.

Unlike her prior commander, Rowena appreciated the banter. A standard patrol lasted twelve hours, unless something bad kicked in. Then they'd get a mid-air refueling and often hit twenty hours aloft. She could rotate some of the operators to the comfortable crew rest seats in the rear, but she never took advantage of that herself.

That created its own kind of trouble. Being labeled as an overachiever pleased the top levels of command but irritated those immediately above her. They assumed she was after their jobs, which she was. The fact that she was smarter than most of them put together, and everyone knew it, didn't help matters.

The man she replaced had aged out, rather than making the grade to Air Commodore. And she'd made her rank five years younger than he had. He'd managed only the barest civility when he turned over the Wedgetail to her command.

Neither Nick nor Grant aspired, both glad to be in straightforward service roles.

Rowena had her eye on those flag posts beginning a single rank above her with Air Commodore.

To make her next step? She had to hone her crew and her half-billion-dollar plane until they shone.

Under the Five Power Defence Arrangements with Singapore, the UK, New Zealand, and Malaysia, Australia helped to keep the trade moving as safely as possible throughout the region.

Australia's Wedgetails had proven to be major assets in achieving that and she planned for her plane to be the most effective one in the fleet.

But now that she was here, sea traffic wasn't her only mission.

"Talk to me about the air." She hit the top right button on the soft-touch pad beside her keyboard to flip her view, relegating the sea to her secondary screen and showing her the surrounding air space.

Nick flipped his screen to match. His three maritime staff specialists would alert him if anything went astray.

"About the same sorry state," Nick groused.

They flew at thirty-nine thousand feet over two of the busiest airports in the world: Singapore's Changi and Malaysia's Kuala Lumpur. The horizon lay four hundred kilometers away in all directions due to the Earth's curvature, and they could see out to nine hundred for aircraft at altitude. Everything from Ho Chi Minh City to Jakarta showed up on the screens—it almost made the clutter down in the Strait look rational. At least the shipping remained on the surface of the sea, other than the occasional submarine. The clutter of the air routes crisscrossed at every altitude imaginable.

But the Wedgetail wasn't called the most capable AEW&C plane aloft without reason. It specialized in sorting the noteworthy from the mundane at sea, in the air, and in near space out to a thousand kilometers. They might be watching the sea today, but if someone lofted a ballistic missile, the Wedgetail could find it before it left the atmosphere.

Rowena scaled her view to the closest hundred kilometers in all directions and began absorbing the patterns—something she did faster than anyone aboard. Always good to set a high bar for the staff.

The magic of her view was created in the back half of the plane.

Past the ten consoles and the small crew rest area, the aft half of the fuselage was closed off. From the wings back to the tail ranged some of the most sophisticated electronics anywhere. They controlled and fed the *Top Hat* radar antenna. The antenna—like a fat-handled dough scraper jammed into the spine of the plane by a giant trying to split the airplane in two—ran from the plane's mid-point to close before the tail and nearly as tall.

This was *not* the thirty-foot-wide spinning disk of the fifty-year-old E-3 Sentry AWACS planes. Those updated the radar view with one sweep every ten seconds. The E-7A Wedgetail's MESA—multi-role electronically scanned array—radar offered a continuous three-hundred-and-sixty-degree view: sea low, airspace mid, and space high.

"The boat's a service vessel. Registered. Called out to assist with a broken Number Two engine," Nick reported.

Rowena glanced over at his console and saw a low-angle satellite image, a static picture of the same boat, and basic registry information. It was one of many kept docked along the Strait like tow trucks pre-positioned on major highways during rush hour.

"Tell him to turn on his damn AIS." Ships were *supposed* to run with their Automatic Identification System transponder operating for just this reason.

After a quick radio call, the ship's ID blinked to life on the screen, reporting that the boat was who she said she was.

"Sounded hungover to me," Nick said in a voice that sounded that way. But then he always did, sober or not.

At her nod, he cleared the screen. One of the techs would keep an eye on it to make sure that it wasn't a false-flag operation or, if legitimate, that the ship they were assisting didn't break the traffic pattern in any dangerous fashion.

Back to studying the air traffic.

Commercial and cargo flights clustered in neat lines toward the major airports. Feeder flights appeared like flowers, their predictable patterns blooming outwards from major airports to smaller fields, then feeding back the other way. The only major field to the south was in Jakarta. Flights to Australia and New Zealand would rarely be routed through this airspace except for directly out of the major cities below.

Every pattern wove together on her monitor to make clear and predictable forms that—

"Who's this?"

She tapped her screen.

Nick glanced over at her console, squinted at it for a second, then turned back to his.

"Small plane," he reported. "Large bizjet class. Crossing at ninety degrees, heading zero-six-zero. Flight Level Four-Zero."

The Wedgetail flew northwest at thirty-nine thousand feet along the far-below Strait. The unknown flight flew northeast at forty thousand feet. Nowhere to the southwest to come from except the vast empty stretches of the Indian Ocean where the Malaysian airliner MH370 had disappeared a decade ago.

"Forty thousand should be a dead zone," she reminded Nick. "Verify."

"Verified."

Eastbound aircraft should be at Flight Level 37 or 41. With the westbound at 39 or 43, that provided a two thousand feet vertical buffer between planes going in opposite directions. Nobody should be at 40 unless they were in transition between flight levels.

"Identity?" Rowena asked.

"No transponder. Radar shows..." Nick kept working his keyboard.

In seconds he'd retuned the big Top Hot radar for Threat Sector emphasis in the direction of the unknown aircraft.

Focusing the entirety of the MESA radar on a single aircraft, vastly increased the detail.

"Bogey is a Dassault Falcon 2000 business jet. Typically, ten passenger and two crew. There's a belly extension I don't recognize. It isn't an antenna."

"Either its lost or—"

Grant slapped off his intercom headset. "What the bloody hell?" He was rubbing at his ears.

"Report?" Rowena asked when he didn't speak.

"Pray I'm hallucinating." He picked up the headset, held it near one ear, then dialed down the volume before pulling it back on. "Jackson? Boller?"

The Wedgetail's pilots' names.

Rowena tapped for the cockpit intercom channel. Nothing.

"What did you hear, Grant?"

"Screams. Like blood-curdling ones. Kind of sound you never want to hear—ever. Jackson? Boller?"

Grant undid his seat harness.

Rowena had been wearing only her lap belt, but out of the corner of her eye she saw Nick pulling on the two shoulder straps to make it a four-point harness. She did the same for herself.

Grant pounded on the door a few times. Then he keyed-in the unlock code on the external keypad beside the cockpit's safety door.

After waiting through the long pause that gave the pilots the option to override the unlock request, the three lights went green, indicating all three locks had opened.

He turned the handle and tugged.

Then harder.

He pulled his hand back and looked at it strangely for a moment, rubbing it. Then he ran his hand around the edge of the door.

Next, he shoved aside one earmuff of his headset, picked up

the intercom phone hung beside the door, and called out the pilot's names. He listened, then hung it up very slowly and turned to face her.

"I think we just lost the pilots."

———

Available at fine retailers everywhere:
Wedgetail
(Coming Fall 20224)

And don't forget that review for Gryphon
They really help.

ABOUT THE AUTHOR

USA Today and Amazon #1 Bestseller M. L. "Matt" Buchman started writing on a flight south from Japan to ride his bicycle across the Australian Outback. Just part of a solo around-the-world trip that ultimately launched his writing career.

From the very beginning, his powerful female heroines insisted on putting character first, *then* a great adventure. He's since written over 75 action-adventure thrillers and military romantic suspense novels. And more than 200 short stories, and a fast-growing pile of read-by-author audiobooks.

PW declares of his Miranda Chase action-adventure thrillers: "Tom Clancy fans open to a strong female lead will clamor for more." About his military romantic thrillers: "Like Robert Ludlum and Nora Roberts had a book baby."

His fans say: "I want more now...of everything!" That his characters are even more insistent than his fans is a hoot.

As a 30-year project manager with a geophysics degree who has designed and built houses, flown and jumped out of planes, and solo-sailed a 50' ketch, he is awed by what is possible. He and his wife presently live on the North Shore of Massachusetts. More at: www.mlbuchman.com.

The Emily Beale Universe
(military romantic suspense)

The Night Stalkers
MAIN FLIGHT
The Night Is Mine
I Own the Dawn
Wait Until Dark
Take Over at Midnight
Light Up the Night
Bring On the Dusk
By Break of Day
Target of the Heart
Target Lock on Love
Target of Mine
Target of One's Own
NIGHT STALKERS HOLIDAYS
*Daniel's Christmas**
*Frank's Independence Day**
*Peter's Christmas**
Christmas at Steel Beach
*Zachary's Christmas**
*Roy's Independence Day**
*Damien's Christmas**
Christmas at Peleliu Cove

Henderson's Ranch
*Nathan's Big Sky**
*Big Sky, Loyal Heart**
*Big Sky Dog Whisperer**
*Tales of Henderson's Ranch**

Shadow Force: Psi
*At the Slightest Sound**
*At the Quietest Word**
*At the Merest Glance**
*At the Clearest Sensation**

White House Protection Force
*Off the Leash**
*On Your Mark**
*In the Weeds**

Firehawks
Pure Heat
Full Blaze
*Hot Point**
*Flash of Fire**
Wild Fire
SMOKEJUMPERS
*Wildfire at Dawn**
*Wildfire at Larch Creek**
*Wildfire on the Skagit**

Delta Force
*Target Engaged**
*Heart Strike**
*Wild Justice**
*Midnight Trust**

Night Stalkers Reload
*Guard the East Flank**

Emily Beale Universe Short Story Series

The Night Stalkers
The Night Stalkers Stories
The Night Stalkers CSAR
The Night Stalkers Wedding Stories
The Future Night Stalkers

Delta Force
Th Delta Force Shooters
The Delta Force Warriors

Firehawks
The Firehawks Lookouts
The Firehawks Hotshots
The Firebirds

White House Protection Force
Stories

Future Night Stalkers
Stories (Science Fiction)

Other works by M. L. Buchman: *(* - also in audio)*

Action-Adventure Thrillers

Dead Chef
One Chef!
Two Chef!

Miranda Chase
*Drone**
*Thunderbolt**
*Condor**
*Ghostrider**
*Raider**
*Chinook**
*Havoc**
*White Top**
*Start the Chase**
*Lightning**
*Skibird**
*Nightwatch**
*Osprey**
*Gryphon**

Science Fiction / Fantasy

Deities Anonymous
Cookbook from Hell: Reheated
Saviors 101

Contemporary Romance

Eagle Cove
Return to Eagle Cove
Recipe for Eagle Cove
Longing for Eagle Cove
Keepsake for Eagle Cove

Love Abroad
Heart of the Cotswolds: England
Path of Love: Cinque Terre, Italy

Where Dreams
Where Dreams are Born
Where Dreams Reside
*Where Dreams Are of Christmas**
Where Dreams Unfold
Where Dreams Are Written
Where Dreams Continue

Non-Fiction

Strategies for Success
Managing Your Inner Artist/Writer
*Estate Planning for Authors**
Character Voice
Narrate and Record Your Own
*Audiobook**
Beyond Prince Charming: One Guy's
Guide to Writing Men in Romance

Short Story Series by M. L. Buchman:

Action-Adventure Thrillers

Dead Chef

Miranda Chase Stories

Romantic Suspense

Antarctic Ice Fliers

US Coast Guard

Contemporary Romance

Eagle Cove

Other

Deities Anonymous (fantasy)

Single Titles

The Emily Beale Universe
Reading Order Road Map

any series and any novel may be read stand-alone
(all have a complete heartwarming Happy Ever After)

For more information and alternate reading orders, please visit: www.mlbuchman.com/reading-order

SIGN UP FOR M. L. BUCHMAN'S NEWSLETTER TODAY

and receive:
Release News
Free Short Stories
a Free Book

Get your free book today. Do it now.
free-book.mlbuchman.com